WHEN THE MUSIC HITS

WHEN THE MUSIC HITS

A Novel

AMBER OLIVER

BALLANTINE BOOKS
New York

Ballantine Books
An imprint of Random House
A division of Penguin Random House LLC
1745 Broadway, New York, NY 10019
randomhousebooks.com
penguinrandomhouse.com

Hardback ISBN 978-0-593-87417-2
Ebook ISBN 978-0-593-87418-9

Printed in the United States of America on acid-free paper

2 4 6 8 9 7 5 3 1

First Edition

BOOK TEAM: Production editor: Abby Duval • Managing editor: Pam Alders •
Production manager: Chanler Harris • Copy editor: Laura Petrella •
Proofreaders: Julie Ehlers, Gabel Strickland, Caryl Weintraub

Book design by Debbie Glasserman

The authorized representative in the EU for product safety and compliance is
Penguin Random House Ireland, Morrison Chambers, 32 Nassau Street, Dublin D02 YH68, Ireland.
https://eu-contact.penguin.ie

For Black girls everywhere and for my family

It's beauty in the struggle, ugliness in the success.

—J. Cole

What's the world for if you can't make it up the way you want it?

—Toni Morrison, *Jazz*

WHEN THE MUSIC HITS

1

It was only mid-May, but it was already hot enough to make the shorts I'd worn under my dress stick to me like a spy suctioned to a skyscraper in an action movie. As soon as Alicia and I got into my apartment, I threw both living room windows open and hoped the breeze would cool our sweat-slicked skin.

The familiar afternoon sounds of my block cut through the transitory quiet. Ambulances blared down Grand Concourse as they raced toward certain tragedy. Old island-born men slung spitfire swear words at one another as they slammed dominoes down on plastic tables. High schoolers fresh out of class lobbed endearments loudly—*stupid*, *big head*, *my heart*, *primo*—like water balloons. To my neighbors, this day was as regular as the last. But for me, this day—one I had been waiting on for a long time—felt morose, bereft of the joy I'd hoped would mark the occasion.

At my celebratory lunch after the ceremony, Mama had called me lucky. Lucky for being the first one in our immediate family to successfully navigate undergrad and, now, grad school. Lucky for emerging from academia triumphant with two shiny degrees in music in tow. But I didn't feel lucky. I felt late and broke.

After lunch, Alicia and I stopped by Mama and Marvin's for a few minutes. Marvin, Mama's boyfriend of the last eleven years, hadn't been invited to the graduation festivities. There weren't enough tickets left for him, so Mama said he'd hang back and give me a gift at the house.

As we entered the two-bedroom prewar apartment, I could see him lying on the beige carpeted living room floor in front of the suede sectional, snapping pistachio shells in half. The opening credits for *American Gangster* flashed on the flat-screen. A half-empty two-liter bottle of Pepsi sat beside him.

Alicia had waved at Marvin, taken a seat at the small wooden table between the sofa and the kitchen, and busied herself with her phone. I waited by the front door. I didn't want to be there longer than I needed to.

"So, Billie," Marvin said. He stood up and gave Mama a kiss, then reached into the pocket of his sweatpants and pulled out a pink envelope. "This is just a little something for graduating. Congratulations."

I accepted it gratefully and secretly hoped he could read the contempt in my smile. I opened the envelope and pretended not to notice the fifty-dollar bill that fell out of the greeting card and floated to the floor as I read. I swept the bill closer to me with my foot to pick it up later. "Thanks, Marvin."

"What you gonna do now that you're finished?"

I'd grown to hate this question. Over the years, too many random people—fourth cousins and great-great-aunts, nosy customers at the CVS where I worked, neighbors—had felt comfortable sharing their opinions on what I should do with my life. But the answer was simple, really. I had wanted to work in music since I was thirteen years old. Music had always found the empty grooves of my body and filled them in with strings and woodwinds, brass and percussion. Nothing but the poetry of words and the rhythm made me feel so thoroughly whole and understood. Everything I'd done so far was supposed to lead me to the career of my dreams. But the road to gainful employment in the industry of my choice was littered with bullshit. I was thousands of dollars in debt. I had taken a year and a half off school to work, stringing multiple part-time jobs together to help support Mama. And I had no full-time job prospects in sight.

I had interviewed at so many different imprints at labels across the city over the past couple of months, trying to line up an entry-level job in A&R,

but I had yet to be picked. It was the same story as when I finished undergrad. HR had told me in emails, *We are so impressed with you and would love to keep you in mind for future positions. Unfortunately, we have decided to go in a different direction.* Later, on LinkedIn, I'd see that someone else got the job instead, someone they thought might fit into the culture better and who happened to be an Ivy League frat boy or the bleached-blonde niece of some executive.

"Well, um. I'm still trying to get a job at a record label. I had an interview at Lit Music Productions a couple weeks ago, so we'll see."

"Well, good luck. And hey, if it don't work out, try something more practical, like a city job. I heard the tests for the MTA is opening up soon. That's a better move anyway, with the stability and benefits."

At my place, Alicia and I sank into the run-down sofa and silently scrolled on our phones, worn out from all the talking and smiling and cheering of the morning.

But I couldn't deny that Marvin's comments had fucked with me a little. I checked my email, just in case an offer from Lit had miraculously dropped into my inbox, but there was nothing.

I sucked my teeth, went to the kitchen, and returned with two cans of margarita-flavored hard seltzer. I placed one on the scuffed faux-walnut coffee table in front of Alicia. I popped open the tab on the other and took a sip, instantly regretting it as the salt-and-metal flavor slid down my throat.

"Do you think Marvin was right?" I asked. "Should I look for other jobs? I mean, I do need to pay my bills, and it's been, like, weeks since I've heard from Lit. It's crazy because I thought it went well, you know? I talked about my passion, mentioned some of the artists they signed that, like, helped form my musical taste. I talked about my internship experience. And still nothing. I don't know what more they want."

"Forget what Marvin said. I don't want you to focus on Lit or any other label either. This day is about you and the fact that you did it, Billie. I'm so proud of you, girl! I know it's gotta feel good to be done after all them years of school."

My chestnut-colored skin collided with her sunbaked sand as I plopped down on the couch next to her. She nudged me back playfully with her shoulder, then slipped off her heels, relaxed into her seat, and slid one leg beneath the other. Awkward as the pose was, her posture was perfect. Years of hip-hop and ballet classes had made her lithe, her muscles taut.

If I was lucky for anything, it wasn't the education—that was all hard work, two or three shitty part-time jobs to survive, and sneaking into late-night artist showcases at bars in the Village, Uptown, the Lower East Side, deep Brooklyn, Flushing—it was that I had a forever best friend who understood me and who had also given herself over to the same thing I had: music, art, the power of our bodies.

"I don't know if *good* is the right word," I said.

"Since when is graduating with a master's not good?" she said, laughing.

"I guess . . . I don't know. Like, I've been giving my all to this, and I thought I'd be further along by now. I'm twenty-four, Leesh. Twenty-five in three months. So no matter what label I end up at, if I even end up at one, I'll be the oldest assistant there. And then it'll be, like, at least five years before I can save enough to move out of this bum-ass apartment. Years before I can make a name for myself. It's all so fucking bleak."

I took another sip of my drink. Despite the taste, I needed the buzz of alcohol to ward off the sense of hopelessness attempting to set up camp in my body.

"It ain't been but six hours since you graduated, and here you go thinking about five years from now." Alicia waved her manicured fingers at me. "You need to loosen up. Celebrate your wins for once instead of worrying about the next thing."

She had a point. I was used to preparing for some future something—music-industry networking events where I could hand out my business cards to executives from the big three, trips to shows where I could try to get an interview with the artist for my growing social media pages, and my dream career plan that outlined my trajectory from A&R assistant to director of A&R.

I first learned about artists and repertoire in middle school. For a presentation ahead of career day, my teacher had asked the class to research careers we wanted to explore and to find out what we'd need to do to pursue them. In my investigation, I learned about what A&R did—how it discovered new talent, helped create new sounds, cultivated and provided guidance to musicians who eventually made an indelible mark on the world. I had been fascinated by the idea of working in A&R ever since.

Alicia said, "Why don't we go out tonight? Let's go to Avia, where we can dance. Once you let that loud music get in you, I know it'll cheer up your depressed ass."

We'd been going to Avia most weekends since it opened a few years ago, and each time it was an adventure. Because their music game was unmatched, Avia was one of the only spots in the city that made people feel comfortable enough to let loose instead of performing thirty-second routines for the internet. They'd bump Top 40, basement house, endless amounts of rap and hip-hop, alternative R&B and EDM and Afrobeat. Underground joints that only a few of us dispersed throughout the space knew.

It was Alicia who first brought me there, before it ever popped on TikTok and Reels. Since she freelanced as an entertainment writer and moonlighted as a backup dancer, she was plugged in. She always knew where the party was, how to find an old friend in a crowd, how to charm people so she could go back to them later to ask for favors. She also knew how to drag me out of a funk when all I wanted to do was sulk and think about how I was going to pay my bills over the next few months.

"Can't we listen to music and chill here?" I asked. "I can order some food and whatever. You know I love Avia, but I'm not in the mood to be standing all night."

"See, now that's where you're wrong. I know exactly where we'll be sitting tonight." A sly smile spread across her face, and I knew I was in for some nonsense.

I threw a side-eye her way. "So you planned this, huh?"

"Nah. It's not even like that. I was on Instagram earlier, and I saw Dre and them say they're gonna have a section there tonight. They were already lit, waving bottles around on Live."

"Dre from high school? I didn't even know you were still cool with him."

"I'm not. We have mutuals . . . and I saw he started dating Raven. Posted her right on his story, all hugged up and shit a few weeks ago, so I added him to see if . . ."

She trailed off, and I knew better than to ask. She was back to stalking Raven's social media. It was an unhealthy obsession she'd cycled through before, one that sharpened the pain of her heartbreak until it broke open again, mangled and bleeding. Raven was the first girl Alicia had ever been with. The relationship had lasted longer than either of them expected—two whole years. It was good until Alicia discovered Raven in bed with a coworker, someone Alicia had been suspicious of, in the studio apartment Alicia had inherited from her grandmother. The next night, Alicia showed up at my house. She was usually dressed to kill, but there she was at my door at three in the morning in a bonnet, stain-riddled sweats, and slides, with fat tears sliding down her bare face.

We ended up lying on the sofa together that night, with a thick, fuzzy blanket spread out atop us, as she sobbed and alternately cracked jokes to make herself smile. We listened to sad music—Toni Braxton, Keyshia Cole, all of Jazmine Sullivan and Kehlani and Summer Walker. We stuffed our mouths with Smartfood popcorn, Sour Power Straws, and cheap vodka and Sprite that we poured into ice cups we'd gotten from the bodega downstairs and hoped the snacks would help stuff down the heartache.

"I know you loved her," I said now. "Probably still do. But the way she did you was messed up. You deserve more than that."

"I know, I know. I couldn't help it," she said. "Ima delete Dre after tonight, I promise."

"Fine, I'll go. For you."

She flashed a smile at me and pulled me into a hug.

Months ago, when my excitement about graduating was fresh and outweighed my pessimism, I had made a playlist for this occasion. Playlists were my thing. I loved the intimacy of curating a musical mood, so I made it my duty to be the one in charge of it in shared spaces—car rides, living rooms, baby showers, sweet sixteens. Today's playlist featured songs about money, confidence, success—all the things I hoped would soon come to me. Now that we were going out, I threw on the playlist, hoping I could channel some of that energy.

The first song on the list poured out of the soundbar and flooded the room with thumping bass. The song came out my freshman year of high school, the same year I met Alicia. Alicia and I would arrive at the metal detectors at the entrance of our school at the same time every morning, carrying breakfast sandwiches, Doritos, and Arizona iced teas in black plastic bags. After we undressed ourselves of earrings, bookbags, phones, keys, and jackets and then redressed, Alicia and I got to know each other on the way to the homeroom class we shared. We ate our food in the back of the classroom to avoid our teacher's detection and became fast friends when we learned that we lived close to each other, came from fucked-up families, and loved all the same songs and music artists.

After the song had been out awhile, Alicia convinced me to make up an embarrassing dance routine with her in the basement community room of her grandma's building. No one but the two of us would ever see it. But the power of the vocals and the thrash of the raucous beat would always burrow inside me like it was brand-new. I would never cease to be bowled over by its genius.

The next song was a Remy Ma joint. I appreciated the way the loud, brash horns announced the beat, similar to the way New Yorkers announced themselves—like there was no way you couldn't pay attention, like there was nothing that could stop you from noticing something so bold.

The first time Alicia and I heard it, we were at a freshman college party, and when Remy's confident flow layered over the beat, we knew, as we rocked our shoulders and raised our cups in the air, that this would be our anthem. "*Nothing could stop me,*" we sang as we drank and danced and hoped, in the back of our brains, that this confidence would see us through to finals.

Remy led into other Bronx rappers. Cardi B with her unmistakable accent and inimitable swag. ScarLip, who professed her love for the city with an old-school vigor. Each of the women gave a voice to people from the Bronx who were too often written off as secondary, insignificant. I'd have killed to work with artists like that one day if a label gave me a chance, artists whose music represented people like me and showcased the spectrum of Black creativity.

Time rolled by slowly as we switched from shitty seltzer margaritas to vodka sodas, listened to more money-making, independent-minded anthems—hoping to inspire myself into a more positive mood. We stalked our old friends and crushes on social media, noting the ones who were still hanging out in front of their buildings every weekend, taking pictures with their weed and their one bottle of Casamigos split among several other grown-ass men.

We got ready leisurely, putting on our makeup and squeezing into our tiny outfits one layer at a time, rotating in and out of the mirror and dancing to the music. No more money-making anthems. I switched us over to something with more bass and shouted, "Ayeee," behind Alicia as she bent over to twerk to Pop Smoke.

Perfecting a full-faced look was an elusive thing beyond my expertise, so I settled on lining my almond-shaped eyes with shakily drawn eyeliner and added mascara too, hoping no one would see the clumps unless they got too close. My twist out had gotten smushed in the back from lounging on the sofa, so I fluffed it into place, then swiped some brown lipstick onto my full lips and topped it with clear lip gloss.

Alicia stood behind me—her head two inches higher than mine—flipped her wavy hair to her back, and blotted a makeup blender covered in tawny-colored foundation on her face.

"So what's good with your man these days?" she asked. "Outside of today, I haven't seen bro in a minute."

I moved out of her view in the mirror and perched on top of the closed rickety toilet seat.

Alicia and Lucas had grown close over the four years he and I had been together. Whenever we all linked, his passion and her verve made a smooth combination that left me contemplative as they debated different sides of a point or exchanged punch lines that left us howling with laughter.

"He been mad busy with teaching at the community center lately. That's where he went after we finished lunch. He been tryna find a venue for Sunsetlandia, too, so our schedules have been a little off. Hopefully I'll be able to catch him awake when I get back."

"Oh, okay. Not your man being booked and busy." Alica carefully wiped away excess eyeliner with a twisted strip of toilet paper.

I laughed. "Yeah, I guess so."

As we inched toward midnight, it was time to make our way to Avia so we could walk in during my favorite part—when the DJ switched from chill vibes to club bangers and people forgot their inhibitions. The part of the night when people stopped their chitchatting, two-stepping, and live-streaming to unleash themselves on the dance floor. I loved watching people's bodies, the way they surrendered to infectious beats, their pelvises thrusting and booties shaking in carnal desire.

The Uber rolled up as soon as we made it downstairs. We slid into the back seat, and the driver switched the music from Panjabi MC's "Dhol Jageero Da" to some new song by another goofy rapper with a forgettable name who couldn't manage to stay on beat. When I'd heard the rapper on SoundCloud last year during my nightly artist research, even with his offbeat rapping, I knew he would pop. He had that kind of sound that was working these days—fun, frivolous, and soaked in nonchalance.

I also knew the underlying reason the Uber driver would think that I'd like this too, that I'd be interested in only a particular sound, a particular kind of music. It wasn't worth getting angry over, but the irritation still simmered beneath. Instead, I focused my energy on the time we were about to have and popped earbuds into my ears. I turned on a new song by an up-and-coming neo-soul singer I found on a Fresh Finds playlist on Spotify the other night, her rasping voice atop a subwoofer bass loud enough to block out the world around me.

As we neared the corner of Eighteenth Street and Eleventh Avenue, I said, "You can pull over here."

Alicia scooted out of the car, and I followed, making sure to check the seats for anything we might have left behind: a phone, a dropped earring, an uncapped lipstick—like drunken lovers or the wet-faced and newly single, such things were no strangers to an Uber's back seat.

We walked off to the side to smoke the rest of the blunt we'd started at my apartment. As we walked, I noticed Alicia's strappy stilettos. I was wearing sensible block heels I could stand in all night.

"Did you bring some other shoes with you? I know your feet gon' hurt with those," I said.

"Damn. I ain't even think about that." Alicia took a pull. "Actually"—she smirked as she passed me the blunt—"we're sitting with Dre, remember? I think I'll be just fine."

"Okay, but, like, you're gonna do all the talking, right? I don't want them to think this is some high-school-reunion-type shit. I barely liked them back then."

Whether it was an old acquaintance like Dre or some stranger, I despised socializing at parties. I hated small talk, the way it never amounted to anything, how devoid it was of real substance. I wasn't interested in any of it. What I really wanted out of a party, out of Avia, was to be taken over by the music. I wanted to dance with abandon. To come out of a song sweating and shaking, my body still caught up in the beat.

Whenever I got stuck in a conversation I didn't want to be in, Alicia, bless her, would see me in distress—my mouth set in a straight line—and press a drink into my hand. She'd slowly switch places with me, her steady smile and direct eye contact a distraction as I made my way back to the dance floor, to the reverberant song pulsing around us.

"Yeah, I got you, girl," she said.

I tossed the blunt to the ground and stepped on it until the orange glow turned to ash.

We only waited in line for fifteen minutes before we were let inside. The club—large and dimly lit, highlighted here and there by red and white lights that flitted around every few minutes—was inundated with bodies, making it feel crowded and lively. At the front of the club was coat check, but when Alicia and I discovered that they had raised the price of each checked item to eight dollars, we scoffed and held on to our jackets and ventured farther into the space.

On one side of the venue was a long, sleek metallic bar. In the middle of the room was a dance floor surrounded by comfy white sofas set up in a U formation so that the bottle-service buyers could be in the middle of the action.

The music was already bumping. The DJ harmoniously blended hits from Megan Thee Stallion to GloRilla, Dua Lipa to Troye Sivan, Tyla to Burna Boy.

Alicia and I got our first well drinks of the night and nursed them through thin straws and scanned the crowd.

As we looked out at the club around us, people were already unleashing. Bodies gyrated close to one another as the beat pulsed through them. Bodies pushed and pulled together, some in sync, some desperate and clinging to one another. The men danced behind the women, especially now that we were in the old-school reggae set—that sultry, wine-inducing music—of the night, and they pushed themselves closer, touched the slick bare skin exposed through cutouts in dresses. Our pale-skinned counterparts jerked to the music in spastic movements. They pumped their fists into the air randomly, unconcerned with rhythm or the personal space of those around them.

"Look." Alicia pointed a silver-clawed finger toward the sofas. A small group of twentysomething men sat on the cushions, some on the backs of the sofas, their feet digging into the plush seats. "There goes Dre."

"Oh yeah," I said, squinting. "That's him. He still got that big-ass head." We snickered. "But he's cute, though. Looks good with a beard."

"Of course he does. Beards be doing the hard work. Will take a man from ninja turtle to fine real quick."

We cackled loud enough to make people look in our direction.

"A'ight," she said. "Let's go over there and see what we can do."

"Ugh, fine. But if they start acting weird, we out."

But she didn't hear me. Alicia was already walking toward the men.

I followed behind her.

All the men looked up as we approached.

"Hey, Dre, long time, no see," Alicia said.

"Oh shit. Alicia, it's been a minute. You're looking good." Dre stood up to give her a hug. "And, Billie, it's been a minute. You're looking good too." He inched in for a hug, and I positioned my body sideways, offering him my left side, the side farthest away from my face. I tried to smile. People liked that.

"So what brings ya here to my spot?" Dre said, smiling wide, motioning toward the other men on the sofa, as if to say he was the leader of this pack.

I tried to stifle the reply that cropped up in my head, but I was too used to the banter that I'd developed with Dre way back when, when sarcastic insulting and flirting were interchangeable. "Oh, this is your spot? Your name written on the sofas or something?" I asked.

"Aha, you got jokes," he said.

Alicia nudged me and glared. "Oh, well, you know, we out here celebrating. Billie graduated with her master's today."

"Oh, word? Congrats. That's dope. Why don't ya sit with us? We got drinks and shit."

Alicia and I exchanged glances. "You ain't got to tell me twice," she said. She grabbed a cup off the clear table and filled it with ice followed by a shot of

Don Julio before topping it off with cranberry juice. She smirked at me as she searched the sofa for a place to sit.

Not wanting to waste a free drink, I made myself one too.

Alicia was now squeezed between two guys who vied for her attention. I spotted an open space on the arm of the sofa near her.

"So," Dre said, yelling above the booming of the music. "What you been up to, Billie? You still writing and all that?"

"Oh wow, good for you. You remembered," I said. "Nah, but honestly, not really. I'm more focused on my TikTok and Instagram these days. I've been building them for a few years now. I interview up-and-coming local music artists, give them a platform to share their music and story and whatever else they want on my Live series. It ain't helped me find a damn job yet, though," I added, almost forgetting he was there.

I took a large gulp of my drink, hoping to get myself to shut up before I revealed too much about my life and struggles to someone I hadn't talked to or thought about since high school.

"Oh. Word. I think I came across your page the other day, actually. I see you be at festivals and concerts too. Got the drip on and all that."

"Oh, so now you got jokes," I said.

He smiled, nodded, and sipped his drink. I looked toward Alicia to see if she could get me out of this conversation, considering she'd told me she'd be the one talking, but she was too busy flirting to notice.

"So let me ask you, since you so interested in music, would you wanna link with my boy Q? He been doing some fire shit with producing. Has a studio down in Queens. Even worked with A Boogie once."

I cut my eyes at him. "Word? What's in it for you?" I asked.

"I'm saying if you get on, and shit pops off with Q, Ima be able to get on at some point too. It's a smooth win for all of us," he said.

"Oh, I see you playing the long game." I smiled. If there's one thing I admire about a New York dude, it's his ability to finesse any situation for a come-up. "Well, what's his IG?"

He shrugged, then said, "MoneyBoyQ."

"Okay, thanks." I finished my drink in two swallows. "I'll follow him, and we'll link."

"Yeah," Dre said, his mouth open, white teeth organized into a knowing grin. "Do that."

He looked across the room at the expanse of bodies, eyes lingering on a group of skinny white women sporting dresses as tight and short as ours, arms thrown to the ceiling as an old Chris Brown song played. They continued their dancing, sticking their fingers in their hair and lifting it off their necks, and returned Dre's stares. Perhaps they too were looking for a free drink.

With his attention elsewhere, I jumped up and slipped past him.

"Hey, do you want to dance?" Alicia said as I moved toward where she sat. We didn't love this song or the man singing it for, let's face it, a laundry list of reasons, despite his talent, but I could tell she had grown tired of the way the men on the sofa looked at her like they would drink her in until there was nothing left.

"And pull you away from all this?" I asked, motioning toward the men beside her, both of them too close to her exposed thighs. "I'm fucking with you. Let's go."

She looked up at me, and the relief I saw in her eyes was palpable and familiar.

•

At some point in the night, I let the music consume me. I shook my hair from side to side and rocked my body to house. I dropped my knees as low as I could take them and twerked to hip-hop as the beats surged through my body. I swayed my hips and sang along loudly to pop and R&B hits like I was the star in a one-woman show. I jumped up and down to electronica and sped-up grunge until my breath went jagged.

It was four o'clock in the morning when we finally left the club, panting and exhausted.

But I was happy to leave. To breathe full again in the open air.

•

"Get home safe, girl," Alicia said. Then she hopped into a rideshare with a voluptuous terracotta-skinned woman with a mass of thick blood-red ringlets whom Alicia had hooked two fingers inside of toward the end of the night. They had leaned against the wall of the only bathroom stall, moans lost to a SZA song booming beyond the doors, while I fixed my sweaty hair in the smudged mirror.

"A'ight, you too, and hey," I said, leaning into the rolled-down window of the car. "Thanks for this. I think I needed it."

"I know, babe." She smiled and blew a kiss at me. I waved and watched the car drive off, then walked the few blocks to the 4 Train.

The train snaked its way through the tunnels of Manhattan until it emerged beneath the Bronx night sky, its headlights cutting furiously through the dark.

Feeling a headache coming on, I lifted my face from resting on my propped-up hand. I grimaced and pulled my phone from my purse to text Lucas. I hoped he was up. He often went to bed early so he could enjoy the sunrise. That was the best time, he always said, to photograph the sun at its truest. But even if Lucas wasn't up, he'd easily stir out of a deep sleep just to walk me home, to make sure that I was safe. He was indefectible like that.

I was lucky to have shared the last four years with him. He was as supportive now as he had been when we met at a Black Student Union mixer my sophomore year and his senior year of college.

It was rare for me to attend events at school. I was always heading to one of my part-time retail jobs, where I tried my best to hide from customers and their stupid questions whenever they caught me on the floor stocking new product. When I wasn't working or taking classes, I tried to absorb all the live music I heard at venues all across the boroughs into my veins like it was nourishment, like it was life-giving, because to me, it was.

I'd only agreed to go to the mixer because Alicia knew some of the people going and there would be free snacks. She was always trying to get me to socialize, to take off the earbuds I wore around campus and connect with the people around me.

When I met Lucas that night, I realized how right she was about the necessity of connection. I'd felt an instant one with him. Alicia and I had snuck into the event fifteen minutes late as Lucas was giving an impassioned speech—about the removal of an African American art class from the curriculum—to

Black students clustered in the middle of the gray-carpeted lounge room. When he was done, he asked people to break up into groups to brainstorm ways to protest the removal.

His passion for our community, for Black art and its impact, how he argued that everyone around the world benefited from our genius, had touched me. Because of him, I would sign a petition or offer a few bucks for the cause, but I couldn't attend more meetings. I had my erratic work schedule to consider, but I also needed to follow my plan, to continue on the path I'd outlined that would allow me to help create art in my own right, to be an A&R mogul worth remembering. As Alicia drifted to the friends she'd come to meet, I said my goodbyes and made my escape.

Lucas had seen me leaving and stopped me, asked me why I was in such a hurry when we were discussing beauty, individual but also of our people. "*By the way, you know that you one too, right? A beauty?*" he asked. I'd wanted to call him corny for the line and for how seriously he took himself, but he was *fine.*

I don't remember what I said after that. All I know is that I had looked up at his big brown eyes and marveled at his high cheekbones, his wide, kissable lips, his moisturized hair plaited in horizontal braids on each side of his head like an homage to Dave East and A$AP Rocky, and I gave him my number. We have been talking art and loving and supporting each other ever since.

•

As the train moved through the night, I scrolled through my Instagram. Then TikTok. And when I got bored of that, my email. I stopped at a new article from a music-review site I used to track local artists across the city. It mentioned a new singer out of Brooklyn, Corryn Blue, whose spacey, ethereal sound was called "a transformative experience." Whatever that meant, I knew I couldn't miss it. I made a note to look at the article when I was sober, to possibly make my way to Brooklyn to see her.

I resumed my scrolling, and past the emails from Fashion Nova offering me tight-fitting clothes at a discount was a new, unopened message from the person I'd interviewed with at Lit.

I sat forward, suddenly alert, and clicked on the message.

From: Sharon.Waters@litmusicproductions.com

To: Billie.Grand@gmail.com

Subject: A&R Assistant

Dear Billie,

Thank you for interviewing for the role of artist and repertoire assistant at Lit Music Productions. We regret to inform you that we have decided on another candidate for the position.

"Fuck," I said, closing the email. The swear slipped loudly from me, causing a drunk man sitting in the corner of the train car to rouse from his sleep. He stood up, wobbly and hunched, and threw slurred swears in my direction. Spittle pooled on one side of his mouth. I couldn't help but laugh.

I'd tried so hard to be everything these labels wanted. I'd pointed to my TikTok and Reels series, MusicallyBillie, and to the fact that I had over thirty-seven thousand followers across platforms and how three of the artists I had interviewed—all of them different genres, from a lo-fi alternative R&B singer to a vibey conscious rapper to a punk-funk genre-bending band that was all Bad Brains meets Kaytranada—were on their way to a big break after being added to dozens of playlists on Spotify and Apple Music a few days after I posted their stories.

I'd gotten a master's, which was more than the bachelor's they generally requested, and I'd had internships at two of the big three. I should've been an easy hire, a shoo-in. Yet there I was again: rejected by another label in New York—the kind of label that boasted exclusive music events and early access to new artists and fresh sounds, the kind of job *I* would kill for, the kind of job that so often went to a trust fund kid who could afford to live and do what they loved without debt and exhaustion bearing down on them—while being yelled at by a man who reeked of days-old piss.

Before I could wallow in my disappointment, I closed my phone and trained my eyes at the twinkling blackness of the Bronx spread out before me. Silently, as I looked out the window, thinking about the future and the past that brought me here, tears trailed down my face.

In the small hours of the morning, the Concourse was transformed. The neighborhood was tucked away after families had gorged on fried chicken and potato salad or arroz con pollo or jerk chicken and peas and rice. The smells of the foods wafted into hallways and permeated staircases, replacing the stench of urine and weed. All that was left of the sounds were car wheels grinding against grimy blacktop.

But aging men were still outside with their Yankee caps atop their buzzed-bare scalps, bottles of Hennessy held at the neck, and ice-filled plastic cups beside them. They lingered in front of the bodegas, as if waiting to be wanted, as if they needed to make their virility known.

I didn't have to wait long before Lucas stepped into view. The night was dark, but the moonlight that sliced through the clouds shined against his sepia skin, the slant of his strong cheekbones, and his lean, muscular frame hidden beneath an oversize hoodie that obscured his face as he tilted his head toward the sky. He always knew how to find it, that light. I loved that most about him: how he so effortlessly glowed. He was the finest, brightest man I had ever known.

"Did you have fun?" Lucas asked. He pulled me closer to him as we walked up the hill, and dipped his head toward my hair. He worked his way through the tangle of coils and planted a kiss at the warm center of my scalp. "*It's nearest to your beautiful brain,*" he often said late at night when we curled together beneath the duvet.

I huddled closer to Lucas in my short black dress, desperate to make myself invisible. Once we were past the men and got into the elevator of our apartment building, I could relax, could stop that old looking-over-the-shoulder thing.

"Yeah, it was packed in there," I said. "The DJ was good, though, so I didn't mind. Oh, and Alicia found some guys we knew from high school. Got us some free drinks and a place to sit."

"Oh, dope. Alicia still coming through with the hookups." He wasn't the type to get jealous and was excited whenever I scored something free.

"Yeah." I didn't mean the waver in my voice, but it came out anyway.

"What's wrong?" He stopped walking and looked at me, his eyebrows wrinkling in worry.

"I didn't get the job at Lit. That was the last label on my list."

He pulled me into a hug. I nestled my face into his neck, longing to get closer to his skin, closer to that familiar scent that calmed me like the bridge of a song, changing the tempo so that my racing heart slowed, and I softened against him.

"I thought a graduate degree would be the cherry on top, you know? Like, if I wasn't enough with the one degree, boom, there's the second. But I'm still fucking unhirable. I worked my ass off to get here, and it's like it doesn't mean anything."

"They are really missing out on you, and soon they gon' realize they fucked up. I mean, honestly, you don't even need them. You been growing your platform by yourself. Finding new music artists. Giving them an audience, making them feel heard, seen. Being authentic. Can't no one take that accomplishment from you. You don't need them to determine your worth or your success." He stepped toward me, away from our apartment door. He locked eyes with mine and pushed a strand of my hair behind my ears. "I believe in you, and it's gon' get better from here."

I nodded and plastered a weak smile on my face so that he'd know appreciation prickled through me. But Lucas—a man who grew up rare in my hood with two working-class, loving parents who instilled in him the importance of self-expression, the freedom to be Black and in charge of his own life—wouldn't understand.

He compiled shifts from all the make-your-own-schedule services—Instacart, Uber Eats, DoorDash—and occasionally taught photography and painting classes to poorly funded local elementary and middle school after-school programs and community centers at a discount, making just enough to cover a portion of the bills while he pursued his real passion.

Lucas grew up in the city, knew it deep in his bones, felt it in the way he moved through the world, but he also had a particular fondness for the sun, Black people, and community.

His love of photography burgeoned once he realized that he was fascinated by the way the sun cast itself brilliant against dark skin, of the people right here in the Bronx. So he dedicated himself to the art fully. I'd often see him contorting his body to catch the way the sun threw color into the world after everything was doused with rain, to catch the way the sun made beauty from darkness.

Once Lucas figured out his own artistic ideals, he never diverged from them. He was driven by them. He'd taken up teaching kids at the community center a few years ago to give the students—bright kids from the neighborhood—a chance to find their niche, to share their own versions of art that represented all that they were, like he had.

Lucas was comforting when I was going through rough patches. He had this way of reminding me that no matter how bleak life got, there was always beauty to be found. We could always connect over art, how it brought us together, how it fed us in ways words could never describe.

Once we were inside, I hung my purse on the linen closet's doorknob and flung off my shoes. I peeled off my sweaty dress, roughly passed a makeup wipe across my face, and plopped into bed. I forewent the rest of my nighttime routine.

All I wanted was to sleep, deep and dreamless.

But as I closed my eyes, the email from Lit played like a low-budget movie across my brain. *We regret to inform you . . .* The line mocked me like a comedian punching down at people who couldn't defend themselves.

I thought about that rejection. Was this what it felt like to be a failure? The side of my face lay flush against the stiff mattress as an idea formed in my head, making me prop myself up on my elbows.

Lit didn't want me. But that didn't mean I couldn't show them what they were missing out on. Maybe they needed to see that I wanted it enough, that I was willing to fight for it.

I opened a fresh email window and began typing a note to Sharon. There was a chance she'd delete the email, sight unseen, but I didn't care. I needed Lit to know that I was worthy, that no matter if they hired me or not, I was going to accomplish my A&R dreams.

2

The state between awake and asleep was one of my favorites. The in-betweenness of the moment—when sunshine is both blinding and beautiful; when fried meat in the pan on the stove follows me, crackling, all the way from my dreams into the waking world; when the birds chirp to one another like lovers harmonizing in a shared shower—is unmatched in the full bloom of day. And Lucas, a person who finished his first workout routine by the time the sky broke open like a cracked egg, had made the in-betweenness of today special.

I sat up in bed and rubbed my temples, feeling the edges of a headache coming on. Lucas's playlist spit out an Orion Sun track. The song was lush and lyrically poetic, her calming vocals calling to me as the smell of fresh-brewed coffee wafted into our room.

I wanted to stay despondent. I wanted to lie in bed and ignore the coming of this day, where the combination of a hangover and encroaching pessimism threatened to knock me off center. But I couldn't leave Lucas hanging. Not when he'd gone through the trouble of trying to cheer me up. I swung my legs off the side of the bed, put on my slippers, and walked to the kitchen.

"Hey, sleepy. Have a seat," he said, pulling out a chair to the small kitchen table.

A vase with flowers had been set upon the table, and I could smell corned beef hash cooking just right on the stove. I swept my gaze around the apartment as I wiped the crust from the corners of my eyes. The art Lucas and I had hung up years ago was still there. On the wall above the sofa was our makeshift gallery—some were photos Lucas had taken of beautifully hued folk of golden fawn and amber, of brown skin cooled with jewel undertones, rich, deep browns of earth and ocher, skin dappled with warm sunlight, bright colors painted around the edges in his careful brushstrokes. The others were mine—a collection of posters and framed art, iconic photographs and magazine spreads of some of my favorite musicians that I'd transferred from my childhood bedroom: Billie Holiday, my namesake, backstage, her hair pinned in florals; the album cover of the Internet's *Ego Death*, an iconic album that I played every night before bed and before I even understood the gravity of the heartbreak and sensuality weaved into their spacey songs; mother of rock and roll Sister Rosetta Tharpe, playing her classic guitar during a portrait session in 1940; an assortment of magazine covers and spreads of Black singers and rappers I secretly hoped I'd work with one day—Frank Ocean, Rico Nasty, Doechii, d4vd dripped in avant-garde designer.

"Babe, you are too good to me." I reached up to kiss him, grateful for his thoughtfulness and his delicate care of my feelings. I broke the kiss and said, "Thanks. I really needed this."

"Feeling better?" he asked and placed a cup of coffee in front of me.

"I fucking wish. I feel like a failure."

"You're not a failure. Like I said last night, this is not a reflection of you, babe. I already know you're that girl. The world gon' know soon too."

I loved Lucas, but sometimes his optimism was grating. I didn't want positivity. I just wanted to eat my greasy food and wallow. I didn't need him telling me that I would come out on top, because that simply wasn't life. Especially now that I'd racked up rejections for months straight, I said as much to Lucas while staring into the coffee mug.

My voice cracked, and I stopped talking. I rubbed my throat, massaging the skin that covered my sore insides.

"I feel you. I do. And I'm sorry." He picked up my hand and gave it a kiss, short and tender. "But you don't need their validation. The money you make from views may not be a lot, but it's all you. You don't need their systems. No one else has creative control over the content you put out. I mean, think about what the ancestors would've wanted. Like, you think they would have wanted us to dream of labor? Of working for them people to get their recognition? Like we need their okay to share our own creativity? Nah. They wasn't dreaming of labor. They wasn't dreaming 'bout none of that. They were dreaming about freedom. About rest. About more than survival. And, babe, with everything you been through in your life, you deserve all that. Not to be in some company controlling other people's careers for their profit."

"A few checks for viral videos isn't enough." I pulled my hand from his, tucked mine beneath my armpits, and looked down at my plate. The corned beef hash had turned gelatinous. I picked around the edges, my appetite depleted.

"I'm proud of what I built," I said, "but it's not consistent. We need money coming in regularly. We need insurance. We need a savings 'cause you know I can't rely on Mama. Beyond that, I don't see joining a company as becoming a conformist or gatekeeper, some shit like that. It's more like, with me there, I'll be able to help bring in more artists of color to the label, support them and encourage them to be their authentic selves. I could maybe eventually be an example for girls like me that want this career for their own futures. This job will give me a chance to work with music and artists in a way I've never had access to before." I lowered my voice and looked into his eyes, hoping he would understand what I meant if couched in softness. "I want this more than I've wanted anything. Once I get it, then I'll rest. But now is the time to fight for it. Like Sunsetlandia is to you, this feels like a calling, babe, and I want to answer it."

Sunsetlandia had always been a dream. When pop-up rooms across the country started to take over the feeds of social media—the Rosé Mansion, Museum of Ice Cream, the Color Factory, all those overly bright, highly stylized, photo-shoot-ready event spaces—Lucas came up with the idea to turn his painting and sunset photography into an event: Attendees would walk through various themed rooms that paid homage to the sun, that broiling star that made light, made life happen on this planet. "*What could be more important than that?*" Lucas had said when I first asked about it, after the idea had tumbled out of him while we were in bed one night, pressed together and trembling under the thin covers as we battled the wind seeping in from the drafty window.

I didn't want to fight with Lucas. Not when everything was so uncertain. I switched topics, knowing that whatever came next for us, we'd navigate it together. "So what's going on with Sunsetlandia lately anyway?"

I pulled my chair over from my end of the table to his. He drew me into a hug, and we cuddled side by side. I listened as he talked about the venue he'd found in the Bronx—some warehouse in the hood that he could paint and set up any way he saw fit. There, his vision would blossom, and it warmed me to think about art, Lucas, all that we could be in this world.

•

My next three weeks were nothing but groom, sleep, and hustle. I continued working morning shifts at the pharmacy in the CVS off Eighty-Sixth and Amsterdam, where people yelled at me because the pharmacist needed twenty extra minutes for their refills or mistakenly gave generics instead of name brands to Upper West Siders wealthy enough to splurge on their health. I picked up a couple of musical theory tutoring gigs I'd found through Indeed and my university's job site too. I applied to smaller companies, indie labels started by music execs who had struck out on their own but who rarely had the financial capital to be competitive in the market. I applied outside of A&R too, hoping to get my foot in the door any way I could—marketing, publicity, consumer research, artist relations—but expanding the search hadn't gotten me any closer to a job.

In between applying to new listings, I worked on my social media. I listened to hundreds of artists every night, parsing through songs with static-laced beats and echoey vocals that sounded like they were captured by a phone pushed up against a speaker or a phone only half-hooked into an aux, to get to the good stuff. The kind of music that was infectious, original. The kind of music that made me pay attention to its melodies, its message, its unique sound. I scoured through social media pages of bars that hosted local artists for free open-mic nights every Wednesday, looking for someone who sparked something deep inside me. That was the thing I loved about live music especially. The way it consumed me, forced itself first into my ears and then into my brain like a beautiful parasite, planting a rhythmic beat or a greasy note plucked from a guitar or a full-throated voice crooning lyrics that sank in deep.

During my search, I came across Corryn Blue again. And I was reminded of her ethereal R&B. She sang of space, of travel and exploration for Black women, of vulnerability in a world that hardens you, of connection and healing from a world that tamps you down.

Corryn Blue's sultry vocals carried me through the long D Train ride down to the part of Brooklyn that was still Black. I parked myself in a dive bar where she was performing, lit up mostly by Christmas lights even though it was almost summer. Dark wood tables and uncomfortable-looking chairs were scattered in the small space. The slab of bar I sat at was moist from a recent dishrag wipe down.

I watched as Corryn Blue took the stage. It wasn't so much a stage as it was a corner of floor unencumbered by a swath of chairs. There was a single mic stand and a stool placed beside it.

Most of the patrons in the bar were unconcerned with the open mic. From what I could tell, most of them had recently gotten off work from a construction site nearby, and their dusty jeans created a cloud around them. They huddled together quietly, drinking four-dollar mugs of unfiltered yellow in groups of two or three, shoulders tense, as they waited for the beer to do its work.

The dull overhead light didn't do much to highlight her deep-brown skin, but still, she glowed. Her hair was in locs, twisted into an updo, and her maxi dress, the color of undulating blue waves, flowed against her skin. She looked peaceful, serene as she held the mic and sang into it, slow and moody, threaded with attitude.

I wanted to find you here
Beneath the clouds and trees
But I found myself instead
Full and open and free
And I wondered, where the hell I been . . .

I closed my eyes to savor her canorous voice, her honeyed notes and guttural humming, the beat rich with the sultry combination of saxophones and cymbals. Goosebumps formed on my arms as I listened to her put tricky emotions into words—that feeling of finding yourself after getting lost in someone else. How it feels to have space to think about yourself again.

When she finished, people clapped dutifully, and she took it with grace, nodded, and whispered, "Thank you." And then she rushed off the stage.

I wasn't surprised by the audience's muted response. In bars like this, people treated these performances like background noise, like momentary distractions from monotony. But they simply didn't have the ear I did. I knew she was incredible. I wouldn't let her talent be lost on me.

Seeing her move quickly through the crowd to reach the exit, I hurriedly finished my glass of cloyingly sweet white sangria and closed out my bill. I walked up to her and pitched my voice loud enough for her to turn in my direction. "Hi, I'm so sorry to bother you, but I thought you were so great up there."

"Thanks so much."

"The way you were so raw, putting all that emotion into the song? It was so dope. I feel like singers aren't willing to be vulnerable these days, to sing from the heart. It's always the singers who whisper sweetly over trap beats who dominate. I mean, don't get me wrong, I like those artists too. But what you're doing here, with your voice, with your lyrics—it's amazing. I swear, I could listen to you sing that way for hours. Anyway, the reason I stopped you is because I was hoping I could ask you a few questions about you as an artist.

"I run an Instagram and TikTok account, MusicallyBillie, where I interview up-and-coming artists so they can share their journey, their style, their art. Whatever they want. I was hoping that you might want to be a guest?"

I hoped this was enough to make her stay and talk. She contemplated me, looked me up and down, from my hair piled on top of my head and secured with a claw clip to my gold jewelry to my baby tee and light-wash baggy straight-legged jeans to my Air Jordan 1s and gifted Telfar bag from Auntie Dionne hooked on my arm. She shifted her eyes up and then back to mine and smiled. She sat at the bar and motioned for me to sit next to her.

"Well, where do we start?" she asked.

•

Even though things were going well—my talk with Corryn Blue on Live had gotten the most engagement I'd seen in weeks—views, saves, and likes didn't really pay the bills.

As we headed into the last weeks of the public school year before summer school started, the tutoring gigs dried up. I forced myself to apply for a second job, where I had to type my resume into the boxes even though I'd already uploaded the Word doc, only to never hear from them again.

In the middle of applying to the Target on the opposite side of the Bronx I'd have to take two buses to get to, I received a call from a 212 number. I picked it up immediately.

"Hi, is this Billie Grand?"

"Yes, this is she."

"Hi. I'm calling on behalf of Lit Music Productions. We interviewed you a few weeks ago . . ."

My heart started pounding hard as I thought back to my hasty email, to the ranting I did in trying to get them to hire me.

Did it work? Or was this an admonishment?

Either way, I suppressed the panic that started rising in my throat and forced myself to respond. "Yes, of course, for the A&R assistant position."

"Yes, well that role is now open, and we'd like to formally offer you the position if you're still interested."

Three weeks ago they hadn't wanted me. And now they were offering me a job. After months and months of rejection and anxiety, I could finally start the career I'd always wanted.

I responded quickly so she wouldn't take my silence for lack of enthusiasm.

"Yes, I would love to join Lit," I said. "Thanks so much for the opportunity."

"Great. Can you start tomorrow?"

Sitting at my desk that was tucked into the corner of our small room, I tried to suppress a squeal, but I couldn't, so I hit mute and raised the hand not holding the phone into the air like I was yes-pastoring at a Baptist church during Sunday service. I unmuted my phone to respond.

"Absolutely," I said.

Right after, I called CVS and quit. Donna, my manager—a middle-aged straight shooter who came in from Long Island on the Jitney and wore dark eyeliner and blue eyeshadow every day paired with fried hair made stiff with half a can of hairspray—wouldn't miss me. She'd been waiting for one of us part-timers to leave so she could give her teenage nephew more hours anyway. Then I called Lucas, who was busy DoorDashing and shooting the sun.

3

Before I knew better, I once showed up to an internship interview at Sony in a cheap starched black suit, my hair slicked up with Eco Style gel into a tight bun. I looked out of place next to girls who exuded quiet luxury, inherited Chanel purses and Hermès scarves adorning them as they breezed into corner offices. Today, I would be more judicious.

I decided on a look that oozed personality but was still professional: two or three chunky silver rings on each hand; thick, medium-size silver hoops in my ears; my silver necklace with a Leo zodiac pendant; my silver script name chain atop a crisp black mock-neck sleeveless shirt tucked into a zebra-print maxi skirt; and black platform mules. I took out the twists I had put in my hair before I went to sleep and fluffed my afro, careful not to disturb the definition. I applied mascara and pink-tinted lip gloss, grabbed my purse, and locked the door behind me.

I put my earbuds in and drowned out the three God-bless-you-mas shouted at me by men lined down the Concourse toward the subway.

I stepped into the bodega next to the train station, opting for mints and a water instead of a small coffee, light and sweet. The spot had been open for hours, bachata blasting loudly from the speaker. The calico cat that usually slept on the bread at night brushed up against my legs as I reached into the refrigerator.

I fished a couple of dollars and change from the bottom of my purse, placed it on the counter, and dashed out of the store.

The train ride to Forty-Seventh Street, near Rockefeller Center, was surprisingly smooth. I escaped the show timers who flipped and twirled on the poles and nearly kicked several people, no sick passengers cropped up, the air-conditioning blew gloriously cool, and there were no train delays—a truly rare day of the MTA working exactly as it should.

I arrived and looked toward the sky—Lit's headquarters was up there, and the building loomed, large and intimidating, above me.

I thought about the sacrifices I had made to get to this early June day—six years of school, three internships, late nights and early mornings of studying, the events and parties I missed to create content, the shit jobs I had to work to cover my half of the bills, all reminders that this was the real endgame. This was what I had prepared for.

•

I stepped out of the elevator and spotted Erykah, the receptionist, at the front desk. She was one of those elder millennials who had found their best look years ago and stuck with it—her stretched hair was pulled up into a bouffant like Janelle Monae in her black-and-white phase, and her lips were painted a deep berry.

"Hi, Erykah. Love your hair," I said.

She looked up from her desk—her eyes lingering on me, from my afro down to my shoes, seemingly in deep assessment—mumbled a thanks, and went back to staring at her computer.

"Uh, yes, so. Today is my first day? I'm here to see Sharon."

"Uh-huh." She angled her body away from me and dialed Sharon's extension. "Hi, Sharon, yes, I have your guest here," Erykah said, then promptly went back to work on her computer.

"Th-Thanks," I said before taking a seat on the stiff sofa in the reception area.

A tall, tanned white woman wearing a dark power suit and bright-red lips, who looked like she had walked straight out of the eighties and rolled into the office, called out my name a few minutes later.

"I'm so glad you're on the team. We're happy to have you. Thanks for starting on such short notice," she said.

"Oh, it's no problem at all. My pleasure."

As we walked to her office, I could see clearly across the open-plan setup. Through the floor-to-ceiling windows, I could make out the Chrysler Building sparkling under the morning sun.

The marbled walls alternated between gleaming white and stark black shot through with gray. The space was peppered with metallic desks and black swivel chairs, in groups of twos and threes.

As we neared Sharon's office, I noticed gold albums encased in clear glass with bronze labels affixed to the bottom. I silently read some of the names on the engraved cases, in awe of what Lit had accomplished since their inception fifty-seven years ago.

We stepped into Sharon's office, and she shut the door behind her.

"So," she said. She stood at the side of her large glass desk, hip hovering over the surface like she wanted to plant herself there if only she had the time. "I'm sorry to start you off like this, but it's a busy time for us. Michael's last assistant left on short notice, so we're playing catch-up here. Why don't we get you introduced to the team and set up right away, yes?"

"Sounds great," I said.

I barely had time to learn what I was supposed to know about the company—its departments, divisions, imprints, company culture—before Sharon was ushering me out of her office and into the hallway.

I walked beside her toward a cluster of desks occupied by waifish women. Most of the offices on the perimeter were occupied by men. We came across the desk that would be mine, the second cube in a row of three, my name already slid into the nameplate.

Sharon allowed me a couple of minutes to put down my bag and grab a pen and pad, each of them marked with Lit's name, before she whisked me off to meet the rest of the team.

As we walked to meet my colleagues, I noticed the conference rooms that lined the halls. They were named after cities around the globe: New York, Miami, Venice, Los Angeles, Paris, Madrid, London. The company's reach extended far, and I was grateful to be a part of something that touched lives and brought music to people all across the world.

I also loved the art. The plaques, the odes to music that seemed embedded in the walls and laced into the interior. There were pop moguls, hip-hop icons, R&B crooners, and rockers splashed in tasteful murals. The lyrics from their most popular songs wound around their images in swirling patterns that seemed to capture the swell and quiet, the bass and rhythm within each one.

First up on the good-to-meet-you tour was Michael, director of the A&R team and my new boss.

"Knock, knock," Sharon said as she popped her head into Michael's office. "I have your new assistant here."

"Billie, welcome," Michael said, bounding over to where Sharon and I stood. "Thanks for starting so quickly."

"Thanks so much for the opportunity, Michael. I'm really looking forward to working here." I shook his hand firmly to let him know that I was ready, that I would be here to stay. I looked him over, mentally cataloging his outfit, from the presumably expensive haircut to the navy Brooks Brothers suit to the cufflinks on his pale wrists and his recently shined hard shoes. He had that look of money, of importance, one that ensured no one would ever mistake another for his role as leader.

Next up was Evan, another white male exec, who wore his shoulder-length hair slicked back behind his ears. He was dressed in a sleeveless fleece vest like a guy who got lost on his way to a hike but decided to stay anyway. His style matched the artists he signed, from what I could see on the Lit website: laid-back white male pop singers who sang about women and life-changing nights spent out in the wilderness, and DJs who blended folk and electronica together like it was some kind of sacred combination.

After that, Sharon introduced me to Kate. There's always a Kate. This Kate was a tall and slender woman with flat blond hair, giant blue eyes, and was dressed in a loose jewel-toned Anthropologie dress. Kate was an exec like Evan, but her focus was on signing white singers who mimicked the style of soulful singers—deep-timbred beauties whose voices somehow sounded like they were honed in a Black choir. Languorous singers whose glamorous appearances only made their sad-girl lyrics more pronounced.

"Hey, Billie. Welcome. Great shoes," she said quickly, then walked toward the kitchen, her large mug gripped tightly in her hand.

"Thanks. Nice to meet you," I said, though she'd already moved on.

I met the other people on the team, whose generic faces and names were a blur, before finally meeting Nina, the only other person of color on my team. She was impeccably dressed in a silky cream short-sleeved shirt, three layered dainty gold necklaces, medium-size gold hoops, and navy wide-legged trousers. Her deep-brown eyes stared into mine, and her button nose was brushed with enough highlighter to make it shine. She had dark curly hair cascading down her back, and her almond skin glistened in the lemon light that filtered through the windows—a sign that she probably kept cocoa butter stocked beneath her bathroom sink.

"Hi, Billie, welcome. If you need anything, let me know," she said.

"Nice to meet you, Nina, thanks so much."

Sharon walked me back to my desk, where there was a mountain of folders and papers spread across the surface that hadn't been there earlier. Before I had a chance to fix my mouth to ask a question, Sharon was already speeding down the hall toward her office. My eyes widened as I read through receipts and invoices totaling thousands of dollars for lunches and dinners at Midtown hotspots where celebrity chefs cooked for only two guests at a time, expensive drinks and seat-side service at exclusive venues, wardrobe selections for shoots from Balenciaga and Gucci, studio fees for recording sessions with producers who worked with megastars.

I'd always known that I would have to work my way to a good salary. I'd been told by professors and short-lived mentors that this was an industry built on passion, that to do this was for art, not commerce. But the evidence of commerce was here in my hands. There was, in fact, money. It simply didn't go to assistants, expendable as we were. But I didn't have time to dwell on that feeling. At least not on my first day, when there were impressions to be made. Plus, I was finally employed in the field I'd longed to join, and I had a 401(k), insurance, and a guaranteed paycheck, no matter how small, every two weeks.

I took a deep breath, reset my shoulders, and rechanneled my focus. I started to shuffle around papers on the desk and look through files in the drawers for a manual or some assistant guide to help me figure out what the hell to do. I was about to give up and look on the computer instead when I came across an unmarked stack of manila folders in the drawer on the right side of my desk.

Curious, I pulled out one of the files and laid it across my keyboard. Inside the file were spreadsheets. The one I was holding tracked upcoming artists in the industry. There was one column each for their names and project titles, a column for their social media numbers and streaming metrics, and a column that decided their fate—whether the artists had been signed or declined. I pulled out another sheet from the file, and as I scanned, I realized I recognized some of the names. At least half of them were artists that I knew had, at one point, been signed to Lit and had exploded onto the scene with a couple of hot singles but hadn't been heard from in years. Next to the artists' names were two more columns that seemed to be dollar amounts. One column was all negative numbers. I couldn't make out what they correlated to, maybe sales? In the last column, where the imprint information went, was a different company name: MHCP LLC. I checked the back of the papers to see if there was some kind of legend to help me understand, but it was blank.

I turned them around and inspected them again, trying to make sense of what I was seeing. When I couldn't find anything, I wondered if they wouldn't mind me taking a deeper look, just in case I could do something interesting with it in the future. Still, I needed to be careful—dedicated as an assistant in this new role first, upward mobility and creativity second. I snuck the list to a sliver of empty space on the corner of the desk where I could go through it later and see what I could eventually make of the artists they'd overlooked.

After that, I switched to looking on the desktop, but my search yielded nothing.

I glanced back at Michael's office. It didn't seem like he was too busy as he stared at the computer screen and leaned back in his chair, his arms linked behind his head. I got up and walked toward his office.

"I wouldn't do that if I were you," Nina said. Her clipped voice stopped me before I made it there.

"Oh, sorry. Is that not right? I thought I would ask Michael about the expenses and stuff on my desk. I'm not really sure how to tackle them, and there's no guide—"

"I know you're trying to get the hang of things here, but Michael really doesn't like to be bothered unless absolutely necessary. Feel free to knock if you want to catch his wrath," she said, her voice dipping beneath her breath.

I hesitated, not sure if she was joking or if his temperament was as bad as she said it was. But there was no hint of a smile on her lips, no laughter in her eyes either. I started toward my desk, but Nina stopped me again and waved me over to her.

"Look," she said conspiratorially, "I'm not trying to be negative or anything, but you have to be strategic here. Ask the assistants around you for help, maybe Charlotte or Jackie. Look on the FIRE database—that's where they store most of the manuals and instructions. It'll take you a while to understand the difference between Michael's digitized and non-digitized files. But basically, you have to figure things out yourself and do it right the first time if you're going to survive at this company."

"Okay. Thanks for the tip." I looked over at a cubicle with Charlotte's name that I had seen as I made the rounds. "I'll ask Charlotte."

Nina smiled, but it was the kind that was polite and cold all at once.

•

I was in the middle of a virtual training for the FIRE system that housed internal records like new-release briefs, tip sheets, marketing and publicity plans, and tour details when my Outlook pinged a reminder for the weekly Tuesday staff meeting happening in fifteen minutes. I knew from past internships that this meeting was where execs presented new artists they were interested in signing and shared updates on clients already on their rosters. At four, people put their computers to sleep, popped up from their cubicles, and made their way to the New York conference room. I followed behind them.

Michael sat at the front of the large rectangular table in the center of the room. The twenty executives—seated on either side of the table—were a sea of mostly white people. The six youngish men were all somehow slack-jawed and slick-haired. Their sleeves were rolled up to show off more of their biceps if they had them, or they wore cotton T-shirts beneath dark blazers. The older men that still thought themselves suave donned well-cut suits, their wrists carrying the weight of expensive cufflinks and watches. Two women at the table were of the Brooklyn transplant variety, the secretly rich ones who cosplayed as working-class, with their Warby Parker glasses and outfits from & Other Stories and Reformation. The other woman wore her wealth proudly, showing off her shiny blowout, diamond studs, wrinkles blasted into smooth perfection. And then there was Nina. The only person of color at the table, a breath of fresh air despite the staleness of the air-conditioning in the building.

The assistants lined up against the walls behind their managers.

"Before we get started, please welcome my new assistant, Billie Grand. She comes to us from internships at Universal and Warner."

I waved at everyone from my place among the chairs lining the wall opposite the snacks. Some people smiled and nodded, others clapped, all made me nervous. I could already feel sweat pooling beneath my breasts. My clasped hands went shaky, so I hid them behind my back.

"Okay, let's start on this side of the table. Evan?" Michael asked, looking to his left, the side opposite me.

I uncapped my pen and put it to the blank page on my branded notepad. Only a few of the assistants standing on either side of me were taking notes, but I didn't want to miss a thing. As an intern, I never had the chance to sit in on big meetings. Not staff meetings, weekly update meetings, or artist meetings. All we got were these bring-your-own-lunch sessions where people from different departments would talk to all the interns about their roles in such vague ways that it never seemed like info I'd need and be able to apply in real life. So I was going to take advantage of this, of the music world and its inner workings laid out before me.

"Uh, yeah. Well, nothing new, but an update on Wren, the pop singer—we made the offer, but he's still deciding with his manager because he has another offer from Republic. I'm going to push for a decision by end of day."

"Okay, great," Michael said. "See if we can sweeten the deal with bonuses. Talk with finance and see what they can do."

Evan nodded.

I had heard of Wren, a nasal-voiced but seemingly sweet "all-American" singer who had become a YouTube sensation overnight after one of his videos went viral. He had the kind of looks and personality that would set white girls on fire—like Harry Styles in his post–One Direction era or Justin Bieber in his prime. And that was, I assumed, exactly what Lit wanted in an artist. Someone who could bring their own fan base. Someone who had the kind of look that would appeal to people in every corner of this country.

In the coming months I'd know exactly who Evan would craft Wren into if he had the chance to sign him. I smiled to myself. Soon, the music and artists that had been brought up here would be real and pulsing and flourishing, and now I had access to the process and a path toward my eventual future as an A&R rep.

"Kate?" Michael asked, calling on people in the order they sat around the table.

"Sure. Um. Nothing new to bring up, but just for the room, there's been some controversy brewing with Lorna Velour. Lorna made a post defending the content on her sophomore album, and then these aggressive women online started attacking her. Michael, can we talk offline about what we can do to protect her? Lorna's lyrics are messy, beautiful, vulnerable, because they are about life. She shouldn't be attacked for that." Kate was getting riled up as she spoke, tears springing in her eyes, ready to flow like the Hudson.

As Kate talked, I had to work to stop my face from twisting up in confusion because Kate had it wrong. She was spinning this in Lorna's favor when everyone knew Lorna had started it.

Lorna Velour, a white woman whose style was vintage Hollywood, was called out because her post was offensive. She had mentioned the names of several successful Black and brown women in music, singled out these women on socials, said that if they could sing and rap number-one songs about fucking and partying and getting money, then why couldn't she write and sing about white women in complicated relationships.

The thing was, none of the artists she mentioned had anything to do with her or her music. They hadn't come at her at all. It was some of Lorna's fans who pointed it out, who took issue with the way she seemed to glamorize domestic abuse. Yet she chose to compare other artists' music to hers like it was their fault she was being held accountable. Now the label was bending over backward to ensure her career would thrive as she attacked the livelihood of others who hadn't even started this.

"Listen, Kate, Lorna Velour is a talent, and we don't want to give her any more ammo to break her contract with us to sign with her uncle at Sony," Michael said as a few chuckles rippled through the room. "I think this will blow over quickly if we just let the chatter die down. But why don't you hang back after the meeting so we can figure this out?"

Kate smiled, bleary-eyed and close-lipped, and nodded. "Okay. Sounds good."

I looked toward Nina, who was seated next to Kate, to see what her face would reveal, but she was stoic, unreadable beyond the tight smile stretched thin across her face.

"Okay, that brings us to you, Nina," Michael said.

"Yes, I've been trying to get in touch with Papi's manager. As I mentioned last week, Papi is a Dominican artist who does Latin trap and reggaeton. He doesn't have a huge following yet, but he made this video a couple days ago that's been getting great traction—he has over two million views across platforms so far. The song is also being used in a ton of Reels and TikToks, so there's some real potential here. I think he could be our answer to Bad Bunny, who's been dominating the charts for years. He's performing at Brooklyn Steel next week, opening for Kali Uchis. I'll see if I can talk to him there."

"Okay. If we could lock him into a deal with a modest advance, that would be great."

Nina shifted in her seat, the corners of her mouth pulled into a near-imperceptible frown. She nodded, and Michael moved on to the rest of the team.

No one else had caught the frown, but I did. Was Papi not worth as much as Wren and Lorna? Her frown made me curious about what it would take to bring new artists to Lit.

I had to find out how Nina had done it before, how she had signed Marcelo and D. Salaz, whose singles became the anthems of the summer before my junior year of college, the background to birthday parties, barbecues, kickbacks, songs that drifted out of Washington Heights and Lower East Side bars and beckoned Lucas, Alicia, and me in, that made us down shots and wine and pop our bodies on crowded dance floors. I wondered how she managed to do that when it seemed like it might be an uphill battle to get them to invest in talent before they blew up, to help develop an icon rather than acquire one.

It's nothing I didn't expect. These labels were about the music but also, unequivocally, about business. Money. Capitalism. And in business, the game is never fair. But I also knew myself. And no matter what I saw today and whatever obstacles might come later, I was going to play the game, and I was going to clear it.

"All right, everyone. Let's stay on target for the next few weeks. We need three more artists for this fiscal." Michael added, "Oh, and don't forget that we're still in talks with Trent and team at Ultimate Records for a possible merger. We haven't come to an agreement on anything yet, but as usual, don't make any mention of Ultimate in your email or even in anything you type. It could work against us in this deal."

He looked around the room, noticed faces streaked with worry, and repositioned his own face into an expression that approximated sympathy before launching into the next part of his spiel.

"Look, everyone, I know we're in unprecedented times and that there might be some changes down the road—budget cuts, restructuring of leadership, imprints, roles. We don't have a sense of all the moving pieces yet, but what we do know is that this merger will make us stronger. It will breathe new life into Lit and usher us into a new era with more inclusivity and diversity and a larger share of the marketplace. It will also revitalize our already strong reputation in the industry. If the transition happens, we'll do all we can to keep the staff and, most important, the integrity of Lit intact as we move forward. Anyway, that's all for now."

With that, people broke off into little groups to return to their desks or hung back to snatch up more snacks from the table. One of the younger executives, who looked like a Glen Powell clone I'd later learn was named Connor, quietly muttered something about the merger to another exec as he grazed. My ears perked when I heard the word *woke* mixed in with *Ultimate,* but I couldn't really make out what else they were saying. I edged closer, trying to understand more, but when I saw Nina about to leave the conference room, I knew I couldn't let her go without saying something. This was my chance at a real first conversation with her. I needed her to know that I was serious about my career here, that I hoped one day I could be like her, that if we grew on each other enough, she would eventually see something of herself in me.

I made a beeline toward her as quickly as I could without being conspicuous.

"Hey, Nina, I just wanted to say thank you. For earlier," I said, gesturing toward my new desk out in the open space. She stood by the table with chips closest to the door, a plate held loosely in one hand.

"Oh, um, no problem." She was distracted, looking off into the distance toward the Midtown sky painted bright, clear blue.

"Yeah. I also wanted to say . . . I really loved D. Salaz and Marcelo. I mean, I must've had Marcelo on repeat that whole summer. Anyway, I'm glad to meet you. I'm a fan of your work, and I'm honored to have a chance to work with you here, and I just wanted to, uh, say that, and I'll . . . leave you to it."

By now, the conference room was empty, and I was grateful to have only Nina witness the feelings that festered within me.

Nina sized me up as I talked and smirked at me like I was a toddler who'd slotted all the shaped blocks into their correct spots for the first time. I would have been insulted if I didn't already secretly crave her approval. I waited as she continued her slow, silent assessment. I nodded awkwardly and turned to leave to avoid further embarrassment. But then she replied.

"Thanks. I'm a fan of them too," she said, breaking out into a smile. "Do me a favor? Hold on to that enthusiasm. You're gonna need it later."

She looked down at her phone, and her face was as unreadable as it had been when she was pitching Papi. "I have to run, but maybe we could grab coffee or lunch one of these days?"

"I'd love that." As she turned to leave, I pumped my fist beside me and smiled. I had shot my shot, and however reckless it was, I knew it was the right decision.

Close to the end of the day, Nina stopped by my desk and asked if Michael had time for a quick chat before he was ready to head out.

I looked toward his office, and since he was at his desk and there was nothing on his Outlook calendar I'd gained access to earlier in the afternoon, I told her it was fine.

When Nina left Michael's office, her face was wiped clean of emotion. I wondered if she used the face often so that it would allow her to take the news from Michael as normal, as though it weren't infuriating enough to burn her alive from the inside.

As I got ready to leave for the night myself, Michael called me into his office. I scurried to his door.

"Billie, I'm about to head out," he said, "but I wanted to say, great job today. Before I leave, there are some things you'll need to know if you're going to be working for me. First, starting next week, I'll need you here every day at seven for the next three weeks so we can close a deal. Also, every Monday and Wednesday afternoon, I take an hour to swim at my gym, so you'll need to schedule a car to get me there and back. I bring in Scooter from time to time, and he'll need to be taken to the doggie daycare. You're not allergic to dogs, right?"

I bit my lip, unsure if all the requests he asked of me were real, but when he didn't laugh, I realized he wasn't joking.

"No, I'm not allergic." I didn't have allergies, but I didn't like dogs either—something about their unconditional love annoyed me. "And yes, of course, I'm happy to help." I nodded my head in agreement to make sure he understood I was up for anything he threw at me, no matter how weird it was.

Michael nodded at me once and resumed work on his computer. I started back to my desk.

"Oh, and one more thing," he said.

I whipped around to look at him, and his eyes darkened as he beckoned me closer.

"I know your desk is a mess right now, and I would appreciate you organizing it, but if you find anything that deals with MHCP LLC, please put it on my desk. Those files are important but also confidential. So make sure to return them to me unread."

"Got it."

"Have a good night."

I returned to my desk drenched in under-boob sweat and grateful I had dark skin so that the blood that had rushed into my cheeks couldn't peek through. It was a good thing he hadn't been watching closely earlier as I inspected the file at my cube. I made a note to put the MHCP file on his desk in the morning.

I took one last look around the office and made my way to Grand Central, near where Lucas had been working for the day, to meet him for our date.

4

Lucas and I planned to go to dinner to celebrate my first day at Lit. We'd taken the 6 Train down to the East Village, where it felt like the New York we'd grown up with. The air was a heady mix of stale beer, sidewalk garbage, and the best dollar slices one could eat when they were broke. Street art was splashed onto brick walls of squat buildings. Artist types chilled on corners and on the stairs that once led to a punk emporium, with their skateboards and Bluetooth speakers blasting Mac Miller and Tyler, the Creator, smoking cigarettes and showing off fresh tattoos. NYU students in blue jeans and dirty white sneakers trailed down the blocks in groups, searching for bars that would accept their fake IDs.

Alicia, Lucas, and I were lucky that we didn't have to leave home for school and got to party in our own glittering city. We spent entire nights there in our early college years, traipsing up and down Saint Mark's Place, slamming five shots each of watered-down rum and tequila in a bar whose floors were perpetually wet and whose bathroom had never seen a mop in its existence. But for only ten dollars per five shots, we let the liquor unwind us, and I led us to salvation—bars whose music made us believe in the profundity of melody and rhythm. I had felt invincible when we were still out when the sun came up. I had the power to make nights last forever.

Now, as we got closer to Avenue A, we stomped our way down the block to prevent rats from scrambling across our feet, and walked up to Miss Lily's 7A. The restaurant was retro-punk East Village cool meets modern take on eighties coastal Jamaican diner. The spot had a long bar with stools, several earth-toned two-tops directly across from that, and aqua-colored booths in the back for larger parties. The lights were dimmed, and it was early enough that people looking to get drunk and dance hadn't wandered in to crowd around the bar yet, so the mood was romantic. Early aughts reggae classics played in the background as the DJ eased us into the evening.

As the food and drinks arrived—two rum punches infused with chunks of pineapple and orange that were presoaked in Wray & Nephew, cod-fish fritters fried to golden perfection with a side of curry dipping sauce, Jerk ramen with pork belly and ackee, and traditional Jamaican oxtail stew that made my mouth water—I finally brought up my day. Lucas wasn't one to push. "*You deserve space to share on your own terms,*" he often said. I loved how he let me be wholly myself, how he let me breathe.

In other words, he minded his business until he knew I was ready.

The melody of the song playing now made some of the women in the restaurant explode into choral harmony as they swayed in their seats and hummed the lyrics Sasha sang, "I'm still in love with you, boy."

"So your first day was good, then?" he asked between bites of of oxtail stew.

"Yeah, I think it was. The office is beautiful, and I have my own desk that's not in a closet. But we had a staff meeting today, and it was weird . . ." I waved my fork in the air and teased my voice into casual because I knew he'd get more bent up about it than me. "Don't ask," I added.

He nodded, stuffed a piece of meat into his mouth. He didn't want to dive into that conversation either.

I took his peace offering of silence and continued.

"There's already a lot of admin work to do, but I expected that. Ima need to figure out the politics here, though. I feel like there's some invisible hierarchy I don't understand yet. And Michael had some weird requests too. Like, I have to occasionally take his fucking dog to the doggie daycare, which, like, sucks, but whatever. Oh, I also heard something about a merger. But I don't know what it was about for real. Other than all of that, it was . . . I don't know.

I was, like, right there in the room where careers are being made. It's sort of surreal. I spend so much time talking and thinking about music, and here everyone is, like, on the same page. They love music so much that they're willing to bet everything on it. They're passionate about what music can do, what it can mean, how it can reflect life back to someone else like it was made just for them. It feels like I'm where I'm supposed to be."

"That's the part I do understand. Like when I'm painting or photographing," he said.

I leaned into him and nodded because I had seen his pensive look in moments like that hundreds of times before, his militant focus.

"I'm always thinking, like . . . how does this feel to me? How will it feel to other people? Does it stir something in me? Art is supposed to mean something, be something that takes you over, pulls you in whole. If there's anything I can relate to about why you took this corporate-ass job, it's that you'll be able to preserve that passion."

"Yeah. One day. . . . There was also the receptionist. She was a little, I don't know, rude? She didn't say hi when I came in, and ignored my compliment. And she was Black. I thought we would have hit it off. Especially 'cause I didn't see any more of us around. Well, except Nina. She's Latina, I think." I stuffed the last fritter into my mouth.

Lucas shrugged. "Maybe she was having a bad day."

"Yeah, maybe. Anyway, tell me about your shoot."

"Well, we was supposed to be in a studio 'cause she said she knew the owner, but she changed it to her crib last-minute. This girl had roaches everywhere. And her cousin kept coming in and out of his bedroom, smelling like straight gas. But her cousin hooked me up for free, though. So it wasn't all bad. Got some on me right now. Anyway, I'm good on shooting with her again. I was only doing it on the strength of David, who's hooking me up with sound equipment for Sunsetlandia anyway."

"Sorry, babe. That sucks. But I have something that will cheer you up."

"Oh yeah? What's that?" he asked, inching closer to me.

"Concert tickets for after dinner. But I'm not telling you who it is. You'll have to find out when we get there." I was pleased with myself when the corners of his mouth pulled up into that easy smile that I loved.

Since we started dating it had been a struggle to surprise him. He knew me too well, and my attempts were thwarted by how acutely he paid attention to details.

He knew my mannerisms, the way my hand shot out from my body and stiffened when I was trying to hide something. He'd laugh knowingly when I spoke in a high-pitched voice different from my usual raspy tone, repeating, "*Wow, that's crazy,*" when a conversation went on too long. I was a bad liar, but this time, I basked in the warm glow of success.

•

The sun sank below the buildings as we walked to the entrance to West Fourth Street station on the corner of Eighth Street that would take us to the concert venue. Lucas occasionally stopped to snap photos of the waning pink light in the sky. Some of the photos were also of me, alternately smiling and hiding from the camera.

We walked up the stairs from the L Train at Union Square and finally got in the line that snaked around the corner from the entrance of Irving Plaza. As we walked, I had to shield Lucas from fans who wore T-shirts that bore the name and image of Wazy, the conscious rapper from Detroit headlining the show.

I didn't really listen to Wazy, but he was Lucas's favorite artist. And though his every word in that grating high-pitched voice made me recoil, Lucas's incessant replays of his debut album, how deeply he felt Wazy's lyrics, his rage, the way he fought for his community and against police brutality, the way he urged Black people to enrich themselves, to weaponize themselves with knowledge because it was powerful, made me like him too. It was a message I could get behind, even while I winced and plugged my ears.

When we got up to the front of the line, Lucas finally realized who was playing. He turned to me and scooped me up into a hug, and I reveled in the feel of his chest pressed against mine, his long arms around me, the stubble that pressed prickly against my skin. He lifted my fro and kissed my neck softly—a gesture that he usually made in the low light of our bedroom that made me feel loved entirely. We moved into the venue, past the throngs of people crowded at a photo backdrop near the doorway, and found a spot close to the stage. It was an intimate space—so close that you could touch the artists, see the sweat streaked across their foreheads and the veins that looked like they were close to popping out of their glistening necks.

There was a decent lineup of opening acts before Wazy was set to come on. I had looked the artists up before the concert so I'd know who to miss if I needed to go to the bathroom. I wasn't interested in any of them so far. Two rappers had gone on already. They weren't affiliated, but their music was basically spiritual cousins. They each rapped two uninspired songs about money and hoes and drugs over deafening beats. I was at least a little excited for the only woman in the lineup. She was a rapper and singer out of the Bronx. I didn't know much else about her yet, but I knew how much talent had grown out of those hoods, how some of those rappers and singers had changed the industry with their naked magnetism.

Samirah was up next, and I was curious to see if she had the kind of fire that ignited stardom. After a few minutes of the DJ playing songs in between sets, the lights in the venue changed. Vibrant colors centered in the middle, and a thin cloud of mist wafted onto the stage. From the moment the lush horns and deep bass blasted from the speakers, I knew this would be the kind of music I'd like—bass that thrummed within me, synth that shocked me into feeling.

Then Samirah ran onto the stage.

"What's good, New Yorrrrrrrk, I'm Samirah, and I'm here to get ya hype tonight." She wore a simple black catsuit, and her hair was slicked back into a long braided ponytail. As she stood on the stage beneath the saturated light, she didn't say another word, yet the crowd quieted, in awe of her presence. She looked composed, cool, like she had done this so many times before, but it never got old, never felt like a chore. It felt like electricity as she cavorted across the stage, bopping to a bright, bass-heavy beat, the kind that made vibrations reverberate through me, and I felt stuck, like my energy was a part of hers. I was caught in her orbit.

Then she started rapping.

Dedicated to this life, paying bills, paying dues
Pay ya homage we coming from Morrison Soundview.

Y'all tryna eat? Bet Ima come through
Got my city on my back, making dreams come true

Samirah held the mic in one hand, her voice raspy, hypnotic, calling out to us as she danced across the stage. It beat out the bass rattling around her so that all that hit me was the punch of her lyrics, her pitch-perfect riffs as she sang the chorus.

Here was music that reflected life back to me, like it was made for me, like I was finally seen.

"Y'all feeling that?" Samirah called out to the audience, breaking the trance she had me in. The people here for Wazy sounded back at her with resounding yeses. She then sang out a low, moody, rumbling note over a euphonic beat. The sound had a gritty, sultry appeal without sacrificing lyrical finesse. It was a song that said that she would never be someone's option, that she wouldn't allow insecurity to be bred into her when she knew she was a prize to be coveted and protected.

In between songs now, Samirah walked from the center of the stage to a stool a few feet away. She picked up a bottle of water that sat on the floor next to the stool and took a sip.

"Goddamn, she's good. Are you hearing this, babe?" I asked, turning to Lucas beside me, giddy and slightly sweaty from dancing and the people pressed too close around me.

Lucas nodded, his braids swinging a little. "Yeah, that was hard. You heard of her before?"

"Nah, I only looked her up for a minute before the show, but shit, I want to know more now."

Before I could say anything else, clashing cymbals and a few low chords on the piano indicated she would be back to singing shortly. "Oh, shh, shh, she's back on," I said to Lucas.

I studied her as she moved into an up-tempo song about success, about what it feels like when people think you aren't enough, but you know that despite everything, you are. The piercing fast-paced beat resounded through the speakers.

"Sing it, sis!" someone shouted from the crowd.

When Samirah finally took her bow, yelling out to New York once again, professing her love for the city and to us for being a part of this experience, and then exiting the stage, the spell had lifted. I was back to my senses, Lucas's fingers squeezing mine. I knew I needed to look her up for real. To see if she was signed somewhere or if I could be the one to help her get there. I searched for her on Instagram, found her page, and hit follow. I'd do a deep dive later.

By the time the DJ started to play Wazy's album hits, the energy in the spot had reached its climax. Lighters and blunts and vapes materialized in people's hands, and the cloud of smoke grew thick above us. Lucas pulled out his own spliff, and we took turns pulling the herb into our lungs. Soon Wazy came barreling onto the stage. He was a pretty boy through and through—short, dark, curly hair; moisturized mustache and goatee; a blindingly white smile against his russet skin; dressed in a sweatshirt and matching shorts set and bulky Dior sneakers. But once Wazy got into the set, it wasn't his looks you paid attention to. It was his infectious energy, the way he bounced up and down in time to the beat, the way he crouched down to get closer to the crowd, the way he said, "This life shit is mine to conquer," and we believed him.

The crowd chanted along with his lyrics, and I did too. But I couldn't help the small part of me that lingered in the before, when Samirah had blown my fucking mind.

•

Three songs in, I was cotton-mouthed, dripping with sweat, and dying for hydration.

I went to the bar, ordered free ice water, and turned away to scan the crowd. As I people-watched and nodded along with the music, a man came toward me. As he got closer, I noticed his deep-brown skin, dark round eyes, and a fade crisper than a McDonald's Sprite. I could never tell which type of guy I would encounter in these dark, crowded rooms—a nice, normal one or someone who'd call me a bitch for refusing his offer—so slowly, as if I were dancing, I moved to the other end of the bar. When he reached me, he leaned back and placed one foot against the wall.

"Hey," he said.

I smiled a half smile, careful to not show too much enthusiasm or hostility.

"Yo," he said. "I'm not tryna talk to you. I know you from Instagram. Quincy. MoneyBoyQ. Dre's boy?" He pointed at himself.

"Oh hey. Okay. You had me ready to fight," I said, laughing.

"Yeah, I sensed that. Anyway, I wanted to come over and introduce myself. When I followed you back on IG, I noticed that you work for Lit, right?"

"Yeah. I started today actually."

"Cool. Cool." He nodded. "So are you, like, looking for new artists and all that?"

I had changed my social media bios earlier in the morning, eager to announce my new job to everyone. I knew good and well I couldn't tell Quincy I was looking for artists when I hadn't even figured out the basics of the job, but I wanted him to take me seriously. I wanted to see what this relationship could bloom into if I told this one little lie that would eventually become truth if I worked long and hard enough at it.

"I mean, not officially, but I'm on my way," I said.

"Oh okay. Well, I do security mostly, but I produce beats on the side. Always gotta have multiple streams of income, you know. Anyway, yeah, let's def stay in touch."

"Do you know anything about that girl who just performed? Samirah?"

"It's funny you bring that up 'cause that's also kinda why I wanted to talk to you. I'm working with Samirah right now. That first song she did was a beat I produced."

"Oh, word? Sis ate up there."

"Yeah, she's got that effect on people. I found her on SoundCloud, rapping to some trash-ass beat. I knew I could make her something better. You got a card or something so I can reach you?"

"Oh, um, I don't have them yet," I said. "But I can give you my number so we can talk later?"

"A'ight, bet. Let's do that." A smile lifted one side of his mouth.

I gave Quincy my number, waved goodbye, and shouldered my way through the crowd to Lucas.

"You were gone a while," Lucas said when I'd returned.

"Yeah. Something good just happened," I said, a soft smile playing on my lips.

He looked at me like he knew something was up, but I wasn't ready to share yet, not until this was more of a concrete thing. Instead, I reached up to kiss him as the hook of Wazy's song, a lovely melody against snappy 808s, coursed through our bodies like the subway rumbling beneath our feet whenever we walked over grates. It pulled me back to the music, back to the moment, and back to this life that felt like it was touching the tip of something bigger.

5

For the next few days at Lit, I felt like an extra who had snuck onto the set of a play on opening night. Here I was, ready to make it big, but secretly I was scared I'd get found and dragged out by security. I didn't want my fate to be like Michael's last assistant's. And I didn't want to waste any part of this world that had opened up for me. So I spent my lunch breaks eating overpriced salads and wandering the halls.

Every time the elevators dinged on the floor that housed the state-of-the-art studios on my way up to the office and I glimpsed into the places where they made the magic of music, I felt tingly all over, like when Lucas massaged my scalp as we watched cheesy music videos from the early eighties before Michael Jackson changed everything. My heart was a radiator, clanging loudly, wildly, in my chest when I caught eyes with Blood Orange, whose albums I'd played over and over again to escape Mama and Marvin's fussing and fighting about unpaid bills, who was in the Madrid conference room for a meeting with a collaborator. I suppressed the impulse to squeal when I saw the release briefs I was instructed to compile for next season's launch. It was for a forthcoming album from Tayari—a three-decades-famous pop star known for reinvention—announcing a rock era that I knew would be powerful enough to coerce people into social anarchy, leather, and spikes.

When I wasn't exploring, I spent the rest of the time getting myself set up. I completed all those tedious corporate-required anti-theft and -piracy courses disguised as trainings, and I was starting to learn the differences between the other assistants. I got myself added to all the requisite distros and had IT set me up in all the systems. I'd printed out images of album covers I loved to post on my cube walls so it gave off a vibe that said I knew and appreciated deep cuts but I was also fun and didn't take myself too seriously. I'd also picked up some cute office supplies from Staples and the good ninety-nine-cent store by the crib that had wide aisles, almost-fresh produce, and a baby-faced cashier that flirted with me and gave me more discounts than he was supposed to.

By the time work ended on Friday, I had learned even more things about Lit. I knew where all the bathrooms and conference rooms were, which copier printed high volumes without jamming, how to answer Michael's calls and forward them to his office, and how to search for an album or tipsheet or artist information in the FIRE database. I watched the other assistants greet guests in the lobby as I walked back to my desk from the kitchen with my crappy pod coffee so I could get it right when someone came in for Michael. I was starting to get my bearings.

The weekend passed by easily. Lucas was off planning things for Sunsetlandia, and Alicia was away for a few weeks on a tour with some pop star. It was also hot as shit outside now that we were in a heat wave, so I blasted the air conditioner and a playlist I'd made as high as they could go and did things I didn't do while Lucas was home. I deep cleaned my side of the bedroom closet. I popped the pimples on my face in the bathroom mirror and pumiced the white, cracked bottoms of my feet while sitting on the toilet. I masturbated with my purple vibrator under the cool air until I came and knocked out for a couple of hours on the sofa.

At night, I did artist research on Spotify for my MusicallyBillie account and threw on biopics about musicians before I drifted to sleep. I adored biopics. I loved seeing the inside view of artists' lives and rise to stardom. I loved the drama and personal relationships. I loved the recreated performances made anew with fresh context. I loved seeing how artists honed their talent, how their music found its way into audiences' hearts.

I started with *CrazySexyCool: The TLC Story* and *The New Edition Story.*

The next day was *What's Love Got to Do with It* and *Ray*. I capped off the weekend with the television miniseries turned Black cult classic about the beloved group Deliverance Desired.

Deliverance Desired was a Black folk collective armed with acoustic guitars and belly-deep voices that had found major success singing to my grandmama's generation about quiet revolution and the ravishes of abject poverty.

The group was fresh on my mind as I trekked down to the office at six on Monday morning when all the overnight workers pretended to be asleep as I slunk onto the train, looking for a seat. Before I went upstairs, I stopped at a nearby bagel place and struggled up to the conference room, cradling an entire continental breakfast for Michael's big meetings in my weary arms.

Once I got everything set up in the conference room, I settled at my desk with my own cup of coffee. Right as I turned on my computer monitor, Michael came barreling down the hallway. I grabbed a pen and pad and stood quickly. I'd learned last week that he preferred to dictate things to me instead of sending emails with clear instructions. It was easy to keep up with him because I'd already been scarred into being a meticulous notetaker in middle school. My seventh-grade history teacher got off on revoking recess if students didn't get all the notes down before he erased them. He was tight when halfway through the quarter, I mastered speed writing and he couldn't do anything about it, when I used recess to go to the student lounge to watch music videos on the school's slow Dell desktop. If only Mr. Malcolm could see me now.

"Good morning, Michael," I said. "Can I get you anything?"

"My office," he said without so much as a backward glance. I followed behind him and prayed his mood wasn't a precursor to bad news.

I stepped in and shut the office door behind me.

"Billie, I'm trying to acquire the rights to Deliverance Desired's works. They're in a little . . . financial trouble, and their catalog is up for grabs."

It had been common knowledge since the nineties that bad business deals in the early days of their career had left them in trouble with the IRS. Michael planned to position himself as their savior, their personal deliverance.

He said, "I need you to schedule a call between me and legal to see if we could reset territory terms. Then I need you to pull whatever public information you can get. Tax information, any liens on property, credit reports, interviews, other bad press. All of it. Get that info to Connor and tell him that whatever comes of this deal would be associated with MHCP LLC."

I remembered the initials from the weird file I'd found on my first day, but I didn't allow myself to think about it further. Michael had already warned me about its confidentiality. For now, although it made me queasy like when I ate eggs loaded with butter for breakfast even though I'd been allergic since I was twelve, I would do as I was told.

I wrote faster to keep up with all his demands as he barked them to me in quick succession.

"Oh, I also need you to book New York from 2:00 to 4:00 P.M. every day this week for something else," he continued. "I also need two reservations for Friday. Pick somewhere nice. Corner booths. No ugly servers. And book me an appointment with Dr. Mads. I'm out of my prescription. Deliverance Desired will be here at eleven, so I need it all done by then."

I waited for more instructions, but Michael was already looking at his computer, clicking through email. He was done dictating, and I had been unceremoniously dismissed.

I started with the easy tasks first. I booked the conference rooms. Then I found Dr. Mads's name in an assistant manual I'd discovered in a stack of files under my desk. Next I called restaurants about reservations and tried to express as politely as possible that Michael didn't want uggos in his section.

When it was time to look into all the things Michael wanted on the group, I tried not to think about how I was possibly helping Michael take advantage of a group that had been singing about Black sorrows and savvy since the seventies.

•

At eleven, Erykah called and let me know that Deliverance Desired had arrived. I was giddy that I'd get to meet the men whose lives I'd watched unfold on my TV screen yesterday, the men whose voices had been the soundtrack of a revolution. I fluffed my fro, fixed the hair in my eyes that had come out of the area where I'd pinned it into the shape of a curly bang, smoothed the front of my midi button-down cream vest dress, and walked to the lobby.

The three remaining living members of the group were dressed loudly, in oversize suits with metallic accents, hard shiny shoes, and wide-brimmed hats. I complimented them on their music, telling them how big of a fan my grandmama was (or so I'd heard in stories Mama told me about her), and did my best to remain calm as I walked them to the conference room.

A few hours later, Michael asked me to bring them all fresh coffee while he stepped out to talk to Connor about something in his office. As I placed the coffees, milk, and sugar on the table and drifted out of the room, they picked up their conversation. I stood quietly outside the conference room door to listen.

"Yeah, this sounds like it might be a good deal, Earl. What you think?" said the one with the red feather attached to his hat.

"Man, this might be the prayer we been asking for. Y'all know we been needing this money," said another in a black suit accented with yellow and silver.

"Let's see what all he talking 'bout before we say yes. But it's looking like we 'bout to eat good to me," Earl said. The light in the room bounced off the gold in his mouth as they all gave one another pounds and erupted into laughter.

I shook my head and walked back to my desk because I knew, considering all the things that Michael had me look up on them, that they didn't understand what they might be giving up for their payday.

I don't know what else happened in the meetings, but after a full week of them, Michael and Connor had emerged triumphant. They had talked Deliverance Desired into a deal that would extend in perpetuity.

Early mornings and late evenings made Lucas and me ships in the night, until I realized it was Friday and we were at the end of my second week. It was time to fill out timesheets for my first paycheck.

I'd wanted to check in with Nina. It would give me a chance to talk to her again and to show her that I was here, already hustling to keep my spot. But she was out with a client.

I decided to ask Charlotte, who looked like she was setting up for a long night herself, instead.

"Hey, Charlotte?" I asked.

She held up one hand to me as she typed with the other, letting me know she'd be a sec. I nodded and pretended to be interested in my gel manicure.

"What's up?" she asked. Her mousy brown hair swung as she jerked her head to me. At this angle, I could see the tiredness under her eyes that she tried to blot out with makeup.

"Hey, sorry to bother you, but do you know if we need to get, like, preapproved for overtime? I've been coming in really early and staying late all week so . . ."

I didn't get a chance to finish talking before Charlotte threw her head back and cackled for a long while before she shook her head no. When I saw her glistening, open mouth, I realized that this was the first time I'd seen an assistant smile here.

"I'm sorry to laugh, but I love that you think we get paid overtime. I mean, don't get me wrong, we totally should and it's super illegal not to. But it's not a real thing here. Think of it as part of professional development. You know, as part of paying your dues."

I groaned. I had hoped it would be different here.

When she didn't say more, only smiled that white-people smile at me and turned her attention back to her desk, I returned to mine.

In for another long night of no pay, I ducked downstairs to charge a slice of pizza on my nearly maxed-out credit card, sent Lucas a text that I'd be home late, and settled in.

•

The next morning, the buzz of my phone woke me out of my sleep. It was Mama. I cleared my throat and answered, hoping this call wouldn't be about her problems.

"Hello."

"Hey, baby. I'm calling to check in. Did you just wake up?"

"Um yeah, Mama, it's mad early."

"Well, you know I start my days at six. It's basically afternoon at this point. Anyway, I was wondering if you wanted to maybe get breakfast or something tomorrow? Feels like we haven't talked in a while."

"I'm running some errands with Lucas, but I have some time at, like, ten if that works?"

"Yeah. That sounds good. I wanted to ask you—never mind, let's talk on Sunday."

"Okay, Mama. I gotta go. See you tomorrow."

I sighed and threw my phone on the bed next to me. A call like this was almost always followed by another call and a request from her. A request for money. A request for my time. A request for my acquiescence. But I wanted to believe that this was innocent. That she missed me and this had nothing to do with the fact that summer started tomorrow.

I prepared myself for her inevitable call back. When my phone buzzed again, I sighed and checked the screen. It wasn't Mama, but a text chain from Auntie Dionne to the family about her annual Fourth of July barbecue in two weeks. I looked forward to it every year. My aunt, who had been like all of us—struggling, working-class—had managed to marry rich. Her gatherings were one of the only times the rest of us family got to escape the sirens, the noise, the hustle, the cramped apartments, the dirty subway, the constant crush of bodies on busy sidewalks.

I replied to the group text, confirming my attendance, and slowly got ready for the day. I took a long shower to ease the tension out of my shoulders. I rubbed myself down with cocoa butter and slathered on a deep-cleansing face mask. I took my time detangling my hair with a Denman brush instead of snagging it through my fingers like usual. I threw on a long black dress, one of my favorites that skimmed my curves. I'd bought three of the same on sale last year when I realized how miraculous it was that they came with a built-in bra and real pockets.

I watched a few scenes of *Lady Sings the Blues* until my hair had dried enough for me to see if Alicia, who was back in town for a couple days for New York– and New Jersey–based shows, would be up for putting my hair into knotless boho braids. I wanted to look good for the barbecue, but I also wanted to shave twenty minutes off my morning routine since Lit had been taking up more and more of my time.

•

"Hey, girl," Alicia said as she opened her apartment door.

She lived only a few blocks away from me in a prewar building that was in different stages of deterioration. Her kitchen had seen the most updates, with its shiny appliances and nonwhite refrigerator, but the paint chipped on the bathroom walls, and the living room ceiling above the sofa had blackened and molded from water damage in the shape of a lily pad or Pac-Man, depending on which way you tilted your head.

It was a sacrifice Alicia endured because the apartment was rent stabilized and her grandmother had dealt with her fair share of real estate vultures. It was a war of attrition we'd seen our whole lives: Developers wanted to oust long-time tenants in favor of those who could afford to move into updated apartments, and our home would be slapped with the label of an "up-and-coming neighborhood."

"Damn, it's hot in here," I said, wiping sweat from my forehead with the back of my hand. I slipped off my sandals and sat down on a pillow on the floor that was placed in front of the sofa.

"Yeah, well. You know a bitch be broke. Plus you just came from outside. You'll cool down."

She grabbed a fan and placed it nearer to me, then sat on the sofa.

I positioned myself between her legs.

"Did you get the hair?" she asked.

"Yeah. Five packs."

Alicia took the hair out of the black plastic bag and placed a tub of gel and hair clips on the seat next to her. She separated the hair I'd bought into smaller pieces, then got to work sectioning the back of my afro into neat parts with gel and a rat-tail comb.

"So," I said, "what's up with you? It's been a minute."

"I know, right? It's been wild. So you know I was on tour doing backup with Rosela Violet, who was opening for Tuff G, right?"

"Yeah." I nodded in anticipation.

She had been touring as a backup dancer since undergrad. It filled in the gaps for money whenever she couldn't find steady work as a freelance writer or when friends were busy getting silk presses instead of the braids she usually installed in the warmer months. She came back from her trips exhausted from the long hours and hard, thankless work of using her body as an extension of another. But she loved telling me the stories of what went down backstage, on stage, on tour buses, in the privacy of dingy hotel rooms, the secrets shared between people who sweat and slept and hustled together every night for months. I was appropriately eager to hear about all the drama. Drama that I was not in was my favorite kind.

"The Tuff G fans treated Rosela Violet crazy. I never seen nothing like it." Alicia said. "They would, like, throw shit at her while she was performing. Or she would be rocking the set, like, really into it, and we're, like, dancing mad hard behind her, and the crowd gave nothing. No energy at all. It was bad vibes all around, bro."

"Damn, that's bugged out." I said.

"It really is. Sad too 'cause she ain't do nothing to deserve it. People just tryna go viral by being assholes. But really I think it's 'cause their vibes don't match for real. The crowd wasn't feeling Rosela Violet's set. It's upbeat and, like, high-energy, which was the exact opposite of Tuff G's depressing-ass music. Anyway, I'm tight because Rosela Violet said she wanted to bring us on for the fall leg of the tour. But with the way that went, I don't know if I wanna go. I'm thinking I might take a break. Be home for a while. Maybe start looking for full-time gigs again. Lord knows I need some consistent money coming in."

"I hear that, girl. I know you'll find something soon. You're too good at what you do not to."

"Yeah. I hope so too. Anyway, how's work now that you at your lil dream job?"

"Different than I thought it would be. Like, being there, seeing how the execs close deals and work with artists is cool. And I really want to get there one day. But it's also been, I don't know . . . weird? I can't figure Michael out, and he gets even stranger whenever this certain LLC comes up. Everyone seems mad standoffish. And I've been working crazy hours that I'm not even gonna get paid for. Plus, I feel . . . icky, I guess, for having helped Michael with the Deliverance Desired deal. I was doing what he asked, and I don't know the details, but I have this, like, gut feeling like Michael did something bad or something. Anyway, I haven't told Lucas. I hate hiding things from him, but I don't wanna hear a lecture on what I should be doing for community right now when I'm still figuring things out and I'm finally at a label after all these years."

"Yeah. I get it, girl. Lucas be on his revolutionary shit a little too heavy sometimes, like, can you be chill? Damn," she joked.

"Word," I said, laughing. "He be so serious sometimes. At the end of the day, everywhere in this industry there's some dirt beneath the surface. So I gotta work with what I got."

"Right, right," Alicia said, focused now on making sure the parts in my hair were even.

I thought back to other things that had happened so far in the office as we settled into quiet. That staff meeting where Kate cried about some bullshit. The look on Nina's face after her meeting with Michael about signing Papi, the way Connor and Michael huddled together in Michael's office as they put together the terms of the Deliverance Desired deal, hushed whispers passed between them. It didn't feel good in my stomach, so I turned to music to distract myself from my thoughts.

I connected to the Bluetooth speaker and threw on a playlist. I turned to my soft-hearted British girlies Rachel Chinouriri, Mahalia, and Olivia Dean first, whose sweet vocals made me think about self-love, self-esteem, the fleeting nature of our youth. The rest of the playlist was a salve that made us feel like we weren't the only ones thinking about how impossible it is to feel solid in your twenties. How everything feels like high-stakes poker, where the possibility of losing, of failing to set up the right path for our futures, is a ghost hand around our throats.

"So what else is happening besides the tour?" I asked.

"Um. Ooh. I didn't tell you. When we got back from the road, I hooked up with Sean, and, *girl*. Let me tell you that this nigga came to the crib with not a single thing I asked him to bring—no food, no snacks, no money for liquor."

"Okay, but . . ." I angled my body toward her, careful not to make her snatch my hair accidentally. "How was the sex?"

"I can't even lie. Like, I really wanted to hate this man because of his bullshit, but, bitch, it was amazing! Some life-changing dick." We burst out laughing until we had to wet our dry mouths with water.

"Like so, so good," she continued. "And he is fine as hell. It's true what they say, a man with no job and nothing to lose is finna hit it better than anybody."

Her laugh always made me feel at ease, made me join in too, because in that moment, it was like nothing else mattered but our joy, how it filled up the room and made us forget that we didn't get much of it elsewhere in this world. "Okay, your turn. What's going on besides work?"

"Well, my mom called."

"She ask you for money again?"

"Not yet. But we're having breakfast tomorrow, so I know she will."

"Can't you just tell her you ain't got it?" Alicia said. "You started that job, what, two weeks ago? You should be stacking whatever leftover money you have for yourself."

"I wish it was that easy," I said. "I mean, you were there. You know what it's been like for me . . . having to save her ass all these years. She expects my help. Counts on me to make up what's missing. What am I supposed to do? Let her suffer?"

"I'm not saying that. I'm just saying, it wouldn't hurt for you to set up boundaries. To let her know that it can't and shouldn't be like that forever."

I would have *loved* to set up boundaries. I would have loved to tell Mama that I would no longer enable her. But I felt too guilty. There was no one else around who could pitch in, struggling as the rest of my extended family were with the cost of groceries, gas, skyrocketing rent that got raised every year. And I knew she couldn't afford the apartment without Marvin's half of the rent. It pained me to think that without me to help offset the lack Marvin created with his summer binges, she'd get kicked out and have to pack up her stuff and head to the local shelter.

"Yeah, I guess. We'll see what she says at breakfast," I said, thinking back to that first breakfast, how it seemed like she hoped syrup and comfort food could counteract the bitter taste of her bullshit.

•

Eleven years ago Marvin moved in with us. In the nine months that followed his arrival, things had been mostly unchanged. We managed. As summer set in, circumstances started to change with it. Mama and Marvin began fighting about money, about him being out all hours of the night. I listened through my bedroom walls as Mama yelled, worried about his loyalty and how we were going to keep a roof over our heads.

A few days before I turned fourteen, Mama wanted to have a serious talk with me about what had been happening. We went to Amy Ruth's, a soul-food restaurant in Harlem. As we sat in the bottom-floor dining room, a cozy space with brown floors and yellow walls with important Black historical figures painted on them, I scanned the menu. Each dish was named after one of those influential Black people. We both ordered the Reverend Al Sharpton. When our food—two plates of fried chicken and waffles—and two glasses of sweet tea arrived, Mama took a deep breath as she fiddled with her silverware. She looked like she wanted to cry.

"What's wrong, Mama? You don't want your food? Looks pretty good to me," I said, inhaling the familiar scents of butter and canola oil.

"No, it's not that, baby. It's . . . um. You may not know this, but things have been . . . hard for me financially for a while. And Marvin, well, I thought him living with us would make things easier." She sighed.

I looked at her, confused. "Okay?"

"Well, things are still pretty hard. And I know you're starting high school soon. So I was wondering if you'd thought about maybe getting a part-time job now that you're almost old enough?"

"You want me to get a job? Why? What about my summer?"

"It'll only be part-time, and to be honest, Li"—she picked up a paper napkin and stretched it with her fingers—"we could really use some help. We're in a bad spot right now. And I know Randall, the manager at the McDonald's on Gun Hill Road, is hiring. If you get hired, I was hoping you could pitch in, only a little from each paycheck, so we can get caught up on bills."

I didn't know what to say. I had never been brought into adult business before. I didn't know that I could even be capable of this much responsibility at my age. I only knew, with her sad eyes peering into mine, that I couldn't say no.

•

After a while, we settled into a rhythm, music pumping around us, Alicia's hands weaving through my hair as I worked on emails on my phone to distract myself from thinking about Mama.

She finished my hair after five hours of separating the quadrants into smaller and smaller sections until she finally ran out of hair to braid. Later, after Alicia snipped off the excess hair from each braid, I tilted my head back into a pot of boiled water, careful not to send scalding droplets down the back of my shirt and onto my already sensitive skin. I pulled two braids to the front, pulled the rest of my wet hair to the back, secured it with an elastic band, and went to the mirror to look at the finished product and fix my edges.

I kept the music going while Alicia picked her outfit and we decided where to go for the night. Alicia pulled on a red halter top and denim booty shorts and I changed into the clothes I'd stuffed into my tote before I ran out of the house—black square sunnies with yellow lenses, a black cropped tee with an image of Grace Jones on the front, a black fitted miniskort, tube socks, a small black shoulder bag, and black-and-white Sambas—and reapplied my lip gloss. When we finished in the bathroom, I turned off the music and grabbed my purse, and we slammed the front door behind us.

6

It was late June, the first official day of summer, but the weather had been warm for weeks. People had already switched out their sweatshirts and black jeans for sundresses and crop tops, Jordans and Dunks, short shorts and corset tops. The Icee lady had appeared on the block like clockwork, selling coco-mango-cherry-rainbow-flavored cold treats in paper Dixie cups. Water gushed into the street from fire hydrants that had been broken open so the neighborhood kids could escape the summer heat. The Puerto Rican man perpetually clothed in a Yankee fitted and a PR flag tank top was set up out there now too, with his table of assorted toys—tiny plastic water guns, watery bubble solution sold in brightly colored bottles, whirring handheld fans that drove parents crazy once they got home. For me, though, the beginning of summer was a time of dread. Summer was when I expected Mama to ask me for help to make up what Marvin spent.

•

Marvin was what most Black people around us considered a stand-up dude. He owned his own business: a long-haul trucking company that transported plastic utensils and paper goods around the country, for which he was paid in lump sums. He was conventionally handsome, with an intact hairline in his fifties, and he had all his teeth. He occasionally did a load of laundry or cleaned the bathroom as a treat. He was as good a man as Mama could get while being a single mother, according to some of my aunts. It didn't matter to them that at the start of summer since I met him eleven years ago, the warm weather and what it came with—the block hot with dope boys flaunting cash, taking long pulls from fruit-flavored hookahs and blunts, with women in clingy sundresses on their laps—made him feral. He'd land home after a long haul, wanting to be good to Mama and keep up with their shared bills, but the magnetic energy of the streets he'd grown up on was too strong. He'd spend the summer months going out with his boys—a collection of other middle-aged men chasing their youth—every weekend, buying tables at local lounges, where bottle girls made them feel like kings, and hitting up strip clubs to prove to one another that they were alpha men, that their women didn't run them, that their money was theirs alone to spend.

By the time he was done with his rampage, Mama was always left to pick up the pieces.

And here she was now, ready to put me in the middle again.

•

I stood in front of Amy Ruth's, trying to ready myself for our breakfast. I looked at Mama through the restaurant window, already seated at the same table we sat at all those years ago. Her eyes were open wide as she held her phone out so she could see it better as she scrolled. I took a deep breath and walked in.

At ten in the morning, Amy Ruth's was alive with chatter. Church ladies who had gone to the early service were seated at various tables, dressed in their Sunday best: pastel pantsuits and matching wide-brimmed hats with faux flowers adorning them. Pearls were strung around their necks, and brooches were pinned to their chests. Men in black suits pressed to the heavens sat in groups with one another, trading wisdoms about life in service to the most high.

"Hey, Mama," I said, walking up to the table.

"Hey, Lili."

I gave Mama a hug, slung my crossbody purse across the back of my chair, and took a seat. Mama wasted no time getting down to business.

"I guess you can assume why I asked you to breakfast," she said.

I nodded and waited for her to continue.

"Marvin . . . he—"

Our server cut in to take our orders. We asked for our usual.

"He did it again," she said. "He said he wouldn't, but he spent next month's rent and some of my savings too. He said it wouldn't be like this anymore, and then he fucking did it anyway."

"Well, he does this every summer. Did you manage to save anything since last time?"

"I have maybe half left. I'm tired. Tired of the same shit."

"Well, you can't be that tired," I said under my breath. Saying it louder would only make her retract, push her back into her comfort zone of silence and denial. It'd also make her want to pop me. "So what you gonna do? Didn't Bill say last summer was the last time before he moved to eviction?" I asked, finally breaking the silence.

"I don't know. I guess I could apply for a loan."

"Can you even get a loan with your credit?" I asked gently.

The slightest bit of anger or irritation that seeped into my voice would send her over the edge, straight into shutdown mode, and that came with rhetorical questions in which she asked who the parent was.

"It could be possible, though." I backtracked. "Where is Marvin?"

"He's at the house, sleeping. He was at Diamond Club last night. Blowing more of our money."

Mama always cared so much when he went on these binges. They wrecked her life over and over again, but she felt like she couldn't let Marvin go. She was still holding on to the early days when Marvin would give her massages, make her laugh after a long day at work, take her to Sylvia's for greens and cornbread and City Island for crab legs and fried fish. He was still the man who made her forget that she had been alone since both her parents had died of cancer before she was thirty. He was still the man who had filled the hole gouged inside her after my father died at the wrong end of a gun because of a mistaken identity—another Black man caught in the wrong place, wrong time.

So I stuffed my feelings down, locked them away so that I could be the dutiful daughter she needed. During my teenage years, I buried myself in music loud enough to drown out the fights Mama and Marvin got in because of his recklessness. Tried not to think about how Marvin had come into our lives and turned my loving, attentive, thoughtful mama into a person who screamed and pleaded for him to change, who pleaded with the building manager to allow us to remain as tenants after all the late payments, who pleaded for me to understand, to hold on because things were going to get better, she promised.

It was then, as a teenager, that music became my refuge, and I started etching out a plan for my future. After work, I would sink into my collection of candy-sweet pop and slow and soulful R&B as Marvin and Mama argued. I turned up the volume to scream along to angst-fueled rock. I danced away the ache to bass-laden hip-hop.

I knew I couldn't pursue music for real. Not in choir or band. Not as an artist, unpredictable as the money was in that part of the business. I had no safety net. I had to make it myself. I decided to get into the business of representation instead. At least then I'd still be surrounded by music. I'd have a hand in creation, and I'd be able to live and help Mama pay bills whenever she came calling.

"Ma, I'm sorry to say this, but don't you think it's time? He's been doing this for eleven years now. How many more years do you need? I mean, I hate to see you this way. Don't you?"

She looked down at her clasped hands for a long while before she said, "Well, I could always play the lotto." A chuckle escaped her, but the smile didn't reach her eyes, and I could tell sadness rested beneath them. She had a way of doing that—making jokes to hide the pain. It was a thing she'd learned from her mother that had been passed down from Black woman to Black woman in our family for generations. Laughter easing hardship after hardship when there was nothing else to lift our spirits.

The server put our plates down on the table, and Mama decided we were done talking about Marvin for now. "So tell me about this new job. You like it?" she asked.

I first loved music because of Mama. On Saturday mornings she would blast songs on the stereo as pancakes got golden on the stovetop. She'd come into my room, pull the blankets off me, and tell me to get up and clean the house—a ritual I still carry on to this day.

Prince blared from the boom box as she swept and mopped the living room. Jay Z got her through scrubbing the toilet, me through folding the laundry. Mary J. Blige and SWV as we took out the trash and washed dishes, counters, the stove. Maxwell and Anita Baker for when we finally plopped down on the sofa, the smell of bleach and Lysol tinging the air.

She was a great singer too. Often, I would hear her belting above tracks as she cleaned. But she never got to use that voice like she wanted. It wasn't practical to be a singer when there was so much working against her: single motherhood, bills, the high cost of childcare. So she ventured into corporate America as an office manager and didn't look back.

"If you talk to Bill or building management, will they give you a little more time? I think I can give you some money when I get my next check. Maybe I could even start a fund only you know about . . . just in case?"

"I'll talk to Bill, but in the meantime, I'm not gonna turn down the help. Just do what feels right. . . . So did you hear that your cousin Olivia is pregnant again? This is her fourth child. I don't know how she's feeding all them mouths when everything's so damn expensive."

It had been years of this dance. We'd gossip about other people in our family, trading secrets about who was pregnant, who was getting a divorce, who lied about being on vacation on a distant island. Mama and I made easy conversation that we had perfected over years, avoiding serious topics, avoiding the fact that Marvin had caused a rift between us, one that made it harder for us to find our way back to each other.

When I was younger, it had become a tradition for Mama to call in sick and pull me out of my day camp one day every summer for us to visit this unassuming record store on Fordham, then hit up the Mexican woman for the mangoes topped with chili powder and sugar-coated churros she served out of plastic containers she pulled out of a blue shopping cart. You'd never guess it if you walked by, but in that old record store—that doubled as a cellphone store, a place to buy ill-fitting T-shirts and fake Jordans, and a makeshift tattoo parlor that also did ear piercings on the bottom floor—were aisles and aisles of records and CDs that spanned back decades. They had listening stations all over the floor, and Mama and I had made it a game to gather three records each and play a song from each album for one another. Once we were done listening, we'd ask each other our favorite things about each song. I beamed with pride when I picked songs that bubbled up memories that made Mama smile wide as she recalled the smell of Grandpa's cigars or the perfume Grandma sprayed on her blouse whenever they all sat in the living room and listened to the sweet melodies of Stevie, to Phyllis Hyman hollering heartbreak and healing, to the irony of War singing songs about peace and friendship. When we were done swapping music, she'd give me enough money to add one album to my color-coded, carefully curated collection.

But one day after our churros and mangoes, Mama said someone was going to pick us up and drop us home. That someone was Marvin.

•

At the end of our meal, I put my credit card on the table to close out the bill.

I looked at the time on my phone and started to gather my things. "Mama, I gotta go. I'm meeting Lucas downtown to pick out picture frames for Sunsetlandia."

"Okay, baby. Have fun. Tell Lucas I said hi."

We gave each other hugs, and then I was off.

I met Lucas at a thrift shop on Eighty-Seventh and Third Avenue that I used to go to after shifts at the CVS so I could sift through the racks for deeply discounted designer clothing.

"Hey, babe," Lucas said, giving me a hug outside the shop.

"Hey."

He caught eyes with me as I formed a wilted smile. "Uh-oh. What happened at breakfast?"

"Nothing different than usual. Mama needs something, so I gotta help her figure out how to get it. I'm so tired of all of it, babe." Lucas held the door for me as I walked inside. I reached my hand out to touch a black stole draped delicately on a mannequin in passing.

The boutique was all on one floor, and it was packed to the brim with racks and racks of lightly worn high-end and inexpensive clothes and shoes; shelves of used books; a mix of mid-century and traditional-style chairs, lamps, and side tables; handcrafted pottery riddled with imperfections; crude acrylic paintings of water and nature settings, with red for-sale tickets pasted on their frames; and a series of funky full-length mirrors that lined the back wall. The picture frames Lucas and I came for were in boxes along the floor beneath a rack of donated fur coats.

We bent down to rifle through them.

"I know. The whole situation is fucked up. But at the same time, you know how it is for people like us. Even my ma and pops needed help sometimes. That year Pops lost his job, I would go to Westchester Square and charge people five dollars to do a portrait of them and save the money, just so I could pitch in at home."

I ran my fingers along the tops of a few frames before I found two medium-size gold ones adorned with sculpted leaves. "What about these?" I said, pulling them from the bunch and holding one up in each hand.

"Oh yeah. Those could work. How much are they?"

"Seven bucks each."

"Cool. Let's find, like, four more and then hit this spot I know Uptown. Anyway, even though I wanted to help, my parents never put that pressure on me. They wanted me to be my own man, to focus on my future. They reached out to their community instead. They leaned on other parents who could help feed me after school. They did odd jobs around the neighborhood for extra cash. They babysat Mr. Robert's sons in exchange for free painting lessons he taught down at the rec center. They made sure that I knew, despite everything, that our people had us. And you deserve that too. So I want you to remember that I'm here. I'm your community. Whenever you need. You're not in this alone."

"I love you." I cradled his face in my hand for a few seconds before we went back to our search.

7

"You'll be staying late tonight," Michael started. I yanked my earbuds out of my ears and paused Hope Tala's "All My Girls Like to Fight" just as she finished singing, "I wish I could throw the first punch." When I looked up, Michael's face was pensive. I didn't want pensive to turn into impatient, so I cued up my work voice and smiled back at him, made myself forget that it was almost noon on Monday and this was the first thing he'd said to me all day.

"Of course, Michael. What do you need?"

His eyes flickered with confusion as he took in my braids, as if he weren't sure that I was the same girl, but he made no comment.

"Trick Mirror is coming in tomorrow morning, and me and Evan are trying to poach them from Atlantic. I need you to pull sales from Luminate, schedule a conference room, pull together a list of potential collaborators, ask marketing and publicity for a preliminary marketing and publicity plan. Grab all of the promotional material and album art from the Tuneups too. That should show them what we can do. This account will be handled by MHCP LLC, so I'll need you to put everything into the MHCP file on the flash drive once you're done since Connor left early. If you need me in the next hour, I'll be at the gym. Make sure my car is downstairs on time."

"Sure. I'll get on it now," I said to the air, my head trailing the path he took to his office as he went, my eyes working overtime trying not to roll at his indifference.

Trick Mirror was a dance-electronica DJ group made up of three white men straight out of Connecticut. By dressing in straight-legged jeans, nondescript tees, and hoodies and showing off brown-eyed blank stares that made people wonder what was behind them, they said fuck you to the stage presence that we expected from musicians. Further communicating that what they were doing was real dedication, a stripped-down-to-its-purpose version of artistry. The sentiment didn't land well with the fans or the critics because their music was about as deep as a line in an ice cream shop when it was brick outside. The latest song they'd released hadn't even charted. It sampled the Isley Brothers' "Between the Sheets," turning the quiet-storm-funk classic into a thumping, multilayered electronic beat.

"Between the Sheets" had already been sampled 161 times to date. Their rendition brought nothing new to it. It was a rehash of a rehash of a rehash that removed the soul that was once infused and made it danceable, but not in a way that moved my limbs.

I was surprised that Michael wanted to poach them. But I wasn't exactly in the best position to share with him that I thought we shouldn't waste our time and resources on mediocrity when there was so much talent out there more deserving. I kept my mouth shut, ignored the sweat that pooled beneath my breasts whenever I was feeling anxious, and prayed it didn't seep through the fabric of my mock-neck shirt.

I booked the New York room, the most impressive of our conference rooms, first, and then I started pulling sales from Luminate. The numbers showed that they were on a downward track. Their streams and sales were down. Ticket sales for their last tour were so bad they were forced to cancel a handful of shows on the West Coast. Nobody was really checking for them besides the fan base they'd built ten years ago.

By the time I got to pulling together a list of collaborators—producers and artists they could potentially work with at our label to further widen their audience and appeal—I was annoyed. The more I thought about Trick Mirror, the more I felt indignant. When I stacked up what I'd seen Michael do to Deliverance Desired and Papi, it made me hot to think that there was always someone willing to overestimate the worth of white men, even when the numbers didn't support it.

Most people had left the office, including Michael, and after I'd pulled together all the things Michael had requested, there was just one last task to complete. I had put it off, trying not to get roped into being curious about whatever the LLC file contained, but it was almost five-thirty.

I sighed inwardly and hoped the weariness I suddenly felt didn't show in my eyes.

I sent a Slack to Charlotte and Jackie, asking where I could possibly find the LLC file. Jackie answered first.

Me: Hi Jackie. Sorry to bother you. Michael wants me to put something in the MHCP LLC but I think he forgot to tell me where it is? I don't see it on FIRE or on my computer. Would you know?

Jackie: Can't talk here. Meet me in Berlin in five?

I responded to her quickly in case she changed her mind. Jackie wasn't really the sociable type. She ate an exclusively liquid lunch—an assortment of green juices and almond milk iced coffees and flavored seltzer waters—at her desk every day without fail and had the blue-eyed, jet-black-hair looks of Megan Fox before MGK inspired her into fake goth.

We sat down in one of the small conference rooms that was outfitted with a bench below a panel of windows facing Sixth Avenue and two side tables with office phones atop them. I looked out at the packed street, watched as people left their offices, raced in front of one another to make sure they didn't miss the train they took at the same time every night. Tourists in flannel shirts, tan shorts, and New Balances that had somehow become fashionable again pointed their phones up at our building, enamored with its size, how it held prestige within. Lit and other well-known tech, fashion, and media conglomerates were scattered among the forty-four flights. For a split second, I wanted what they had: the freedom to be in awe one moment and to walk away from it all the next. But I knew I shouldn't feel anything but lucky, lucky, lucky like Mama said. So many people from where I'm from never even had a chance of making it to the point I was at then. I turned my attention to Jackie, who had already taken a seat on the bench.

"Thanks for helping," I said.

"Yeah, no problem," she said, distracted. We'd only been there two minutes, and she was already responding to new emails that poured in. After a while of furious typing, she put her phone down on the bench next to her, and then she got up to peek her head out of the booth, turned her head both ways.

I looked back at her, perplexed.

"Have to make sure no one accidentally hears us," she said. "Anyway, I can't be away from my desk that long. Michael keeps . . . certain files that can only be accessed on a flash drive that's in a drawer of his desk that requires a key. Ever since the merger was announced, he's been nervous about keeping things on his computer, worried about what IT or legal can see. The key is easy to find if you know where to look. I've been here longer than any of the assistants, so I know all the secrets." Her eyes glinted beneath the fluorescent lights, and an odd little smirk snuck onto her face.

"The key is taped under his desk, on the left side below the monitor. These files are extremely sensitive. If you want to keep your job, make sure you don't look at anything beyond what you need. If Michael finds out that you were digging where you don't belong, he will make sure you never work in this business again. You got it?"

"Okay," I said, nodding slowly. "I won't."

I thanked her again, and she hurried back to her desk like she was scared someone would catch my scent on her. I went to Michael's office and got on my knees, careful not to make myself ashy as I felt around the grainy underside of his desk for the supposed key.

The key was where it belonged. I opened a smaller drawer within a bigger drawer, pulled out a black flash drive, and stuck it into Michael's computer. I took a deep breath and opened the only folder named MHCP LLC on the drive. That folder contained several other folders. One was labeled with a music artist's name I vaguely recalled hearing before, but I couldn't remember where. I hovered the cursor over the folder, preparing to click as curiosity clouded my thoughts, when Jackie passed by Michael's office and startled me.

"See ya later, Billie," she said, throwing me a look I couldn't decipher as she walked to the elevator. My heart dropped into my stomach like after I'd endured the drop on the Kingda Ka roller coaster at Six Flags. I loaded everything from today onto the drive and put it back where it belonged—I retaped the key and shoved what little I'd seen into the back of my brain.

•

It was seven when I finally finished work and turned my phone from do-not-disturb to regular mode. My phone pinged with four missed calls and a flurry of texts from Lucas.

"Fuck," I said aloud as I scrolled through his texts and jabbed the elevator button. I'd forgotten that I had agreed to meet him at some event in the South Bronx. Lucas's boy who he played ball with whenever they found each other on the court was debuting his attempt at a singing career now that he was free from the rigidity of army life.

As the elevator doors started to shut, a purse swung through the semi-open door, and Nina stepped in behind it.

I tried to relax my furrowed brows, but Nina could sense the frenzied energy coming off me, like I was a kid who had gotten lost in a department store.

"Hey, Billie—are you okay?"

I relaxed my eyebrows and smiled. "Oh yeah. I'm just late for a thing."

"Same." A pause, then, "So how are things going so far?"

"It's been good, I think. A little different than I expected, but it's so cool to be a part of the process, you know, and see how an A&R's vision can help shape music and artists."

"Nice. I'm glad to hear. Well, if you ever need advice or anything, let me know. I've been here awhile, so I can give you the real."

"Thanks so much. I might take you up on that."

Nina smiled and nodded. The elevator doors opened, and we said good night to each other as we exited the building.

Once Nina had walked in the other direction, I hurriedly opened the texts and sent one back saying I was on my way. I made it to Grand Central, and the 6 Train was miraculously waiting on the platform.

•

From the outside, Beatstro looked like any other restaurant that slung greasy cheeseburgers, baked mac and cheese, and sweaty pitchers of sweet sangria. But inside, the restaurant was a cross-cultural haven that blended the best parts of the Bronx and placed hip-hop at its center. All across the restaurant were homages to the birth of a genre that started right here in this borough. The walls were lined with original vinyl records, portraits and art that honored the four pillars of hip-hop: deejaying, emceeing, graffiti painting, and breakdancing. Toward the back of the space was a DJ booth with enough space for performers to do their thing and for patrons to crowd around them when they weren't at their tables.

It filled me with pride to be from here, to know how many people from my hood had changed the culture. I called Lucas as soon as I walked into the spot. "Don't Wanna Be a Player" blasted around me as I squeezed through the dancing crowd and waited for him to answer. I spotted him in the back, at a table with his friend, sipping on Coronas rimmed with lime.

"Hey," I said breathlessly. "Sorry for getting here so late, babe. I got caught up at work. Jalen, good to see you again." I gave him a small wave.

I took a seat next to Lucas in the booth and leaned in to kiss him. He gave me a short kiss as if one more second might singe his skin, and then he smiled at me like nothing was wrong. I tilted my head in question. He waved his hand at me in that way that said he wanted to talk about it later. I hated public arguments too, the way they reminded me of reality TV where an innocuous phrase or perceived slight could launch a series of thrown drinks and physical fights, so I kept quiet. When the waitress came by, I put in an order for a pitcher of margaritas for us to share.

"Did you go on already, Jalen?"

"Nah, I'm up after the next three performers."

"Oh yay. I'm glad I didn't miss it," I said.

The event featured performers and artists of all kinds. Slam poets. Dancers. Rappers. Singers. They were all here to prove that they were special. That they were budding stars. But it never took me long to tell the difference between hard work, creativity, and natural talent and ego and false bravado. Between people who wanted fame over those who wanted to be heard, to be seen because if they weren't, they might never feel like their truest selves.

The first rapper to go on was all ego. He rapped about money, but mostly about his own dick, interested in the myriad ways women could please him. The icy vibe between Lucas and me melted as we locked eyes and laughed.

The next person to go on was a singer, but she wasn't much better than the rapper. She sang with heart, from the diaphragm too, so it was loud and dripped with passion, but she had the kind of voice that could only be appreciated in a private karaoke room in K-Town with supportive friends.

The last person before Jalen went on was a twentysomething man named Roman dressed in a caramel-colored snakeskin T-shirt, tan pants, and round-rimmed gold glasses that framed his chiseled face. His shoulder-length locs were pulled up into a fanned ponytail. He looked every bit of Good Humor Toasted Almond fine. When he hit us with a silky-sounding "How y'all doing tonight" as he stepped onto the area of floor that had become a makeshift stage, I could already feel myself slightly mesmerized.

The set began with a slow song about love that highlighted his range. He mastered the electric, romantic cool of Steve Lacy, topped it with the slick swagger of someone like Brent Faiyaz, which resulted in his own unique, alluring vibe. He didn't rap-sing, didn't shy away from the emotion, from invoking feeling deep enough for listeners to be transported, swept up entirely by the melody. He belted out haunting high notes and tumbling runs with ease. He even rolled his hips a little as he sang, making his set all the more intoxicating. He was all sensuality and charm and charisma, and I knew then that I had to give him my card to see if we could potentially work together. It wouldn't be now, but when the time came, I'd hopefully have a roster of artists I'd started relationships with.

After he finished his two songs, he walked off the stage, and it was like he knew he killed it. He had the kind of confidence—with the way he tipped his head up and licked his lips at the women closest to the performance area—you couldn't manufacture. The kind that said he was untouchable in his craft, in the distinct way he carried himself. He was exactly the kind of artist that would be good for Lit. Someone who had enough presence, intrigue, sex appeal, and talent to captivate millions, and I wanted to be the one to help Lit snag him before someone else did.

"Where you going, babe? Jalen is up next," Lucas said, throwing his arm around my shoulders.

"I know. I'll be right back." I shrugged off his arm, scooted out of the booth, and crossed the restaurant to where Roman was standing around a table of friends.

"Roman?" I asked.

"Oh, uh, wassup?"

"What a great performance up there. I'm a fan."

"Oh, word? Thanks so much." He touched his arm to the back of his head and smiled sheepishly like he was waiting for me to ask for his autograph.

I had made it this far on nerve and margaritas, but now that I was standing in front of Roman, I wasn't sure where to start. When I ran into Quincy at Irving, he had approached me, impressed by my position at Lit. I couldn't handle Roman the same way, all casual confidence and reserved cool. I had to be careful. I had to come off professional, like I was someone who could offer opportunities, even when technically I couldn't just yet.

It also didn't help that I had felt the edges of intoxication closing in around me. I focused on getting out the spiel I had practiced in my head, clear and to the point.

"Do you have a second to talk? I'd love to link with you to discuss future opportunities. I think you have a sound that's working right now, and if we play around with the vocals a bit, I could help you get into local shows across the city, help get your songs on playlists on streaming, maybe even get you on small stages on festival circuits if you stick with me," I said.

"Sorry. Maybe I missed it. What did you say you do again? If you're a fan, I have some shows in the works. You can follow me on IG if you wanna know what I got coming next."

"No, no, sorry," I said, waving my hands. I realized I'd never introduced myself. The familiar heat of embarrassment enveloped me, but I couldn't stop or let it show on my face. I was in it now, and this was the practice I'd need if I was ever going to sign artists on my own. I continued on. "I meant that I work for a record label, and I'm interested in your music."

"Ohh, well, then. That's a different story." He rubbed his hands together. "Yeah, we can definitely talk business. I'm a little busy right now, but do you got, like, a card or something so I can get in touch with you later?"

I reached into my purse and pulled out the business cards I made myself two weeks into the job at Lit. I'd lifted a logo from the letterhead I used to draft letters for Michael, printed my info on some card stock I'd snuck from the supply room, and painstakingly cut them into neat, symmetrical rectangles at my desk before I escaped into the night.

"I do. All of my contact info is there. Looking forward to connecting soon."

He looked down at the card, his eyes lingering on Lit's name. "Bet. Me too," he said. He shifted his glasses on his face, smiled with his wide, bone-bright teeth, took the card from my hand, and turned back to his group of friends.

•

When I got back to the table, Jalen had already begun to prepare for his set, but Lucas was sour-faced, like he had stuffed a handful of pickles in his mouth. "What was that about?"

"I wanted to see if I could maybe work with Roman down the line at Lit. I gave him my card."

"Oh, wow," he said. He put down the margarita he had been holding and shifted back in his seat.

In between the acts, the DJ played current and throwback hip-hop and R&B hits. Aaliyah's "We Need a Resolution" blasted around us, and it felt like a bad magic trick how keenly the lyrics applied to our current situation. "So while I'm here tryna set up some time for us to chill because I haven't seen you for real in three weeks, you over there working? You can't spend two hours not doing things for Lit?"

I looked around at the other four-top tables and surrounding booths. People were starting to look in our direction. I lowered my voice.

"Are you really gonna do this right now?" I said, narrowing my eyes at him.

"Look, all I'm saying is I'm worried about you. I know this means a lot to you. I want to support that. But . . . sometimes it feels like it's all you care about these days. I just want you to remember that you don't owe your whole life to that job."

"Well, I appreciate your concern. I really do, babe. But it hasn't been that long. For now, I need to do what it takes, and I also need your support in that." I reached out for his hand and looked into his eyes. "I know you're used to having me to yourself every other night, so three weeks feels like a long time, but I promise it won't stay like this."

Softly, after what felt like an eternity, he said, "Yeah, babe. Yeah."

Jalen walked onto the performance area for his turn, and Lucas pulled me closer to him. I stretched his arm farther around my waist, inhaled the scent of his warm woody cologne, and watched as Jalen performed a soul-infused ballad, the passion in his voice surprising me enough to make me lean in and pay attention.

•

When we finally made it into our apartment, our shoddy kitchen appliances whining miserably in the dark, I went straight to the shower. The alcohol and vibrations of the music left me warm, in anticipation of something more. As the scorching water ran along my spine, the tension in my back and hips loosened. I thought about the nights Lucas and I used to grind against each other to Lil Baby and Future, like our bodies were made for only that. I closed my eyes and remembered his warm breath against my ears, the music throbbing behind me, his "*You're so gorgeous*" or "*I want you*" igniting something inside me. I opened my eyes to find my hands had found their way below without me noticing. I quickly dropped them, realizing it'd been a while since we'd had sex. Lit and all the things I was willing to compromise for it—my time, my ideals, my work-life balance—had been all-consuming, and I hadn't noticed until now how much I'd been missing Lucas's closeness. I would not end the night without knowing the distance growing between us could always be closed.

When I finished my shower, I wrapped a too-small towel around me and walked into the bedroom. Lucas was lying on our bed, scrolling through his phone. He looked up when he heard me.

He watched as I dropped the towel to the floor, his eyes clouding with lust, slowing scanning from my red toenails to the pomegranates on my chest I could thank my mother for to my ass that was fat in all the right places.

I grabbed my phone and threw on a playlist filled with slow, sexy songs to further set the mood.

"Wicked Games" by the Weeknd came softly through the portable speaker on my nightstand.

As the Weeknd crooned, "Give me all of it," I moved my hands over his muscular chest and planted wet kisses down his abs until my mouth reached his V-cut where it met the base of his dick. I pulled him out of his basketball shorts and boxers, feeling it throb and grow with my touch, and took him into my mouth. When that became too much for Lucas to bear and he groaned out whoas in time with the music, he pulled me up, and we switched positions. "Just tell me you love me," the song said as I looked down at Lucas, who mouthed, *I love you*, to me before he sucked softly on each nipple.

The song changed as Lucas teased my thighs with his quick tongue. "Helps my body to unwind. Don't waste time," Cleo Sol sang when Lucas dipped his tongue inside me. I pushed his head closer to me. My eyes rolled back, my body pulsating against him. Then finally, slowly, he eased himself inside of me. I sighed as our bodies moved together. My moans were cut short as he kissed me deeply. We kept that position, my legs wrapped around him, arms akimbo, until we both were breathless, satisfied.

"What was that about?" Lucas asked from his big-spoon position. "Not that I didn't enjoy it."

"I . . . wanted to feel you again."

He turned my head toward his so I was looking in his eyes. I pressed into him and let my tongue explore his mouth.

"As long as we're together, you will," he said.

"I know." A slow smile spread across my lips. The distance I was worried about wasn't too vast to overcome. Lucas was there, his heart beating against my back, and he was mine.

8

After Michael and Connor had emerged triumphant in the poaching of Trick Mirror, the next two weeks slipped by like water through a sieve, and things had mostly returned to normal. These days I was only in the office until six or seven, and thankfully I hadn't had to use the key taped under Michael's desk again.

Mercifully for me, today was a half day before Fourth of July weekend. The office had already emptied out as colleagues, even the ones cosplaying working-class who took this job for the prestige, snuck out of the office early so they could reach their summer houses by sunset. I expected the day to be quiet, but when Erykah called to let me know that Walter Winters had dropped by unannounced and was now waiting in the Lit lobby to see Michael, peace went right out the window.

Walter Winters had won Grammys decades ago, when white men wore big hair and tight pants and believed in trickle-down economics. He had loyal fans who faithfully bought his Christmas and greatest-hits albums that eked him onto Billboard Hot 100 the last few weeks of every year, but he was decidedly a has-been. Lit, however, still treated him like the sun rose and set on his ass. He got the time, the patience, the budgets that'd make someone else's career more than a few times over, and, apparently, the ability to come in whenever he wanted.

I sighed and hoped he wouldn't berate me like he did whenever he called to speak to Michael about some problem. He'd start off polite, not wanting to immediately break the idea of that polite Southern etiquette bred into him, but his ego wouldn't let him keep calm when Michael was busy. He turned nasty and demanded things that he and I both knew were above my pay grade: renegotiation on his royalty rates, additional cover options for his half-baked albums, better accommodations while he was on tour. I wouldn't have minded helping him if he'd had a better attitude or if he were actually fighting for better terms, but he was already getting the best of what Lit could offer. His demands weren't need, only greed and self-aggrandizement.

I could already feel the anxiety building up. I was a kettle ready to whistle. I sucked in a breath and blew it out with as much force as I could muster. I reasoned that the whole thing could be simple. I had only to seat him in the conference room, get Michael in there, and then get out. The tricky part was to try to be invisible, inconsequential, so I wouldn't get caught in his web.

I let Michael know that Walter was there, then greeted him in the lobby and tried not to laugh at the fact that this man looked like a real-life Doug Dimmadome. His all-white ensemble, complete with giant hat and cowboy boots, made people stare as we walked to the conference room. Walter and I exchanged pleasantries on the way, and I was relieved he hadn't come in guns blazing.

I grabbed Michael and then circled back to the kitchen for a carafe of water, a cold can of Coke, and a specific brand of barbecue chips we ordered special from Mississippi and kept on hand for Walter.

When I got back to the room, they had already dived into discussion, and I didn't want to get caught in the cross fire. I put the refreshments on the table and backed away slowly like that meme of Homer Simpson disappearing into bushes.

"Billie, now what do you make of this," Walter said. My back was toward them and my hand on the doorknob, but it was too late. I had been too slow, and now I was forced to stay and listen.

"You know. People think 'cause you add a banjo or an acoustic guitar that it makes your song country. But I've been in this business forty years now. I know what country is and what it ain't."

He wagged his calloused fingers in the air as he continued. "These so-called artists don't know shit about what it is to be an American. A patriot. What it means to love your country and the land. All they do is complain. Seems like we can't even say nothing about it either 'cause of all this damn cancel culture, these liberals with their agendas. But sometimes you just gotta say what needs to be said. And I think what we really need is to bring American values back to country. We need to stop letting all these people like Sha Nasty ruin it with their bull crap. With their rap nonsense. That ain't what country is about. And it ain't the country music that America wants."

Michael said nothing. Only nodded and sipped his scotch. He hadn't agreed with or denied anything, but I felt like something noxious was bubbling up in my stomach now that we had ventured into tricky territory.

"Now, Billie, what do you think about all this?" Walter Winters asked, aiming his fingers at me in condescension, like a professor bestowing me with knowledge they felt I should have known already.

I stalled, trying to come up with something that would encapsulate all the emotions I felt about country—how I personally wasn't a fan, but respected how Black people had made the genre, had forged legacies in the South, had spent lifetimes planting seeds for the next generations in the soil that were now blooming, growing beyond belief. And still, we weren't allowed to tell our stories the way we wanted. We weren't allowed to sing about land and freedom, the way some of us were rooted there like trees, branches ever reaching toward something that seemed impossible until it wasn't.

"You want to know what I think?" I asked.

"In fact, I do, little lady. What do you make of Sha Nasty? Do you think he's country? That he can represent my genre?"

People like Walter had been gatekeeping country for decades with racism and ever-moving goalposts. But the crazy part was that there was no way Sha Nasty was anything other than country. He was indisputably country. He was fucking country personified. All his songs were about the earth, the land, the open space—early morning hoeing and nights spent under the stars in fields of corn and animal shit, things my city ass didn't know anything about. But it wasn't enough to sway people like Walter Winters. They preferred us in their predesignated lanes so they could keep a thing that wasn't even theirs, to claim it for themselves.

I forced myself to laugh, light and airy, like I took no offense to the very offensive thing that he was saying, because my career depended on it.

"Well . . . I mean, I think you're right in a way. This kind of country hasn't had a chance to shine this bright in a long time. But it's always been there. There have always been singers who have brought in musical elements from hip-hop or jazz or blues to the genre, but made sure that the core of the music was country, at its center. I think that kind of creativity and innovation should be honored. Isn't that what art is about? To me, it seems like a way for country to be what it is, but also open it up to new listeners, which is a good thing for the genre and artists overall," I said.

"Country don't need new listeners. What we need is to stick to the classics. Give the people what they know and love," he said. He slapped his thigh for emphasis, and I turned my head away at the sound.

I realized then that Walter Winters was playing a humorless game with me. A game that reinforced the idea that he and others like him were the ones with the real power. A game that would force me to agree with him, my one Black voice standing in for the whole of the community, giving him validation for his bigoted ideas.

I gritted my teeth together in a way that vaguely resembled a smile if you didn't look closely but also said, *Fuck you*, if you were really paying attention. "Yep. I guess you do have a point there. The classics always sell."

"From the horse's mouth, am I right?" He smiled a smarmy smile at me and lifted his drink toward Michael to cheers.

I made my escape as they continued their conversation, my opinion gathered, my existence no longer necessary.

•

I rushed to the bathroom and hated the uncontrollable tears that ran races down my cheeks. I wasn't usually a crier, but Walter had pushed me to the brink. I needed to let it out before I returned to my desk for the last hour of work. No matter how badly Walter had gotten to me, I couldn't let Michael know that I couldn't handle it. I didn't want to seem weak. Tears may work for white women, but they didn't do much for Black women. It only amplified the thoughts they kept secret—that we were incompetent and should be grateful we were hired in the first place.

I cried as silently as I could into a wad of tissue in the bathroom stall and tried not to smudge the mascara I'd swiped on this morning. When my ducts were dry enough to be seen by the general public again, I exited the stall. At the sink I scrubbed my hands as if that'd erase the last twenty minutes, and as I looked at my reddened eyes, I caught sight of Nina in the mirror. In my crying, I hadn't even noticed that someone else had entered the bathroom.

"Hey, Billie," Nina said. "Are you all right?"

I sniffed in some of the snot that dripped from my nose, dabbed it with a rough paper towel, and cleared my throat. "Yeah. Nah. I'm good. It's been . . . a weird day. But it's almost over, right?" I said, like caring about my feelings was only a bit I was playing at.

"Yeah, only one more hour," she said, tapping the Apple Watch on her wrist. Nina grabbed some paper towels, dried her hands, and made her way to the garbage can near the door.

Nina's hand was on the door handle, the door ajar, when she turned back around to me suddenly. "You sure you're good?"

"Yeah. I think I'm gonna be okay. Thanks for asking." I smiled weakly.

"Well, I've got a little time to kill before I link up with a potential artist at Dumbo House. Do you want to grab lunch? This is your chance to ask me anything. I was Michael's assistant for five years. And I saw Walter in the conference room. I know what you're going through," she said.

I didn't even have to say yes for her to know that I was already on board. She smiled at me, then told me to meet her in the lobby after we wrapped for the afternoon.

Walter and Michael had walked out of the office together at 12:25 without much interference from me. Walter was pleased that Lit was going to give him everything he had asked for, same as they always did, and Michael was happy to oblige. Walter was one of the first artists he had worked with when he joined Lit thirty-six years ago, and he loved to kiss up to a man who had helped sing his praises enough to get him to the seat of director. Plus, Michael was already late for the car I had scheduled that would take him to the airport for his vacation in the South of France.

With that done, I packed up my stuff and got myself together to meet Nina.

"So," she said, once we were both on the elevator, "getting the hang of everything?"

"It's good. I feel like I'm getting to know the systems a bit more. And I feel like things are going well with Michael. I mean, I haven't gotten fired or anything, so that's a good sign."

"Yeah . . . I've been seeing you hustle. Fend for yourself. It's that kind of fire that'll keep you in a job like this. The last girl Michael hired, the one you replaced? She quit after a couple weeks. Couldn't handle it. I don't blame her. A lot of people can't. This job doesn't allow for softness. I mean, I made it, but it wasn't easy. Working for Michael before I was promoted was crazy hard and involved way more bullshit than necessary."

We arrived at the bottom floor of the building and walked to the cafeteria. This would be the first time I ate here. I typically took lunch at my desk like Jackie, but instead of a liquid diet, I convinced myself I was full from meals I put together to stretch my paychecks: peanut-butter-and-jelly sandwiches paired with a side of Cheez-Its, almost-rotten leftovers from when I meal-prepped at the beginning of the week, a bag of pretzels, and a cup of hot water I dumped two sugars and squeezed lemon into to trick myself into thinking it was lemonade.

As we looked out at all the food stations, from ramen to poke bowls to Mediterranean to chopped salads to barbecue, littered across the floor, she said, "Let's get food and regroup, yeah?"

"Sounds good. I'll grab a table," I said.

Nina settled on food from the cold bar and a seltzer water. I got a slice of pepperoni pizza, the cheapest thing you could get from the cafeteria, and we sat at one of the round tables that were spread out across the expansive space.

This opportunity to learn from Nina had dropped into my lap like a gift when I least expected. I wouldn't waste it. I got right to the point. "So how did you get your start here? What was it like to work for Michael all those years?" I asked.

"Well, I'm from Brooklyn. Crown Heights. Been there my whole life. It's changed so much from when I was growing up," she said wistfully.

Back in the nineties, even into the early aughts, Brooklyn belonged to us. The people who had lived in this city their whole lives, whose families had been there for generations and had thrived, laughed, danced, sung, fought, cooked, and made up with and looked out for one another. Now things had changed. Crown Heights was plagued with people who wanted to turn the Brooklyn Nina knew into a personality-less play town indistinguishable from the basic hometowns transplants pretended they wanted to escape from.

"But it was always a place full of music, you know? Jay. Kim. Fab. Their songs were always on—blasted from the bodegas and out of cars as they rode down the street. Floating out of windows as people did chores on Saturday mornings. Bumping at the block parties when it was hot out and kids jumped around in them giant bouncy houses. It made me love music."

"Yeah, I get that. I'm from the South Bronx, which is apparently being renamed by some as SoBro. I can't even think about that for too long without getting tight. . . . anyway, my mom was big on music, but I was also inspired by the neighborhood. The old heads blasted music every weekend—Motown, hip-hop, house, reggae, salsa. And people would be laughing, dancing, having a good time, you know—like music was the one thing that helped them, healed them when everything else was messed up. It's part of the reason I want this career, to help bring music into the world from people who look like me, that come from where I come from."

"Yeah," Nina said. "That's exactly it. It's like . . . I was just so proud to be from the same place as all these artists who were making music that represented my life, the people around me, that told our stories. So I worked hard and ended up getting a full ride to Columbia. I did some internships, and now I'm here. I feel lucky that I sometimes get to do something meaningful with my life. I'd always dreamed of being the first Honduran Dominican A&R exec to rep brown people, give them the opportunities the industry been refusing them from jump. I'm working on that still."

At the end of her story, her tone changed from wistful into sadness, anger seeping in too, and I wondered if it had anything to do with Papi and others she may have tried to sign like him. With the ways she was told that his story, his music, didn't matter to the "right" people.

"Well, you being here is inspiring. Makes me feel like I might be able to do the same thing."

She was nodding across from me now, like she was starting to understand me, my hopes and motivations. Like she could see that I was serious about being here, about being prepared for what was to come.

Unexpectedly, she leaned into me like she was giving me a secret warning and pointed to her arm, to her skin. I immediately knew what she meant. There was trouble ahead for someone like me, like us, and I'd better be prepared for it.

"I'm gonna keep it real with you, Billie. Because I feel like it's my duty and I think you might have what it takes. . . . I don't know what you know about the Ultimate merger. But when these labels consolidate like this"—she shook her head, then looked me straight in the eyes like she could see through me—"it's usually not a good thing. People lose their jobs. Whole imprints shut down. Budgets get slashed. Bosses get cut. It can be really brutal. It's happened once since I've been here, and I made it through. Want to know how to survive it?"

I nodded hungrily, like her next words would be my last meal.

"Work. Your. Ass. Off. Make yourself indispensable. Master the admin work you do for the team. Be willing to do anything this company asks of you—within reason. Don't do anything that'll put you in jail, girl, or in danger . . . but yeah. It'll take everything—all your time and every damn ounce of your patience, and that part sucks. If you survive it, you'll get to do what I know you've always wanted to do. You'll get to help put good music, good art, into the world. And then there'll be more of us, people like me and you, here doing that work. And that's when we can make real change. Gotta keep your eyes on the prize, sis. Don't let Michael's ignorant artists get in your way. Here you'll have to choose your battles. That's how you'll win the war."

Despite the years of bullshit and the impending merger, Nina still seemed exhilarated by this work. It was a wonder Nina had let me in at all, that she had let me see how much of herself she had wrapped in this intricate, messy, wondrous business. I wanted that experience too—a chance to become a part of and then change the ecosystem, a chance to be remembered as part of culture, history.

"Thank you so, so much for being honest with me and for telling me all of this. I'm ready and willing to do what it takes," I said.

"Yeah, no problem. I'm always happy to share some wisdom. Listen, there is another thing I want to tell you."

I leaned in closer to her.

"Michael is a good person to learn from. He's been in this business a long time, so he knows everything and everyone. But he's also involved in things you do not want any parts of. If you see anything you shouldn't, you better act like you didn't."

I nodded slowly as she looked at me somberly.

I paused, thinking about whether this was the right moment to ask for more advice after all she had already shared, but before I could lose my nerve, I decided to blurt it out.

"Got it. I will mind my business, I promise. But . . . I have one last question for you if you don't mind . . ."

"Shoot," she said.

"So let's say I stay in my lane with Michael, everything goes well with the merger, and we're all safe. How soon would I be able to scout artists while I'm still an assistant? I feel like I could be an asset to the A&R team if they let me."

"Oh, you're an eager one. I like that," she said, laughing. "I would say after you've been here a year, Michael might let you work with him directly on some of his artists' projects. A year or two after that, he'll maybe start trusting you to scout for a very small roster on your own time. Now there are *some* people here who get to do things on a different timeline." She rolled her eyes at the last statement, but she didn't let me in on her meaning. I wouldn't pry. If she'd wanted to tell me, she would have. I made myself a sponge instead. I wrung myself out of questions and waited to absorb whatever advice she wanted to impart.

She continued, "But for the most part, that's the timeline. And when they give you that opportunity, you better hit the ground running. You need to have already been going to shows around the city on your own time and be plugged in to what's poppin' on the internet, on Instagram, YouTube, SoundCloud, Bandcamp, podcasts too. It's one thing if you have the ear for talent. But you have to prove yourself. You have to have that fire in your belly to go for what you want."

I felt warm at the growing trust between us, at the work I'd already started that would soon be met with results. After how hard it had been to land this job and then navigate things at Lit so far, after that trash meeting with Walter and

Michael, my fire had been reinvigorated, flaming anew at the possibility of learning more under Nina's guidance.

Nina stuffed the last bit of salad in her mouth and looked down at her watch. She gathered her trash and crumpled it onto the lunch tray.

"Hey, I've gotta get to my thing," she said. "But this was nice. We should do it again sometime. I hope you're feeling better than you were earlier?"

"Oh. Yeah. Definitely. Again, just thanks so much. You have no idea how much this means to me." I smiled wide at her like a kid next in line for a theme-park ride, enthusiasm cracking through the cool exterior I'd built up. She smiled back at me, and then she was gone.

I sat at the table alone, still cheesing and thinking about my future.

I had made the connection and gotten the advice I'd wanted from Nina. I would have to be the best assistant Michael had ever seen. And I was up for the challenge. I would work hard. I would make myself indispensable. All I needed was thick skin, a good ear, and a little patience.

I gathered my stuff and made my way out of the building, into the muggy Midtown air, my mind clear, my goals set.

●

After the day I had, all I wanted was to chill. I wanted to change into a comfy lounge set and throw on slow, soulful, swooning melodies. The kinds of songs that made me feel like the rhythms and timbre, percussions and brass, were somehow a language calling back to the history, to the ancestors deep in my bones. But as soon as I opened my apartment door, I was met with water. Water was flowing from the bathroom sink onto the floor. The entire hallway was soaked. It seeped into our bedroom too, drowning the clothes that had fallen off the chair we tossed our clean but unfolded laundry on, and making them stink of mildew.

I already had so many issues with this apartment—appliances that hadn't been updated since the seventies, walls that peeled, roaches that had the decency to stay hidden during the day but got bolder as the sun set. I didn't need to add sinks that could apparently burst at any moment to the list. But this was one of the few places Lucas and I could afford. I sighed and called the super.

While I waited, I grabbed a mop to sop up the water in the hallway and placed a bucket beneath the sink to catch its dripping.

After the sink had been fixed and I had mopped up the dirty footprints the super had streaked across the hallway, I put on a superhero movie I'd seen too many times to count. Superhero movies were comforting for their formulaic nature, their predictability. I knew the heroes would always eventually win. Disaster would always be averted. These movies, with their neat endings tied up all nicely until the next adventure, always did the job of making me forget about everything I had going on—with Mama, with my career, and with the appliances in my apartment that had gone to shit.

Lucas joined me when he came home thirty minutes later and made my favorite: homemade adobo-seasoned popcorn. But I only paid attention to a few scenes before I started thinking back to my conversation with Nina, to her emphasis on hard work and patience.

Honestly, to hell with patience. I wanted to throw it smooth out of the window. I already felt so behind, an assistant two months away from twenty-five. I was good at making things happen, not waiting around for them to happen to me. I hadn't heard from Roman and I knew it was time to close the book on him and move on to someone else—Samirah. Samirah had been on my mind ever since I saw her, because I knew she had *it*. I knew she had the potential to be a star, and waiting two years until I could bring her to Lit felt too long. Felt like I'd lose her to another label. She could be my ticket to making myself indispensable, to showing them I have an ear, that I have the grit, hustle, and determination to stay in this industry. So what if I was a little early on the timeline? I would make myself the exception.

I pulled my laptop from beneath the sofa pillows and flipped it open. When the screen whirred to life, I typed in Quincy's website address that was linked in his IG profile.

I expected to find a website with incomplete information and stagnant photos of old artists he worked with, but the website was professional. He had a place for his bio, a tab for archival tracks, photos of his studio space, and toward the bottom of the page was a music player where you could hear the latest beats he was working on. Some of them were even for Samirah. My interest was piqued. I grabbed my earbuds.

The tracks were all so different, and as one of the songs played, it became clear that Quincy knew how to cut through the crowd with his own style. His instrumentals had the rattling high hats, 808s, and massive sub-bass of drill music; the horns and electric pianos that were popular in the nineties; classic boom-bap beats that were the unyielding pulse of New York hip-hop for generations; and the melodic jazzy undertones of R&B. Before long, I was nodding my head along with the music. I hadn't heard mixes like this before, the way each song was its own vibe. It reminded me of other producers, when they were new and shiny, shaping the culture and absolutely everywhere. Like when the Bronx's own Swizz Beatz bolted onto the scene, inflecting his beats with fluttering bells and whistles, jangly woodwinds and sped-up drums. Or when Pharrell infused hazy guitars and his signature four-beat intros into futuristic-sounding beats. Or maybe someone like Metro Boomin, whose trap beats with their deep 808 bass, high-hat rolls, and triplets introduced a new era. Even now, when it seemed like so many things had been done in music, so much so that it felt as if nothing new could still possibly emerge, Quincy knew how to take one part of a beat and make it his own, something fresh, inviting, all-encompassing. He was clearly untapped potential, and I wanted to be a part of it.

Quincy must have sensed that I was listening to his beats, because not long after I had started playing the tracks, my phone vibrated with a DM.

MoneyBoyQ:

i lost ur number

my fault

but I wanted to stay in touch

hit me back when u get a chance

I needed to play this smart so that I could build rapport. So that when it came time for me to sign artists, I could go to Quincy first, ask that Samirah work with me—not some other A&R exec—based on the strength of my continued and persistent interest.

MusicallyBillie:

hey

glad you reached out

how is Samirah?

still thinking about her after sis slid at Irving

MoneyBoyQ:

oh yea

havent seen her since the show

but she straight

y u ask. u tryna chop it up with us?

A connect? I didn't think it'd be that easy. I was prepared to bust out more of my charm that I kept in reserve for moments like these, but he was already interested. Now I had to see if he'd be willing to go a step further.

MusicallyBillie:

you can connect us?

that would be dope

when would ya be free?

MoneyBoyQ:

whenever u got the time

hmu whenever

Just as I sent my last message, Lucas noticed I wasn't looking at the movie and tapped me, his eyebrows raised in question.

"Quincy. That producer guy I met when we saw Wazy," I said and removed my earbuds to hear Lucas better.

Lucas nodded. "Oh. Word? Ya gonna work together or what? I know he gotta be impressed by my baby girl."

I smiled and nudged him playfully. I didn't want to be distracted by his compliments. If I let him, Lucas would launch a compliment attack, throwing sentiment upon sentiment at me until I was overwhelmed with love. I put down my phone and let myself fall into his arms sideways as he sat on the sofa next to me.

"I think so. He said he can connect me and Samirah. As far as I know, she's unsigned. If I get someone like her, even at this stage of assisting, to take me seriously without implying I'd sign her then and there, I think that would set me up well for when I actually can."

"Yeah, I can dig it. I see the plan. I see the vision. Soon you'll be taking over Lit. There's finna be so many artists up in there they ain't gon' know what to do wit' 'em," he said, smiling.

It wasn't golden hour in the apartment, but when I looked at him in that moment, he looked brilliant, gilded.

I gave him a kiss, and then he pointed his lips at the TV, making sure I would stop working and make space for myself to relax. I closed my laptop and turned my focus to the movie so that we could finish watching superheroes save the world and repeat until we fell asleep with all the lights on in the apartment.

9

"What do you want me to get?" I asked into the phone, waiting for Mama to respond on the other end. Lucas and I had left the house early, racing against time to get all our errands done before we had to hop on the road to Auntie Dionne's barbecue. We had shoveled two bags of dirty laundry into the washers and dryers at the laundromat down the street and run to the supermarket for groceries for the next week and ice and the two eight packs of Sprite Auntie Dionne requested. The liquor store was our last stop to pick up a bottle for us and for Mama so we wouldn't show up empty-handed.

"Get vodka. You know they love them some light liquor," she said. I could hear the smile in her voice, the way she was anticipating a good time. She laughed her fullest laugh in the company of her first cousins. They were the ones who knew her best, who shared the same cherished memories, who existed before the harsh realities of adult life latched on to them.

"Yeah, that works," I said. "Okay, I'll call you when I'm about to head out."

"Okay. Later," she said.

Lucas and I walked the few blocks back to our apartment and started getting dressed. Lucas put on a white linen shirt over a tank top and topped it with a silver Cuban-link chain. I put my hair in a half-up-half-down style, secured a stack of gold anklets around my left ankle, and picked out an all-white outfit to match. If we were pictured together later, there'd be no doubt that we were a couple that did the most. I could see us now, color coordinated and cuddling at a table in some deserted part of Auntie Dionne's backyard.

"Hey, Lucas," I said as I slipped into a white sleeveless top with a matching pleated tennis skirt.

"Yeah," he said, entering our bedroom as he pulled on white jean shorts.

"I was thinking about your mom the other day. She usually invites us to y'all's yearly family reunion this time of year. Is it still happening? I gotta put it in my calendar so I don't miss it."

"Oh, nah. I didn't tell you? They decided to go on a cruise to the Bahamas to celebrate their twenty-fifth anniversary. Ma said it was about time they went somewhere romantic since they never had a honeymoon."

"Aww. That's adorable. I'm happy for them. Tell Rose and Charles I said hi. Hopefully we'll get to see them for Thanksgiving. I need some of your mama's baked mac and cheese."

"You and me both," Lucas said.

"Yeah, at least we'll eat good today." I looked at the time on my phone on the nightstand. "Shit. We're gonna be late if we don't hurry."

We quickly finished getting dressed and headed to Mama's apartment. We heard the arguing before we even reached the door. I knocked hard and waited, but they couldn't hear me over the screaming. I whipped out my spare key and let us both inside.

There in the unlit kitchen I saw Mama near the light switch, flipping it up, then down, then up again, the dimness in the room unchanged. Marvin was in the living room, which could be seen from the kitchen, his face contorted in anger, lit by the sun beaming through the windows.

"Uh, what's going on in here?" I asked, looking between the two of them.

"You should stay out of grown folks' business, Billie," Marvin said.

"Marv, please. Not right now. I'm going to take this here bottle and get going. And since we grown"—Mama threw a pointed look toward him—"I would hope that the lights are on when I get back."

"Yeah, whatever," Marvin said. He picked up an amber bottle that sat on the floor near him and downed a swig of Malta as he plopped onto the couch. "Bring me something back. You know Ima be hungry."

"Yeah, yeah," she said. "C'mon, y'all. Lili, grab that potato salad out of the fridge and let's go."

•

Mama climbed into the passenger seat of the car Lucas had rented for the day.

A few blocks in, Mama turned the dial and blasted the air conditioner as high as it could go, guzzling expensive gas as we neared the highway.

"So is everything good, Ma? Did you get the money I Cash Apped you? You didn't hit me back," I said from the back seat.

"Yeah. Thanks, baby. I got it. We still need a little more for the light bill, but we're gonna figure it out. I've been meaning to call you, but between dealing with Marvin and training the new girl at work since Tracy died, it's been a lot going on."

"Oh my god. Tracy died? That's so sad," I said.

"Yep. She had a heart attack. She was four years away from retirement. Damn shame. And she was replaced in less than a week. Can you believe it?"

I'd met Tracy a few times, when Mama brought me to her office on bring-your-child-to-work day. She'd been working at Mama's company since before I was born.

A shiver ran through me as I considered the luck of people who had given their lives over to work only to expire before they got to do anything outside of it. I wouldn't let that be me.

"Anyway, since the lights are off right now, the air-conditioning not working. Y'all got an extra fan I can borrow?"

"Babe?" I asked.

"Yeah, there's one in the linen closet near the Christmas ornaments. It's small, but it's battery powered, so it should work. I used to take it with me on camping trips," Lucas said.

"Thanks, honey," she said.

"I'll have Lucas bring it down when we get back." We were just forty minutes into the drive, but traffic was heavy. "Let's put some gas in this car now, though. Think it's running low," I said. I took out my credit card, the closest thing to cash I had on me most times since my salary barely covered my portion of the rent and student loans, and handed it to Lucas. We pulled into the nearest gas station, where Lucas got out and filled the tank. I couldn't help but think about the facts. About the fact that Mama still needed my help even though she had a decent-paying job. About the fact that many Black families were only one generation—hell, one paycheck—away from poverty. About the fact that even if one of us did make it, we felt obligated to pull our families up with us. It's the same reason so many rappers talk about buying their mamas their first homes. They—and a lot of Black families—had never had a leg up on anything in this world, including the workplace and generational wealth. But that would change with me for me and Mama and Lucas . . . hopefully.

We drove for another forty-five minutes and watched as the buildings downsized, the trees grew larger and more formidable, the sky opened up vast and clear, the air free from the stench of garbage, urine, and sweat. It was a drive I'd loved since I was a kid, the kind that gave me serenity and peace in exchange for the life and energy the city provided to keep me measured.

We pulled into a cul-de-sac in Nyack, where the houses all looked the same: manicured lawns, large oak trees, classic suburban homes with white siding and red brick. It was one of those movie neighborhoods—the type of homes you'd see in a family film that housed a four-person unit and a beloved pet and walls that didn't peel and sinks that never leaked.

As we approached Auntie Dionne's backyard, I could already hear Will Smith's "Summertime," a barbecue classic. We weren't the first to arrive, but right in the middle—after the time we would have been called upon to help set up, but before we could officially be called late.

Now in the backyard, with the music changing to songs from Earth, Wind & Fire and Kool & the Gang around us, Mama, Lucas, and I made the rounds. First, we walked over to Auntie Dionne, who was busy putting out extra napkins.

"Hey, baby," she said, giving me a hug, her ample bosom pressed up against my stomach. "You're so big now. Looking all beautiful. I love it. And with that nice young man too. Come here," she said, gesturing toward Lucas.

"How're you doin', Mrs. Dionne?" he asked.

"Aww, I'm good, chile. I'm good. Well, don't y'all look stunning. Hope to see some marriage coming soon," she said, looking over the rim of her glasses at Lucas and me.

"Oh yeah, soon. Maybe after I've worked for a while. I just got a new job at this cool music label."

"The job will always be there, but your eggs, they ain't gonna last forever," she said, amused by her own comment.

Intricate horns and sticky guitars announced Parliament. Then the velvety vocals of the Spinners cut through the air as a false laugh flitted past my fake smile.

It didn't matter that I had recently graduated from grad school or got a new job, started a career, even, but that was expected from the older folks. Older family members were only ever concerned about the maternal things, about which domestic roles I could play that would make me a good and proper woman.

She hugged Mama too and asked her how she was doing but left out any mention of Marvin. I assumed they had already had that talk many times over.

Next, we walked over to Uncle Charlie, who was busy manning the grill. He always talked out of the side of his mouth that didn't have a cigar placed in it, and he gave Mama and me hugs and Lucas a congenial slap on the back.

"Listen here, Mellie." Uncle Charlie was one of the few who called my mother Mellie, short for Melanie. "If you need me to handle Marvin . . . you just say the word."

"Oh, Unc," Ma said, feigning laughter. "I'm good. Don't worry. Now, what you need to worry about is them cigars. You know them things will give you cancer."

He laughed his rollicking laugh, followed up with "Don't you fret about me. I'm fitter than some of these youngbloods out here," and then he told us to get a drink and settle in.

After that, we said hello to the rest of my aunts and uncles we called "the regulars," the ones we could expect to see at all the family functions, and chose a table away from their judging eyes. My cousins hadn't shown up yet, so the fun had not officially begun. I asked my mother for her drink order, and Lucas and I walked over to the bar area.

Once we got our drinks, we sat back at our table, listened to Shalamar and Slave, Chaka Khan and Stephanie Mills, drank and munched on hot dogs, hamburgers, and spicy sausages until it was time to pile our plates high with barbecue essentials—potato salad (Mama's famous recipe), pork ribs, corn on the cob, and baked beans.

After a while, the volume of the music had been turned up, and my aunts and uncles ventured onto the grassy makeshift dance floor to two-step to Dennis Edwards's "Don't Look Any Further."

As the classics kept coming, the ones played at nearly every Black barbecue across the country, the ones that seemed so tied to Blackness that we knew them in our minds, limbs, and hearts—Luther Vandross's "Never Too Much," the Gap Band's "Outstanding," Keni Burke's "Risin' to the Top," Maze's "Before I Let Go" (blended into Beyoncé's version), McFadden & Whitehead's "Ain't No Stoppin' Us Now"—I smiled. These were the songs of my childhood, the songs that were a permanent part of the culture, of me. They connected me to something bigger than myself. Generations of my family grooved to these songs through the decades, and even when the world around them didn't love them, these moments, with music stirring through them while they were surrounded by loved ones, they were enough.

Soon, as the classics gave way to newer hits, my cousins arrived in clusters and plied themselves with food and drinks at a table near ours.

"Heeyy," Selena and Sade sang at once.

"So tell us everything," Selena said.

They each sat down in the open chairs next to me, drinks in hand. Lucas had already gone to hang with my male cousins.

"Tell you everything what?" I asked.

"You know, have you met any celebrities? Can you get us into some parties? Some studio time?" Selena said.

"Yeah, girl. This the perfect opportunity to get some clout," Sade said as she danced in her seat.

"Y'all funny. I'm really not that important. But give me a few years, and Ima be on it."

"See, that's what I'm talking about. All you gotta do is slide us in there, and we up," Selena said.

"Yeah, like I said, we'll see. I can probably give you some advice, and I can, like, listen to material if you have it ready. But that's about it. Might be different when I get promoted. But if you have, like, basic questions, I can answer them," I said.

"Basic questions? This girl thinks she *Vogue* or something," Selena said.

"Yeah, Li, you ain't gotta be like that. Don't be acting all bougie and shit now that you got this lil job," Sade said.

"I'm not. I swear. Yo, why y'all coming at me like this?"

"We not coming at you like anything. We just saying. Remember where you came from. That's all," Selena said.

"Yeah. A'ight. Ima get another drink," I said. I lifted my cup toward them, and although it wasn't anywhere near empty, I made my way to the bar.

Now that I had this job with access, with the illusion of success, I knew people would start expecting things of me. But they didn't know the details. They didn't know that I worked all the time, that I barely had enough money to cover my monthly expenses, that I hadn't stepped inside the studio in the office at all, that I didn't have any real power yet. All they saw was glamour. The Lit name.

My phone started to ring as I took a sip of my drink and surveyed the backyard now suffused in orange light, the sun beginning to set.

I answered, and Michael's voice rang out immediately, his tone wrapped in urgency.

"Billie?" he said.

My stomach lurched, already anticipating the worst. There was no way that a call on the holiday weekend meant anything other than trouble.

"Sorry for the noise. I'm at an event right now. How are you, Michael?" I asked.

"I'm fine. . . . Billie, I know it's a holiday, but I need you to do something urgent for me."

"Sure, Michael, what do you need?"

"Roxie Larue is missing something from her rider, and the venue is unable to get it. I need you to go down to the office to grab it and then go to Madison Square Garden to give it to her team."

Roxie was technically Kate's client, but Kate was already on vacation, and her assistant was out because of Covid. It was up to me. If we didn't get everything on her list of requests that she presented to the venue, we'd be in breach of contract.

I wanted to say no, but then I heard Nina's voice saying, "*Make yourself indispensable.*" I imagined one of my artists on stage winning a Grammy and thanking me right after God and their mom. For that, I'd do anything.

"No problem," I said, careful to keep my tone cheery, joyful, gracious, even if I felt the opposite.

"If we don't get this to her before her show starts, she's threatening to break her contract. This is her biggest show of the season. We need to keep her happy. Got it?"

"Got it."

"Great. I'm emailing you the details now. Pay close attention to it. If we forget anything, it's our asses." He chuckled, but the sound was humorless.

"No problem. I am on it," I said, but I was talking to the air. Michael had already hung up.

Off the phone now, I caught Lucas's eye across the backyard. He raised his hands in question.

I shrugged and mouthed the word *Lit*. Seconds later Lucas was beside me.

"What's going on?"

I leaned in close so he could hear me over the music.

"That was Michael. He wants me to go to the office for something. I have to leave now or I'm not going to make it to the show."

"Are you deadass? You have to leave right now? It's a holiday," Lucas said. I could see the flash of anger on his face that cinched his eyebrows close together, that pinched his mouth tight. He didn't want this for me, this career that pulled me away from living, from being in the moment, free of anything at all.

"I'm sorry, babe. My family will understand. But if I don't dip now, I'm not sure Ima still have a job when the office reopens on Tuesday," I said.

"Okay, how you gonna get to the office then? It's wild far."

"Ima just ask around for a ride. Olivia be leaving all these events early for work." I glanced around to see if she was anywhere in the backyard, but she wasn't there. "Lemme see if she still here. I'll check the house."

I moved to make my way inside when Lucas shifted and blocked me and grabbed my hand.

"Babe, you shouldn't have to do this. This is your time off after mad weeks working, like, every day. Spend time with your family. Recharge. Be here. With us. With me."

"Lucas, stop. Please. I can't. I promise I'll make it up to you later."

I gently pulled my hand from his right as the beat to Cameo's "Candy" came through the speakers. This was usually my favorite part of our barbecues—when everyone, young and old, would get up at the sound of the synth bass and shimmy onto the dance floor to participate in the line dances. I had been electric and cha-cha sliding, cupid shuffling and wobbling since I was a kid, and I loved being swept up by the gentle current of generational ties that spread through us as we danced together.

I knew I had to leave. If I ever wanted to help create music that was passed down like heirlooms, I had to keep this job.

I gave Lucas one pleading look and threw a glance Mama's way as she mingled with her first cousins to see if she'd notice my departure before I turned to go inside and look for Olivia.

•

Olivia had been in the kitchen as I suspected. She was packing up leftovers for her three boys when I cornered her and convinced her to give me a ride. She lived in Brooklyn, so my office wasn't close to her destination. In order to get her to drive me, I had to bribe her with promises to check out the new single her current boyfriend had made and Cash App her twenty dollars for gas.

We made it to the office in fifty-four minutes, her speeding down the highway with the windows open and bass-heavy music blasting as the kids' iPads screeched with nonsensical YouTube videos.

The office lobby doors were locked when I arrived. There was a lone security guard at the front desk who seemed like he was there for show. No one was expected in. And technically, neither was I.

I banged on the door and held my work badge up to the glass to get his attention, relieved it happened to be in the purse I was carrying.

"Hi, sorry. I just need to get upstairs for something," I said.

"It's Independence Day, yuh know," he said, eyeing me suspiciously as he held the door out beside him. The musicality of his accent, somewhere Caribbean, dripped from his tongue.

"I know. Sorry. It's sort of last-minute. Can . . . I go up?"

He nodded and stepped to the side. I glided in sideways, careful to avoid more of his concerned judgment.

At my desk, I looked through the folders in the FIRE system for the rider and prayed that I'd find her record fast.

Roxie was a huge moneymaker for the label. She was a pop star who commanded the attention of adult men and teenage girls alike, with her cheerleader-style dance moves, songs about sex disguised as cutesy, infectious high-energy beats, pitchy vocals, and impossibly catchy lyrics—the kind of shit that'd go viral with the quickness. Her last album went double platinum, and she had debuted her third album earlier in the week, landing at number one on the *Billboard* charts.

Failing to get an artist like that everything she needed would absolutely cost me my job. And at this point, it didn't matter that I had to leave my family, that it had cost me money I really didn't have to hurry down there. All that mattered was that I handled this so that I impressed Michael and had the opportunity to see this career through.

After ten minutes of searching, I found the rider in one of the digital files incorrectly logged in the 2026 season. The rider wasn't the most extensive list, but it was incredibly specific. She wanted a teacart with chamomile and mint tea (absolutely no black tea) and wished to have the water boiled to exactly 104 degrees Fahrenheit. There was a list of an assortment of foods and snacks and a request for four bottles of the best possible local white wine. Whatever room they put her in was to be draped in white to avoid looking at any undesirable walls, and a maple bourbon candle was to be lit in each corner of the room.

The last item on the list in bold red was the thing that was missing—two vinyls of the album she released before she signed to Lit. She wanted to smash them with a hammer seconds before she went on stage because she said it gave her good luck. It made her think about the trajectory of her career, about the way her domineering, definitely creepy former manager controlled her and stopped her from making music after that first album because he owned the beats, wrote the songs, and provided background vocals in the form of enthusiastic sound effects. But really, he stopped her because he could, because the industry rewards toxic behavior from terrible men. Now that she was out from under his thumb, she wanted to remind herself that she had broken free.

I looked down at my phone to gauge the time. I had twenty minutes to search for the album and needed the other ten to get to Madison Square Garden.

In the assistant manual I'd found weeks earlier, there was a document outlining what to do in situations involving Roxie, including when things went wrong with her rider.

It said that Michael kept his bottom desk drawer full of vinyls and physical CDs of his favorite artists—the ones who had made his career a success from the eighties until now.

I made my way to the drawer and ran my fingers across the tops of the cardboard cases until I found Roxie's. With the vinyls in hand, I grabbed my purse from my desk and ran to the elevator. I called an Uber on my way down, thanking the universe that Wi-Fi here worked in the elevators.

By the time I emerged from the building, the car had canceled. The streets were completely gridlocked because there was another bomb scare in a city park. If I called for another car, I'd never make it.

I knew what I would have to do. I took a deep breath and then started sprinting down the street. Thankfully, this was New York City, and not a soul cared that a sweaty Black girl was speeding down Sixth Avenue.

I had to stop and catch my breath for a few seconds every three blocks I ran, because sweat was pouring from my scalp onto my face and my chest heaved from the exertion. I hadn't worked out like this since I was forced to take a PE credit in order to graduate college. But as I stood in front of the Macy's display, with its summer scene—mannequins dressed in polos and shorts, collared sleeveless tennis dresses, bikinis and swim trunks, beach balls and umbrellas beside them, atop a bed of fake sand—wheezing like a pug with bad allergies, Madison Square Garden came into view.

I gulped more breath into my greedy lungs and ran the last few blocks to the side entrance where the backstage crew entered.

When I made it to the door, sweat glistened from every part of my body. I probably looked like a deranged fan, and the bouncer, dressed in all black, looking serious and holding a clipboard in his right hand, used his left to aggressively point to the main entrance.

"Hi, actually, my name isn't on the list, but I have to get something to Roxie Larue on behalf of—"

The bouncer waved his hand inches from my face. "If you're not on the list, you're not getting in."

I sighed. I didn't have time for this. I was achy and tired and wanted to get this thing to Roxie so I could finally go the fuck home.

I dug into my purse, found my work ID at the bottom, and flashed it to the bouncer. "Look, I work for Lit Music Productions. I want to make sure Roxie Larue gets what she needs," I said, projecting a polite smile onto my face. "Please," I added, because it always helps with their ego, their wanting of our need.

The man stopped and took the ID from my hands, looked closer at my picture, at the embossed Lit logo that reflected silver under his flashlight. His eyes returned to my face once more, and then without a word, he jerked his head to the side and handed my ID back to me. I squeezed past him and through the black metal doors.

I affixed my ID to the top of my shirt as I walked through the doors and followed the white tape on the sticky gray floors. I flashed my ID at anyone who stared at me too long, and walked confidently, like I knew where I was going, but under my breath, I muttered the number of Roxie Larue's dressing room over and over, shifting my head and peering down long hallways.

As I speed walked, I almost passed Roxie's dressing room, but when I saw an entourage of backup singers and wardrobe assistants taking turns knocking on the locked door, I knew Roxie was in there. As I approached, breathless, hair sticking to my face, sweat still pouring from my skull, I heard crashing coming from inside the room.

"Where is it? I'm not going on without my ritual! I will cancel this fucking show, I swear," she yelled.

A white woman with wavy hair dyed a red that almost looked natural rapped on the door. "I'm so sorry, Roxie. We're working on it. I'm sure it's here somewhere," she said.

I ran over to the woman while taking the records out of the taupe tote bag I carried it in.

I quickly threw some charm into my voice so I came off as nonthreatening, as someone trying only to defuse a tense situation.

"Hi, I'm so sorry Lit wasn't able to initially provide the album for Ms. Larue, but I have them right here. There's no need to cancel—I bet all of her fans would be so grateful to see her. She puts on such an amazing show."

The woman sighed and pulled me into a hug. "Oh, thank fucking God."

"Happy to help!"

It wasn't the truth, but it was what she wanted to hear, what all people who ask things of you that you cannot actually refuse want to hear.

She nodded and rapped on the door again, this time telling Roxie Larue that she finally had the records.

The woman didn't have to say anything to me for me to know that my part in this night was done. I had run through Midtown looking an entire mess, but I had also done what was asked of me: I saved the concert and Lit from a broken contract. And though I was sure I wouldn't get any of the credit for this from Michael or Roxie Larue or her team, I still felt pride swelling in me that let me know I could do this. If Lit let me, I would make sure that the artists I signed were happy, that I could give them everything they needed to thrive, that I could grant them the same comfort, the same peace of mind Roxie Larue had gotten from her soothing rituals.

I texted Michael to let him know the deed was done and made my way to the subway.

•

I hadn't heard from Lucas after I left the barbecue. But when I ascended from underground, I realized he had been blowing up my phone for the last hour. Most of the texts were variations of *Where are you?* and *Hit me back, babe.*

My phone was at 3 percent, and it wouldn't last long enough for me to call him, so once the train pulled up to my stop, I hustled up the hill, up the stairs, and into my apartment.

I could hear a deep voice harmonizing with a melodic beat carrying through to the hallway and knew Lucas was still up. He waited for me in the living room, a blunt lit in his hand.

"Billie, I was worried 'bout you. What happened?" he asked, closing in on me for a hug.

I moved my body away because I felt sticky and moist like when a Band-Aid decides it has had enough of trying to shield your skin from more disaster.

"Ugh, you do not want to touch me right now." I started to undress right there in the hallway. "Did Mama get home okay?" I asked.

"Yeah. She's good. I drove us back. She knocked out in the car, and I think Marvin was already asleep when she got in. . . . So is everything good with you?" He took another pull of his blunt and looked at me, his eyes caught halfway between desire and worry.

"Michael had me running through the city to get a record to Roxie Larue that was missing from her rider. If she didn't get it, she would break her contract."

I twisted up my face to let Lucas know that I wasn't in the mood to debate after the day I had, but he pressed on.

"Damn. I'm sorry, babe. It's kind of fucked up that you can't even spend a weekend without thinking about work. You shouldn't have to give everything to a corporation that doesn't give a fuck about you or their artists."

"They're doing what they're supposed to do. They're making deals and making music. I can't control how that gets done. Not yet at least." I realized how it sounded as soon as it came out—morally sketchy but practical, like buying a knockoff bag from the pushy sidewalk vendors in Chinatown, but it was the truth.

"This company is making a profit off deals that fucked people like us in the first place . . . I don't know. Something doesn't feel right at Lit. I feel like you're losing sight of what you came there to do. I don't want you to get lost too."

"Baby," I said softly. "This is all . . . temporary. I can't snap my fingers and get things to change like that. I have to pay my dues. Work my way up. If I show enough dedication, enough willingness to do what it takes, then I will get my chance. This is me getting mine."

Lucas looked at me then, suddenly serious. I stopped trying to slip off my socks, and he gently pulled me closer so that my back was against his stomach, my neck brushing against his lips. He slowly moved my hair from my neck to the front, and I turned my head to meet his behind me.

"I hear you. All I'm saying is all of this . . . it better be worth it," he said.

And I nodded because I needed it to be true.

10

Back in the office after the holiday weekend, the location of a photo shoot in SoHo for an artist had gone awry, which left Wren over-dressed, styled in custom high-fashion pieces underutilized in ninety-degree weather.

I knew I couldn't walk into Michael's office, hoping he would give me some advice on the best course of action for my shit-gone-wrong list. He'd tell me to figure it out, that it's what he hired me for, much like he'd told me before, his tone wrapped in layers of easy confidence—the kind of confidence only found in white men who were taught that these were the spaces they could own.

After my talk with Nina, I knew it was on me to master the job. I sprang into action.

I hit up Alicia first and asked her if she knew of any places that would be cool enough to schedule the shoot. It had been a while since we last talked in person. She had been holed up in her apartment, feverishly sending out pitches for weeks. She was stuck, she complained to me over a series of voice notes and FaceTimes, going from company to company, trying to find a place that would hire her as a full-time staff writer.

"*I'm giving them my best pieces, Billie. I don't know what else I can do. It's getting depressing,*" she'd said. I tried to cheer her up, but there wasn't much I could say that would contradict the reality of her situation. Journalism was a dying business, and I felt awful for her. She'd spent her whole life reaching for a career in an industry that was falling apart, that had become a sad shell of its former self.

She did manage to point me to her most recent article on *Curbed* about office spaces that had been turned into cultural hubs and art galleries around the city. I picked the L out of the lineup, a sprawling spot in Williamsburg with a sweeping view of the New York City skyline—and persuaded the manager to let us use the space in exchange for free swag and promotion through our channels to other artists. I organized cars to pick up the stranded artists, and off they went to the borough of reinvention.

Later, I had to take care of an artist who was late for their studio recording session. There wasn't much to do there besides ensuring that they were all set with hot coffee and black tea with honey to keep their brains and throats working, moving, pulsing with the creativity needed to record in the studio on the fourteenth floor.

When I finally looked up from my computer, dusk had colored the sky a darker shade of blue than I had expected. I realized I hadn't had time to text Quincy like I had planned after our little chat over the weekend. I pulled out my phone and shot him a quick message, hoping to set up something with Samirah soon.

Quincy:

wanna come thru today?

gonna be in Miami for a min after next week

I looked at my phone, and it was past seven already. I'd finished most things on my to-do list today, and the few remaining tasks I could do at home. It was late, but if this was my chance to get more info from Quincy on Samirah, I had to take it. We decided to meet at eight-thirty.

I had shut my computer down, but fired it up again and searched for all the latest intel on Samirah.

•

Quincy's studio was deep in Queens. When I got off the E Train and appeared above ground on an avenue, boulevard, and street all at once, it took looking up directions on my phone and walking the wrong way twice to figure out exactly where I was going.

By the time I reached the studio at the end of a quiet street surrounded by warehouses, I was sticky from the suffocating humidity, and panting. I pulled out the water bottle I'd stuck in my bag earlier and sucked from it deeply.

I turned my phone camera on selfie mode, applied a quick swipe of gloss, and fixed my natural hair I'd packed in a slick bun with a small brush I kept in my purse before pressing the buzzer to the fourth floor.

"You made it," Quincy said as he opened the door.

He had a fresh fade, the edges lined up perfectly, and he was wearing a black Hellstar tee, a gold chain that flashed bright against his dark skin, and a pair of all-black Balenciagas. This fit, all of his fits really, at least the ones I had clocked from his social media, made him seem like his style was endless, like he was the kind of guy who would simultaneously stand out and fit in among dudes from around the way or almost superstars who wandered into his studio.

"Hey. My bad. Sorry I'm late."

"Nah, it's cool. It's just that Mirah has been here for a minute. I wanted to properly introduce y'all."

"Oh," I said. I pitched my voice lower and got closer to Quincy. I had the research I needed, but I hadn't at all expected to meet her this time. I was going to have to wing it and hope my passion and charm made up for anything lacking. "I didn't know she was going to be here."

"Yeah, my fault. I forgot to mention it, but I figured it was cool since you wanted to link with her anyway. It's not a problem, is it?" He looked back and forth between me and the studio behind him.

"Nah. It's all good. I'm excited actually."

"Well, come in."

I hadn't been allowed in the studios at the office—I was much too junior for that—but when I stepped into Quincy's studio, even though my body was begging for rest, I suddenly felt alert, like someone had taken a taser to my nerves.

I swept my eyes across the room, taking in the dark carpeted floors and a section of the wall near the soundboard papered with snapshots of prolific producers like Timbaland and J Dilla taped next to Tay Keith and Boi-1da while they were making the beats for iconic songs. A black leather sectional was pushed up against the back wall, and a large glossy black coffee table sat in the center. Across from the sofas was a mixing area, equipped with a long black slab that had knobs and levers, buttons and dials, and I wanted to know what they did, how Quincy controlled them to make beats I'd never forget once I heard them. And finally, after I'd eyed everything else in the room, I looked toward Samirah in the isolation booth. She was composed, with her eyes closed, head bopping, hands stretched out beside her like the music was right there in her hands, and she was just as when I saw her at Irving: mesmerizing, an entity I couldn't tear my eyes from.

"You want something to drink?" Quincy asked. He turned around toward me from his place at the mixing station.

"Um. Nah, I'm good."

Quincy nodded and turned back to the mixing board, pressed a button that connected to the isolation booth, and stopped the organized clattering of the beat.

"That was good, Mirah. Now this time, could you give me a little more at the end? Really put all you got into those last three *yeahs*."

Samirah side-eyed him in mock annoyance, laughed like she was Janet Jackson at the end of a song, nodded, and tried one more time. She took a few deep breaths before singing again, placing her hand on her abdomen for support.

I didn't want to ruin this vibe, the feeling in the room like we were on the edge of greatness, so I stayed quiet, let the music take over, and thought about what I would say to her when she finally came out. How was I going to impress someone with this much presence and talent?

After a few minutes of listening to Samirah yell *yeahs* into the mic melodically, Quincy paused the music and let her know it was time to take a break.

Samirah appeared from the isolation booth, jet-black hair in loose barrel curls that went down to her waist, eyelashes that looked glamorous but heavy on her lids, dressed in a black-and-lime-green cropped track jacket and matching shorts. Nothing about the lighting in the space changed, but it was like she sucked it up wherever she went, sparking a path to her that said, *Pay attention or you'll miss something good.*

"Aye, so, Samirah, I'd like you to meet someone." Quincy motioned for me to join them by his chair near his equipment. Samirah looked over in my direction.

I smiled awkwardly and walked to where they stood near Quincy's workstation.

"This is Billie. She works at Lit Music Productions."

"Samirah," I said, holding my hand out. "So good to meet you. I saw you a couple months ago at Irving. You were amazing."

I'd never been starstruck before. I had encountered a number of stars as they rolled through the Lit offices, but somehow this felt different. It was like Samirah was already someone whose autograph I wanted to keep safe, like it was a valuable, precious thing I couldn't risk losing.

Samirah shook my hand firmly. "Good to meet you too. Thanks so much. That was actually the biggest show I've played so far."

"Oh, dope. I totally couldn't tell. You were a natural up there."

"Thanks. I'm still getting the hang of being on stage and whatever." She shifted her weight from one foot to the other. It occurred to me that she might be nervous to meet someone from a record label. I could use that to my advantage.

"Yeah, so . . ." I drew out the words slowly, trying to think back to my conversation with Nina about preparedness, trying to recall what I overheard Michael asking artists on calls, but I decided that the best way to persuade her was to be myself, to keep it simple and direct.

Quincy invited us to sit on the sectional while he sat at the mixing area. Samirah sat but I chose to stand so I could look at her head-on.

"Before we get into you, I wanted to share a bit about me. As y'all know, I work at Lit. But before that, I obtained my master's in music with a concentration in musical theory in May. So I intimately understand music on many levels, from production to writing to music history. It all comes in handy when trying to sign artists in this business. Alongside that, I been running my own social media accounts, MusicallyBillie, that have thousands of followers. I interview up-and-coming artists about their music and stories. I've dedicated my whole life to music, and I'm passionate about shining a light on and helping Black and brown artists, talented local artists like you, thrive. I've heard hundreds of thousands of tracks, live shows, demos, but nothing like you. And I think with time and hustle, we could eventually make magic together. So, yeah. That's why I wanted to link with you in the first place. I think you are really special, and I'd love the opportunity to bring you into Lit if I can. If you're feeling that, I have a couple questions I'd like to ask if you don't mind?"

She nodded.

"Cool. Yeah. I'd love to know more about you as a person. Your style and inspiration behind your music. So my first question to you is how did you get your start in music?"

"Yeah, that's actually a crazy story. A'ight so, boom," she started.

I smirked, loving that she started her sentence with the quintessential Black story-time phrase.

I looked toward Quincy, and he watched her rapturously, waiting for her to go on. He knew what was coming, like this was the very story that made him want to continue making beats for her.

"I'm in the lunchroom. Sixth grade—by that time everyone knew me as the girl with the headphones. You know, them big-ass Beats that went over your head? I always had them plugged into my iPhone playing, you know, whatever was hot, Lil Wayne, Kanye—before he started doing the shit he's doing now—Nicki . . ."

Samirah's eyes gleamed as she spoke and touched her hand to her face. She was fully immersed in the memory now, thinking about the beginning of it all.

"I used to sit alone, scribbling in my little notebook or whatever as I mouthed the lyrics to what was playing. So this dumb boy comes over one day and pulls my headphones off my ears, on some real grimy shit. Says something like 'You think you a rapper or somethin'. Let me see that.' Then he grabs my notebook. I try to grab it back from him, but he was tall, so I couldn't reach. And by then, there's mad people watching. The boy started reading one of the songs I wrote in the book and starts clowning me. But I flipped it on him." She laughed, her hand shooting to her mouth to cover her spreading smile, took a beat, then, "Yo, so I hit the dude right in his balls."

"Ayoooo!" Quincy said. I had forgotten he was here for a moment, spellbound as I was by Samirah, but when I looked over at him with his laid-back laughter, the liquid in his cup sloshing around in his hand, it was easy to see why people gravitated toward him.

"Yeah, bro. Right in the fucking balls. Not gonna lie, it was hilarious after the adrenaline died down," she said. "Anyway, so, I grab my book and, in the loudest voice, recite the rap as I heard it in my head. When I tell you that the lunchroom was so silent . . . I was honestly scared. But then everybody went right back to what they was doing before that all happened. I was lucky they didn't laugh my ass out of there. Then later that day, people kept coming up to me during recess, like *Yoooo, that was fire.* And from there, I kept it going. Made lil songs on my computer once I got one. And once I was in community college, I started doing open mics. And basically, here we are now."

"Ayeee. Okay. Now that is a good come-up story. I can see you telling that on podcasts, radio shows, easy." I laughed.

I could imagine how her personality would play in an interview, how they'd be enamored by the way she blushed, the way her smile spread as she thought about her passion, the way she was unabashed in who she was and where she came from.

"So what are you trying to say with your music? I ask because there are so many artists out there. But so few make it through, you know. So being unique and knowing what you want to say to everyone listening is important."

Samirah took a moment to think, the whites of her eyes on display as she looked up toward her brain. "It's hard to get noticed with so many people doing they thing on the internet. I used to rap in the subway actually to get a little money so I could help Moms with the bills. I'd sell little snacks in school so she never had to worry about giving me pocket change or money for school trips. I'm independent, and I hustle. Writing about stuff that means something to me. Being a woman. Being a woman in America, a Black one at that. Growing up in the hood but wanting better. Something more than what life had given me. So I got that serious stuff. But I also have fun party music. A lil somethin' y'all can twerk to."

Samirah twerked in the seat and stuck out her tongue, and I knew what she meant. That the weight of being a Black woman in this world meant a dual existence.

"Yes, I love that," I said. "Can I hear more tracks? I want to get a sense of how I'd pitch you. Where you'd sit in the market. Based off the song you recorded earlier and the ones I heard at Irving, I'm thinking of somewhere between Flo Milli and Leikeli47. Maybe some Lauryn Hill too with the singing. I think if I know how that all blends together, we could pitch you as someone energetic and lyrical, confident and thoughtful but still playful."

"Yeah, we got, what, maybe one more song right now?" Samirah said, looking toward Quincy. "Let's play that one for her."

Quincy nodded and turned his attention to the mixing board. He pulled up Ableton Live on his laptop and hit play on the song.

A rattling beat with deep bass inflected with claps, cymbals, and warm guitar flooded the room. It was a complex beat, and I took it apart as I heard it in my head, singling out instruments and sounds layer by layer so I knew what made up the whole. Samirah gestured the lyrics to the song from her seat as it played.

"That is so good, y'all. Like, wow. It's got a nice, deep groove. And the quick high hats make it sound bright. I like that. But can I play around with it real quick? I have some ideas."

Quincy looked at me, smirked, and got up from his chair. "Yeah, let's see what you got, then." He sat next to Samirah on the sofa.

I hadn't been in a studio since college, back when I made beats and created new songs for my composition classes. Though it had been years, it came back to me now easily. I took a seat at the workstation in front of his laptop and started to play around with the beat. I programmed in a guitar sample and stretched it to make it sound more sensual, sexier. I added a piano riff in G minor to complement the melody. I spaced out some of the high hats to give it more texture.

When I was done, I turned in my chair and looked at them on the sofa. "What do you think?"

Samirah and Quincy exchanged a glance with each other, then looked back at me.

"Oh, so this what you meant when you said you know music intimately. I didn't know you knew how to make it for real. My song sounds so good," Samirah said.

I laughed. "Nah, I'm all right. I just hear a song or a sound and know what it needs or what it doesn't. That instinct to, like, help shape something or someone, or help them say whatever they want to say in the best way they can, has helped me a lot in my career. It's part of why I think I can help you get signed."

"I'm listening," Samirah said.

"Okay. So if we were to try to get you signed, first we need to think about you as a package. Something unique and appealing so that the label can't say no. So I think we should put together an EP with some of the songs Samirah has out already. The song you just played is fire, and with the adjustments, I think it could be your leading single. We should add a couple more new songs to the EP too. I know the label responds to stuff that's fresh, tailored for them."

"Yeah. I think we could do that," Quincy said. He leaned forward, his elbows resting on his thighs. He gestured with his hands as he spoke. "I'm working on a few beats right now that would be good for you." He tilted his chin toward Samirah.

"Yeah, that sounds great, honestly. I'm wit' it."

"Let's do it," I said.

I had convinced Samirah that I had potential. And that I would turn her potential into a possible record deal. Launching Samirah's career would set up my future, for our future together.

"Well, while y'all are working on the EP, I'll plant the seeds at my office so that when we get this thing poppin', we can hit the ground running. Would six months be enough time to complete the project?"

Samirah and Quincy exchanged glances and nodded at each other, a silent agreement that solidified our partnership.

"Okay. Well, if you have any questions at all, want to link up or anything, you know where to find me."

I said my goodbyes to Samirah and Quincy, grabbed my bag, and headed home. As I walked down the stairs, my mind raced with ideas of what to do for Samirah. I was buzzing, like when I pumped the swing too high in the park and my stomach lurched at the anticipation of bigger thrills, the violence of a potential fall to the ground somehow making it all the more exhilarating. She could possibly be my first artist as an A&R rep if everything went right, and I felt warmth swell in the center of my heart as I contemplated my future.

11

On the second day of Leo season, the CEO of Lit Music Productions emailed all the senior staff across imprints in the New York office about an emergency meeting that would happen today. I was on the email thread only because I had been enlisted to take the minutes for our department. There were no further details given, which, naturally, sent the office into a frenzy. People had been shuffling around all morning, gathered in groups of twos and threes, whispering. They gripped their coffee mugs tightly in their hands, held equally tight smiles on their faces as they reassured one another with shoulder pats and weak hugs.

When it was time for the meeting, people shuffled into their seats around the table, still murmuring, trading rumors about the future of the label.

"Good morning, everyone. So I'll be straight with you," Stanley, the CEO, started. He sat at the front of the room with the four division heads, including Michael, next to him like they were a panel of experts at a conference. The light from the window poured into the room, shrouded his bald head in light that made him shield his eyes as he talked. He motioned for someone to close the blinds. I was sitting in the front row of chairs. Michael signaled to me with his eyes, and I hurried over to the windows.

"You know a merger between Lit Music Productions and Ultimate Records has been in the works for some time. The merger has gone through successfully."

From where I was standing, I could see the faces of almost everyone in the room. Some people went wide-eyed, hands shot up to cover their mouths split open in shock. Others furrowed their brows, crossed their arms, spat curse words beneath their breath. Even my own heart dropped into my stomach as I contemplated what this new company would look like, how it would change my plans. I'd just gotten an in with Samirah.

While it was true that Michael had been mysteriously private—heading out every day at noon for the last four weeks to secret meetings I didn't book for him and having closed-door conversations with the CEO near the end of the day, where they leaned into each other, their voices pitched low—I hadn't expected it to happen so soon into my tenure. I hadn't expected that so much about Lit was about to change.

Ultimate Records was an independent label run by Trent McCarthy. Trent started out in A&R in the late eighties at Universal, working his way up from assistant to president in record time. When he left Universal and started Ultimate, he funded the venture partly with the salary he had amassed over the years and with start-up money gifted to him by his actor parents. Ultimate had become successful, a well-known name in the music industry and the country's second largest independent label in the mid-nineties for plucking artists from obscurity, turning street kids into stars at a time when hip-hop was in its infancy. Unlike other companies, he curated his label with care, giving his small stable of artists fair deals and creative reign that allowed them to thrive artistically. The problem, however, was that when Trent had launched artists' careers, they left after the first album, seeking fatter advances and greater financial security. Trent, for all his care and purposeful leadership, couldn't compete with the likes of the big three. But now we were in a new era, where listeners clamored for authentic representation and demanded that big labels put their money where their mouths were.

Stanley explained that the acquisition of Ultimate would be a step toward that, a shiny new direction for Lit. It would give Lit greater diversity, larger market share, and would quiet critics of the label who had called Lit predatory for Black and brown artists, though he didn't say that last part aloud. It would also help Ultimate not lose artists to one of the big labels—that was what Lit had in spades—the finances, the resources, the right connections to make artists' careers last a lifetime.

After that, Stanley asked us to direct our attention to the television behind him, where someone pulled up a video conference on Teams.

Trent, a fiftysomething white man with sandy-brown hair and thin lips, wearing a black blazer over a white shirt with RUN-DMC across it, appeared on the screen.

"Trent, welcome. We're wrapping up our meeting here on this thrilling acquisition, but it'd be great for you to introduce yourself to the team."

"Thanks, Stanley. So I just wanted to come on today to say that I am beyond excited to be merging with Lit. Lit has been a pioneer in the music industry for decades, and I've long admired the roster and commitment to art. With my back catalog and with the resources of Lit, I believe we can really make a difference in this industry and do something new that will get listeners excited to hear everything that comes from us and keep them coming back for more. I'm looking forward to making that magic happen with you all."

"Thanks, Trent. Us too. Can't wait," Stanley said. He waved goodbye, and the screen returned to black as the video conference ended.

I looked around the room again and saw anxiety flicker across my colleagues' faces, frustration creeping into their eyes, their features caught in discomfort, confusion that made it look like a question had formed in their minds but they didn't want to be the one to ask.

For all the good they said would come out of this deal, we knew that mergers meant layoffs. And no matter what Michael might have said about keeping everyone employed when I first started, I wasn't sure I or anyone else believed him.

The room was quiet for what felt like a long time before Connor raised his hand and cleared his throat. He didn't have the same look of concern as the rest of us. Even Evan had the good sense to keep his mouth shut, to take this news with a smile until we could share our thoughts confidentially. But Connor, with the breezy way he walked through life, didn't need to worry about consequences or job security or even success. He never needed to worry about a single goddamn thing.

"So what does that mean for us? Do we all still have jobs?" he asked.

Stanley rubbed the bridge of his nose and sighed. He exchanged a look with Michael, who answered the question in his stead. "We're still in the early process of the merger, so we haven't nailed down personnel changes just yet. But for now, let's all focus on the work, focus on making big acquisitions to account for the overhead and other expenditures. Artists you know who will make us a profit."

The whole thing felt practiced, like Michael knew he would have to have answers, to try to make us feel like he would have our backs, and be sincere about it too. But I couldn't trust that he was telling us the truth. I felt certain he was spewing bullshit because he wanted us to carry on, business as usual.

"Well—and I think we're all thinking this—will the Ultimate employees be moving into this office?" Evan asked, emboldened by another white man speaking his mind.

"They will. But not until the new year when their lease is up."

The collective murmur started again as people grumbled to one another about limited office space, open-plan setups, the idea of cohabitating with colleagues that used to be—would still be—competition.

"Okay," Stanley said. He ignored the current of dissatisfaction that swept through the room and continued on. "We will be sending around a memo with further details later in the week. All right. Thanks everyone."

•

"Uh, Billie," Nina said once she'd caught up to me leaving the conference room. We were a few feet from my desk, and she had her arms up. "Couldn't give me a heads-up?"

"There really wasn't much to tell." I turned back toward Michael's office to see if he was paying attention. Though he was on a phone call, I lowered my voice. "I knew Michael was up to something for a few weeks, but I wasn't sure if it was the merger. He's been hush-hush about it lately."

"Yeah. Well, I guess it's not your fault." She touched her hand to her chin. "Shit. This just . . . doesn't seem good. Who knows how this will affect us in the next few months."

"Yeah, I'm worried too," I said. "Do you think there's gonna be layoffs? Or, like, will there be less to work with when signing artists?"

"I don't know, girl. All I know is I'm gonna get to work. If anything around here changes, I wouldn't want to be caught on the bad side of it."

I nodded solemnly, thinking about all that I had left to do, to prove, as Nina walked back to her desk.

After the meeting, I wanted to know more about Ultimate Records and its owner. Was Trent really all about diversity and authenticity like the CEO said? I scoured Google for ten minutes and couldn't find any scandalous or damning information on him. All six of the articles I read reiterated Trent's commitment to supporting artists from all walks of life in as many genres and musical forms as he could. I breathed a sigh of relief. It was a short-lived breath. My mind immediately turned to Samirah next, to what I could lose if this merger forced our division to make cuts or, worse, if our imprint was folded into another, stunting the little bit of ground I'd gained thus far.

I tried to do work, make the most of what had been handed to us. I started to respond to the marketing team about some social media assets for Wren, but I was too distracted to finish. Now that the future here was up in the air, I had to adjust my plans.

I pulled out my phone and shot a text to Quincy to set up a meeting with Samirah as soon as we could.

The hours dragged on glacially following the big meeting, and for a while there was nothing but chatter—people loitering in front of one another's desks, exchanging whispers and holding their coffees close like it would somehow bring them comfort. But after hours of this, we all had exhausted our anger and frustration, and all we were left with was low morale and noiseless unease.

I wanted more time to fester in the unease. I'd wanted to sneak home early to sleep away the anxiety that eclipsed this day. What I hadn't anticipated was Connor needing something from me before the day ended.

Connor had never needed me for anything before. He only ever came to my desk to see if he could speak with Michael. But here he was now, staring at me from the front of my desk, an arrogant smile on his face.

I spit out my normal line, thinking he might still want to talk to Michael.

"Michael's unavailable right now, but I can—"

Connor laughed, walked over to the side of my desk, and placed his hands in the pockets of his slacks. "Billie," he said. His voice was collegial, pleasant.

Warm like we had been friends, buddies, who enjoyed each other's company this whole time.

I was suddenly a combination of suspicious and curious. I stopped myself from cutting my eyes at him and waited to see what he'd say next.

"I actually wanted to talk to you. I need your opinion on something. It won't take long. Maybe fifteen minutes or so. Just want an extra set of ears down in the studio."

The studio was the one place I wasn't allowed to be, and now, with an exec specifically requesting my presence, this was my chance to go. I would finally see where some of my favorite artists had made music. I would finally be able to show someone at Lit that my opinion had value, that I had an ear, that I was worthy of being there.

It was kind of strange that he needed it from me at all since I wasn't his assistant. But for an opportunity to see what the studio was like, how artists laid down tracks and came up with melodies, how they perfected the chorus or inserted a bridge, or how producers mixed songs and interpolated samples to make something new, I was willing to cast aside almost anything, even my lingering suspicion of Connor.

"Okay, sure," I said.

"Great."

He swept his hand out beside him like he was leading the way, and together we walked to the elevator and got on, avoiding chitchat as we descended.

We entered and my eyes widened as I took in the studio. The room reminded me of Quincy's, but it was larger, grander, breathtaking, really. The tan-paneled walls were gilded with gold. A modern chandelier that was all gold metal lines and bare bulbous lamps hung from the ceiling. Large chartreuse sofas were in the seating area. Tall carafes of sparkling and tap water and a few glasses sat atop the counters.

Scanning the rest of the room, I laid eyes on the isolation booth, and in there was a man about as average-looking as the blue-shirt-wearing men who wandered Wall Street during lunchtime. He wore a green cable sweater over a white collared shirt. His jeans were a mid-wash blue, and he wore navy Converse on his feet. Though I knew better than to judge someone based solely on what they wore, I couldn't help but think about how white men could wear and do what they wanted without people giving it so much as a cursory accusatory glance. It was unclear where he'd fit in, but it began to crystallize as Connor signaled him out of the booth to meet me.

"Hey, and who might this baddie be?" the man said.

"Oh hi. I'm Billie. I . . . uh, assist Michael."

"Oh yeah, yeah. I've met him before. Anyway, nice to meet you. I'm Juda, though I'm sure you knew that already," he said.

I did not.

He flashed a smile at me, and his top teeth encased in a grill—diamonds encrusted in gold—glinted in the light.

As I looked at the inside of his mouth, I laughed to myself. He looked like a business-casual version of Jack Harlow, who was already of the overhyped white-boy variety, or Macklemore if his career had survived the tens. And that wasn't a compliment. So I smiled instead and kept the internal screaming inside.

"So," Connor said, clapping his hands. "Why don't we play back the track and then take it from there?"

"Bet," Juda said.

Connor picked up the receiver of the phone that was atop a table in the corner of the room.

The sound engineer moved around levers and pressed buttons until a heavy bass in a classic boom-bap beat filled the room, followed by woodwind instruments I couldn't place. Before I could decide if I liked the beat or not, Juda's voice flooded the room.

The first few bars of the song only consisted of two lines that Juda repeated over and over.

Shake that ass, mami, shake that ass, mami
Make it clap, mami, make it clap, mami

As I sat on the sofa, I had to work hard to keep my face straight. This man, who couldn't decide if he belonged to the hood or the suburbs, was rapping about ass cheeks in a style that had been falling out of favor since 2018.

When the song finished, Connor looked at me expectantly.

"Okay. Thoughts?" he said, standing up.

I paused, thinking of the right thing to say. I knew I couldn't be completely honest. If I were to tell them I thought this whole charade was absolute dogshit, they wouldn't be pleased. If I told them that Juda was likely the kind of guy that'd never wear grills or play his music in front of his parents, his original community, that he was someone who only put on Blackness like a costume, that this music was a mockery, they wouldn't be pleased about that either.

I decided to make my thoughts palatable for him, inoffensive. I needed to keep my reputation at Lit intact, and I hoped Connor wouldn't be able to see through it.

"It was definitely something," I said.

"Okay," Connor said. "And what exactly does that mean? Billie, I asked you here because I wanted to know if this *slaps.* If this is something you would twerk to in the club with your girlfriends. Give me something other than *something* here," he said. He threw up his hands, exasperated by my vague response.

I resolved to be strategic, diplomatic about my response so he couldn't tell I hated every ounce of this exchange.

"Okay. Um. How do I say this. The song isn't the problem," I said.

"Well then, what is the problem?"

"It's . . . This all seems kind of . . . inauthentic, no?"

"Nah, this is me. You either fuck wit' it or you don't fuck wit' it," Juda said.

"Okay. Well, um . . . the beat is good. High-energy, catchy."

Using the opportunity to pull out my phone and get out of this situation, I looked down at it and checked my email. None were urgent, but I flashed my phone to Juda and Connor anyway.

"I'm so sorry, but I have to get back to my desk."

"Okay. Well, uh, thanks for coming down, then," Connor said. He touched his hand to the back of his neck as he and Juda exchanged glances.

I exited the room swiftly and avoided looking back as I walked to the elevator. I didn't want to be reminded that I had been used. Not for my skill. Not because he needed a fresh set of ears. But because I was a Black woman who could validate them.

I should have anticipated it. I should have known that Connor wasn't shaken by the merger news and suddenly needed outside opinions. He was carrying on as though nothing had happened.

I shook my head and cursed my naïveté, cursed myself for believing that it was somehow an honor to be invited to the studio.

When I got back to my desk, Michael was still on the phone in his office.

Desperate to talk to Nina about what had happened with Connor, I walked to her desk to see if she was there, but her cube was empty.

"Yeah, she left around lunch. Think she's out for the rest of the day," Kate said. She typed furiously at her desk as she spoke, her eyes never leaving the computer monitor. I suspected she was feeling the way we all were: fearful, anxious, like life had been upended in a single day. I had never seen her move this quickly before, and yet here she was, toggling between emails and Excel sheets.

"Oh okay. Thanks."

For a moment, I thought I'd ask her how she was feeling about the merger, but before I could decide, my feet had already made the decision for me and carried me back to my cubicle.

Done with his call, Michael swung by my desk and dictated a long list of tasks to me before he left for the day. I wrote all the tasks down as he talked, but I knew there was only so much my brain could endure after the day I'd had. My mind was not in this office with this bullshit.

I pulled out my phone and texted Quincy again to see if he was around. I had to keep up the hustle.

•

Quincy had agreed to meet me at a bar in the Lower East Side. He was already there when I arrived at the bar and took a seat on the sofa across from a pool table. I greeted him and gave him a hug. The surrounding area reminded me of my great-aunt's basement—seventies themed, a fireplace painted pale pink sat across from the sofas, and board games with missing pieces, worn boxes, and tattered instructions littered the tables, the air an odd mixture of lavender and cheap cognac.

Even though it was a Monday night, there was a DJ in the corner of the room, who played Top 40 hits as people cozied up with one another. The space seemed like one for lovers, for people who knew what the other hated and desired, cherished and detested, an unusual place for the pairing of people that Quincy and I made together.

"So I have an update," I started. "And this is confidential, so don't tell anyone."

Quincy nodded, leaned in close.

"Lit and Ultimate Records are merging and—"

"Word?" he said. "Damn, that's crazy. Always something going on in this music shit." He shook his head and took a sip of his drink.

"Yeah. Tell me about it. But listen, I think we can use this to our advantage. If we can try to get Samirah signed prior to that happening, it would give us a good chance of sliding in and making her a priority artist on the roster. I was hoping we could possibly move up our timeline for new music from her."

"I think we can make that happen. When do you need new material?"

"Ultimate will move into the Lit building sometime in January, after the holidays. I'm assuming three-ish, maybe four months to put everything together before everything is official. Can you handle that timeline?"

"I think so. Ima hit Samirah up ASAP. See what she thinks. Knowing how hungry she is, I bet she'll be down," he said.

Despite the moved-up timeline and the surprise news, Quincy was still chill, relaxed, a guy utterly unfazed. He seemed ready for whatever was thrown at him. It made me wonder who Quincy was outside of his role as producer. Whether his life had been easy or hard, whether he had developed this persona so that he'd be able to breeze through life almost the same as Connor, but with actual talent instead of white skin that made mediocrity seem like genius.

I nodded. "Cool, that's good."

"Is there anything else we should do in the meantime, though?"

"Yeah, we need to make sure she keeps performing, keeps building her fan base, keeps engaging with people on social. We also need to get her in some articles. Build some buzz around her name. And we will need to do a photo shoot. A couple changes of outfits. Make them look real professional so we can use it for the cover of the EP we'll put together. We'll bring the pictures and articles about her to the meeting—don't worry, I'm going to work to secure that—both in hard copy and on a tablet. We'll need to have her tracks ready on the tablet as well. I have a good Bluetooth speaker my mother bought me for Christmas one year. We can bring that too, 'cause you never know what could happen with the audio in conference rooms. We get all of that, and all Samirah has to do is shine."

As I listed off the things I would need to get ready for Samirah, I realized I actually sounded professional. Like I knew what I was doing. Like I had some kind of expertise. I was impressed with myself. It made me feel lightheaded but assured, like a balloon bopping in the wind yet tethered to the earth by the unwavering death grip of a child.

I had listened closely to Nina when we had lunch. With the merger on the horizon, I couldn't afford to slack in my assistant work. But more important, I couldn't afford to lose with Quincy and Samirah. I simply had to convince them that I was willing to do whatever it took to get them signed. And I knew in my gut I was good enough to do both.

"Okay. Sounds like a good plan. Ima get on making some fire shit they can't say no to," he said, rubbing his hands together.

"Ayeee. That is exactly what we need. I think Ima head out, though," I said.

I wanted to get home as soon as possible to show Lucas that I was making progress with my way of doing things. I wanted to show him I had done something that could potentially take my career to the next level, that could secure my spot at Lit as things changed with the merger. I also wanted to ask for his help with the photo shoot, because there was no way I'd have the connections or budget to book anyone else in the timeframe I'd laid out to Quincy.

Outside, we hugged goodbye, and I shot Lucas a text that I was on my way home as I walked to the subway.

12

Everyone at the office was working harder than ever to prove their place with the merger news, and I'd been too busy with tasks for Michael and Samirah to come up for air until Labor Day weekend.

Labor Day had always marked the beginning of fall for me. Pumpkin-flavored everything had appeared in stores at the end of August. Oversize sweaters and blazers and turtlenecks were dusted off for quick use. New Yorkers took the Metro-North up to orchards and farms to pretend to enjoy picking apples for social media.

Now, Lucas and I sat across from each other on our living room floor, cross-legged and relaxed. There was a small tray of half-eaten edibles—a pan of brownies I'd laced with a powerful tincture I'd bought the other day at a smoke shop in Harlem—next to us, and Wazy played softly around us.

I grabbed his hand slowly, brought it to my face, and kissed him on the fleshy part of his hand before I threaded my fingers between his and laid our hands in my lap.

He had put his feelings for Lit aside and agreed to do a photo shoot for Samirah.

"Okay. So what's the plan again?" I asked.

"Well, with me dividing my time between Sunsetlandia and my other gigs, I'm thinking we'll do it in a couple weeks?"

"Yeah, that's fine. As long as we get it done and I secure this deal before things are final between Lit and Ultimate, that works."

We were quiet for a while as we cuddled next to each other, as the music switched from Cash Cobain to JID, but then Lucas sighed, and I knew he was about to change the subject to me, to what I was doing at Lit. He hadn't mentioned it the last few weeks.

He hadn't bothered me when I was up at four in the morning answering emails. He hadn't bothered me when I scoured the internet for a backup artist if Samirah went wrong. But the deeper he got into painting and photographing for Sunsetlandia and all the things it stood for—art as an essential part of self-expression—the more he resented this job that he thought wasn't healthy for me.

"Babe. Do you think they'll even go for Samirah? I mean, you've only been there three months and you seen the shit Nina has to go through. I don't want you to get your hopes up for nothing."

I pulled away from him and mulled it over in my head, imagined the taste of failure, bitter and salty, on my tongue. But I knew I couldn't give space for that thought to grow. I shook my head, letting the thought go with it.

"I know. But that's why I'm trying to get Nina to eventually be my mentor. If I could get her to work with me on Samirah, then they'd have more reason to trust me too. They wouldn't be able to deny hard work and talent when they see it. I know what I'm doing, babe."

I could hear him clear his throat, could see the wheels spinning as he thought of how to respond next, but then there was silence. Maybe he could sense that I was not in the mood for one of his self-righteous speeches.

We exchanged small, polite smiles that hid thoughts that would break this cozy mode of loving we were in. Lucas laced his fingers back into mine and squeezed.

"Wait. Before I forget," he said.

"What?"

"Your mom dropped by earlier to give you this." He grabbed it from the coffee table next to him and placed a thick white envelope into my waiting hands. The clear window revealed the sender as Mama's landlord. I turned the envelope around and lifted the flap cautiously. It opened easily, letting me know that Mama had already taken a peek. I unfolded the papers within and read.

I hadn't talked to Mama since the barbecue, just a good-morning text here and there to be sure she was alive. She was upset I'd left, and I was annoyed because she knew that it was this job that helped her pay her bills in the first place. It was hard to stay in consistent contact with her when my fury so often bled into my love for her.

She was a part of the reason I had to work this hard. She was the reason I didn't have a home to fall back on if this whole music thing didn't work out. She was the reason I could not fail. So my love and rage and care for her tangled, a single mass of weight that threatened to bury me if I let it.

I didn't know how to fix what was wrong with her, with this cycle that she was in. But until Marvin was gone, until she was ready to let him go, this would always be my burden. It would be my job to make her feel better. It would be my job to carry her to the top once I finally made it and got us both out of the hood and into homes no one could ever kick us out of. It would be my job to help save her, because there was no one else.

"What happened?" Lucas said. I flashed the papers at Lucas, pointing to the word *eviction* written in bold red type at the top of the page, and hastily walked to our bedroom.

I threw on the first sweater I could find—a ratty gray thing I fished from the heap piled on the clothes chair—pulled it over my sports bra and leggings, and charged down the stairs and then up the stairs in Mama's building to her apartment.

It was eight on a week night, and she was bound to be home, her hair wrapped up, glass of wine in hand, reruns of *Judge Mathis* playing on the flat-screen.

At her front door now, I knocked hard, not caring if the neighbors heard my wild banging. They had already heard so many sounds come from this apartment anyway that I doubt they would even register my knocking as alarming.

"Why'd you come down here knocking on my door like you ain't got no goddamn sense?" The pajama set and matching bonnet she wore were as rouge as my insides felt.

I ducked under her arm that was holding out the door and walked inside, turned to her with my hands on my hips, and aimed my words at her like missiles, heated and precise.

"You gave this to Lucas?" I asked, holding the papers out to her in my hand.

"Yeah. I've been calling you about it all day. This felt like the fastest way to get to you since you can't seem to answer your phone."

"Sorry, Mama. I've been busy. Work is crazy. I have so much to do in the next few months—but I don't want to get into that right now. . . . Why did they send this? What's going on? You said everything was good except the light bill and a few others, not that you were close to eviction."

"Come, have a glass with me," she said. She moved silently through the kitchen as she looked for wine glasses, whipping open cabinets and opening and shutting drawers as she went. She pulled a bottle of vinho verde from the refrigerator and doled out a large pour for each of us.

Together, we curled up on the sofa, holding the wine like it was that therapist ball—the one that grants the person holding it the right to speak—only the wine seemed to be the opposite. The more wine we drank, the less we talked.

Once we had each drained our glass, I knew this would be my chance to talk to her for real. I turned to face her full on and placed my hand atop hers on the sofa.

"What's going on?" I asked softly.

"I lied, okay? Everything isn't good. I didn't want to bother you with it, but I really need help. That money you gave me, baby, it was just the tip of the iceberg. I need a whole lot more than that. Marvin found the stash I had at the house. I had been peeling off some of his cash over the last few weeks to make sure we had enough to catch up on the bills, but he found it. And he promptly spent that shit on booze and strippers. He couldn't wait to fuck us over," she said. She slammed her wine glass onto the table, and it shattered in half, just collapsed into itself like it hadn't known what caused it or why it sat there, sad and broken. I took it to be a sign. I wouldn't let this break her. Not while I was there and willing to do something about it.

"Mama, don't you know? You got you. You are strong. And smart. You've got a good job, and you're funny as hell—"

"Hey," she said, throwing a stern look at me and my swear word. She hated when I swore in her presence.

"Sorry, sorry. But it's true. You're gonna bounce back from this. *We* are gonna bounce back from this."

"Thank you, baby. But how're you gonna be able to help me when you haven't even helped yourself? Have you saved money? Are you somehow rich now and I didn't get the memo?"

"I don't know," I said. "I'll come up with a plan."

"Yeah? Well, you would have to figure it out fast 'cause they're about to put me *and* all my shit out."

"I've been at Lit a few months now. And they match my 401(k). It's not a lot in there, but maybe I could take out a loan and you pay me back later? How much would you need?"

"Well, I'd need at least twenty-five hundred on top of the regular rent. You gonna give all that to me? I can't accept that. I'm supposed to be helping you. Not the other way around."

"I know, Mama. I want to help. Especially if this is what it takes to get Marvin out of the picture."

"Let's not get into that right now."

Here she was, thirty days from eviction, and yet she wasn't ready to condemn him. I wanted to scream, to break her rules about raising my voice in her house, so I could tell her just once that she was being stupid, that she was better than this, that she deserved more.

"Well, when is the time, Ma? You're three seconds from eviction, and all you can do is guilt me into giving you money? You are letting this man walk all over you like it's nothing. Like it don't hurt that he got you out here scrambling every year. Don't you be stressed? Fed up? If he really cared about you, he wouldn't do this. He wouldn't put your lives in jeopardy because he can't control himself. All this just to have a man is not worth it. Your life would be so much easier without him. Don't you want that for yourself?"

"I don't know nothing else, Li," she said. Her voice cracked, and she looked like she was on the verge of tears. She got up to grab the rest of the wine. A new glass poured, she took a sip, and looked up at me, hurt clouding her eyes. "I . . . don't want to be old and alone. I want someone to hold me at night. To love me the way he does when things are good. It's hard to stop wanting that when you're raised to want it. Love ain't a faucet. I can't turn it off whenever I want. We've been together a long time. And I need time to deal with that. That's all I'm asking. I will talk to him. But for now, let me be."

We sat quietly for a spell, watching the television as the plaintiff argued her case: She was suing her husband's mistress for damages after a fight broke out during the infidelity. Before I understood that this show was a kind of fiction, I loved watching it with Mama whenever I had stayed home sick from school, captivated by the way Judge Mathis doled out justice with humor.

I laughed as Mathis called one of the women a crackhead, but my head snapped in the direction of the front door when the sound of the key turning the lock announced Marvin's arrival.

It was late now, after ten, and as soon as he took a few steps into the place, I knew that he was drunk. Somehow the sight of his stumbling reignited the rage I'd carried into this apartment after seeing the eviction notice.

"Hey, Marvin," I said from the sofa.

Mama looked over to me, pleading with her eyes for me to shut up.

Marvin looked up with surprise in his bloodshot eyes. "Oh, hey, Billie."

"Mama told me about the eviction," I said.

"Yeah? Well, it's not really your business."

I got up and moved closer to him as he took off his Timbs by the door.

"I think it is. Can't you see how what you're doing is hurting y'all? How y'all even supposed to make it to retirement like this? How am I supposed to live my life when I'm always looking backward, worried about how y'all gon' make it?"

"You ain't lived the years I lived. Ain't seen the shit I seen as a Black man in this world. You ain't seen what I witnessed growing up in these streets. What I go through on the road. It's hard out here. Sometimes that shit gets to me. There's more behind it than you'll ever know," he said quietly, looking toward Mama for help. "But I hear you."

"I don't know if you are hearing *me*," I said. "It's been hard for me too."

"Billie, I think it's about time for you to head home. It's getting late," Mama said, her hand on her hip as she now stood in the kitchen.

I looked between them, hoping that there would be more words, but I had apparently said enough for all of us.

I nodded incredulously, then brushed past Marvin on my way out. I took the stairs to my apartment and relished the feel of Lucas's hug as he opened the door.

13

Since the merger was announced, things in the office had been dialed up to eleven. Michael's days were a never-ending stream of meetings, coffees, and lunches. Artists and managers called him daily to make sure they weren't being dropped from the label. My colleagues at Lit emailed me incessantly, hoping to snag a ten-minute meeting with Michael to secure their futures at the company, to ensure that they too weren't being dropped.

The news had rattled everyone—from assistants to upper management—and prompted them into action, into being even more present and productive. Though Michael had promised no personnel adjustments for now, we couldn't ignore the nagging feeling that everything was about to change. Before the news, people would stroll into the office hours after the official nine o'clock start time, but now people filtered in early. The smell of freshly brewed coffee permeated the halls as pot after pot was made.

As soon as I walked into the room, I was cornered by the A&R reps who hoped that I'd have some new info for them. But there was nothing to share, nothing that I could say to instill confidence in them.

As for Nina, I had seen less of her in the last few weeks. I assumed she was out there trying to get a big artist like Michael had asked. The next time I caught her at her desk, I would ask her out again, get some insight on how to handle Samirah. I'd talk to her about it all: Connor, Juda, Quincy, Samirah. And hopefully she'd give me advice on what to do next.

•

After work, I emerged from the West Fourth Street station and pulled out my phone to double-check the address where I was supposed to meet Alicia. The weather was perfect—a slight breeze, bright sunlight skimming my skin, the air as clear and fresh as it could get in this city—and people in the West Village around me knew to take advantage of it. People wore their best fits to sit sidewalk-side at trendy cafés and sip dirty martinis. The men who played basketball in the park across from the IFC Center were deep into a game, their shirts sweat-stained, their calves bulging as they performed different jump shots. People were lined up outside the gate that surrounded the court to watch them. As I walked to the venue, I watched groups of folks hanging out on corners and holding ice cups or ice cream cones and laughing loudly, mouths spread open in delight. I smiled, warmed by the city after the cold of the office. I still loved this energy that couldn't be duplicated elsewhere.

When I got to the entrance of the venue, the usually empty storefront had been transformed to accommodate the launch of a new makeup line co-owned by an artist one of Alicia's friends was the dance captain for over the summer.

Outside the venue, people waited for their chance to walk the red carpet that ran the length of the ground in front of the store. A couple of photographers snapped photos of people as they posed in front of a backdrop with the makeup line's name and their numerous sponsors plastered onto it.

I stood off to the side of the entrance to wait for Alicia. It took her ten minutes to arrive before I saw her speeding toward me, her hair swooped into a slick, long, straight low pony, dressed in a cream top and silky champagne-colored trousers.

We gave each other one-armed hugs. "Sorry I'm late, girl. I was actually already inside before, helping bring products in. Then I went to get something to eat. It's been a day."

"It's cool. I haven't been here long. I'm happy to be out of the office. The energy in there is not it."

"Oh, it's a lot more than not it," Alicia said conspiratorially.

I looked at her quizzically.

"Let's go inside. You gon' need a drink for this," she said.

I shook my head and followed behind her as she walked up to the security by the red carpet and flashed a laminated tag affixed to the metal tab on a red lanyard.

We stopped to pose for photos before going inside, and I tried my best to smile like Tyra taught me all those years ago on *America's Next Top Model.*

A few clicks of a camera later and we were in the event space. A waiter walked by with trays of pink cocktails made with gin and garnished with lychee. Alicia snatched two glasses off the tray and passed one to me.

Once we had our drinks, we parked ourselves at an open cocktail table. I swept my eyes around the room and took in the different stations in the store, each area themed according to which element it enhanced—lip bar, eyebrow island, shadow sandcastles, highlighter heaven.

Another look around proved the sneaking suspicion I'd had when we first walked in: We were the only Black girls at this party. The attendees all seemed to look the same—tall, fashionable gazelles draped in slip dresses, with perfectly tousled hair that swayed against their milky shoulders. Their skin, clear and smooth, mocked mine, which was currently mottled with blackheads as it always was the week after my period. This party, it seemed, was for a particular kind of person, and Black girls weren't the target demo.

"Where's your dancer friend?" I asked.

"Probably in the back somewhere. She got roped into helping them put together the gift bags. But yo, let me tell you what she told me about Lit."

"Ooh. I can't wait to hear this."

"Yeah, so. My friend was on Valencia Grace's tour, right? Her team had hired mad Black dancers and other people of color, 'cause you know they're trying the inclusive angle right now. Anyway, one night the dancers were all talking, and the merger came up. Char knew about it beforehand because she used to fuck with an artist who was almost signed to Lit. He ended up turning down the deal because Lit had offered him one of the shittiest recording contracts of all time. I'm talking low rates on publishing rights, trying to take majority shares of songwriting credits, working in the right to license merchandise without the artist's approval. Shit was crazy. What's even crazier, though, is that the artist wasn't the first or the last to receive a contract like that. Apparently, Lit been doing it, mostly to other Black and brown artists, for years. They been able to keep it quiet for so long because they've threatened anybody who wants to talk publicly about it."

"Oh my god. That's crazy. I knew they were on some fuck shit, considering what I've seen so far, but I didn't know they were on that type of timing. I been so hopeful that there were enough good people out there that could outweigh the bad, but this is crazy. Shit, shit, shit."

"Yeah, girl. The tea is that's why they're bringing Ultimate in. To make their reputation look better in case any of this comes to light."

I started to put two and two together in my head. I thought about the flash drive, the weird files. The secret meetings between Michael and the CEO. The litany of untalented artists that Michael and Connor and Evan signed to hit a trend that never lasted more than a season. I wondered how I could continue to work at this place knowing what dirt went down. Maybe Lucas was right all along. Maybe this path I was on would only make things worse for the artists I wanted to lift up.

"Damn. This is low-key heartbreaking. I get into this industry only to find out I'm basically working for the devil," I said, shaking my head, my heart beating fast in time with the house music playing in the background. I chugged the rest of my cocktail and looked around for a waiter, desperately wanting another drink to wash away the metallic flavor that started building up in the back of my throat.

"What do you think I should do, Leesh? Should I quit? I still got Mama's eviction to worry about. Not to mention rent. But this is kind of making me sick."

"I don't know, girl. It ain't like these other giant corporations aren't also doing bad things behind the scenes. These days, we gotta just go with the lesser evil. What I can tell you is that this would make one hell of an exposé."

"Word. It dead would." I looked across the table at Alicia, who looked like she was in deep thought, like she was thinking she could be the writer of such an exposé.

"Please tell me you're not thinking of writing about it."

"Well, why not?" she asked. "Getting an article like that placed could land me a full-time job. Put me on the map. And it would help artists not get fucked over like they are at Lit."

"Yeah, but. Think about how that could fuck over everyone there who is trying to do some good. Nina. Me."

"What if there's a way we could absolve everyone else except the main ones causing the problems? That way Ultimate comes into Lit and makes things better, and the people responsible for the bad deals get fired. Would be a win-win for everyone."

The flash drive came to mind again. Maybe I could sneak some of the files to her. But was I really that willing to throw away the career I worked so hard for so soon? I wasn't sure.

"I don't know. It sounds risky."

"Maybe it is. I'm only thinking about it for now. Not gonna do anything. But think about it, sis. You on the inside. This could be your chance to be a part of the change you always wanted."

"Yeah, I'll think about it. Anyway. What else is going on with you?"

I needed to change the subject. I didn't want to think about it anymore. I had enough guilt to deal with. I resolved only to drink and ignore everything else that had been going wrong lately.

"Eh. It's been better. Right now, I'm temping at *Kulture Magazine*. The job is fine. But I'm in the office three times a week, and my coworkers are insufferable. They're always going on about Zero Bond or their random vacations. This one girl kept talking about the time she booked a trip to the Maldives because she'd put in too much overtime that week. She said that shit so casual too. Like it's normal for people to just be picking up and traveling to whole-ass countries on a whim."

"Yeah, it's crazy how different people who work at the same company live," I said. My mind drifted to the execs at Lit who had parents and spouses who bankrolled their passions. But not all of us had that luxury. And I felt it so acutely here, among the fancy curated drinks and beauty products so far out of my price range that I laughed when I checked the tag on a tube of matte red lipstick in passing.

"So what else is going on your way? You said your mom is getting evicted? What she gonna do?"

"Yeah, she has two weeks to pay all the back rent or they're gonna kick her out. She says she doesn't want my help, but I can't let Mama be homeless. I was thinking of picking up tutoring, taking a loan from my 401(k) now that there's some money in there."

"But don't you gotta pay that money back every month? That's not gonna eat at your check?"

"Yeah, but what other choice do I have?"

"Billie," Alicia said softly, turning to look me in the eyes. She put her drink on the table and touched her hand to my shoulder, leaned in close so I could hear her over the cacophony of noise. "I know you want to help. You been helping her for a long time now. And, like, I get it. You know what it's been like for me since my mama passed. Same type of shit. But this isn't your responsibility. You know that, right? Don't be so hard on yourself. You're already doing a lot as it is."

"I know it's not my responsibility," I said, my voice cracking as I slammed a fist on the table. A couple of people from the table a few feet away turned their heads toward us. I lowered my voice, but I couldn't keep a quiver from seeping in. "But if not me, then who, Leesh? There's always this pressure or, like, expectation, for me to hold everyone up, hold everything in while I'm doing it too. And it's like, who am I if I'm not saving people?" Tears started to form in my eyes. "Who am I when I'm not killing myself to help? It's one thing after fucking another. Lit. Money. Mama. It's too much sometimes. . . . I don't know if I can keep going like this. Maybe Lucas was right. I'm starting to wonder if any of this is even worth it."

I picked up my glass and threw back a big gulp, then dabbed the tears that streamed down my face with a napkin.

Alicia, being the best friend she was to me, knew that this moment didn't need words. Didn't need solutions either. She pulled me into a hug instead, and we clutched each other as hyper pop music bumped around us.

I sniffed and blew my nose in the napkin. I requested a loan from my servicer right there at the party and left Mama a voice note, one finger plugging my ear so I could hear myself above the music. I said, "Mama, I'll have the loan ready in a few days. I hope this will give you what you need to get on track."

I turned to Alicia. "Fuck it. I'm giving her the rent money. But I'm telling you now so that I don't renege on it later: This will be the last time. I need to stay focused on work. I don't want to be worried about my opportunities to grow there if shit starts going left. And in order for me to do that, I gotta secure an artist they think has potential, or at least that's what I think will get me there the fastest. Samirah could be that artist for me. But she's gotten little to no press so far. I think she was featured on *Okayplayer* some months ago after her show at Irving. Do you think you're cool enough with the editorial director for her to let you pitch Samirah for a roundup?"

"I'm not sure. I'm only there because someone is on maternity leave. But I do get to go to the editorial meetings. I'll see what I can do."

"Thanks, girl," I said, giving her another hug.

"Let me know where and when she's going to be performing next, and I'll try my best to get the details to the editorial director."

I didn't want to think more about Mama or Lit or Samirah. I wanted this moment for us. Me and Alicia in an exhale. Here, among the islands of beauty and endless champagne. It was time to disconnect from all the things expected, required, of us.

"Okay, cool. Will do. Now, let's stop talking and drink," I said.

"Yeah, speaking of that." She tapped on the shoulder of a waiter that was nearby.

"Yes, hi, um"—she flashed him a toothy smile and looked down at the name tag on his crisp white shirt—"Patrick." She held up the media pass her dance-captain friend had gotten her. "Would you be able to send a full tray of cocktails to this table? There are a few more people from my team coming, and I'd like them to be well hydrated," Alicia said, oozing charm and sex appeal that was somehow still professional.

"No problem, ma'am," Patrick said.

Alicia thanked him, and off he went to retrieve the drinks.

I lifted my eyebrows toward her, and Alicia shrugged.

"What? It's free! One, the gin company is sponsoring this event, and two, these motherfuckers are rich, do you hear me? They won't miss it at all."

We both threw our heads back in laughter, and it was swallowed by the swell of hyper pop music that surrounded us as we indulged in a second cocktail that we picked up from the tray as Patrick dropped it off.

"Let's enjoy this party and forget about everything else—I think Valencia Grace might perform later, and they're giving out gift bags at the end of the event, so take it all in," she said.

And take it in we did until we each made our way home to our respective corners of the Bronx.

14

The vibration of my phone buzzing beneath me stirred me out of sleep. The lack of sun through the shades told me it had to be really late or really early. I fished for the phone in the bed. The time read four-thirty, a full hour before my usual alarm. I was annoyed and wondered if someone I knew had died or gotten into an accident or something for me to be getting calls this early. I looked again, and the screen said, "Michael." There were four texts and two missed calls.

I cleared the raspiness from my throat and answered when the phone rang a third time. "Hello?"

"Billie, I need you to pick up something from Dr. Mads. He's going to meet you in front of our office building in forty-five minutes. I'll be waiting for you upstairs. Also, I have Scooter with me. I'll need you to take him to Pups and Stuff as soon as you get in. Don't be late," he said. Then he hung up. I let out a deep breath.

I didn't want to leave my warm bed, let alone take his big-ass greyhound to doggie daycare, so I allowed myself a couple of minutes of staring into space before I got up. I took a seven-minute shower, scooped my hair into a puff, and slipped into all black—a turtleneck, jeans, and square-toed booties—like a worker at a Victoria's Secret. I wouldn't make it to the office in time without an Uber, but I didn't have the sixty-three dollars in my bank account to get me all the way there. I rode the train to 149th Street and took a car the rest of the way.

When I got out of the car, it was still dark. In front of the building, I could make out a well-dressed man, also in all black, holding a smallish brown paper bag. Michael must've given him a description of me, because as soon as we locked eyes, he started waving me over with his pale hands.

"Hey, you're picking up for Michael?"

"Yeah, Dr. Mads, right?"

"Yeah, yeah," he said, fidgeting with the brown bag. "Here. Tell Michael to send the rest of the money when he gets this." Dr. Mads darted his eyes around, side to side and up and down the block. "I gotta go." He placed the bag, the bottom of which was coated in a white film, in my hands. He was gone before I could say thank you.

When I got upstairs, I was expecting Michael and his giant, panting dog to be the first things I saw, but it looked like no one was in. The motion-sensor ceiling lights flickered on as I walked to my desk. From there, I could see Michael and Connor in Michael's office. The door was cracked open, and Michael pointed a stiff finger at Connor as he leaned into him. Scooter sat on the floor beside Michael like a good boy.

I didn't want to surprise them in the middle of the tense situation they had going on, so I walked loudly, hoping they would hear me approaching. I heard some of their conversation as it floated through the semi-open door.

"We can't have artists talking to anyone about our MHCP deals. Do you understand what could happen if this gets out?" Michael slammed his hand down on the table. "I need you to fucking handle this."

Connor nodded like a bobblehead, looking shaken for the first time since I'd worked here. "I'll take care of it," he said in a small voice.

They hadn't heard me, so I cleared my throat and knocked on the door softly to alert them of my presence. "Um, sorry, Michael," I said.

"What?" Michael sneered. When he recognized that it was me, he called Scooter's name, and the dog stood to attention. At the same time, Michael held his hand out for the package. I grabbed the dog's leash and placed the brown bag in his hands.

"Go. Now," he said.

When I looked back as I pulled the dog along to the elevator, I saw Michael empty white powder onto a folder on his desk, hold down one nostril, and snort the substance through the other. I hurried out of the building into the dewy September air.

After a twenty-minute walk to the doggie daycare on Fifty-Third and Second Avenue, during which Scooter dragged my short self along while he peed on every tree he saw, I headed back to Lit.

When I walked in, Michael called me into his office. "Don't ever mention anything about this morning to anyone," he said without looking up from the contracts he was signing.

"Done," I said. He looked up at me now, unamused, then dictated tasks for me to handle for the rest of the day, like nothing had ever happened.

•

"Okay," Michael said once we had settled into our seats for the afternoon staff meeting. He sat at the head of the table, dressed in a light-gray suit as he leaned back in his swivel chair.

"Good afternoon, everyone. Connor, why don't you start."

Over the last few months, the way Connor carried himself in the office had started to irritate me. I hated the way he walked around, like he owned everything and everyone in it. I hated the way his looks worked magic on the women of the office, making him seem charming even when he was handing out extra work to the assistants that he didn't want to do himself or when he took credit for something he didn't execute. I especially hated how clear it was that he had bad taste and no real ear, yet would still get support for his artists because he made them seem like musical geniuses. I knew that they were actually contrived, unoriginal, and uninspiring acts that hopped on trends that passed too quickly.

But Michael didn't care about any of that. Connor was golden. A young white man with the right kind of pedigree, the right amount of money, properties where he could throw parties and invite all the execs for exclusive afterwork hangs, the right legacy from his family. His parents' names were chiseled into the walls of the Ivy League college halls they donated to. So he was able to sign artists who didn't care about artistry, whose music was copies of copies. He signed artists regularly but didn't care to cultivate them or push them to be their best or grow their careers. All that mattered was that he had signed someone with buzz, someone that everyone else wanted, all that mattered was that he had won. Those artists being a hit was only a bonus. A bonus for which he was handsomely rewarded. He was, despite his shortcomings, the kind of person that always came out on top.

He sat in a chair near Michael and nodded at his assistant to start his presentation. He stood up and motioned toward the screen.

"This," he said, "is Yung Curren$y, and he's the next big thing in rap."

On the screen was a video of a dark-skinned young Black man with pink dreadlocks surrounded by surlier Black and brown men who stood together on the stoop of a brownstone. As the video played, it became clear that it was Brooklyn, perhaps Brownsville or East New York—neighborhoods that had yet to be gentrified.

The lyrics to the song and the video were in perfect sync—when Yung Curren$y talked about guns, the screen showed the men holding guns, mimicking shooting. When he talked about getting hoes, some of the motley crew gathered onscreen and got sturdy while others threw money at the twerking women around them.

The song sounded good enough at first. It had the kind of deep bass that immediately garners attention, the jolting ad-libs that build excitement, but something about the track and video was unnerving. I wasn't sure why, but it seemed off, Blueface-esque in a way, like somebody playacting at being a rapper. It was missing bars and lyricism. It was missing the hard-earned grit. It was missing that New York energy and spirit.

I decided, as the song played, that I didn't like this video. I didn't like this artist. I especially didn't like the way Connor was elbowing enthusiastically along with the music. A sneer almost snuck up on my face as I watched this bullshit happen, but I caught it before it could spread across my lips. Instead, I looked toward Nina, hoping to catch her in a sideways glance, but Connor stopped his dancing and started his spiel before I could lock eyes with her.

"As you can see from the video, Yung Curren$y is speaking to the perfect market: Gen Z. They're social media influencers, they're young and desperate to show how accepting and tolerant they are," he said.

This was another Connerism, as I liked to call them. He had this tendency to make gross, sweeping generalizations about entire groups of people as though they were nothing but data points and numbers on a chart that got him closer to his six-figure bonus. It always left a bad taste in my mouth, like leftovers that passed the smell test but went rotten when you took a bite. Didn't Connor care how Yung Curren$y could affect rap? How he and his artist were treating it like it wasn't a game worth being good at, like it was no big thing to make a mockery of the genre. After months at Lit, I was hoping to see a few worthy artists get signed so I could say I was in the room when it happened, but so far it had only been mid artists with weak positioning and generic music.

". . . but also *not* exempt from liking party music about drugs and sex and reckless culture. So I gave this guy a sort of 'hood treatment' in the same way we've done for other artists," Connor continued.

"Now, Yung Curren$y is actually from some suburb in Pennsylvania—but that's the appeal on our side, right? He's clean-cut and articulate, but with the 'hood treatment' he'll have the right look. Plus his cousin lives in Brooklyn. We borrowed a bunch of his cousin's guys and shot this video. I really think it's going to be a hit. He already has hundreds of thousands of followers and active listeners across platforms. And all the right people are into his work—college kids, frat boys, sorority chicks across the country with Daddy's cash to spend on merch, festivals, concerts, you name it." He paused for dramatic effect. "So," Connor said as he slammed his hand down on the table. "Thoughts?"

It was clear as day Yung Curren$y wasn't from the hood. Anyone who was Black would be able to tell by looking at him. There was an innocence, a look of suburban content to him that didn't mesh well with the lies he was purporting about his lifestyle. But in music, at Lit apparently, it didn't seem like that was important. Black male artists were all the same here. Formulated to lack substance and dedication to craft. Meant only for white consumption.

I glanced around the room to gauge the other A&R reps' reactions, to see if anyone objected to this parade of Black degradation, but people were decidedly into it. Jackie and Charlotte were alternately whispering to each other and watching the screen as they stood against the wall. Evan smirked while nodding his head and threw a thumbs-up Connor's way. Kate nodded to the beat and looked out at the city through the window. Michael was also watching intently. He didn't dance or nod, but I'd learned to tell when he liked something. He'd squint his right eye like he was trying to figure out the least amount of money he could offer to artists to make them want to sign with us.

Me? I was furious because surely no one could be good with this, surely someone else here was worried that he was ostensibly pitching this Black man rapping about disrespecting Black women and murdering people to exclusively white listeners, but everyone just smiled and nodded. I looked to Nina, the only brown face in the room, and instead of connecting with her, I found her blank expression, devoid of a smirk, smile, or frown to help me understand the thoughts that ran through her head.

"Good work, Connor. Yung Curren$y seems like what we need for the roster," Michael said. "Why don't you make him an offer and leave it on the table for twenty-four hours? We'll talk offline then."

"Sounds good," Connor said. He smiled, pushed himself back in his chair, and opened his legs wider. He didn't say anything more, but I knew from his change in posture that he was proud of what he had done. I pressed the tips of my fingers against my throbbing temples.

•

"Hey, you got a sec?" I said, standing over Nina's cubicle after the meeting. I had to let some of those feelings, dark and disconcerting, out of my system.

She pulled her earbuds out and nodded. "What's up?"

"I . . . uh, was in the meeting, and um, did you see and hear what I saw and heard?"

Nina inched in close to me, touched her hand to my arm, pitched her voice low.

"Of course I did. Connor's gonna be Connor. I mean, why even get upset at this point, you know? The label supports it. Supports him," Nina said.

Nina said she wasn't upset, but she'd rolled her eyes like this was still a soft point, a bruise that seemed healed but vibrated with pain when you accidentally pressed against it. I knew there was frustration buried beneath the facade. There was no way she wasn't frustrated about how she seemed to bust her ass for this job and Connor did half as much and consistently got his way.

I wanted to hear more about her frustration. I figured it'd make me feel better about my own. Plus, it would let me know what I'd be up against when it was finally my turn. "But why do they support that, though? I've been looking at, like, all the A&R reps' rosters for research, and his artists don't even stream or sell well. They're hot for, like, three seconds, and then they're gone. How can that even be considered successful?" I asked.

"Because that's what this label, this industry, does. Or least how it functions these days. Us A&R reps are meant to follow the numbers, the trends, and play it safe, especially since so many artists are putting their own stuff out online. So we find someone moldable to make music that will appeal to most people. Anything too out of the box, anything not easily categorized, is a risk the label isn't necessarily willing to take."

"So then, how do you push back? Sign artists that are actually about something?"

"When there's someone you really want that you know is good and marketable, fight for it. But also know when to let things go. Some battles aren't meant to be won. At least not until there's more of us at the top to change things around here," she said.

For a minute, I was speechless, deflated, like a soufflé that never reached its potential. Or defeated like my hope whenever Funk Flex dropped too many bombs on a song I wanted to hear but knew he wasn't going to let play full through. I hadn't expected her directness, but I shouldn't have been surprised. That's the thing about New York women: We always know how to get straight to the point. I wished she had commiserated with me, though, that we could have had a moment to stew in our anger together. But she had been here too long. She had experienced too much to let these little instances rile her. She had come to expect it. She had come to ignore it because it would only distract her, it would only use up the energy she needed to fight for the artists she did believe in.

I had to remember that I was on the opposite end of the spectrum—I was only just getting started.

Nina nodded and smiled softly. The tough-love part was over, and now she felt bad that it was my turn to learn things the hard way.

"Look, I know things seem a little bleak now. But if you keep your head down and focus on your goals, you'll get there. You know what, why don't we grab drinks tonight? I'm gonna be booked up for the next three weeks after that. Maybe I can share some of my happier stories? Might give you something to look forward to," she said.

At the prospect of gaining wisdom from Nina outside of the office, I smiled.

"That would be great," I said. And I meant it.

•

"Hey," I said, bounding over to reception. Nina had mentioned taking me somewhere special, exclusive, and I felt giddy at the thought of going somewhere far fancier than anywhere I'd ever been or I could afford on my own. "Got caught up trying to finish something. You ready?" I said. But Nina hadn't heard me.

She was too busy laughing with Erykah to notice I'd even stepped into the space. For a moment, jealousy pierced through me. But then I remembered: I was still the new girl. Yet I couldn't shake the irritation I felt when I saw Erykah laughing. She had never warmed to me, and I couldn't understand why.

We had all been the *only* at white institutions, at work before, and that was a lonely existence. It was an existence that required a splintering of self. But with one another, with other Black people, we could be any amount of Black we wanted. We could be hood. We could be angry. We could be depressed. We could be free. Didn't Erykah want that with me too?

"Hi, Erykah," I said cheerily. I hoped that would ease me into the conversation. But she gave me a firm half smile and turned back to Nina.

I took a seat at the chairs near the door and pulled out my earbuds to scroll on my phone, but as soon as I placed them in my ears, I heard Nina edging out of the conversation.

She walked over to me, still laughing, and motioned for us to get on the elevator.

As the elevator pinged on its descent to the lobby, I had to ask. It had been at the tip of my tongue so long I feared I'd swallow my words along with my courage.

"So I get the feeling that Erykah . . . maybe doesn't like me?"

Nina let out a long, luxurious laugh. "You noticed that, huh?"

"Kind of hard to miss."

"Well, why don't you ask her to lunch so you can find out?" Nina said. She winked as we walked up to the open door of an art gallery.

Placed in the center of a large horizontal space with walls painted stark white were four avant-garde sculptures directly next to one another. Each tall, metallic structure looked like a collection of smooth-textured metal pipes tangling with one another as they reached for the saturated faux sunlight above. It was a metaphor for New York City and all the ways the poor were battling the rich for control, for comfort, for space at the top, where everything was open and limitless.

In front of a piece of abstract art that was all hard-edged shapes stood a tall man in a black suit.

"Watch this," Nina said.

She walked up to the bouncer and demurely whispered the word *illustrious* into his ear. From behind the bouncer, a door had appeared, open and waiting. I couldn't yet see what lay beyond the door, but I smelled the familiar scents of gin and sweat. As we walked into the spot, I realized that we were in a speakeasy.

The candles on the tables scattered throughout set the small space aglow. A porcelain claw-foot bathtub sat in the middle of the room, and a jazz band played soft music at the front of the bar.

A hostess with a short pixie cut and well-muscled tattooed arms showed us to a booth, its surface covered in sumptuous burgundy velvet.

"This place is . . . wow," I said.

Nina and I slid into the booth, and the hostess placed thin menus in our hands.

"Right? I found it one day when I was scouting locations for one of my artists' launch parties," Nina said. "So what you want to drink? It's on me. Well, Lit. I call it corporate reparations." She smirked and flashed the company card she pulled from her wallet.

The menu was filled with exotic cocktails that had sophisticated ingredients like honeydew melon, star anise, and rosemary, and as someone who drank the cheapest spirit on any menu, I felt both entranced and out of place.

I ordered a nineteen-dollar cocktail infused with vermouth, cucumber, lime, and raw sugar—their version of a caipirinha. Nina ordered a drink called the champagne mami, a colorful concoction that swirled pink and orange whenever Nina moved her straw.

After each of us had taken a few sips, the caipirinha made my tongue loose. "Okay. So tell me about some happier times at Lit," I said.

"For me, the good days are when I have a chance to work with *my* artists. I get to direct them in the studio. I get to help them select the best tracks to make a fresh and cohesive album. I get to be their liaison, helping them get what they deserve from Lit. Good days are when I get to be fully immersed in music, by all the things I help create."

The good days sounded worth it. The good days were all I was ever hoping to do. I wanted to know more. I envisioned what it would be like to be in the studio again with Samirah, to help with her sound, to help her hone the talent I already knew she had. I wondered how it felt for Nina that first time in the Lit studio, whether it was as magical and fulfilling as I imagined it to be.

"Who was your first artist? You worked for Michael for a while, and then?"

"D. Salaz. I scoped him out at a bar in Spanish Harlem. Talked to him after his set, and I was so fucking nervous I was shaking. But he didn't know that. To him I must've seemed confident as hell. And it worked because he hit me up a couple days later," she said. Blood rushed to her cheeks, her cocktail and nostalgia painting them with rouge as she smiled.

It was nice to see her this way—her smile real and infectious. It was nice to see that she sometimes got precisely what she wanted.

"How did you convince him to sign with you?" I asked.

"To be honest, I was just honest with him. I told him that I loved what he was doing. How important it is to me to get more Black and brown people signed at Lit and in the industry overall. How he could fit into that. And he was into it. I made sure to show him that I had a creative vision for him and that I really cared about making him successful and impactful. I had a business plan.

It's a matter of, like, staying authentic to the music and the artist, and executing that in your own way and then getting the execs to see it that way too," she said.

"Oh okay. Yeah. That makes a lot of sense." Vision. Plan. Authenticity. I etched those words down in my head so I'd know what to do with Samirah, so I'd know how to convince her that she needed to sign with me because I was committed to helping her perfect her craft, to making her a success.

"So yeah, before I brought him to Lit officially, I helped him with his sound. D. Salaz had been all over the place before then. All of it was good, but none of it distinct. He was Latin pop, he was reggaeton, he was Latin trap, he was bachata. We had to be strategic about how we wanted to pitch him, because, of course, this industry loves to put people in boxes. You can only be one thing, can only do one thing."

She looked at me here, and she was all hard lines and cold eyes. Another nerve had been touched, and her anger had flared like a house cat—her teeth bared, lethal, as she readied her words to read the industry for all the ways it forced her to be docile.

"I mean, think about it, our division at Lit, the artists we are allowed to sign. There's no room for artists who exist in the in-between, you know. And I don't want D. Salaz to get stuck, you know? It's easy for an artist to get trapped into a sound. The label don't care about real representation, so it's my job to. Because who else will?"

The frustration in Nina's voice was crystal. This job was a battle, and with every win there were casualties along the way.

I said nothing. We let the quiet fill the space between us. Both of us thinking silent thoughts.

"Well, I definitely remember hearing that first D. Salaz joint in college," I said. "It came on at one of the dorm parties at my school, and it was wild. It dropped earlier that week, I think, and all of us went crazy for it. It must've been amazing to see him have that effect on people," I said.

"Yeah. That's what makes this all worth it, you know? I don't think I'd ever be able to do anything else."

"That's what I want to do too. I'm glad you're here," I said. Hearing Nina talk made everything seem possible.

"Is that what you want, Billie? To be like me?" she asked. There was a smile there, a sly one that dared me to answer her question.

"I mean, yeah. I've done my research. There ain't that many of us at the top. There's Simone Smith at Atlantic. Diana 'Winn' Barnes at Interscope. Mya James at RCA. And maybe three handfuls of others. But considering all the men, especially all the white men out here getting successful off things they didn't even have to fight for, and you're still here doing your thing? It's inspirational. If I could do a fraction of what you do, I'd be grateful."

She smiled big, and her teeth shone through the candlelight. The staccato jazz music that was low before swelled around us now, disjointed, but trying to find its groove, same as us.

"I like you," she finally said. "And I think you might have what it takes to be here. But keep being a good assistant to Michael."

"I can do that," I said. "But if there's an artist I think might be for good for Lit, would you take it into consideration for your own list? And maybe I could, like, shadow you on the project?"

Nina narrowed her eyes at me, carefully assessed what I suggested. She didn't look taken aback, impressed, or even surprised. It was like she was waiting for the right time to let her emotions show, a permanent poker face in play, but then she laughed, and it immediately got lost in a swirl of saxophone sounds.

"Why don't we say it's tentative for now. Gotta see what that ear sounds like," she said.

Nina seemed loose now, different, like she was willing to reveal more secrets about the business. But I didn't want to push my luck. I had gotten so much from her already.

She looked down at her phone and sighed. "Okay, I gotta get home. Gotta meet Alana Negrita in the studio in the morning."

After we closed out our check and drained the rest of our cocktails, Nina called a rideshare on the company card to each of our apartments, and I thanked her again for everything, for taking me under her wing, for connecting with me and calming me down, for letting me know this was a place I could belong, even when it didn't feel like it, and for the free drinks that helped wash away the bullshit of earlier today.

"Anytime, potential mentee," she said, leaning into the car window as I adjusted myself in the back of my Uber. "Looks like that's me," she said, motioning to the street behind me.

"See you tomorrow," I said. And then she was gone.

I plugged my earbuds in as we pulled off, pressed play on an FKA Twigs song that featured a clashing and discordant but somehow pleasing beat—sort of like how it was working at Lit, with its faulty ideologies and rare slices of beautiful art—and texted Lucas that I was on my way home.

15

After taking the 4 Train down, Lucas and I were on the 2 Train up to the first location we had mapped out for Samirah. It was near Morrison Soundview but also close to Southern Boulevard. I had suggested we take pictures near Samirah's neighborhood to best capture her, and Lucas obliged. He also wanted to get at least one shot of her standing in front of the Bronx sign spray-painted near the train station that white people loved to pose with whenever they dared to venture Uptown.

"So what should I expect from her? She gonna be hard to work with?" Lucas asked.

"Nah, she's chill. It'll be good. Don't worry," I said.

I thought back to that meeting at Quincy's. How Samirah had smartly described her music, why it was important to her, how it fed her soul, and how she wished it did the same for her listeners. Lucas would like her.

I smiled at the thought of my two worlds colliding, becoming entangled in the best ways.

Lucas nodded and reached for my hand. I threaded mine through his and laid my head on his shoulder until we got off the train and made our way to the location.

"Yo, what's good?" Quincy said, hanging out the window of his car as we walked up.

"Hey," I said.

Quincy motioned for us to get in the car, and I stepped into the front seat. Lucas sat behind me in the back. I leaned in to give him a quick hug. "Lucas, Quincy. Quincy, Lucas."

"What's good, bro?" Quincy said as they dapped each other up.

"Yeah, so Mirah texted me. Said she's gonna be, like, ten minutes late. But she's on the way. In the meantime, ya want something to drink? Or ya tryna light up?" he asked. He pressed a button on his phone connected to the aux, and a slow, melodic, lush, heady beat poured from the speakers. Quincy said it was something he was working on for Samirah.

The beat, with its insistent percussion and mellow rhythmic interplay, took me back to another time. I was in the desert in the scorching Arizona sun with Lucas. We were in the middle of the Grand Canyon in the quiet of the vastness. It was a spontaneous trip—instead of beating ourselves up about what little money we had, we had taken advantage of the first cheap Spirit tickets we could find. Just us, the sun, the scorched rocks, and ruminative lyrics brought to life by a bewitching voice, similar to the music playing now. It felt like a dream then, like nothing but the sun shining against our skin mattered, and here we were in the dream again. I looked behind me, and Lucas and I exchanged knowing glances, our minds likely lingering in the same memory.

Today was a big day for me. One that would start a chain reaction that led to the outcome I most desired, so I probably shouldn't smoke. But damn if I didn't want to take a pull of that indica deep into my lungs to ease my mind, to stop my thoughts from racing, thinking too much about the possibility of things going wrong.

"You know what. Fuck it. I wasn't going to smoke today. But since we're here and you're offering, and it could get my creative juices flowing . . . roll it up," I said.

"Already done," Quincy said, holding a blunt in his hand.

We took turns passing and pulling from the blunt, the sweet taste of the strawberry strain on my lips as I blew out plumes of smoke. And as the plant worked its way through my body, loosening my limbs so that they felt gelatinous, making the pulses and vibrations of the music flow through me as I swayed along, I rode the waves of the high.

A few minutes later, Samirah walked up to the car, rolling a small green suitcase behind her.

We all stepped out to greet her. She had already given me and Quincy hugs before she turned to Lucas. "Wassup, y'all. Lucas, right?" Samirah said, shaking his hand.

"Yeah. Nice to meet you. Excited to work with you today. I see you came prepared."

Samirah flipped her flowing hair back and laughed. It had changed since the last time I saw her; this time it was a long black body-wave lace front, edges laid to the heavens.

"Yeah, you know. Gotta look good for the shoot. Anyway, so what's the moves?" she said, gesturing toward me.

"Lucas is gonna run through the plan. You should have already gotten the link I sent you with his work," I said.

"Yeah, I got it. Looked through it before I got here. You got some skills," she said, laughing again, throwing a look Lucas's way.

"Thanks. I be trying, you know. Anyway, all you gotta do is look good, and I got the rest. We're gonna shoot by the sign first, and then we'll head up to around your old neighborhood after that. If there's anything important or meaningful to you in that area, let me know, and I'll work it into the shoot. Sound good?"

Their exchange reminded me of college Lucas. The Lucas I fell in love with. The Lucas that took photos of me randomly whenever we were together that last year, he on his way to adulthood, me entering into a new phase of freedom, catching the most intimate parts of me that I didn't like to show, illuminated by slivers of amber light—a collarbone jutting out of one of his shirts two sizes too big for my frame, knees that were aggressively undainty peeking out beneath distressed jeans. It was the way he saw the parts of me that I tried to hide, the way he captured beauty in the innocuous that kept me enraptured by him. And here he was, seeing me again. Except I wasn't the one in front of the camera. He was seeing me as I am now. A businesswoman, standing near another woman who held my metaphorical dreams in a series of soon-to-be snapshots, buzzy articles, and upcoming shows.

"A'ight, so we ready?" Lucas asked.

"I stay ready so I never have to get ready. Feel me?" Samirah said.

Lucas smiled, clapped his hands together, then reached into the car to grab his equipment.

"Let's get it," Quincy said. "I don't really know nothin' 'bout this whole photo shoot thing. Ya already know my thing is creating the beats, making the magic and all that. But Ima provide the vibes if nothing else."

"My guy," I said.

•

It was always a treat to see Lucas work. The way he dove to the ground to catch the right shot, unafraid of the grime that stuck to the sidewalk. And Samirah, a gem if there ever was one, knew her angles. She knew when to look fierce, knew when to stare into the sun, eyes slightly averted, so that she glowed, regal and proud. She knew when to look playful. She knew when to smile, close-lipped and demure so that she looked seductive against the colorful backdrop.

If I hadn't known any better, I would have assumed she was a model, assumed that some esteemed agency had snapped her up, eager to sell products to the masses via her image, but then I remembered that we all were models in a way, primping and preening for social media, showing the highlights, only the good stuff that kept followers coming back for more.

After some photos had been taken, Samirah and Lucas huddled above the small screen on his camera, flipping through photos, looking for anything that might need adjusting. I moved closer to Lucas so I could see too.

"This one is perfect." Lucas pointed to a picture that showed Samirah washed in sunlight, her skin glistening like a Black kid slathered in Vaseline on their way to the first day of school. Her face was lifted toward the sun's rays, her arms flowing freely in the air above her. She looked peaceful, tranquil, like the cover art on one of those neo-soul records that wanted you to know that the artists were deep, that there was a well of emotion rumbling beneath them and only through listening to the songs on their record could you reach their depth, learn about the things that broke and restored them.

And it was all wrong.

Samirah's music wasn't serene or calm. It was gritty, it was soulful, but raw. It was rough, but hopeful.

"Hey, Lucas. These shots are fire, but it's not really what we're going for. I'm thinking Samirah should look more powerful and confident rather than free and flowing, you know? That'll better reflect the music," I said.

"A'ight, let's try it like this," Lucas said. "Stand over there for me, Samirah."

He redirected Samirah again for a few minutes, but when we stopped to look at the pictures again, it was still giving soft-girl vibes—all positivity and happiness, not the passionate, moody, confident girl I'd seen perform at Irving and who mesmerized me at Quincy's studio.

Lucas wasn't looking beyond his own art at this shoot—he had captured Samirah as if she were another subject for Sunsetlandia, had revealed her dignified beauty as she shined beneath the sun, but it wasn't what we needed.

"Lucas, I'm sorry, but this direction isn't right. Can I show you what I'm thinking?" I said, reaching for the camera in his hands. I remembered watching Samirah as she posed and feeling moved by one of her expressions, but it passed too quickly for me to respond then. I wanted to search the camera to see if it had captured that split second.

He loosened his grip, and I pulled the camera gently into my hands and scrolled through the photos. Most of them were warm, Sunsetlandia vibes. But there was one that struck me immediately. Samirah stared directly into the camera. Her expression was sharp, severe, but somehow snarky, playful, despite the angles her cheekbones cut. This was what I had been envisioning. This picture made a statement. It's exactly what her EP needed.

"Hey, Samirah, Lucas, look at this one. This is the vibe we're going for," I said, motioning them over. "We should do more like this."

"Ooh, yeah, girl. I look mad good here. Imagine how it's gon' look after the edit too," she said.

"I don't know, Billie, shouldn't she look happier, though? I feel like we don't see a lot of that on EPs," Lucas said.

"Oh, you know what, he's got a point, though," Samirah said. "I'm not tryna look like I take myself too serious."

"Yeah, um, let me talk to Lucas real quick, Samirah. It'll just be a minute," I said, pulling Lucas away.

"Look, I know you're only trying to help. But this isn't Sunsetlandia. We have to get the cover art for the EP right so that it matches Samirah's sound so that we can continue to build her audience, you know? We're making a product."

"First off, she's a person, not a product. And I thought she looked good. What's the problem?"

I sighed and tried to soften my tone. Lucas wasn't my enemy. In fact, he was doing me a favor. I just had to get him to see it from my side—that whatever we did now would set the tone, would signal to her audience who she was, what she was about, why they should care about her. And we couldn't spread that message if she put out an EP with the wrong image.

"Okay, she isn't a product per se, but what we're putting out in the world is. It matters that we pitch her a certain way. It matters that as soon as you see her, you have an idea of what to expect. That's what we need to market her. To position her in a way that best fits what she needs to stand out, but also what the people want from her."

"Did you ever consider that she don't need someone from a label, even if it's you telling her what she needs? I mean, it's her art, her image, right? She can't decide that?"

"I know, but there is some helpful tailoring done, even in art, to help the art reach the right audience, like how you decide what paint colors to use for images. It's a framing, same thing I'm trying to do here. Babe, if we want her to work, it's gotta be a team effort. And it would be so good to have you on my team. Can you do that for me?"

I pleaded with my eyes, looking into his, hoping he would see how much this meant to me. How I didn't want to fight with him. All I wanted was to do right by Samirah.

He stared into my eyes for what felt like a long time before he finally said, "Yeah. I can do that for you."

"Thanks, babe," I said.

He nodded, and then I laced my fingers into his and gave them a squeeze before I shoved my hands into my pockets.

"Samirah, so I talked it over with Billie to make sure we got the right vision. I'm thinking we take more photos in this vein?" he said, showing her the photo we discussed during our little sidebar. "Give us more of that Bronx attitude. That toughness. The sexiness that comes with that. I'm thinking we could get it quick since we have a couple like that already."

"Bet. I'm always tryna rep for the Bronx girls anyway," she said, tossing her hair.

They went to work again capturing photos, and this time, I could tell they were the right mood. Lucas had listened, and I sighed in relief that this part of the equation was nearly finished.

After they were done and I'd looked at the photos again to make sure we'd gotten what we needed, Lucas started breaking down his equipment. As Lucas organized his things into the bags, I conversed with Quincy and Samirah about next steps in the process. Even if Lucas and I weren't on the same page yet, my plans for Samirah at Lit were underway, and I was thrilled that I was much closer to completing my goal.

16

It was seven on Halloween night, and for once, I had nothing extra to do for Lit after work. I picked up a giant bag of mini Kit Kats from the Walgreens a few blocks from the office before I made my way home, excited by the prospect of pure leisure. Lucas was out doing Instacart. Halloween was usually a busy night for him, with people ordering last-minute candy, costumes, and liquor for their events. I planned to eat the chocolate while watching scary movies in my fleece-lined pajamas on the sofa until I fell asleep.

I had been home for an hour and was watching a scene where a young Busta Rhymes beat the fuck out of Michael Myers in one of the *Halloween* movie sequels when I heard a knock on the door. I hadn't ordered anything from Amazon, and Lucas rarely forgot his keys in the house. I got up from the sofa and looked through the peephole, then unlocked the door.

"What are you doing here?" I said to Alicia.

Alicia was dressed like an Olympic track star, wearing long colorful nails with gems and dangly bits hanging from them, hip-length knotless braids, spandex, and a fake gold medal around her neck. "Hey, girl," she said, walking farther into my apartment. "Get dressed. We're going out."

"What? No. I'm not paying an entry fee to stand in some crowded bar next to eight men dressed like different versions of the Joker. I already have plans," I said, pointing to the flat-screen as Myers plunged a chef's knife into a busty woman's chest.

Alicia put her jacket down on the sofa and pulled something out of the reusable shopping bag she carried. "I got you this," she said. She handed me a pair of black cat ears. "Oh, come on. It'll be fun. It's free entry, and there's open bar until eleven. This guy I'm talking to is the one throwing it. He's the DJ."

"But I don't have a costume."

"You can be a slutty cat. Put the ears on and wear something black and tight."

"You're lucky I got that in my closet. I'll go, but I'm only staying a couple hours."

"That's all I need," Alicia said, then stuck her tongue out.

I threw on some music while I got ready. I put on tight vegan-leather leggings, a black-and-silver bustier, and a cropped leather jacket. We downed a shot of vodka each before we got into an Uber.

Forty-seven minutes later, we were in Bushwick, freezing our asses off in front of the club as the bouncer looked for our names on the VIP list.

When we got inside, it was a little after ten. Not many people were in the venue yet, but the DJ Alicia was hugged up with in the booth played Halloween-inspired hits as people took advantage of the open bar. I let Alicia have her moment and ordered a mojito.

As the minutes ticked by and I added a mental tally to my list every time I saw another girl dressed like a cat, I got closer to wanting to go home. After a trip to the bathroom, I planned to make my exit. Before I could announce my departure, Alicia introduced me to someone she had been talking to by the DJ booth—a dark-skinned man dressed like an NBA player in a jersey and matching shorts, who had come to watch DJ Rob's set.

"Hey, Billie, this is Hanif," Alicia said.

We shook hands.

"Hi, nice to meet you," I said.

"Hanif was just telling me that he had a record deal with Lit years ago." Alicia gave me a knowing look.

"Um. Yeah, it was kinda crazy," he said. "Some guy named Connor DMed me on IG where I was blowing up. Came to see me at the Delancey one night when I was performing some new shit. Within days, he made me an offer. It wasn't a lot of bread, but what would I look like turning down an opportunity like that? They wanted me to write for a few of their artists before I could put out my own stuff, so I wrote, like, ten songs. I did some demos too hoping they would let me keep my vocals on the tracks. After a while, when I pressed them about me recording an album, they dropped me from the label. Fake tweets of me dissing them started appearing online. Corny shit I would've never wrote. The whole thing was weird. Put me off big labels. That's why I'm independent now. I recorded something with Rob for his album coming out next year."

I tried to keep a straight face as I heard his story, but the metallic taste building in my mouth made me want to throw up. I never should have come to this party. "Wow, that's messed up," I said. "I'm sorry that happened. But good luck on the song, though."

I turned to Alicia. "I gotta get out of here," I said. It was all I could manage before I pushed through the costumed crowd to the exit and into the cold air. Outside, I put my hands on my knees and dry heaved a few times, but nothing came up. After I collected myself, I put my earbuds in and spent the walk to the L Train wondering if working at Lit had possibly made me complicit in their fucked-up schemes.

•

I was still thinking about what Hanif said two weeks later when all of us at Lit got wind of what happened at Ultimate early that morning. Ultimate Records had called a last-minute meeting, rounded up an imprint's worth of employees into a conference room, and unceremoniously told them that their positions had been terminated. The employees had been labeled redundancies since Lit already had Wavy Records and didn't need another electronica imprint. It happened at their offices, so we hadn't seen it in action, but the impact was still felt—some of our execs had absorbed their clients and doubled the workload for all of us, Nina included.

I wrote to Nina on Slack, hoping that she'd still be down to potentially take on Samirah as things fractured like cathedral windows around us.

Billie: Hey Nina. How are you holding up? Did you get some of the Ultimate clients?

Nina: Unfortunately, yes. It's been insane lately.

Billie: Ugh, I'm sorry. That sucks.

Billie: Do you think they'll start shutting imprints down here too?

Nina: Maybe. It kind of feels like when Lit bought Noir Records in 2018.

Nina: It was pretty much like this. They fired a bunch of people, shuttered a couple imprints, and spread the work out between whoever was left.

Labels had been doing it for years. Big three buying smaller labels. Midsize labels combining with other midsize labels. Never enough staff to handle all the work. All it does is create a monopoly so they could be the ones in control.

Nina: But that doesn't mean we should slack. You never know if we're really in the clear. Happy to do lunch again if you want to talk more?

Billie: I would love that. I was hoping to run something by you for an artist I think has real potential too.

Nina: Ooh interesting. Yeah, let's talk.

Billie: Cool. I think I can grab lunch in ten. Let me check with Michael tho.

I knocked on Michael's door as he clicked around on his computer.

"Hi, Michael, I'm running out to pick up lunch. I'll be gone for twenty minutes at the most. Can I get you anything?" I asked.

He looked up from his computer at the sound of my voice, his eyes burning with anger. "Do you really think that now is the time for you to run off? You need to be here. Doing your job. If you don't want to do that, let me know. I can get someone who actually wants to work in here as soon as tomorrow."

"No, um, sorry, Michael. I will . . . I will get right back to work."

"Yeah, good call. And close my door on your way out," he said.

As I walked back to my desk, I felt the anger building inside me, coming fast and loud like the train when it skips my stop when I'm running late, a roaring mockery.

I had given so much to Lit already. I'd taken last-minute trips across the city to get our artists what they wanted and acted like a damn Black ambassador for colleagues whenever they needed validation. But Michael didn't care about that.

All that mattered was that I got the job done. At whatever cost.

I wanted to throttle him. I wanted to go to his office and let it all out, to cry and scream and tell him how much I'd been busting my ass for him, for Lit.

But I knew I couldn't respond that way. I had to be calm. Kate and the other white women in the office had their tears, tears that often worked in their favor, evoking sympathy whenever they weaponized them at their target. Tears would not work the same for me.

I took a few deep breaths, dabbed a napkin at the corners of my eyes, and got back to work.

After I'd been working a few minutes, Slack pinged a notification on my computer.

Nina: Uh, hey? We still picking up lunch?

I looked back toward Michael's office to see if he was watching, but he was still on the call I had patched through, laughing as though his anger had only been fleeting, a gift just for me.

In my anger I'd actually forgotten about Nina. But then I felt relieved that I'd have to cancel, that she didn't have to see me broken.

Billie: Hey, sorry. Wish I could. Michael needs me to stay here. I think Ima be chained to my desk for a while.

Nina: Oof. Yeah. Been there. Wanna pick this up later? Maybe at the holiday party in a couple weeks? Feels like things would be calmer then.

Billie: Yeah, that sounds perfect.

I put my phone and chats on my desktop on do not disturb and busied myself with work. Today would not be the end of my story at Lit.

17

"Billie," Michael called from his office.

I got up and walked the short distance to his door.

"Are things all set for tonight?" Michael said as soon as I stepped into view.

I was in charge of organizing the company holiday party happening tonight. I was surprised we were even having one considering the merger, how many things were up in the air come the new year. But in one of our little dictation sessions, Michael had said that this would be a morale booster. People loved an opportunity to get dressed up and eat and drink free shit, he'd said. I took the task seriously, meticulously planning it out with Iris, the event coordinator of the venue. More important than the party, though, was that today I was going to bring everything I had done for Samirah to Nina, and it all had to go smoothly.

"Yes. I've arranged for the rental company to be there at two, followed by the catering company at three. I'll meet them over there at four to hang the lights and arrange the tables. The flowers have already been delivered."

"Great. Could you schedule my car for five? I want to get there early to greet a few people."

"Got it. Will do."

I started to walk away before he called out to me again.

"Billie, could you also make sure everything is all good with Trent?"

"Of course, Michael," I said. I offered a small smile before I walked back to my desk and called Trent's assistant to confirm the details.

Things had quieted down a bit as we got closer to the holiday season. Most people were going to be out of the office next week, on the way to their hometowns or cozy, mountainous locales for skiing and nightly dips in outdoor Jacuzzis, away from the slushy streets of the city. But I'd still be here hustling.

I would be lying if I said it wasn't a relief that I never had to travel for the holidays. I didn't have to worry about delayed planes or travel fees or even awkward family dinners. Most of my family lived here in New York but usually had their own plans with their immediate families, so Mama, Lucas, and I were left to our own devices.

Lucas and I had made up our own traditions over the years. On Christmas Day, we typically cooked a holiday-themed breakfast together, featuring candied bacon and French toast made with challah rather than the Wonder bread we used on regular days, followed by lounging on the living room sofa occupied with our gifts as Nat King Cole, Johnny Mathis, and Eartha Kitt crooned Christmas tunes in the background.

I would usually use some of my time off to wander the city. The emptiness of it made even the most unbearable places in Manhattan—well, Times Square couldn't be saved by the holidays—a little less crowded, a little more breathable. But this season, I didn't have time to wander. I needed to use my time wisely, efficiently. The next month before the merger was official was crucial, and every minute of it mattered.

Now that I had gotten Quincy and Samirah on board with my plans, all there was left to do was to talk to Nina to see if she would want to sign Samirah and let me shadow her. And the holiday party was the best place to do that. She'd be in work mode, but she'd also be more relaxed, loosened by passed hors d'oeuvres and endless glasses of wine and champagne, spiked eggnog, and sparkling cider. If I spoke to her at the right moment, I was sure I could glean some info about how to get Samirah into the office, and then to get her and Michael into the same room.

It was twelve-thirty now. I had three hours to check all the items off my to-do list before I went to prepare for the party.

I filed expense reports for my team; stuffed materials into special-made mailers for the radio and press, alerting them of Lorna Velour's sophomore album world tour; and scheduled and coordinated five meetings to discuss album-release parties and press conferences, all while chugging cups of bitter coffee in between my rapid typing.

At around three-thirty, I hit send on my last email of the day. I let out a deep sigh, releasing the tension that had built up inside me like carbonation in a soda unknowingly shaken and opened too quickly, grabbed my bag from the small closet at my desk, and bolted to the bathroom.

First, I used a toothbrush to wash away the sour taste that lingered on my tongue. Looking at my reflection in the mirror, I swiped on red lipstick and pulled an edge brush from the inside pocket of the bag. I swooped the baby hairs into perfect swirls that matched my curly updo with a smidge of gel.

Minutes later, I was out in the brisk December air as I waited for my Uber to arrive.

•

Setting up hadn't gotten off to a good start. The caterer was thirty minutes late. The flowers had initially been delivered to the wrong address. And my hair had already started to get puffy as I waited for the car, bundled beneath my bubble coat. But I was proud of what I had done to transform the space.

Bouquets of birch branches, juniper, tulips, and snapdragons sat atop the cocktail tables. String lights had been hung from the ceiling by me and the event team that came with the space. Waiters were at the ready to pass around appetizers like baked Brie with cranberry sauce, salmon crudo, antipasto platters, and stuffed mushrooms, while assorted chocolate-dipped desserts and fresh fruit sat on a table, artfully displayed buffet-style near the glimmering holiday tree.

Half an hour later, my colleagues had begun to arrive in cliques. The higher-ups slipped in loudly, talking excitedly among themselves, followed by the assistants, who arrived one by one, looking devastatingly relieved to not be in the office past seven.

Now that the party was officially underway, and Michael was tucked in a quiet corner with Trent and a few of his colleagues, I could finally relax.

I looked around the room and flagged down a waiter for a glass of white wine and a few appetizers and waited for Nina to arrive. When she got there, I'd be ready.

Quincy had sent me sample songs that would go on the EP earlier in the week, and Samirah made it her mission to apply pressure with these songs. In each of them, both three-odd minutes long, she brought riffs and belts and lyricism like I hadn't heard in years. As I curled up on my sofa one night, soundbar blasting, hair raised up on my arms as I listened, I nodded along to what she was saying, felt it in my core when she hit deep notes. Even though the full project wasn't ready, from the snippets I'd heard, I could tell they were songs that would be long-lasting, that would outlive the fifteen minutes of fame a viral song on TikTok would provide.

As I sipped my wine, I spotted Nina at a table with Erykah and Charlotte. I hadn't had a chance to talk to her over the last few weeks in the lead-up to the party, and now that my chance was finally here, I wanted to make sure everything went right.

I tallied up all the things about Samirah I knew would get Nina's attention—her social numbers and engagements; her media coverage so far; her earnest, raw personality, a magnetic thing that made you never want to look away; her impeccable stage presence, a plus for someone so early in her career as an artist.

I pulled in a deep breath to center myself, then walked over to their table.

•

Nina was dressed in a silk ruby tie-waist vest with matching wide-leg pants and black satin boots. A slick low ponytail and gold hoop earrings completed the look.

"So what usually happens at these things?" I asked, trying to slip into their conversation like I'd been standing there the whole time.

"I mean, it's an office party. So some drinking and eating. Socializing. Ooh, but sometimes one of our colleagues will get an artist to perform a song or two if we're lucky," Nina said.

“Cool,” I said, nodding my head.

With Samirah on my mind, I didn’t want to chitchat, I wanted to get down to business. I had to get Nina alone, so I finished the last of my drink quickly to make the excuse more believable.

“Well, I’m going to go grab another drink if anyone else wants to come with,” I said.

Erykah and Charlotte were too deep in a conversation about a reality TV show where people got engaged to strangers they’d never seen face-to-face to even hear us.

“Sure. I could use another,” Nina said. She set her empty glass on the nearby cocktail table, and together we walked over to the bar.

We ordered cranberry Christmas punch and faced each other as we leaned against the side of the bar.

“So how are you?” I asked.

“I been busy as hell. Trying to keep my artists on schedule, staying on top of deadlines. Always trying to find talent any way I can,” Nina said.

As she looked down at her drink, I felt the vodka in the Christmas punch burning in my stomach and my hands getting clammier by the second, but I wouldn’t let that interrupt my flow. I was so close to getting what I wanted.

I looked around me to see if anyone would catch our conversation, but when I didn’t see Evan or Connor nearby, I felt safe to go into my spiel.

“So, Nina, I was hoping to talk to you at this party because I have something I’ve been working on that I’d love to share with you.”

She looked back at me and raised an eyebrow. “Okay, well, spit it out.”

I bit my lip out of nervousness, the vodka still burning my stomach, my insides squirming because I wasn’t sure if she’d think me advantageous, focused only on my own goals when things were at their busiest with the merger.

“Around the time I first started at Lit, I went to this show at Irving Plaza. There was this artist there, Samirah, who opened for Wazy. And she was amazing. I’m telling you, the girl had it all—style, presence, musical talent, crowd engagement, originality. I really think she’d be perfect for the roster.”

“Okay,” Nina said. Her voice was neutral, and I couldn’t tell if she was already judging me or open to hearing the rest of what I had to say. But there was no backing out now. Especially not since I promised Quincy that I could possibly get Samirah a deal.

"Long story short, I've been working with her on getting a polished EP together, helping her with her socials, trying to make sure she gets some buzz in the media with some help from a friend. Since I'm not in the position to sign artists, I was hoping that I could maybe shadow you if you like what you hear and see of her. And then we bring her to Michael when she's ready. Or whatever you think is best. Of course, I'll do whatever you think makes sense here."

I could feel Nina's eyes on me as the seconds ticked away slowly, painfully. She moved her hand to her chin and cocked her head to the side, her eyes squinted, her posture closed off.

"Billie," Nina began.

I leaned in closer to her, eager to catch every word amid the sounds of Christmas music, laughter, and the clinking of glasses.

"You've got a lot of heart. I'll give you that. And I know the merger got a lot of us shook. But listen, you should have asked me first before you did any of it. It's always better to go into a situation with as much knowledge and experience as possible. At the end of the day, neither I nor you can know if Michael will let us make her a deal. I mean, even I can't get things past him sometimes. This shit is an uphill battle. Always. Remember when I tried to sign Papi months ago?"

I nodded because I knew she couldn't take Papi any further than the shitty deal Michael had told her to offer, no matter how right she was about his mass appeal. No matter what vision she might have had for him.

"He had all the right things too," Nina said. "All the things you're saying. But it didn't work out. It happens, and it sucks. But that's why you gotta be careful. You getting to know them so personally and putting so much of your own energy and resources into her is a great quality to have in this business, but it could also get their hopes up. It could give you a reputation as a liar, someone who says they can do what they cannot do. And as you know, reputation is everything. But . . ." She looked at me then, right into my eyes like she could see to the core of me. Though she had had several drinks, her eyes were intense, focused like she hadn't had a single drop of liquor in years. "Show me her work. If she's as good as you say, I want to hear for myself."

"Oh," I said.

I hadn't expected her to listen to it here. But luckily, I was prepared for anything. I took my phone from my clutch and pulled up a new single as my heart galloped wildly in my chest.

She popped in an earbud she'd taken from an inside pocket of her purse as the song queued up. "Rudolph the Red-Nosed Reindeer," the Temptations version, played in the background, and Eddie, a man known for his flawless falsetto, sounded distorted to me, deep and strange and totally unlike him. I realized then that it wasn't the music at all. It was just that everything around me slowed in the half a minute it took for Nina to listen, to judge my ear, my taste, me.

"Okay, Billie. I have to admit, I'm impressed," she said.

She was frowning as she said it, but I could tell this was the good kind. And then all I felt was relief. My heart that had been beating maniacally eased its way back to its regular thump, thump. Everything around me in the room seemed to come back to normal pace too.

Nina was impressed by Samirah. By someone I scoped out. I knew I needed this validation, but the way satisfaction crashed over me like a wave, pulling me into a brighter mood, surprised me. Made me feel warm like the confidence I sometimes had in myself, in my dreams, was warranted.

"Samirah is talented for sure. I'll check her socials, streaming metrics, and all that later. Shoot me an email with all the details. I think I'll also need to see her perform live so I can measure her stage presence, crowd engagement, and whatever before I make any moves. But this is a good start, Billie." She playfully grazed her shoulder against mine.

I was sure that this meant that she would let me shadow. I was sure that this meant that she thought Samirah was the next big thing the same as I did. But I wanted to hear her say it aloud to make it real.

"So just so I'm clear, you're saying you're willing to take Samirah on and have me work with you?" I asked.

"Well, not exactly. Let's see her at a performance, and you'll have my answer then. But good job on this, really. I respect the ambition." She laughed, and it was like a saxophone swooning my ears with its music.

I squealed, and a smile stretched across my face. I wasn't usually a hugger, but I suddenly felt the urge to pull her close, to spread some of my gratitude to her, skin to skin. I suppressed it as I tried to keep it cute and professional, and settled for saying thanks instead.

"I promise you're not going to regret this," I said. "The next thing on my list is getting another performance set up. I'm thinking right after the holidays but before the merger."

"Sounds good, Billie. Keep me posted on everything, and we'll follow up in the new year."

"Will do," I said, still giddy.

"A'ight. I gotta do some mingling now, you know how it is, but come find me later, though," she said as she made her way over to the other execs.

As the night wore on, I shuffled from table to table, making small talk with some of the assistants I never got to grab lunch with in the office. And even though I hated small talk, nothing could take me off this cloud of positive vibes I was riding on. Nothing could take away the joy and immense relief and pleasure from what I'd accomplished tonight, from what I hoped for the future.

Standing with the assistants now, I listened to Charlotte, Kelly, and Jackie complain about their bosses.

"It's like they don't even think we're people with feelings," Jackie said following a gulp of prosecco.

"Exactly. Like, I get it, we're assistants. We get the coffee. We schedule the appointments. We answer the phones. But for fuck's sake, can they please stop yelling at us in front of everyone? It's so embarrassing," Kelly said.

A chorus of quiet yeses rang out from us all as we nodded our heads in agreement. As we continued to drink and complain, the music turned from holiday to the latest hits, and most of the higher-ups had taken cars back to their new-money/old-money/more-money-than-I'd-ever-have homes in Chelsea/Tribeca/Upper East Side. Each of us had our grievances. Jackie, with her complaints that Evan made her pick up his dry cleaning and micromanaged her down to the minute even though she'd been his assistant for three years. Kelly, with her complaints that her manager commented on her outfits so often that she knew that when Sam said, *You look tired. Are you okay?* it meant that she'd better have a cup of coffee and apply more makeup ASAP. Kelly made sure to keep a makeup kit and several outfits in her desk closet, just in case. And then there was Charlotte, with her complaints about Connor and his isms. His sexism, his racism, his elitism, his classism. There wasn't a day that passed that Connor wouldn't make a comment that seemed innocent on the surface but bubbled with malice beneath its glossy tone. I was all too familiar with Connor and his isms. Especially after that afternoon in the studio.

As I thought back to that recording session, lost in the swirl of that ignorant moment, Connor stepped out into the middle of the room.

"Hey, everyone. I want to thank Michael for this party. Everyone having fun?" he yelled into the mic. He wobbled a little as he held his arms out in drunken delight. A cup of something dark, whiskey or scotch or some other drink that made him seem like he had more taste than he actually did, was in the hand not holding the mic, and it sloshed over his fingers and wet his forearms as he outstretched them. He pushed up the sleeves of his black button-up, a couple of buttons undone at the top, before the rest of the liquid could seep in.

As I looked at him, my mouth twisted up into a snarl-like smile, I heard a few of my colleagues enthusiastically yell out in the crowd—Evan, Sam, Jason, all the male execs who ran in a pack and filled up the offices with their mediocrity and undeserved confidence. Others, the assistants I'd small-talked with, stared at him wide-eyed, taking small sips of their cocktails as they waited to see what came next.

"All right. That's what I like to hear," he said. He smiled that smug smile of his, basking in all the attention centered on him. "I have a little surprise for you."

Thundering bass began to play from the speakers, followed by background vocals that repeated the word *yeah* over the beat in varying whispers that sounded vaguely like sex sounds.

Something about this beat felt familiar, like I'd heard it before in passing. Maybe in a car commercial, or it caught my ear as it drifted from an open door of a store while someone was leaving. As I tried to think of where I had heard this beat, Juda waltzed into the room and began rapping as he strolled to the center.

As he walked, I clocked his fresh haircut, the grill in his mouth that sparkled beneath the bright lights in the room, and the only thing that popped into my brain was a single question—*Are you fucking kidding me?*

I had always known that Connor would continue working with Juda no matter what I said, but I didn't expect to find him at our holiday party, brazenly rapping about asses, putting on a Blaccent and offending everyone in the room.

"Oh my god," Charlotte said. "Juda is here?" She looked in his direction, her eyes bright as she focused on him.

"I love this song!" Jackie said. Her voice shot up three octaves higher than when she was talking about the things she hated.

But as Charlotte and Jackie looked on excitedly, I realized that they weren't offended at all. They were fucking overjoyed. They didn't find anything wrong with this whole charade, how easily Juda could slip into another culture and thrive on it.

I turned my attention back to Juda as he launched into the verse following the hook.

Shake that ass, mami
What will you do for me
You looking sweet like honey
Now I'm about to throw that money

I looked across the room toward Nina, remembering that I had yet to tell her about what had happened that day I visited the studio to listen to Juda with Connor, but when our eyes connected, it was as if she knew. Her lips were upturned into a smile, but her eyes were cold, staring as though she'd witnessed something she wished she could unsee. Erykah was standing next to her too, face all tooted up, her eyebrows also raised. When our eyes met, Erykah and I tilted our heads toward each other in that what-in-the-white-hell-is-this kind of way. It was the first time Erykah had regarded me like I was part of her community, our community. It was the first time I felt acknowledged by her. I wondered what this meant for our relationship going forward. If we'd see each other in the hall and exchange words that made me feel less lonely, less like she was another landmine on the way to success.

But at this moment, Nina, Erykah, and I were three brown faces in a room made of alabaster. We were the only ones in the crowd not nodding along. The only ones not amused by this caricature. I decided then that I had had enough of this night, enough of this party. Plus, I had already accomplished my goal: Nina was that much closer to helping me. And that was all I needed to end this night in the right mood.

I put down my drink on the bar before I gathered my coat and purse from the coat check. I walked over to Michael, asked if he needed anything, but he waved me off, told me to enjoy the rest of my night. I was officially off duty. Iris, the event coordinator, would handle the cleanup.

I walked to the train, waited forty-five minutes for it to arrive, and rode in a subway car that was freezing and reeked of body odor, but all I could think about was how good it felt to hear Nina say she respected my ambition.

18

In mid-December, before I was off on vacation for the holidays, I'd spent most of the work week collaborating with Quincy to get a performance set up for Samirah. Over the weekend, Lucas and I bought a beat-up tree from the guys in the parking lot of the White Castle on Fordham.

I also sent out dozens of cold emails asking venues to give me a deal or a hookup to rent a space for a Samirah show. In exchange, we'd give them some of the proceeds from the tickets. But in the end, it was Quincy who found us a space at a lounge near Third Avenue in the Bronx, managed by some guy he used to hang with back in the day when he took classes that one semester at Borough of Manhattan Community College.

We set the event for mid-January before the merger, when the city would be bustling again, teeming with people grateful to be back in a city that didn't know all of their hometown secrets.

Samirah was off writing new songs. Quincy was busy mixing and polishing the beats and vocals. Alicia was trying to pitch Samirah for her magazine, and Lucas was working on the EP art. Now that the event was set, Nina had invited me to Alana Negrita's album-release party so I could see what happened at events in order to be better prepared for Samirah's.

"Just so you know," Lucas said, holding a cup of coffee close to his lips, "I sent the edited pictures to Samirah a few minutes ago. The ones *you* liked. She should be posting them soon."

"Oh, that's great, babe. Thanks. I was getting worried," I said.

I'd clocked Lucas's tone, the slight irritation in his voice when he said *you*, but it was far too early to get into another fight about art, selling out and the definition of success. I let the shot go unchecked to keep the peace.

"Are you doubting my skills this early in the morning?" he said, his mouth swept up into a grin.

"Nah. It's not that. They had that round of layoffs mid-November, and everyone's doing double the work and on edge. I want everything to go right."

Lucas put his cup down, grabbed my hand from across the kitchen table, and stared into my eyes like he didn't care that they were still crusted from sleep. "It will," he said.

"Thanks. I'll cross my fingers for now and hope that lands well with her fans. We really need them to show up, 'cause Leesh might have a couple people from *Kulture Magazine* come through, and Nina is gonna be there. There's just . . . a lot riding on this. . . . Anyway, enough about me. How's prep going for Sunsetlandia?"

"It's been busy. I shared it on socials to get the word out. I got Chris and Jeff promoting too. I still gotta get my VIP guest list ready, and I have maybe two more sets of shots to develop. But I got the liqs on deck. Junior gonna DJ. I mean, that nigga owes me, like, three hundred dollars, so he basically had no choice but to do it." He laughed. "But yeah, everything is painted. Most of the other photos are in the boxes there already, so it's not gon' be too much to set it up that day. You should come early so I can give you a lil private walk-through."

"Yes, of course, babe. I can't wait to see it." I got up and kissed him before I put the dishes in the sink and got ready for work.

•

All morning I waited for the photos to pop up on my Instagram feed. In between emails and phone calls at my desk, I discreetly pulled the screen down on the app, forcing it to refresh and refresh in the hopes that Samirah would appear in all her musical glory. Finally, as the morning turned to noon, two posts from her appeared at the top of the page. One was a collection of photos strung together as a reel with a Samirah song as the background music. The other was a regular collage of pictures. I put three fire emojis beneath each of the posts and saved them to my profile for extra engagement. Soon enough, other likes and comments began to come in, praising Samirah's look, complimenting the music track uploaded along with the post, noting their excitement about the upcoming event and enthusiasm for an EP that might be on the way. Seeing the like count climb higher and higher with each passing minute, I knew I needed to hit up Alicia for the last part of my plan.

Billie:

you seeing this?

Samirah posts are poppin off. Twelve thousand likes in the first five minutes

holy shit

Alicia:

i'm looking girl

this is perfect timing too

we have our brainstorming meeting today

Ima suggest Samirah to Janet

she loves looking into new "urban" artists

makes her feel like she's a good person cuz she supports brown people every now and then

but she be the main one talking slick when she thinks no one's listening

Billie:

smh

okay thanks

the event is set. Ima talk to Nina about it on thurs at Alana Negrita's party

Alicia:

I mean, that's good that she's gonna help you get set up and shit

but you sure you can trust her?

what if she cuts you out of the deal altogether?

I looked back toward Nina, who was on the phone with a client, but when she caught me looking at her, she smiled and threw me an upward head nod.

Nina had only ever been my ally. I had to believe that she was on my side. I had to believe that we would have each other's backs.

Billie:

yeah

I think I can

I returned the smile.

•

Tuesday and Wednesday flew by quickly as I focused on work. I dutifully answered phone calls, went on coffee runs for the team, scheduled meetings and recording sessions for upcoming artists, packaged hundreds of press kits for Connor until my fingers were laced with tiny paper cuts that stung furiously whenever I washed my hands, and did lunch runs for Michael so that I could be on his good side again, hoping that the anger he threw at me a couple of days ago was merely a speck, a small snag in our future relationship that I imagined would stretch into years. It was an exhausting week that left me cranky and puffy eyed as I rode the train Thursday morning, pulling my sunglasses over my eyes to avoid any accidental human contact.

Once I got to the office, I'd have to redo my mascara since it had smudged during my attempt to brighten my eyes, and I'd have to reapply the lipstick too—hell, I'd probably have to touch up my whole face. Alana Negrita's album-release party was later this evening, and if I wanted Samirah's event to go well, I had to take notes—and look good while doing it. I needed to know what made a music-release party special. Obviously the music was the key component, but I needed to know what made it something memorable, something that made people want to buy Alana's album and call themselves a forever fan.

If I wanted to make Samirah a star, I'd have to learn from one.

I dug into the rest of my work, eager to knock as much off my list as possible so that I could make it to the event with Nina early. I wanted to see what setup looked like, what breakdown looked like, what the energy was when people stepped inside the venue. Samirah's event would be scaled way down. We were planning it with next to no budget in some corner of the Bronx, but if I could apply a little of what I learned tonight, it might make the difference between a good event and a disaster.

Alana had scored success over the summer with two top-ten entries into the Billboard 100 list, and her ascent to the top, and Nina's satisfaction that came from her success, was part of what made me determined to stay in A&R, to get everything right for Samirah.

Nina had signed Alana two years ago and put everything she had into making sure that everything she did for Alana was authentic to Alana's vision. In the environment Nina had created for her, where Alana felt free to embrace her Afro-Latina roots, she thrived. Alana's music was full of life, vibrancy, energy, and laughter, her fluttering voice blending harmoniously with the tracks. She filled her music videos with supple dark-skinned people who took up space, who were proud of all they were. She felt free to wear her afro, to sing about the struggles she faced, about how no one considered her Latina or American enough. She was one of the only Afro-Latina, deeply melanated female artists to hit the top 100 in an industry full of Rosalías and JLos.

I could tell that whenever Nina talked about Alana, it made Nina proud that she could help bring Alana's light, her voice, into the world.

In the bathroom now that the end of the day had come, I triple-checked my makeup and the rest of me for stains, lint, or anything else that didn't belong, but my outfit—a structured oversize blazer, dark silk camisole, high-waisted cargo joggers, and black booties—was fine. I made my way over to Nina, who had already called a car that was waiting downstairs.

"One thing before we get there," Nina began as we slid into the back seat. "Don't get all starstruck at this event. Say hello and keep it moving."

I knew I couldn't come off as too green, too eager, so I nodded, confirmed that I'd be on my best behavior. But inside, I was squealing. This was the part of the job that hadn't been revealed to me before, the part I longed for most—to see the impact Alana made, to know that Nina had been the one to help shepherd her into her world.

Soon, I'd have that for myself, for my own legacy.

As we pulled up to the venue, a glitzy club in Tribeca, I knew we were about to enter an extravagant, star-studded event. Outside the venue a red carpet had been rolled out, and ornate jewel-toned flowers hung above the walkway like a canopy of colorful stars. Photographers descended upon the carpet hungrily like a pack of drunk girls over some fries after a long night out, waiting to get their pictures of the celebrities as they emerged from their luxury vehicles.

After Nina and I had checked our coats, I looked around at the space, clocking details that made this event feel special, remarkable in its decor, in its ambiance, so that this night would be etched into the minds of the attendees: Huge jewel-toned orbs giving seventies-era opulence hung from the ceiling like a forest of overgrown mushrooms, a photobooth area with a merlot backdrop accented with gold sat in a corner near the VIP area, and both the stage and the bar had been lit so that the vibrant lights mixed with the lightly vanilla-scented air-conditioning, creating a thin layer of fog that shrouded the room in mystery.

As we walked to the bar, waitstaff moved about the room, straightening the pillows on the sofas. They swept the floors and wiped down surfaces, ensuring that people could see their reflection in the black of a tabletop or in the glint of a glass as they sipped a cocktail.

"Should we get a drink first? You know, to loosen up?" I asked.

"Definitely. It's free and curated—look at this," she said, picking up a menu from the bar and reading aloud. "Die dreaming—a modern take on morir soñando: vodka, fresh-squeezed blood orange juice, oat milk, and cane sugar. Pass the hookah—Brugal, a rum with notes of chocolate and caramel, ginger beer, cinnamon stick. May emit plumes of vapor from dry ice.

"What do you think of the drinks? I wanted them to represent the culture, something that reminded Alana of home, but also had that element of surprise and elevation."

Home. Culture. Elevation. Nina was methodical about Alana's music and image, but she also cared about every little detail, made sure that every part of Alana was reflected in what she did, that what she put out in the world paid homage to her culture, to her people. I would have to think on it later, the things that would best represent Samirah.

"I love it. I'm coming for that pass the hookah," I said, laughing. "This is, like, what we need more of. A&R reps who know how to execute an artist's vision because they have similar lived experiences and can understand the little nuances. I feel like that gets missed a lot in this industry."

"Thanks. That's what I'm all about. Making sure my artists feel seen and understood. Making sure they feel taken care of, because they deserve it. Because we all deserve it," she said, a smile creeping across her lips.

"So," I said. "This is Alana's debut album, right? How does an artist like that get money from Lit for a party like this?"

"Well, first, you need someone like me within the company to fight like hell for it. Remember when I said to choose your battles? Alana was one of mine. She just had this presence, you know? Like you couldn't look away and you didn't want to. I was on her before the *Hip-Hop and Me* guest spot too, when all she had was an Instagram filled with grainy videos and unsynched audio. But when I saw her say on the show she wanted to follow in the footsteps of some of the greatest Afro-Latinas before her—Celia Cruz, Oscar D'León, Tego Calderón—I knew I had to sign her fast. I basically threatened to quit if they didn't sign her, and they really needed me at the time because I was recently promoted to an exec role, and there were no other people of color and barely any women at all in power there. So they let me sign her, and then Alana and I worked on the first couple songs, and it all trickled down from there. When it really comes down to it, the label just wants to know that their investment would be worth it. And I made sure that it was. That said, not everyone gets the same treatment." She took a sip from her drink and leaned back against the side of the bar.

"What do you mean?"

"Well, I knew I couldn't make an offer before her *Hip-Hop and Me* appearance. It only mattered after she'd already built her audience there. They didn't care about some brown girl singing about brown shit before that. She wasn't as valuable." She looked thoughtful as she took a sip of her drink. "As you move up at Lit, keep that in mind. Remind them that we have value whether they think so or not."

I nodded solemnly, agreeing with her, because that had always been my plan.

We'd reached a lull in the conversation, so we stood quietly sipping our drinks, hips swaying a little as Romeo Santos played in the background. After a few minutes, people began to trickle into the venue—social media influencers I recognized from Instagram and TikTok who together boasted millions of followers—and walk over to a series of sofas marked VIP AREA THREE.

Nina and I exchanged small talk in between people watching after that, sharing details about the bullshit we endured at work, so I didn't notice Alana had finally made her way into the venue. As Alana approached, attendees pulled out their phones to film her. An entourage of security surrounded her as she walked. She looked radiant, dressed in a shimmering gold dress and stacked heels, her hair fluffed out into a gorgeous afro adorned with an orchid at her left side. Her makeup was glamorous, impeccable. She was, simply put, a vision, a sight to behold, the baddest of bitches, in the words of Trina.

"*Hola. Como estas?* Nina, this party is *fabuloso,*" Alana Negrita said, moving toward Nina for a hug. "Thank you for everything," she said, clutching Nina's hands in hers.

"*Pero por supuesto.* Anything for you, babe. I'm glad that it all came together. Oh, and before I forget, I'd like to introduce you to my colleague Billie."

"Billie, nice to meet you," Alana Negrita said. "I hope you're enjoying the party?" She moved toward me and gave me an air kiss on each cheek once she was close enough.

"Nice to meet you too. Oh, absolutely. . . . I'm a big fan, by the way. Nina let me have an early listen of the album, and it is so good. I can't wait to see you perform tonight."

"Aw. Thanks so much, hun," she said. A dimpled smile skipped across her face. "Can't wait for you to hear it."

"Sorry to steal you away, Alana, but why don't we do some mingling. Talk to the press. Talk to some of your important friends here, if you know what I mean. Ooh, and look who made themselves comfortable in VIP."

I turned toward the area and saw Anitta, also dressed in a metallic ensemble, outfit on theme and flawless.

Nina touched her hand to my shoulder. "Will you be okay by yourself?"

"Oh yeah, totally," I said.

Nina and Alana Negrita chuckled and ventured over to the VIP area.

Over the course of an hour, I watched as Alana schmoozed. Eventually, after I had downed a couple of glasses of die dreaming, I took my seat on one of the sofas in the area Nina had sequestered and watched as Alana Negrita moved from celebrity to friend to social media influencer, sharing her inspiration for making the album, talking about her journey to fame and what it was like to live in LA away from her family in Washington Heights, and snapping pictures until it was time to take the stage to perform songs from her album.

The lights dimmed, and it was so dark that if you reached out, it felt like you'd touch nothingness. The only light in the room now was golden and pooled in the center of the stage, a mic stand in the middle. As the music from Alana's first hit single started to play, she slinked onto the stage, swaying her hips, and picked up the mic. And in that moment, it felt like Alana was the only person who could lift us out of the darkness, whose radiant joy could overtake anything.

"Thank you, everyone, for coming tonight," she began. People in the crowd whooped and clapped. Some of the celebrities, the ones Alana had grown to call friends, raised their glasses and cheekily stuck out their tongues. "I never thought I would be here. I grew up surrounded by love. By my family. Surrounded by music, whew, they could sing and play instruments. The genes are strong, y'all," she added with a chuckle, her brilliant mouth twinkling in the light.

"But things were tough. Papi worked two jobs. Mami had to sew all our clothes—" She stopped to take a breath, tears pooling a little in her eyes. "I am just grateful to be on this stage today. I am grateful I have a chance to show you that Afro-Latinas are out here. That our voices matter. That we are talented and we have something beautiful to give to the world."

When she finished her speech, I clapped along with everyone else but probably harder than I should have. Red as my hands were now, I was glad that I had come here tonight to witness this, to witness her. To see the ways a good A&R rep could change an artist's life, could help turn their art into legacy, into the soundtrack of a people or a mission. It's why I knew I couldn't miss with Samirah—so that I could get her here.

As Alana Negrita started singing empowering lyrics over an upbeat Caribbean pop track, the bass knocking behind her, I imagined it was Samirah, that all of this, the glamour, the access, the impact made to the culture, that it was real for Samirah, for me—the future was so close.

Alana soon switched to the next song, and people were up dancing in their sections, their bodies moving in time to the beat. When Alana finished, a DJ took over and played Top 40 hits, the crowd cheering when Alana's tracks were mixed in with them, and I smiled. I would never forget this night. It had given me everything already, and now that I knew more about what made Alana's launch prodigious, I knew what I had to do for Samirah.

I pulled out my phone and sent her a text and hoped that by the morning, I'd have the answers I needed to make my next move.

After an espresso martini to wake myself up, charged to the company card, I said my goodbyes to Nina, who was busy leading Alana from media person to media person, and climbed into the back seat of a rideshare with a new vigor, a clear vision for what was to come.

19

The first week of January was the coldest it had been since winter started. At nineteen degrees, frigid air blew through me on my way to work while I rubbed my hands together to speed up their race to warmth. Yet at the office, it always managed to be only a hair above freezing. Though it had been hours since I had entered the building and warmed my hands with my first cup of caffeine for the day, I pulled my office cardigan on and sipped from my mug, waiting to feel that familiar tingling as my hands defrosted. It was bullshit that offices were still set to temperatures made "standard" in the seventies because mostly men wore three-piece suits and controlled the agenda. As I sipped my afternoon cup of tea, Connor suddenly appeared at my cube, causing me to spill black tea on my desk, the brown liquid seeping deep into the papers and folders strewn on the surface.

"Shit, I didn't mean to scare you, Erykah," Connor said.

He knew good and well that I was not Erykah. I had worked at Lit for seven months, had even spent time with Connor one-on-one, and yet he still managed to fuck up my name with the only other Black girl in the office. Erykah was slender, long-legged, and light-skinned like the color of Latto without a tan, and I was more Tanerélle, closer to chestnut, with wide hips and thick thighs. I knew that this could only be a direct attempt to make me feel small, insignificant, like I was interchangeable. Instinctually, I balled my fist tight, hoping I'd have a chance to "accidentally" punch him if he got close enough, but I let it loose as he walked the few steps to his office and grabbed a roll of paper towels. I didn't need the trouble that my anger, my seething, would cause. So I did what I always do—I forced a tight-lipped smile and cataloged this for the future, for when I'd have the power to do something about it.

"Whoops," he said, handing me the roll. "I also didn't mean to make a mess. Just wanted to see if I could get a quick chat in." He gestured toward Michael's office, where Michael was busy listening to something on his computer.

I blotted the folders now riddled with brown stains as well as I could, searching for the right way to respond to Connor, to face him as I thought about the shitty things I'd seen him do. I stared at him, eyes burning. "I . . . um." I finished blotting the papers as Connor stared, waiting for me to finish cleaning up his mistake, and pulled up Michael's calendar on Outlook.

"He is in a meeting now. He'll be free in about five minutes. Want to swing by then?"

"Great, thanks, Erykah," he said.

It was the second time he'd used the wrong name, and I knew I couldn't let this go on longer. I could handle a mistake, but this was an attack, this was him, again, trying to exert his power over me, over this office, and I would not let it stand.

"Actually," I said, loud enough so that he'd turn around to hear the rest of my sentence. "It's Billie. You're thinking of Erykah at reception." I worked to keep my voice controlled as I spoke, careful to remain light, to drench my anger in molasses, sticky and sweet.

"Oh." He shook his head and laughed heartily, like I'd told a joke he had been waiting his whole life to hear, write down, and regurgitate at some company mixer. "You two look so alike with this hair," he said. He pointed to my twist out, his hands so close they grazed a strand of my hair as they flailed inside his laughter.

Before I had a chance to respond, he walked back to his office and shut his door. Anger spread through me as I stared at the sad brown stains on the paperwork I'd worked hard to collate, and I racked my brain for the resemblance that Erykah and I supposedly shared. I could find no discernible likeness between us beyond our natural hair, Blackness, and storied names. Flustered, my heart racing so fast it felt like I'd spew it up, bloody and wildly beating, I pulled out my phone to text Quincy and Samirah, hoping to trade this moment for a moment of joy.

If I couldn't get Connor to respect me, I would upstage him. I would make him regret his disrespect when I was the one who came out on top.

As we planned, I typed out *January 18* to confirm the event date, and it sounded vaguely familiar, like I'd saved the date in some far recess of my brain for something important, but looking through the calendar on my personal email and finding nothing, I switched back to my text app.

I texted Alicia right after I finished with Quincy and Samirah, running down Samirah's new social media numbers, the date of the event, and the venue, and put down my phone to finish the rest of my work.

•

It had been two days since I was mistaken for Erykah, and I still couldn't get Connor's casual racism out of my head. But what bothered me about the whole conversation, microaggressions aside, was that it reminded me that Erykah and I still weren't friends.

Since the holiday party, Erykah had started saying hello back to me whenever I spoke to her, and I was grateful for the interaction. But we still hadn't shared a laugh, we hadn't complimented each other's hair or outfits, and we hadn't tilted our heads at each other and recognized when something offensive was happening before our eyes.

It was eleven-thirty now. Around the time people started making their lunch decisions. I had only half an hour before Erykah left her station at the front desk like clockwork, so I sent her a note on Slack.

Billie: Hey Erykah! I hope your day has been going well. I was wondering. If you're free. If you'd like to go to lunch with me in the café today?

I kept my note simple, but the message was clear—I wanted to get to know her. I'd reserved this time for her while Michael was out to a lunch with the Ultimate execs, and I knew it'd be three hours before he came back. All I had to do was wait for her reply. As I waited a minute and then another, watching for the dots that indicated she was typing to pop up on the screen, my heart did its butterfly thing. It fluttered like it had when I first met Lucas, when his calm presence unnerved me, easily broke through my icy facade, through the walls I was so used to putting up.

Erykah: Hey. Sure. Lunch sounds good. 12pm?

Billie: Works for me. Will meet you by your desk then.

I filled the half hour with sending and responding to emails, desperately trying to reach that coveted inbox zero. I caught Erykah's eye as I approached her desk. She looked pensive, eyebrows furrowed, arms folded.

Erykah and I made small talk on the way to the café about the weather and our weekends before we settled at a sun-shrouded table by the window.

We eyed each other cautiously as we started nibbling at the food we'd picked up from the barbecue station. After the holiday party and what happened with Connor, I had to make the first move if I wanted things to be different. I had to be the bridge that crossed us into new territory.

"So, Erykah. I, um, noticed that when I first started, you seemed kind of . . . I don't know, distant toward me. I was wondering if I had done something to offend you? I don't know what it is, was . . . but I want to make it right."

Erykah paused her eating and looked at me. "Billie, do you know why I am the way I am?"

"Well . . . no. I guess that's why I asked you to lunch," I said, not sure where she was going.

"Yeah. I thought so. Billie, I have been here for ten years. Ten years. It's a long-ass time for anyone to be somewhere. And every day I come in, and these people treat me like trash. They treat me like I'm nothing 'cause I just answer the phones, 'cause I'm just the receptionist, 'cause I'm not here making deals and signing talent and whatever. Anyway, I don't know the details, I've seen the way Michael operates. The secret phone calls I've had to patch through to him. How Connor follows in his footsteps. It's made me not want to fuck with whoever worked with Michael directly, knowing that he might be up to something shady. It even took a while for me and Nina to be friends until I knew she was a real one. I just didn't want to be involved. I do not get paid enough for that."

"Yeah, I get it. Knowing too much complicates things," I said.

"Yeah. It does."

"Yeah. Well, anyway. I wanna change how we are with one another, you know. I'd love to be friends. And speaking of change." I leaned into her so no one passing by could hear me. "Michael and Connor have been acting weird. . . . Something seems off about the way they do some of their business, especially with the merger being finalized in a couple weeks."

"Honestly," she said, getting closer to me too, "I have noticed. Michael has been getting sloppy. Leaving printouts of MHCP files in places where people can find them. He's been losing his temper more lately too. Let's just say, I wouldn't be surprised if what they're doing gets exposed soon. There's been whispers in the industry, you know. About his bad deals. It's only a matter of time before more gets found out and shit hits the fan."

"Damn. That's crazy," I said, touching my hand to my chin.

"Yeah, so you better watch your back. In case," she said.

Thinking, I nodded and chewed the barbecue chicken in my mouth until it turned to paste. I sipped my drink to wash it down.

"Thanks. . . . Oh, by the way. Do you know that Connor mistook me for you today?"

She sucked her teeth. "I'm not even surprised. You would've thought he learned when Amara came up in here a few weeks ago and he thought she was Nina. He was tight when Amara called him Chris for the rest of the meeting."

We both threw our heads back as we laughed, and something in me finally clicked into place. A sense of ease and lightness working its way through my limbs as the tension between us melted.

"Yes, see. I need all these stories in my life. Anyway, tell me about you. Where'd you grow up?" I asked.

For the next twenty minutes, I learned about Erykah's life: How she was the only girl in her family, so she had to help her mother raise her younger brothers. How she had a fourteen-year-old son who she hadn't planned on having so early in life but who ultimately led her on the path to this job, the path to being the one who made it out of the hood back when it was possible to snag a job without a college degree she would have been paying off for the rest of existence.

Even in our differences, our distinctly unique pasts, we shared in the Blackness that connected us: backyard and curbside barbecues filled with classic R&B and, as the nights wore on, house music and hip-hop and the sound of the older folks arguing when someone reneged during a game of spades wafting into the air; Easter Sundays when our moms sat us down in the kitchen—Kirk Franklin or Donnie McClurkin on in the background and a chair between their legs—greased our scalps, and took a hot comb to our hair, its sizzle inches away from searing the tops of our ears.

As we parted, on the way out of the elevator, we laughed, recounting moments from our childhood and adolescence and when we first became enraptured by music. I felt buoyant. Lunch with Erykah had been everything. With her I got to be real, got to peel back the layers of performative whiteness, free to use the mannerisms that came natural to my limbs and phrases easy on my tongue. It reminded me why I needed to be here, why I needed to be part of the establishment in order to change it from within.

•

As I lay in bed at home on Monday morning, a few days later and the week of the event, I switched between checking email on my phone and surreptitiously checking my Messages app, waiting for Alicia to text me back. She had promised to let me know when the article that featured Samirah would go live. I didn't know how she managed it, but she had convinced Janet to include Samirah in a lineup of new artists in shows around the city. Alicia told me the article would post an unspecified amount of hours from now, but I couldn't stop myself from trying to pinpoint when, texting her on a thirty-minute basis.

Alicia:

Bitch you betta stop blowing up my phone like you my girl or something

I promise you

it's gonna come out on the site this afternoon

Billie:

Okay. Last time. My bad.

This is pretty much my only chance for Samirah to get enough attention to make Lit notice.

If she doesn't get signed, I would have to start all over again and hope I can get someone on before Ultimate fully integrates.

Alicia:

I know. But girl, relax. Everything is gonna be good. Deep breaths.

And don't text me again about it, I got you! Love you.

A laugh tumbled from my throat, and I was grateful that she had pulled me out of a spiral.

I checked the site again when I picked up lunch, and sure enough, the top story of *Kulture Magazine*'s online page was the mention of Samirah in an article among five other newly discovered artists:

SAMIRAH OFFERS THOUGHTFUL LYRICS; JAZZY, GRITTY BEATS; AND A FRESH, SULTRY VOICE. CHECK HER OUT ON JANUARY 18. THERE WILL BE FREE DRINK TICKETS FOR THE FIRST FIFTY GUESTS. HAPPY DRINKIN' AND TWERKIN'.

Although the writer, Caroline Evergreen, whose name I was sure belonged to some white woman straight out of a Waspy Connecticut suburb, basically reduced Samirah's art to twerking music—to be fair, she wasn't entirely wrong, there were some bops that could fit in the category—I clapped my hands together softly, quietly celebrating this victory.

Then I texted Alicia. No matter how many times she playfully cursed me out, it was worth it because she always came through. I knew by the way she made me laugh, how she was the only person to bring me out of my family funk, that this would be the kind of friendship that would last forever. She would be the one I'd count on even when there was nothing to count.

Alicia:

Don't ever say I ain't do nothing for you sis!

Billie:

I would never. You are the best. Drinks on me next time we link.

Alicia:

Bet.

I hit Quincy and Samirah in the group chat, and it was more of the same—pure elation. I texted Nina the article too, hoping she'd finally have the ammunition she needed to bring Samirah in as a viable artist during the meeting next week, setting the last piece of the plan in place.

Later, as we both wrapped work and Nina had dinner with a potential client she had been eyeing since November, she texted me back confirming the details. She was direct and to the point. She'd done this too many times to be prematurely excited about it.

•

Taco night started back in college, when all Lucas and I could afford on date nights were those Old El Paso taco kits and a pound of ground beef. We'd gather in my mom's kitchen, and I'd throw on some music, something thumping and percussive, and we'd get to work stuffing our tacos with meat and cheese, and if we were lucky, sour cream left over after my mom made pound cake. We carried on the tradition after college, because with my two jobs and MusicallyBillie and Lucas's various gigs, we could never get the timing right to have a proper meal together. So we made it a thing, turned it into an oasis of comfort and guac.

We added more toppings in recent years—avocado crema, tomatoes, onions, cilantro, lettuce, and freshly warmed tortillas.

Lucas was at the kitchen counter now, carefully dicing onions on the cutting board we "borrowed" from Mama all those years ago. Thinking of Mama, I'd been fighting the urge to check in with her about the money, the apartment, but I had done my part and needed to let it be. We still had our brief chats, but it seemed like neither of us wanted to be the one who crossed the line.

"Did you remember to pick up the grape tomatoes?" he asked. He turned his body away from the counter, toward me, onion-riddled knife in hand.

I pulled my head from the fridge, holding the tomatoes up beside me. "Yep," I said, maneuvering around the other flimsy paper bags filled with the rest of the groceries I hadn't yet put away.

"Thanks," he said. He grabbed the container from me and began halving the tomatoes. He threw seasoned ground meat into a sauté pan and let it simmer with the diced onions. I continued filling the shelves of the fridge and cabinets, praying the food would last until my next paycheck.

"So," he said, "what's good with the Alicia thing? Did she get them to write that article?"

"Actually, yeah. She came through. The article is up. So hopefully that gets more eyes on her. Nina is going to come too. I'm excited."

"Aww, shit. Is my baby 'bout to be a big deal out here?" he said, smiling.

I laughed. "I'm not famous yet, and I wouldn't want to be. But if I happen to get to know a lot of celebrities and get invited to cool parties in the process, then that's just good fortune." A sly smile spread across my face as I sat down at the kitchen table.

"When's the event again? I'm assuming, as the very important boyfriend, that I get a free ticket?"

"Oh yeah. Def. I got you. I want Leesh to come too since she helped me with this whole thing. The event is on the eighteenth, so save the date."

Still standing in front of me, Lucas changed his whole demeanor. The smile he wore before had receded and was replaced by an expression that scrunched up his face, that stiffened his body, that made his arms go up beside him.

"Are you deadass?" he asked.

"What—what happened?"

"You really scheduled this for the eighteenth when you know that's when Ima launch Sunsetlandia?"

"Oh shit. I am so sorry, babe. I thought I told you. I must've forgotten to tell you with everything else going on." I moved closer to him by the stove so I could reach out to touch him, hoping it would bring him back to himself. But he snatched his arm away. I pulled my hands back too, stunned by his rejection, and stuffed them beneath my armpits.

"What time is it again? I think I can still make it toward the end," I said.

"I'm not gon' hold you, Billie. You kinda got me fucked up right now," he said, reaching up to rub the sides of his face, his braids pushing in different directions. "I told you mad times the date was the eighteenth for Sunsetlandia. You already know how hard I been working to get this shit off the ground, yo. And you know I always wanted you to be there. That was the plan, right? Us doing this art thing together. But this. This is some other shit. You been losing yourself for months. We been distant and unconnected. You spend every second of your time on Lit. Your morals are all fucked up. And you promised me, fucking promised me, that you'd come up to Sunsetlandia to see how I'm doing. Do a walkthrough with me. But no, you've got your head so far up Lit's ass, up Samirah's ass, that you can't even be bothered with mine. And even with that, did I trip? Nah, I let you do you. Now you gonna miss my show for what? Something that might not even pay off? Because that's the only way you'll be valuable to this shiesty company? Nah, that don't sit right with me," he said, shaking his head.

"Lucas, are you serious right now?" I backed up from him again, my shoulders raised, my mouth pinched so that I looked like an angry thing, ready to pounce. "It was a mistake. You're OD'ing—"

"Oh, I'm OD'ing? So you not the one that's been checked out? Coming home late all the time? Waking up at three in the morning to answer emails? You not the one that's missing something I've been building for us for years?"

"Lucas, first of all, calm down 'cause you're doing a lot right now. Second, you always think everyone can do their own thing. Be a one-person show all the time. Get your head out the fucking clouds, bro. There's always someone to answer to. And me doing that now at Lit, with Michael, so people who look like me can win later is a problem? I-I don't even know what to say right now.

You over here accusing me when I'm tryna do the same as you. Put our community on. Help make art. Just because it's not what you would do doesn't mean we're not on the same path. Look, I fucked up on the date, but it wasn't on purpose. That was the only day available, and I didn't realize the conflict. It's too late to change it now. What you want me to do?"

"You need to figure out your priorities. Figure out if that job that got all your time is worth losing this relationship you been basically absent from. Is that job with them racist people and their narrow thinking what you want? I mean . . . you see what happens to Nina. You want to be fighting with them like that for the rest of your career? Trying to get them to see humanity in your people just so they can make some fucking music? Couldn't be me, Billie. And it shouldn't be you either. This isn't at all how I saw shit going."

"Yeah, well. Me neither. But I'm sorry, okay? I really am. I never meant for this to happen."

"Well, it did. Look, I need a minute to cool off. I need to think." Lucas turned toward the door, grabbed his coat, and left.

In the kitchen, I built my tacos alone. I took my plate with me to the table, and as I sat down, I glimpsed the Samirah article still pulled up on my phone. I turned my phone face down on the table, then pushed it away from me. It slipped and hit the floor, but I didn't even check to see if the screen cracked. In the silent solitude of the kitchen, my eyes let go of the tears they'd been holding, my appetite quickly forgotten.

20

I dreamed that night. Dark and vivid dreams of failure, of being fired from Lit mercilessly, the kind of firing that involved HR walking me out, watching as I packed my things, watching to make sure I hadn't taken something valuable, something they deemed me unworthy of having. I dreamed of being ridiculed for daring, for dreaming of being someone, when really, I was nothing at all—a girl from the Bronx who thought she could be significant to the world, carving out a tiny section where she could thrive, but it wasn't meant for me.

In the low light of the morning, I woke up sweat-drenched and panting, reaching out for Lucas's comforting hug, the feel of his warm skin against mine, but he wasn't there. There was no sign that he'd even made it back home—the scent of his hair oil, earthy with a hint of spice, didn't linger on the pillows, and his workout gear remained disheveled and untouched near the closet door. I checked the nightstand where my phone sat. The screen was dark and unresponsive. I plugged it into the charger and checked the time. Six-thirty. Soon, I would have to make my way to the subway alone, with no moment of intimacy to hold on to, to carry me through the fuckery I knew I'd encounter at work.

As I thought back to what Lucas said last night, my breathing turned heavy, my heart was beating loud. Here he was leaving me when I needed his support, when I was about to have a turning point in a career I'd worked my ass off for. But I didn't even know where he ended up last night. It was the one thing we'd always made sure of—that we wouldn't leave the house angry with each other, and it hurt like hell that he'd left after basically calling me a corporate shill, like I hadn't waited my whole life for this opportunity. I grabbed my chest, trying to massage the tightness.

I knew I'd fucked up. That we were supposed to be in this together. But couldn't he see that my intentions were pure? He was supposed to understand me. He was supposed to know my heart. But he was too blinded by his own ideals to recognize that it felt like this was my only shot.

My alarm went off, snatching me out of my anger long enough for me to get dressed. I held back tears as I swiped on mascara and lip gloss. Still vibrating frustration, I tugged on my coat and made my way to work.

•

I spent the morning at Lit organizing meetings, mailing packages, routing contracts internally, putting together Excel sheets, submitting our artists for prestigious awards, and making sure no one interrupted Michael until he was ready. It was only a couple of hours until the meeting where Nina would bring up Samirah, and every task was punctuated with excitement. This would be the first time I'd have a voice, feel like I was important, be everything my dreams last night said I wasn't. In preparation, I had given Nina everything she needed—the *Okayplayer* article from last year, the article Alicia helped secure in *Kulture Magazine*, Samirah's social media numbers, forthcoming event details, and the tracks that would go on the EP—to convince Michael to let us consider Samirah as a viable artist.

When it was time for the meeting, as everyone shuffled in with their papers and stats, and executives sat at the table and assistants stood against the walls, looking like they'd rather be at their desks, catching up on their never-ending work, I stood behind Nina so it'd be easy to chime in, easier for everyone to see me and pay attention.

"Hello, everyone," Michael said. He turned toward Connor, who was seated next to him, dressed in a plain black tee with a blazer thrown over it, smug smile hugging his face like any other day.

"Connor, do you want to start?"

"So an update on Kyrie Kash, you know, the one from a few weeks ago who dropped that 'Work Dat Ass Out' video on YouTube that got half a million views overnight? We're close to signing her. We're negotiating terms, but I think we're close to a deal."

Kyrie Kash was a straight-up Nicki Minaj knockoff. She had the wigs and multiple personalities queued up, like the guys who waited outside sneaker stores on Two-Fifth to cop a fresh pair, like that was the thing that would set her apart. The real problem was that she couldn't rap for shit. She was beautiful, shapely, the kind of woman that could turn heads, but she made the kind of music you wanted to turn off. It was all corny bars and punchlines that didn't hit. And outfits that looked a decade out of style. I appreciated her hustle, how she rose out of the trenches, but she wasn't someone who would last. And Connor knew it too. He knew what mattered in this industry was the moment. And he only ever planned for his artists to hit that moment, and whatever happened to them once the industry had chewed them up and spit them out was none of his concern.

"Great work, Connor. When are you thinking for her album release?"

"Well, she'll be one of the lead artists in 2027. Maybe slate her for summer—she's gonna get the girls twerking, am I right, Nina?"

Everyone around the table laughed as Connor delivered his joke except Nina and me. Connor only ever talked like this, slicing his generally Ohioan colloquialisms with slang, when he was referencing Black artists. He never referenced the booties of white female artists' fans, even when the music was the same, the kind of high-energy, thumping music that got people onto dance floors. After spending months here, I knew that no one would say anything to Connor. He'd be free to spout jokes like this whenever he wanted. And if anyone dared to complain, they were regarded as merely myths, redacted in HR records, never to be spoken about or accounted for again.

Michael called on people around the table, who shook their heads with nothing to bring up today, until he finally called on Nina.

I took in a deep breath and reassured myself that Nina would crush this.

She'd take what I'd given her and turn Samirah into someone they'd want to know more about. I'd seen what she'd done for Alana Negrita. How the room had been in awe of her. I could trust Nina to do that here. She would show people why we needed to be heard. Still, as I waited for her to speak, my heart fluttered. I pressed my hand to my chest discreetly, hoping to hold in whatever was trying to come out.

"Yes, I have something," she said. "This is actually an artist I found out about through our lovely assistant Billie." She paused for a second, moving her body slightly to the side so people could see me.

My heart flopped in my chest like a suffocating fish as people turned their eyes toward me. Unsure if I should speak, I waved a small wave and smiled.

"Anyway, I'm talking about Samirah. She's recently been featured in a couple articles, *Okayplayer* and *Kulture Magazine* to name a few. She's got a niche following at around fifty thousand across platforms, but her TikTok and YouTube Music shorts often reach over a hundred thousand views. Her fans are streaming her content on Spotify, Apple Music, and SoundCloud at high rates with her song 'Let Me Get On' and her newly released single, 'Two Ways.' She's a rapper and singer, and she's got this funky, jazzy, soulful throwback kind of style with a modern upbeat twist—I think she can be big. We'll see how she is on stage when Billie and I see her for a performance on the eighteenth."

"Hmm. Seems like she could be similar to Kyrie Kash. Especially if we put them in seasons near each other . . . but it might be worth a meeting if she's as good as you say. Report back after the performance, and we can talk then."

In another division at the label, they had seven different white cisgender femme pop stars, each singing their own similar brand of sexy upbeat songs with repetitive hooks, synth-laced beats, and nasally harmonies. Why couldn't there be two Black women on the label who, by most standards, weren't similar at all? I wanted to say as much, but how could I when I held no power, no title, no weight of a reputation as one of the *good ones* that would give me enough room to tell them that they were full of shit?

Nina mumbled an okay, and I wished I could see her expression. I wondered if she had the same impenetrable look she wore when Michael lowballed her on other artists she tried to sign. Michael moved on to the next person.

Thirty minutes later, I was back at my desk, answering emails and stuffing my emotions down like Mama said I should. Her words, the ones she used to say to me to prepare me for the real world, rang in my head, lulled me back into calm: "*Don't let a minor situation get you out of character and further away from what you tryna accomplish. Okay?*"

But the enthusiasm I had felt moments ago had been tarnished. It turned out that I hadn't had a chance to speak at all. I was as powerless and voiceless as I'd been before. But if Nina worked her magic, soon I would do the thing I'd always dreamed of—I'd succeed.

I shot off a few more emails and swung by Nina's desk, eager to talk about Samirah. I caught her at her desk, browsing through *Billboard* on her computer.

"Hey," I said.

She swiveled toward me in her chair, and as she stretched her legs outward, shaking them a little to get her blood circulating, I caught sight of her soles.

"Hey, girl," she said.

"New shoes? Those are cute," I said, pointing my finger at the red-soled heel and then her.

"Yeah, I ended up treating myself to them because I signed this new artist I was after, but also because—" She looked around and lowered her voice. "Okay, don't tell anyone, but I ended up interviewing for a position at Ultimate. They're planning to create a new division with Trent at the helm."

My mouth hung open in surprise as I listened to her news, but I could tell she wasn't finished. I waited for the rest. I was happy for her, but with the Samirah event coming soon, I worried that she'd leave before she had a chance to help me through the process.

"I wasn't really looking for it," she continued, "but they reached out to me and eventually made an offer. I didn't end up going for it since it was a lateral move, but it makes me think about what else might happen with Lit."

I couldn't think of anything to respond with, in shock as I was, so I simply nodded and hoped she'd say more.

"Girl, close your mouth," she said, that laugh that effortlessly tumbled from her throat trailing her words. Like she could read my thoughts, she said, "Don't worry. I'm still here and I'm still going to help you with Samirah."

I mirrored her laugh, letting out relief with it, and tried to turn my own grating one into the kind that charmed in the way hers did. "Oh, thank God," I said. "But very interesting that they're trying to bring people over to their side, especially after laying some people off. Something to think about for sure. . . . Anyway, I came over because, um, well, I wanted to thank you for everything you've done so far. I am so, so excited for you to see Samirah. I hope she blows you away."

"I'm sure she will."

"Yeah. I just hope everything goes right."

"Well, try not to worry about it too much or it'll drive you crazy. Focus on trying to make the event go the best way it can." She crossed her legs, picked her mug up from her desk, and took a sip. I eyed her Louboutins again as she settled into her chair.

I was suddenly self-conscious, fingering my gold name chain. I adjusted my under-fifty-dollars-total outfit—an oversize cream sweater atop black straight-legged jeans and dark Chelsea boots. "Yeah. You're right. Anyway, I'm sure you have a lot to do. Let me let you get back to it."

"Yeah, you know, always some fire to put out. But let's figure out a game plan sometime early next week?"

"Sounds good," I said.

As I moved to return to my cube, I thought about turning back to Nina to tell her my frustration at what Michael implied at the meeting, but seeing her face, how she held in a smile that I was sure would light up this corner of the office if it had been suddenly plunged into darkness, how the acquisition of a new pair of shoes worth more than a month of my salary graced her usually modest-priced-shoe-covered feet, I knew that she had recently gotten good news, most likely about a new client, and I wouldn't take that joy from her, even if it would help me feel better to release.

21

In what felt like the longest, coldest month of the year, the heat in Alicia's apartment was off. Even though it was under forty degrees, her landlord had decided that his tenants, locked away within the thin walls of their apartments, could pile themselves with blankets, dress themselves in layers upon layers, to keep warm. And on Alicia's sofa, bundled beneath heated blankets we bought at Duane Reade with gift cards we'd received from distant aunts over Christmas break, she and I huddled together eating lemon-pepper chicken wings straight from the bucket.

"How many we got left?" she asked. A bit of seasoning was smeared on her lips and covered her hands. She picked up a napkin from the table in front of us and pinched her fingers to wipe off the grease.

"Three," I said. "I think you've had more than me, so all of these might be mine."

She reached over to my lap, where the bucket sat. "Not if I can grab one first." She quickly snatched a wing as I tried to shield the bucket with my body.

"Well, damn. If I had known you was gonna eat mine too, I would have ordered more."

She laughed closemouthed as she masticated, then said, "Yeah, I had to work through lunch today. I'm starving."

"Ooh. Yeah. Been there."

After months of waiting and planning, organizing and persuading, it was finally Sunday night, the night of Samirah's show—a day I had been waiting for since I saw her at Irving Plaza with Lucas last spring. I had hoped to spend this day with Lucas, listening to our favorite songs as we moved through the apartment, dancing and eating, drinking and laughing, preparing and dressing until it was time to leave. But in the four days leading up to his own event, he had been preoccupied, and we still hadn't properly made up since our fight. Things felt distant between us, and my heart felt his absence. My chest tightened when he got up for his workout and didn't leave my cheeks, my shoulder blades, my lips, savoring his kiss. I hated that we couldn't share an embrace when he slipped in late at night covered in paint, telling me to go back to sleep whenever I woke from the noise and peeked up at him through my wild afro. I wanted to tell him that I was sorry again, that I missed his encouragement, the way he offered gracious words generously. But I was still angry at him. For his coldness, for all the ways he didn't agree with my career choices when I was trying to make a life for myself, a life for us.

Alicia noticed I'd been holding a fry to my lip for a few minutes as I went on an inward Lucas spiral, and threw a pillow at my head. "Billie? Are you okay? You been frozen like that for a while."

"I don't know. I keep replaying everything that happened with Lucas this week. I feel shitty and annoyed but also just want to be in this moment, with me, with you, and the possibility of tonight."

"You know I love Lucas, and you low-key did mess up the date, but we're here now. I'm here and have always been. Remember the nights you crawled into my window from the fire escape and I got excited thinking it was my crush but it was your ass escaping your mom and Marvin's arguments?"

"Or that time we stress drank too much coffee studying for finals and almost sent ourselves to the hospital? But it was just what you needed to apparently finally share with me that you were bi—as if I'd care." I laughed.

"Or"—Alicia's voice took on a different tone—"the time you were there for me when my mom was first diagnosed with throat cancer. You were there for me when I needed you most. And I'll always do the same for you. Our bond is unbreakable. You're the sister I never had. So like I said, I love Lucas, but we got us."

She was right. Alicia was my family, and she was more than enough to get me through the night.

I looked down at my phone. It was three hours until showtime. We needed to start getting ready so I could be there early to set up, to create the atmosphere that would make people want to come to the event even though the news told us this morning to anticipate two inches of snowfall tonight.

"We should start getting ready," I said, turning toward Alicia. "You can have the other two."

"Thanks," she said, seizing the wings before I finished speaking.

I pushed the covers off me, walked to the kitchen, and put my hands up to the oven that we had turned on to spread heat throughout the apartment. I rubbed them together and pushed them as close to the open door as possible, hoping to warm them enough to perform the tasks needed to get ready for the night: unraveling the twists in my hair that I had meticulously sectioned and moisturized with leave-in conditioner, saturating my skin with cocoa butter so that it glowed, slipping into the outfit I had bought for this occasion, paired with rectangular-shaped medium-size gold earrings and a pair of gold pumps.

Wanting to set the mood, to get myself amped up, I yelled to Alicia as I walked to the bathroom, "Put the playlist I made on."

"Gotchu," she said.

Soon the silence in the apartment was replaced by hard-hitting bass. As Alicia and I got ready, oscillating in and out of the bathroom, we dressed, did our makeup, and sipped glasses of cheap sweet white wine we had also picked up at Duane Reade. I made a mental note to text Samirah, Quincy, and Nina when I was done.

"So how are you feeling?" Alicia said.

We sat beside each other in our outfits—she in a black bandage dress and hot-pink heels, I in an olive-green blazer with a built-in corset and A-line skirt set and black fold-over knee-high boots—waiting for the Uber.

"I mean, I'm excited, but I mostly feel like I'm gonna throw up. And I . . . I wish Lucas was gonna be there," I said, admitting the thing I had been holding in since I walked through her apartment door.

"Yeah, I know, girl, but y'all will get it together. He has his thing. You have yours. I'm impressed by all y'all's creativity, honestly." She laughed.

"Nah, but for real, y'all both tryna accomplish shit and ain't nothing wrong with that. You'll see him later at his event, and I bet everything will be back to normal then."

"Yeah, normal sounds good," I said.

•

Alicia and I were the first people to arrive, and I felt raw, as scraped out as an Italian ice with those wooden spoons, as I surveyed the space, wishing Lucas could see what I'd done, who I became when I was doing the thing I was made to do.

The venue had been cleaned, and the surfaces that were usually covered in grime shined under the light. The stage that sat in the center of the back wall had been lit with a kaleidoscope of color that would only enhance the ensemble I saw in the picture Samirah had texted me earlier.

I pulled out the drink tickets I had bought from the good ninety-nine-cent store and looked around the space for the manager. I caught eyes with him right as he appeared from the back, holding a water bottle in his hand.

"Keith, hi, I'm Billie. I work with Samirah. We spoke on the phone a couple days ago?"

"Oh, yes, hey," he said, shaking my hand.

He positioned himself toward the stage and gestured to it with his hands. "So Samirah will be performing over there. There's a room for changing in the back. It's small, but it'll do the job. We're gonna set up a table at the front to check for names on the guest list and provide wristbands for people who will get drink tickets—you got those, right?"

I handed him the roll of tickets, and he cradled them in the pit of his right arm.

"Okay, we'll give two tickets to each person who paid for the event. Drinks for you and your crew are part of the package." He looked around the rest of the room as though he were searching for something. One of his staff members caught his eye, and he called out to them. "I have to take care of some other things, but if you need anything else, let me know."

"Sounds good. Thanks so much."

He nodded and walked off.

"Ayeee," Alicia said once he was out of earshot. "Look at you settin' up whole-ass concerts like a big shot."

"Thanks, girl. Quincy helped too. Teamwork makes the dream work. . . . Speaking of teamwork, will you help me set these up on the tables?"

From the reusable bags we'd lugged into the venue, I pulled out the food I'd negotiated with an acquaintance who had a side business selling plates. In exchange for two hundred dollars that I covered with tutoring money, she supplied me with creative remixes of hood classics that matched Samirah's vibe: deconstructed chopped cheeses, beef patty bites atop a bed of oxtail fried rice, mini mac and cheeses with fried wingettes.

Alicia and I also put together gift bags last weekend that held shot glasses inscribed with *Samirah* and lighters we'd glued glittery rhinestones onto.

Alicia and I set the food and bags on the table near the back of the venue. After we finished, Alicia wandered off to get a drink, and as she walked to the bar, my eyes trailing her, I saw Nina coming through the door. I caught her attention and waved her over to me.

"Hey," I said. We dipped in to give each other hugs, and I caught a whiff of perfume, a cinnamon, honey, vanilla concoction that I realized she only put on for special occasions, recalling the smell of her the night I went with her to Alana Negrita's album-release party.

"Hey, girl," she said. "I like this lil setup. The food and gift bags and stuff. Nice. Did Samirah get here yet?"

"Thanks! I be trying, you know," I said. "But nah they're not here yet. . . . Matter fact let me shoot her a text and make sure she's not gonna be late. She was linking up with Quincy, and they were gonna drive over here."

"Got you this," Alicia said as she walked up and placed a drink in my hand.

"Oh, thanks, girl."

She fake-coughed and darted her eyes toward Nina, who stood on the opposite side of me, likely trying to figure out who it was standing next to her best friend in such close proximity.

"Oh, I forgot you haven't met before," I said. I met Alicia's stare and mouthed, *Be nice,* to her before I tapped Nina. "This is my best friend, Alicia. Alicia, this is my colleague Nina."

"Nice to meet you. I've heard so much about you," Alicia said, putting on her best customer-service voice and reaching out to shake Nina's hand.

"Alicia. Likewise. So nice to meet you. How are you ladies? Y'all ready to get into it? I know I am, considering how much Billie has talked this girl up." She swayed her hips, not so much that it constituted dancing, but enough that she looked like someone ready to unwind, ready to take down her hair that was swept up into a taut topknot, shake it out, and slink onto the dance floor, unbridled, body surrendered to the beat of a song.

"As soon as Samirah hits the stage, it'll be a vibe. You'll see," I said.

I looked toward the entrance again and saw that people had begun to filter in. Samirah's fans hailed from all of New York City, and the audience tonight reflected that in their outfits. Uptown girls were dressed in short, tight dresses and primary-colored heels, and I imagined that they were used to this kind of thing—freezing their asses off as they made their way to the venues, sacrificing warmth and comfort for free drinks and guaranteed entry to a place that deemed them sexy enough not to have to wait in line with the rest of the commoners. There were men too, in their T-shirts and jeans, sprinkled throughout. And then there were the white girls, the ones who wanted to prove they were underground and edgy, who looked scared, as though they should never have ventured to the Bronx at all. They all wore outfits that matched in theme and color—black tops, oversize light-wash straight-legged jeans, and white sneakers—like they had planned it so they wouldn't lose one another, as if they were spread out across a theme park and not a lounge in the hood.

I swept my eyes across the room once more, taking in the way people stared and pointed at the gift bags and the way they excitedly walked over to the food table or the bar, eager to down a free drink or two.

I joined in Alicia and Nina's conversation that had turned toward Kyrie Kash's new video, where she hopped on a remix of a new single from Nena Flame, another rapper. In a series of garishly decorated rooms, Kyrie Kash and Nena Flame rapped about their sex lives in gratuitous detail. As I thought about the women dressed in skin-tight animal-print outfits rapping about the wetness of their privates, the way they could entice men with their superior sex skills, the way they reveled in receiving well-deserved pleasure in the deepest parts of themselves, it made me think of what Samirah would be up against. These new rappers—women who had achieved new heights of success in the genre, had fought for and were committed to their own sexual agency, and repped their hometowns fiercely—still faced scrutiny, scrutiny from their male peers who deemed them less than for talking about the same things they did, for daring to delight in femme desire, for selling sex like their music labels and their audiences demanded. They would be her competition. And Samirah would be compared with them, pitted against them, made their official enemy, because the industry couldn't stand to see women working together, making room for more than one at the top.

As I thought about how I could make sure Samirah got the treatment, media attention, and company resources she deserved, she and Quincy texted me in the group chat that they'd be at the venue in five minutes. I gathered Nina and Alicia, who had been immersed in a conversation about all the famous women who had appeared in Kyrie Kash's new video, and directed them toward the room in the back so I could be ready for when Samirah arrived.

•

There are some moments in life that move in slow motion. Things somehow seem sleeker, brighter, like someone has taken a remote to your eyes and moved the timer to half speed in order to catch whatever ravishing thing had consumed your attention. That is what it was like when Samirah walked into the venue with Quincy. Her black hair—that flowed seamlessly into a blondish gray and that was adorned with rhinestones at the hairline—swayed behind her. Her glam beat was impeccable. She was shrouded in a long white faux-fur coat, but beneath was an ice-gray two-piece—a crop top and leather shorts—paired with thigh-high leather platform ice-gray boots. She was the most sickening person there.

The crowd, busy mingling among themselves, stopped to look as she walked, as she flipped her hair, smirked in a way that said she knew she deserved all their attention, and glided over to us. It was captivation at its finest.

"Samirah," I said. "Wow. You look amazing."

"Well, it's my first show with the industry folk, so you know I had to gag them real quick," she said.

"Yeah, well, whatever you were going for, you did that shit," I said. "Hey, Quincy, good to see you too."

"What's good, Billie? You ready for tonight? Shit is about to be a movie."

"After all these months of prep? Hell yeah. I got Nina in the back. My friend Alicia's there too. Let me take y'all there," I said.

Nina and Alicia were already situated in the room the size of a Lower Manhattan studio apartment when I knocked on the door and announced Samirah and Quincy. I could tell by the way Nina's eyes roved over her, like she was calculating Samirah's presence, that a good impression had already been made.

The five of us crowded in front of the vanity that had three out of six lightbulbs lit up above the mirror like it only believed in the sanctity of odd numbers. The room was sparsely decorated, with a small love seat, basically a glorified chaise, in the left corner; a money-green leather sofa, a callback to nineties-era opulence, cracking in spots, leaving behind the gray of its dull fabric beneath; and a stack of beat-up boxes housing any number of trinkets in the corner opposite the chaise. The smell of recently used mops that permeated the air made sure I'd never forget the scent of something damp and rotting.

"Okay, so now that we're all here," I said, looking from Quincy and Samirah on my right to Nina and Alicia on my left, "introductions. Quincy, Samirah, this is my colleague Nina. I've told her all about you both."

"Yes, she has," Nina said, reaching across me to shake their hands. "I'm excited to see what you've got, Samirah. And, Quincy, I'm sure she'll be backed by some of your beats—I'm impressed by what I've already listened to, but I bet hearing it in person is going to be even better." She flashed a smile.

"Thank you, thank you," Samirah said. "I just want you to know that I'm a star in the making. No one's doing it like me right now. I know you haven't seen me perform yet, but I promise you when I finish, you're gonna want more."

Nina laughed. "You're confident. I like that. I'm sure I will." Nina touched her hand to Samirah's shoulder.

"Yeah, I'm feeling myself today. You got to if you want other people to, you know?" Samirah said.

"Good point," Nina said.

“And this is my best friend and media coordinator extraordinaire, Alicia Reynolds, who works over at *Kulture Magazine*.”

“Hey, girl. Big fan. I made sure my boss put you up on that listicle on the site so we could get more people to the event tonight. I can’t wait to see what you do,” Alicia said.

“I already know Ima shut shit down. ’Cause that’s what I came here to do. But right now. I just appreciate y’all’s love, you know? Ain’t too many women out here looking out for me. So the write-up, this event, just everything. I am so grateful for it. It makes me happy that for once Black women are in charge. We need y’all, ’cause sometimes it feels like—oh and Quincy too, my bad,” she said, nudging him next to her.

He shook his head playfully, then, “Nah, you good.”

“But yeah. Sometimes it feels like no one’s got our back. No one’s willing to put someone like me on, willing to see potential in people like me who no one ever gave a real fuck about. It makes me feel like ain’t nobody ever gonna be down for us but us. And that Black sisterhood—shit, ain’t nothing else like it in the world.”

This was everything I wanted A&R to be. Samirah’s gratitude, how she felt heard and seen, it was the thing that had fueled me all this time. She knew that I was in her corner to protect her, to build her up, to be there for her in a way no white exec like Connor or Evan or Michael could. I saw her. We saw her. All of her. So the warm and vindicating feeling that rose up in my chest, spread through me, and threatened to spill out of my throat? I never wanted to let that feeling go.

“A’ight, a’ight. On that note, I think that deserves a round of shots. Let’s make a toast.” Quincy pulled a bottle of Casamigos and plastic cups from a bag and tipped the bottle into each cup, counting to four with each pour, and handed them to us one by one. “To all of us, and to a good fucking show.” He raised his cup in the air.

The rest of us raised our cups with him too and tilted them back into our throats.

“Woo,” I said, wiping remnants of the liquor from my mouth with the back of my hand.

“Okay, we’re going to give you some alone time, but break a leg! You’re gonna be great. I know it." I moved closer to her and gathered her into a hug. Once we pulled apart, I ushered Nina, Alicia, and Quincy out of the room, leaving Samirah with a final wave.

•

After fifteen minutes of downtime spent with my makeshift crew, drinking and talking about the state of things, about the particulars of what it meant to inhabit a brown body in this industry, in this world, the MC for the night stepped onto the stage—interrupting the beginnings of a conversation about the top five rappers over the last three decades that I was sure would lead to an all-out argument in the middle of this life-altering event—and made introductory comments to the crowd. When the MC finished getting the crowd riled up, he called Samirah to the stage. As Quincy and I had planned, a cacophony of lights illuminated the stage along with a shroud of light fog. Samirah made her way to the front, and one of her songs started playing in the background, announcing her musical arrival.

Bouncing onto the stage in large, confident strides, Samirah addressed the crowd.

"Wassup, New York," she said. "Damn, y'all look good. . . . Thank ya for coming out even though it's brick as fuck out there. Before I get into any of my songs, I also wanna thank ya for riding with me. For supporting my shit. I wouldn't be where I am now without y'all. And I want to thank each and every one of you from the bottom of this Bronx girl's heart. Now, are ya ready for a good fucking show?"

A raucous cheering rippled through the room.

Her gaze swept the crowd, a smile splashed onto her face.

She motioned toward the DJ behind her, who threw on the beat to her newest single. It was the single I'd helped fine-tune—rich, energetic, bass-heavy beat that fluttered with warm guitar and quick high hats. She bopped her head forward as she danced from the right side of the stage to the left before she started singing. The song was about a date gone wrong, a man gone wrong. And as she sung about a man who couldn't handle her success, the way she was perpetually undeterred no matter what social media hotep leaders spouted, I could see people getting into it. They started to raise their drinks in the air, sway their bodies, their hips swinging in time with the four-four measure. They started to unwind.

I looked toward Nina for the first time since she started, and she was captivated. She looked rapturously toward the stage as she nodded her head. I saw Nina take in Samirah's dancing, the riffs she added into the song after the hook. The small smile that Nina held on her face as Samirah walked on stage, that widened the more she watched. After studying Nina all this time, the way her face could sometimes be impenetrable, I knew this time she was fucking loving it.

As she continued performing, a cloud of weed smoke went up in the air, and it was clear people were vibing. They were feeling this joint. The song was unequivocally a hit.

I wanted to feel like them—taken fully by the music, by the performance—but there was a restless unease working its way through my body with each minute that passed. I knew that my win tonight came at the cost of Lucas, his show, his art that he had hoped to share with me.

I shot Lucas a text to let him know that no matter what, I would support him.

> Hey babe. I just wanted to say good luck with Sunsetlandia tonight! I am so proud of you. I hope you know that you inspire me every day. Your passion. Your creativity. Your resolve. I am often in awe of you. And I want you to know that after all we've been through the last few years, I won't let a few bad months change that. I can't wait to see Sunsetlandia later. I know it will be great. Break a leg.

I sighed and turned my attention back to the stage.

When the song finished and the applause had quieted, Samirah's playful, upbeat demeanor changed into something serious. She stood solemnly in the center of the stage as the beat died down, commanding the audience to attention. She walked over to the mic stand situated at the corner of the stage and brought it to the center as she prepared to launch into the genesis of the next song.

"A'ight. This one is a change of pace, y'all, but I wrote this one when I was living out of my cousin's basement and eating noodles and frozen pancakes for all my meals. Y'all know them times. Them times when everything's going wrong. Job's got you fucked up. Relationship ain't going right. Living situation's a mess. But you know what? I ain't let that stop me. I put all that, that emotion, that hurt, that down-and-out, into this joint on paper and then into this single, and it gave me peace and solace when there wasn't any, and I'm hoping it does the same for you."

A slow, trumpet-filled, piano-heavy song began to play about a woman on the verge of a breakdown because of pressure—pressure from her mother, from her friends, from life, the way it forces people to deal with things breathlessly, endlessly, because, as they say, it stops for no one, and as she sang, with the spacy, heady beat behind her, I could see people swaying in the crowd, their faces contorted in concentration, in smiles that hid the pain buried beneath.

Once that song finished, she moved into one about self-esteem, one that honored her body and her mind, that had a pulsing, warbly bass and featured futuristic high-hat sounds that made for an irresistible beat to twerk to and one that made the faces that were momentarily pinched in pain turn up into easy smiles, into mouths pried open from joy, elation at being proud and free, liberated from worry, if only for the duration of the song.

As Samirah sang and grooved, Nina and I had been exchanging glances, turning toward each other whenever she had been relatable, engaging, or entertaining, showing the telltale signs of a person capable of captivating a crowd. I could see that Nina was interested by the sway of her hips and hair, the curve of her smile, the wave of her shoulders.

Nina was sold.

When Samirah finished her set, uttering a heartfelt goodbye to the audience, I turned to Nina, who was standing next to me. "So what did you think?"

"You know, she's a little rough around the edges, but the girl has got big potential."

"So that means she's a go for a meeting at the office?" I asked. I clasped my hands together and focused on my breathing so I wouldn't pass the fuck out from my excitement.

"Yeah. Definitely," she said. "And congratulations to you too." She had ordered a drink, and as she finished her sentence, two drinks appeared, the waitress handing one to me and one to Nina, a rum and Coke and a vodka soda, respectively. "Not everyone has the ear for good artists. People say they do, but when they put it into practice, things just . . . fall apart. But Samirah." She pointed toward the now-empty stage, where the MC was doing his stand-up bit. "That is someone I would have scoped out when I first started in this industry. Someone I would scope out now too, actually. I'm impressed, girl." The yellow lights momentarily spliced her face in half, leaving the left side shrouded in darkness, the right drenched in canary, and the whole of her smile dazzling and broad.

I smiled back at her, hoping it was as disarming as hers had been following her kind words. "Thank you. I really appreciate that."

I felt that familiar wave of relief that left me feeling drowned, immersed in the glow of accomplishment. I looked around and spotted Alicia and Quincy closer to the table and sofas where we first sat when Alicia and I arrived. I said, "Why don't we go tell Quincy and Samirah the good news?"

Together we grabbed Quincy and Alicia and walked to the small room in the back to meet Samirah.

•

"Hey, you were amazing out there!" I said, opening the door to the room. Samirah was standing in front of the vanity, wiping down her face that dripped with sweat.

I ran up to her for a hug, arms outstretched.

"Thanks, sis," she said, laughing, pulling me into her.

"You're welcome. You deserve all the praise," I said.

"You sure do," Nina said, stepping nearer toward where we stood. "You were so good."

"Ayeee, that's wassup. I already knew my girl was gonna kill it. So what's next? We setting that meeting in the office soon or what?" Quincy said, suddenly next to us and pouring the four of us shots as he had earlier in the night.

"Yes, soon. I need to get the director to sign off when I report back on the performance, Samirah's crowd work, stage presence, and all that. After that, Billie and I should be able to schedule a sit-down from there."

"Yes. That's what I'm talking 'bout," Samirah said.

"Yep, so more soon. But hey, listen, guys, enjoy this night. Enjoy the fact that you just killed it out there." Nina lifted the sleeve of her blazer and checked her watch. "I have to run to meet another client now, but Billie can run down the details for y'all about how to prepare. Good night."

Quincy and Samirah waved goodbye, and Nina walked toward the exit.

"Oh, nice meeting you, Alicia. Bye!" Nina said, opening the door, leaving, and Alicia entering after peeling off from the group to use the restroom.

"Nice meeting you too," she said. "I see it's a celebration going on in here. I'm guessing that it's all good news?"

"It is," I said.

"Yay! Samirah, you were so good, oh my god," she said.

"Thanks. Performing is like a high, you know, and knowing that we're 'bout to take it to the next step, that we're 'bout to be official, yeah, I'm feeling extra good," she said. A smirk spread across her heart-shaped face.

"Second toast of the night. Billie, since you helped hook this thing up, you take Nina's shot," Quincy said.

"Oh, nah, I'm good. I need to get to my boyfriend's art show in one piece. Speaking of which . . ." I pulled my phone from my clutch. "Shit. I didn't realize it was so late."

I bit my lip as I thought about Lucas. About the way we still hadn't gotten back to ourselves, about how we were focused on everything but each other.

"Yo, you good?" Quincy asked.

"Damn. I was supposed to be there, like, thirty minutes ago. I'm so sorry, y'all, but I gotta leave, like, right now," I said.

"It's cool. Samirah and I were going to a party my boy is throwing in Brooklyn. Alicia, you can come through too if you want?"

Alicia said that she was down.

"Okay, y'all. Sorry again. It sounds like fun. I'm there next time. And I will be in touch about the meeting first thing tomorrow."

"Cool. Thanks again for everything," Samirah said, pulling me into a hug once more.

“Of course,” I said.

A twinge of something unnamed, maybe regret or the salt of bittersweetness, settled into me as I gave Alicia and Quincy hugs, and I was reminded I couldn’t celebrate this moment longer or linger in the success of the night.

I ignored that feeling as I gathered my coat from the chaise, thinking about Lucas, about art and the way it could change everything. I made my way into the night as snowflakes started to fall to the ground. I pulled my hood over my head and waited for my car.

22

Hearing Lucas talk about what Sunsetlandia would look like over the last few months—the lights, the photos, the walls, the ambiance—gave me a sense of what I could expect from the event, but I wasn't prepared for what I walked into when I stepped into the venue.

There were at least two hundred people crowded into the space, even as the event drew closer to its end. Some sat and stood at tables near the bar and danced near the DJ booth, others lingered in the rooms and savored his work with hungry eyes. And the walls, themed by room, were engulfed in color. In one room there were brilliant blues and emerald greens, in another vibrant reds and yellows, the next bursting in lilacs and violets, and finally magentas, oranges, and hot pinks. The colors were a part of paintings on the walls that showcased the various glories of nature where the sun rose, hung, and fell beyond mountains and plains, over knolls and hills, behind skylines and dusty backroads. Then there was his photography. Each themed room dripped with photos that showcased the opposite of nature—they showed Black people doing everyday things in the Bronx as the sun illuminated them: people bathed in soft sunrise light as they descended the subway stairs at Grand Concourse on their way to work. Lustrous mornings that haloed mothers hanging clothes on racks that sat on their front porches in Longwood. Sunset that illuminated Black and brown kids who ran through sprinklers, threw sand at one another, and climbed jungle gyms in the fleeting days of summer at Pelham Bay Park. Golden hour as the light reflected off the glass of the barbershop in Castle Hill while some men got and others waited for haircuts. Bright-yellow moonlight that made the tricks the teens did at the River Avenue Skate Park even more impressive. Sunsetlandia, with its tribute to light and nature, city life and culture, had highlighted our community beautifully. In that moment, as I looked around, catching glances from curious brown faces, I fell in love again, could feel my insides swelling with pride that I knew and loved someone who could create beauty like this.

I started to take out my phone to capture my surroundings on social media but remembered that I was already so late. I opted to call Lucas instead.

I called three times, but my calls went unanswered. So I went searching for him through the rooms. Eighties music played in the background as I walked and touched my hands to the walls, tried to feel him within. I searched for the exact brown of his skin in any man matching his height and build. I longed for a glimpse of his freshly braided hair that grazed his shoulders. Finally, I found him in the magenta room, surrounded by a group of men and women dressed in bold colors and brash patterns, snakeskin and croc, paisley and seventies-style stripes, that somehow looked like they would effortlessly match every room they walked into.

Lucas stood in the middle of the crowd, gesticulating with his hands. Between the crowd and the colors that swirled around us, he hadn't seen me enter. I walked closer to the group, praying that I broke in at the tail end of someone telling a joke so that I could insert myself into the conversation without the awkwardness of trying to be interesting and relatable. Thankfully, as I got closer, the group started to disperse.

"Hey, superstar," I said, standing opposite him, the space between us now devoid of other bodies.

"Hey," he said. "I see you finally made it an hour away from closing." He looked at me, smile on his face, but no light in his eyes, a bite in his normally playful banter. He shifted from one foot to the other, one hand in his front pocket, the other casually at his side.

"I'm late, I know, but I wouldn't miss this for the world. Honestly, Lucas." I took on some gesticulating of my own. "This is amazing. There are so many people here! You really did your thing. I'm so proud of you," I said. I moved into him for a hug and prepared myself for rejection, for any slight movement that meant that he'd rather not be near me, touching me when all he really wanted was the distance between us.

"Thanks, I appreciate it. But, babe. You missed my opening speech," he said softly, hugging me back. In his eyes was the hurt that I hoped wouldn't be there.

"I know and I'm sorry. I wish I could have caught it. I really do. How can I make it up to you?"

"All of the major stuff is done until we have to break down. Come here," he said, grabbing my hand. "I want to show you something."

We started walking slowly through the exhibit, peering into each room until we arrived at a room I hadn't noticed before, a room the color of flames. We stopped in front of a photograph of a sunset in the West Village, hills painted on the walls behind it. I stared at the picture, trying to understand why this one felt familiar to me, like perhaps I'd lived and breathed in that moment now hanging on the wall, as Lucas stared, waiting to catch my reaction. When it finally hit me, I realized it had been taken the evening of my first day at Lit, and if I looked to the right of the photo, which showed a tree-lined street, cars parked on either side, I saw myself in the reflection of a window, smiling.

I gasped, and my hand moved to my face on its own.

"I brought everyone into this room and gave this whole speech about how you inspired me and you weren't even here," Lucas said, finally breaking the silence. "Told them that you were sharing art in another way, your own way, but now I'm not so sure that's even true. We've just felt off. Look, I love you, Billie. I want you to be happy. But it feels like maybe you lost something. Like all you care about is money, success for yourself at the cost of success for other Black people. This is not you. You never been about that all these years I knew you. I've seen the way you help your mom. I know you want to help people. But I can't see how this is a part of that. I can't see how this is not sellout behavior. But if you tell me this is what you want, what you really fucking want, I will believe you, but Ima have to figure out how I still fit in all of this."

"Lucas," I said. I thought back to that feeling caught in my throat when I watched Samirah perform. When Nina had seen what I saw, and then I knew. I knew nothing else would make me feel this way. Nothing else but music would be enough. "Tonight was one of the best nights of my life. I can't describe to you how fucking lucky I felt to be doing what I've always dreamed of doing. Like what you're doing here. It's where I belong. God, it's so fucking exhausting. But it makes me happy. I want you to know that. I want you to know that through everything, I would choose this again. And I would choose you to be on this journey with me. I know we're not us right now. But I need you. I need you to be on my side. So that we can do this life together.

"I know you think we see things differently, but I don't actually think that's true. You care about art existing as freely as it can, and for many musicians, singers, songwriters, the right kind of launchpad and financial backing can help them do that, live more freely in their creativity. I want to be the conduit, and yes, Lit damn sure has its flaws, and who knows if I'll stay there or try for another label. But what I do know is I want this life, of discovering new music and bringing it to the world. It's that simple. Not the bad deals, not the corporate bull, but it is a part of the journey to me figuring out my place here."

"Okay," he said. "I believe you, and I support you, but I do need things to change between us. For you to figure out how to make me, us, a priority again too. It really hurt looking into the crowd and not seeing the woman who'd been the light for me out there."

"Again, I'm so sorry. To make it up to you, I've got something to show you when we get home." I stared into his eyes intensely and then pulled him in for a passionate kiss. We stood in the middle of that fiery room, holding each other until another group of people filtered in, and another and another. We, it seemed, were never going to let go again.

●

When we got home, I made Lucas lock himself in our bedroom so I could prepare his surprise. After our big fight a few days ago and me missing most of Sunsetlandia and being absent from our relationship over the last few months, I knew I had to make it up to him in a big way. I'd gone down to Michaels on

Twenty-Third and Sixth and picked up candles, streamers, a custom banner I preordered to hang across our walls, construction paper, two glue sticks, and a large foam presentation board.

I placed the candles all around so the whole apartment was cast in incandescent light. I hung the colorful streamers and banner on the wall with tape. It read, WELCOME TO SUNSETLANDIA PART II. On one of the walls opposite the kitchen table, I mounted the foam presentation board. I cut up yellow construction paper to mimic sun rays and glued them to the edges of the board. Then in the middle, I glued pictures I had developed of me and Lucas that we'd taken over the years: a selfie of me and Lucas as we studied in our school's library; a picture of us the night we moved into our apartment as we sat on the floor, laughing and eating pizza straight out of the box; a picture of us at the Grand Canyon that one year, earbuds shared between us as Lucas stared out into the expanse; a picture of us cuddled in Central Park during a fall picnic where cheap white wine spilled all over my shirt and he gave me his flannel so I wouldn't have to walk around the city with a wet top; a picture of us with my hair sweated out, Alicia whooping at the camera while Lucas smiled at me, holding me in a side hug, his eyes rimmed with red after a crazy night out. I pasted these and a dozen other photos artfully on the board.

After thirty-six minutes, everything was ready.

"Hey," I said, entering the bedroom. "My surprise is ready for you."

Lucas looked up from his phone. "Yeah? What you got for me?" He smirked, and I wondered for a second if he'd heard me cutting paper and gluing things together like a madwoman.

"You'll see. Close your eyes," I said.

He obliged, and I grabbed his hand to lead him out into the living room. "Okay, you can open them."

He stood in the middle, taking in everything around him. Then his mouth curled up into a smile. "Babe, this is—wow."

"So what do you think? Obviously, this can't compare to the original, creative, amazing Sunsetlandia from this evening, but I wanted to do something to show you that what you created matters. Your art matters. And I'm sorry again that I missed it. But I also want you to know that you and I, that matters to me too. I wanted this opportunity to celebrate us. As Black folk trying to find light and love in this world. But also to celebrate light that has existed in our relationship all along."

I walked up to him and grabbed both his hands in mine. "I know I have been acting like an asshole. Not seeing you or hearing you. But that stops now. I'm committed to us. To you. And no matter what happens at Lit, I don't ever want to forget that again."

Lucas pulled me into a bear hug. "I love it. Thank you, Billie. Really," he said, holding me closer to him by my waist. "I love you. And I hope that from now on we can talk to each other. Even when we don't agree or if one of us fucks up. We're in this together, a'ight?"

"I know," I said.

We hugged again and then looked at the gallery of our love glowing in the candlelight.

•

Lucas and I ended the night making up. Usually our sex was sensual and passionate, all tender kisses and gentle caressing, but tonight, we fucked furiously, him pulling me toward him, me on my knees. We moved together. Our tongues explored each other's slippery skin, each of us working out our frustrations until we came at the same moment, heads tilted toward the sky. When I woke in the morning, sore but gratified, our bodies were still intertwined.

I grabbed my phone from the nightstand and looked at the screen. It was almost time for work. I untangled my body from his, careful not to disturb him as he slept and ignored his early morning workout, and hurried to the shower, texting Nina on the way there to talk more about strategy.

Billie:

Hey, do you have time to strategize re Samirah meeting sometime today

Nina:

Let's touch base first thing. Can you get here before nine?

I would have to skip coffee at home and hope there was no train traffic, but if all things went smoothly, I could make it.

Billie:

Yes. See you soon!

•

I made it to the office in time. I pulled off my coat, threw down my bag, and made my way to the kitchen.

"Morning. Thanks for making coffee," I said, already filling my cup. "So about Samirah. What are you thinking? I know we already mentioned her at the meeting last week. When do you think we should bring it up with Michael?"

"If everything is ready to go, I think we should go to him ASAP. Maybe even today? We only have until the end of the month until Ultimate moves in."

I racked my brain, trying to think of what Michael had on his schedule for the day. When I couldn't remember it off the top of my head like I usually did, my mind still fuzzy from the shots and sex from last night, I pulled up my calendar on Outlook on my phone.

"Looks like he has a free half hour around three. We could try for then. Could I get your advice on my pitch? I know you're going to lead, but I was thinking I could lean into Samirah as a person, like what she uniquely brings to the table beyond the music, how she's hungry and smart and versatile, how we could help shape her but keep the part of her that will be true and resonate with fans, you know?"

"Yeah. That sounds good. Let's emphasize that, and I'm gonna comp her to some contemporary artists that match her style and vibe to give him a sense of how she could play in the market. We gotta throw in some big names to get him interested. You know they don't be knowing our Black-famous stars. Anyway, I'll give you a heads-up when I'm about to kick it over to you. If we do everything right, the sit-down could be the day we make her a deal."

I raised my hands into the air and shook them like I'd just gotten selected as a contestant on a game show—a bundle of excitement and hope and a hint of desperation. I broke out into a wide grin. I had come this far, and we were almost at the final step. I would need all the luck I could muster when I walked into Michael's office later.

"Sounds good to me," I said.

She reached out to touch my arm, then nodded and walked out of the kitchen.

"Oh, and"—she whipped back toward me—"just remember that we've prepared all we can. Now is the time to trust our ears and our instincts, and we'll take it from there."

"Thanks, Nina," I said. I walked back to my desk with her and focused on my task for the next few hours—stuffing mailers with promo material for Trick Mirror.

As I prepared the mailing, answered the phones, and coordinated future meetings, I started to feel my nerves ramp up, and I began thinking about the what-ifs. *What if I wasted all this time trying to build Samirah and Michael hates her? What if none of this matters, because I am a nobody at this company? What if I get fired for my insolence? For thinking I could do this thing that I was never equipped to do, never smart enough to handle?*

Those thoughts circulated in the back of my brain as I worked until lunchtime, when I decided to write out the bullet points for Samirah on my notepad, trying to get the doubt, the what-ifs, to stop.

Looking at the facts of Samirah laid out plainly, simple and resolute, I felt better, like I could handle whatever was to come, because I had done all I could to back my shit up with evidence, proof that she could be as good as some of the clients on my colleagues' rosters, that she could be someone fans would care about deeply. Now feeling as calm as I looked on the outside, I finished more items on my to-do list as the clock ticked toward three.

•

I knocked on Michael's door right at three. I made sure to time it after he'd had his afternoon coffee and ensured that he wouldn't be in a bad mood, dismissing us before we even had a chance to argue our case.

"Yes?" he asked.

"Hi, Michael?"

He looked up from the contracts he was signing, his pen hovering over the pages.

"Billie, what's up?" He leaned back in his chair and folded his hands like he was a professor waiting on his student to argue their dissertation, thinly veiled judgment and condescension beneath his stare.

"Well, I was wondering if now is a good time for you? I have something I'd like to discuss if that's okay?"

"Okay," he said. "What is this about? Someone on the phone?"

"No, not at the moment. Actually, I have an artist I'd like to bring up. Nina should be in this meeting as well. Let me go grab her," I said, quickly dashing out of his office.

I called her name, and she got up quickly and walked over to us.

We stepped into the office and eased the door shut.

"Michael, hi," Nina said. "Loving that suit today."

"Thanks. Have a seat. I hear you two have something to discuss?"

We sat in the two chairs in front of his desk, my eyes darting toward the grand skyline through the large windows behind him.

"Yes, we wanted to bring up the artist we mentioned at the staff meeting last week. I'll let Billie give you the pitch, but, Michael, I have to say, Samirah is a real artist with something to say," Nina said.

Michael looked at her, eyes squinting. "Real artists are good. Great, even, if we want to get a chance at the Grammys in the next season. But real artists don't pay the bills, Nina."

"I know. But that's why I'm only bringing you the best. People with big potential. And Samirah is it."

Michael raised his eyebrows curiously. Then he motioned for her to go on, his interest at last piqued enough to try our case.

"She's already getting buzz in magazines and blogs. She's media-genic and gaining followers fast on socials. Her streaming is going up on all the platforms. Last I checked she was at over two hundred thousand monthly listeners on Spotify alone, and that's all grassroots promotion. Imagine what we can do with her with some marketing and publicity. Imagine what sales can do when they have someone they can build. Someone who is more than a one-hit wonder," she said.

She was talking about Connor. About longevity and how whenever it didn't work out with Black artists, with brown artists, he phased them out. Tried a new batch. Rinsed and repeated. Nina was not Connor. What Nina brought, consistently and successfully, were artists that kept you interested and wanting more.

"Okay, so what's she like?" he said.

"Well, Billie discovered her last summer. And since we've been working with her, I've gotten to know her style. I'm seeing shades of Doja Cat with her playfulness and lyricism. She also has that Cardi B appeal—sexy, down-to-earth, funny, topical. Even though they have slightly different audiences, I think the main thing that holds them in the same space is their agency in their music, how they hold dominion over their own stories. I think people are hungry for that right now. Right, Billie?" she said, turning to me.

When she said my name, I jolted out of my trance, me staring at Nina, studying how she works, how she casually showcases her skill, her thorough knowledge of the industry. I pulled in a deep breath and focused on trying to emphasize Samirah in the way that Nina had—bringing her talents to the surface, showing him why she deserved it all.

"Yes, so," I started, "I've been tracking Samirah's career over several months. I first heard about her accidentally—at a concert I was attending with my partner. And she was incredible. People were there to see Wazy, but they responded well to her even though they didn't know her music. It was really something to watch. Anyway, I connected with her producer that night, and since then, I've been working to help boost Samirah's social media and presence in the hip-hop scene as well as a few new tracks she premiered at an event yesterday." I looked toward Nina, hoping I was hitting the mark, and when she nodded in a way only I could see, seemingly in approval of how I was handling the meeting, confidence settled into my bones, and I sat up straighter and continued.

I moved my eyes to meet Michael's, and he was squinting in the way he did when he was trying to analyze something. It was the first time he'd looked at me that way. Like I was saying something worth his mental calculations. Feeling like I had more control over the meeting now, I went on.

"She had a performance yesterday that blew everyone away. A few people from the press were there. People in the audience posted all over social about the food, curated drinks, and gift bags I put together for the event, and of course the new songs Samirah revealed that night. Samirah is just . . . captivating, and her songs are raw and real and original and not like anything that's out there right now."

I felt Nina glance at me, sensitive as I was to her every movement, waiting for her to complete our already-compelling argument. "And that is why I think we should set a meeting. We know the fans are there. We know the press is catching on. We know people are liking the music. The last step is just for her to show you what we already know. . . . What do you think, Michael?" she said.

Nina's question hung in the air as I watched Michael, tracking his eyes as he darted them between us and considered the duo Nina and I made. As sweat began to build beneath my breasts, soaking my good bra, I practiced taking slow, deep breaths, trying to avoid passing out from anticipation.

Sweat snaked down my stomach as he tried to decide which one of us was the lead, which one of us would run the meeting and help Samirah through the signing process. Knowing Nina's track record already, how he had once put his faith in Alana Negrita and D. Salaz, he nodded at Nina. Then, "Okay. Great pitch. She sounds interesting. Send me all you have, and I'll listen tonight."

"I will send it right after this meeting," I said. I stifled a smile, telling myself that this was only a beginning, a jumping-off point toward negotiation. But I couldn't help when the corners of my mouth turned upward ever so slightly.

"Great, and, Billie, get a meeting on the calendar for tomorrow. You know my schedule. Find a good time."

"Absolutely. I will take care of it ASAP," I said. "Thanks so much, Michael. Looking forward to the meeting."

"Yeah, thanks, Michael. We hope you'll love her," Nina said.

"Yeah, we'll see," he said.

Nina and I stood and walked back to my cube together.

"Oh. My. God," I whispered loudly. I stood and tried to quiet the squeals that wanted to escape through my open mouth.

Nina and I had run through the pitch like an oiled machine. The feeling working through me was only rivaled by the first time I'd gone to a music festival.

I'd managed to take off time from my two jobs to go to Afropunk when it was still true to its cause, when it was still a refuge for Black alt and soul music, for artists that didn't find their music on airwaves but instead in the ears of those that didn't mind digging to find treasure. I'd taken the train deep into Brooklyn and was surrounded by beauty from the moment I stepped into Commodore Barry Park, the music sometimes melodious and deep, other times loud and thick with angst, washing over me—it was my favorite day of that entire year and a memory that I recalled often so that I'd never forget the way it filled me like I had been nothing but hunger before then.

"Thank you so, so, so much," I said.

If Nina was feeling excited, she was playing coy about it. Her smile was demure, muted as she locked eyes with me. But when she said, "Feels good, don't it?" giving me a shoulder hug, I knew that she was feeling positive about what we'd done back there.

"Go ahead, bask in it," she said. "But remember that there's still a chance Michael won't want to sign her. Either way, just make sure you, Samirah, and Quincy are prepared for tomorrow."

"I will. Can't wait."

I sat at my desk and did what Michael had asked—I found an open slot and plugged in Samirah's meeting. Then I sent all the materials I had on Samirah to Michael.

I sent a hurried text to Quincy and Samirah, writing *urgent* in all caps, letting them know to drop everything for this meeting.

They texted back in seconds, at record speed.

Quincy:

Let's fucking goooooo!!! Mirah what I told you that day I made that beat for you? We almost there *brown strong arm emoji*

Samirah:

I can't believe we did it yo. Ahhhhh we out here!! Ima start practicing Two Ways for the performance part of the meeting. Ima kill that shit tomorrow!

●

On the way home, the D Train stopped in between the 125th and 145th stations for seventeen minutes, where the internet didn't even try to meet us halfway with at least a couple of bars of service, but that couldn't shake me. Not even the man who stood in front of the doors and shouted at people about Jesus and how we were all probably going to go to hell bothered me as it usually would. I was too pumped about this deal.

Once I was off the train, I practically ran home to tell Lucas in person the news that I had alluded to in my texts to him earlier.

"Babe," I said.

"I'm in here," he yelled from the kitchen. "Got your text earlier, babe. I'm really proud of you."

I walked over and gave him a hug. Then grabbed some red wine out of the fridge and poured us each a glass.

"Thank you. That means a lot," I said. "Anyway, how did everything with Sunsetlandia really go? Are people talking about it? How much did you make from the event? Tell me everything!"

"Yeah. It's all over Instagram. TikTok too. Did you see? Check the hashtag."

I pulled up Instagram on my phone and clicked on the account he had created for the event and encouraged people to include in their posts via signs at the venue as they walked through each room. Hundreds of people had tagged the account, taking pictures and videos of the walls; of people dancing as the DJ played Black music from every era, every genre that celebrated Blackness, the way its genius was everywhere, sick percussive house, bounce, and Jersey club music that inspired people to put in footwork, to nineties and early aughts classics shouting out the Bronx—"Uptown, baby, we gets down, baby"—to sultry modern songs that made people slow dance together and rap that made people chant, "They not like us," along with the music; and of his photography in all its colorful brilliance.

I touched my hand to my heart. "Aw, babe. This is amazing. Would it be crazy if I liked and shared every one of these posts?" I asked.

"Uh, yeah. A little bit," he said, laughing, me joining in with him.

"Yeah, you're right, but Ima do it anyway," I said.

"You do that." He nudged me playfully beneath the table, his knobby knees brushed up against mine. "Yeah, so. The page I made for the event has mad followers now too. Everything said and done, I'm happy about the way it turned out. Better than I could have imagined . . . except for a small detail," he said. "Anyway, before you got there, I was talking to some lady. She said that she was impressed by the event and that she sponsors up-and-coming artists. Think she might have worked for the same people that did the Happy Place experience out in LA. Said she wanted to talk with me further. Not sure if I should. This whole time I've been on you for working for some corporation. And now I got this thing in my lap that I don't know if I even want . . . I-I always wanted my art to be mine. Said I'm not gonna let no one change my work. But the funding she has to offer, Billie? It's hella bread. Hard to think about that number and turn it down."

"Oh my god, Lucas." After all this time he'd spent being angry at me for wanting to be a part of something bigger than myself, to give myself over to the cause, here was the same opportunity laid before him. Maybe now he'd finally see that there were good people out there who wanted to help bring art into the world. Maybe this time he'd see that not everyone around him was there to take. Maybe some of them were there to give.

"I mean . . . think about it like this. If you get to keep creative control and they're willing to pay you that much, why wouldn't you take it? You get more visibility. You get your name out there. It's everything you've wanted, right? The money gets you closer to generational wealth. The visibility gets you possibly famous and us out of this bum-ass apartment. What's better than that?"

"You already know what the problem is. How do I know they won't take my shit? Turn it into something I don't even recognize? If there's other people involved, how do I know it's real? That it's still from me? I don't want to be another sellout. Another artist who's only in it for money. For fame. That's not what I'm about."

"I know, baby. I . . . I'm just saying. Maybe this could be good. Talk to her. Get all the details. If you don't think it's right for you, fine. But it can't hurt to hear her out." I reached my hand across the table and sat it atop his.

"Yeah. I'll think on it. . . . Anyway, tell me about your day. It seems like your meeting went well?"

I thought back to the way Nina and I were in sync, how my nerves made it so I'd have to throw my good bra into the laundry.

"It did. I was nervous as hell. But our meeting with Samirah is tomorrow. I don't really know how it's gonna go, but I'm excited. And a little scared? But mostly excited."

"Well, good luck, babe," he said. "I really hope things work out for you." He reached out to kiss my forehead.

"Also, have you talked to your mom? Tell her I got something for her," he said. He handed a white envelope to me. Inside were five one-hundred-dollar bills. "It's part of what I earned with Sunsetlandia after the overhead. I know it's not a lot, but I know how much you help your mom. I figured I could ease your burden."

I was suddenly reminded that I hadn't talked to Mama in a while. I had been busy with Lit, and whenever I wasn't tied up with work or Samirah, I occasionally sent her memes and video clips on social media, but I'd otherwise avoided her. I didn't want to get caught back up in her life again now that things had calmed down since Marvin was done with his summer spending. After the eviction had been settled, Marvin was back to the regularly scheduled programming he always did after the season, making up for his transgressions by offering Mama gifts, backrubs, handling more than his share of the chores so he could get back in her good graces. It was nothing more than him love-bombing her, pretending that he didn't let his own bullshit get in the way of their lives together. But I couldn't get Mama to see it for what it was. Not when Marvin had already been around for more than a decade, offering attention when she felt that no one else in the world took her thoughts, feelings, hopes, seriously, even as he left their lives crumbling, hanging in the balance, as the weather around them turned frigid.

"I'll give this to her when I go see her after the Samirah meeting. There's something I need to say to her face-to-face." I hugged him. "But thank you, babe, really." I looked at him, eyes sparkling with love. We talked more too, me giving him the details of Samirah's event, the meeting with Michael, and what would happen tomorrow; him telling me more about the details of the Sunsetlandia opening, about how it had felt like people were dancing, were looking at his soul on those walls.

Once our food had been eaten; our plates had been scraped; I had laid out my clothes and my hair had been washed, conditioned, and twisted; and Lucas had showered and reviewed recent pictures he took for his next few posts, we collapsed into bed early, both of us thinking of each other as our paths for the future lay ahead of us.

23

As I got ready for work, I caught sight of myself in the bedroom mirror. Nothing about my face had changed. I still had the same arched eyebrows and button nose, the same almond eyes and thick kinky hair, but somehow I felt different, like I had entered a new phase of adulthood.

Eight months ago I had felt hopeless, certain that things would continue on the streak of bad circumstances, but here I was getting ready to lead a meeting at work for the first time today. Here I was ready to set boundaries with Mama. Here I was doing something I had only dreamed about until now. I stopped putting bobby pins in my hair and took in the moment.

•

I got to work early and took the extra time to print out nine sets of the packet I'd created for Samirah—which included recent photos of her, mentions of her in the media, data on her socials and streams from SoundCloud, ReverbNation, Apple Music, Spotify, and others—and put them in the manila folder next to my desk. I had bought a new pack of pens for the occasion and placed them atop the folder. I pulled out the company-issued tablet that Nina had loaned to me for the day and loaded it with Samirah's music, both the new EP that we were pitching to Michael and the rest of the team today and a few of her most popular tracks from earlier projects.

Everything ready, I turned my attention to work and tried not to think about the what-ifs, the doubts that snuck up again as I prepped. *What if this meeting doesn't go over well? What if Samirah and Quincy hate me forever?*

Whatever I was feeling had to wait because I had to show up for her.

I pushed the what-ifs aside, walked to the kitchen to get some coffee.

Nina strode into the office, hair up in a bun, wearing a wrap dress, looking chic as usual.

"Hey," she said, stopping in front of my cube, sipping coffee.

"Hey, you look great. . . . Anyway, I've got everything ready to go. I even brought a backup speaker in case anything goes wrong with the audio in London," I said. I had other backups too. A backup shirt. Backup shoes. Cough drops in case my throat became inexplicably dry. I wanted to be as prepared as possible for my ascent to the rest of my life.

"Good. I'm glad you're prepared. One last thing. After this long at Lit, I know that the best approach to any pitch isn't just passion. Our job is to sell Samirah as the next big thing. It's why I keep a poker face on when I'm in this office, to show them I'm not leading with feelings. I'm leading with good judgment that I can back up with stats and talent. Keep that at the front of your mind when you're in that room, and you're gonna do great," she said.

"Got it. Thanks, Nina. See you in there," I said.

•

I had been watching the clock for hours when I finally got the call from Erykah, who let me know that Samirah and Quincy were now waiting for me in the Lit lobby.

I thanked her and walked to the London room to fill carafes of water and set them on the table. Then I called Michael and let him know that our guests were here and sent an email to everyone else who would join the meeting—Jason from marketing and promotion, Sam from branding, and Gary from publicity. I let Nina know too.

"This is it. Moment of truth," she said.

"I know." I mumbled a sound of excitement as we walked together to grab Samirah and Quincy from reception.

"Hey, Quincy," I said, giving him a hug. He was dressed sharper than usual in a cream henley that showed off his muscles and felt soft against my skin, dark jeans, and loafers. His gold necklace gave the fit a final edge.

As I hugged Quincy, Nina greeted Samirah.

She too had altered her look into artsy business casual—a long tan trench coat adorned with gold buttons that she wore atop her shoulders, Gucci sunglasses, layered gold necklaces, a black shirt tucked into fitted leather pants, and shiny stiletto boots, with her hair in black-to-blond Fulani braids that hung long to her ass.

She looked fierce. Professional. But also like herself, like she was in full possession of her wits and knew she'd have to come with everything she had in order to make an impression.

"Ayeee. Y'all look amazing," I said.

"Yeah, girl. Gotta come prepared. They see me pull up in this fit with my talent? They not gon' even know what to do with me," she said.

"Ha. I like the confidence," Nina said.

"Yeah. I gotta show them why I deserve to be here. Being nervous is not gon' help with that," Samirah said.

I nodded and hoped her words would help me with my bubbling stomach.

I tried to put the thought aside, to quiet my insides that rumbled loudly, before I launched into my speech.

"Okay. So everyone should be in the conference room right now. I had tech set up the room so that I could include the slides I made that match the packets," I said, motioning toward the papers I held beneath my arm.

"I'm going to lead it off. Give y'all an introduction, then Billie will jump in, then we're gonna throw it to you guys to seal the deal," Nina said.

Samirah and Quincy nodded.

"Now, they may ask you to perform a song or two, Samirah. Billie should have told you about this already. You know which songs you'll go with if they ask?"

"Yeah, I was thinking on it last night. Ima do 'Two Ways,'" Samirah said.

"Perfect," Nina and I said in sync.

"Bet," Quincy said. "Let's get it."

With that, the four of us were off to London.

When we arrived at the meeting room, all the conversation between everyone seated at the table ceased. I trained my eyes toward the back of the room, where a baby grand piano sat, trying not to make eye contact and give away the fact that I was terrified to be running the meeting along with Nina, terrified that this could be the thing that got me fired from Lit and ended my career before I'd had the chance to make my mark.

I started to nervous sweat, perspiration pooling in my pits, threatening to show through my shirt beneath my blazer, as I placed a packet in front of everyone seated and finally sat in the chair at the head of the table opposite Michael, next to Nina. Quincy and Samirah sat at the middle of the table so that everyone could get a good look at them.

"Okay, looks like we're all here," Nina began. She paused to study each of the faces in the room and smiled, and I marveled at her confidence, how she commanded the room with style, with an ease that felt natural, unrehearsed.

"Thanks so much for coming, all. I'm excited that you could join me and Billie so that we can share with you the talent that is Samirah. She's an up-and-coming artist from the Bronx. And she's been absolutely killing it over the last few months."

There was a pause, and Nina suddenly threw her eyes in my direction, signaling for me to jump in.

I'd written out what I wanted to say in the meeting, the things I wanted to highlight about Samirah, but as I was trying to recall, my mind somehow emptied of everything I thought I'd never forget. I opened my mouth to speak, hoping that whatever came out of it would make sense.

"Yes, exactly, Nina. I discovered Samirah a few months ago, and she has impressed me at every turn. Her music is deep and smart and unforgettable. There's a real magnitude to it that I think will appeal to a wide range of listeners. And beyond that, Samirah is just a vibe. Anyway, without further ado, here is Samirah."

Samirah moved back in her chair, slipped a quick smile to Nina, cleared her throat, and waited until people's eyes had snapped in her direction. "I just wanna say thank you so much to everyone here today. Thank you so much to Billie too, who found me at one of my shows and, like, took interest in me like no one else did. Gave me help when I didn't even ask for it. I'm grateful to her, to Nina, to you all for taking this meeting. If there's anything I want ya to know about me, it is that I'm hungry, I'm determined, and I'm a star, baby. Plain and simple. I write all my own music and put everything I have into this, and that's what you'll get if you sign me. My talent. My vision. Me."

"By the way," Quincy cut in, "I've been working with Samirah as her producer for a minute now, and I've never seen someone so talented and determined and just ready to put in the work to be best at what she does."

"Great. Thanks to you both. So," I said. I stood up, then, "If everyone could direct their attention to the slides that correspond with the packets in front of you, I'd like to show you why we should bring Samirah into the Lit family."

As I spoke, the data I presented about her socials and the articles seemed to get no response. I saw blank faces around the table, even some tending toward boredom. I watched as Jason yawned and then tipped back in his chair and laced his hands behind his head, and it made me wonder what people were thinking. It made me wonder if what I was doing was good enough, if I was good enough.

"And now, since we've gone through all of that, I'm sure you want to get down to the real thing—the music."

I touched a couple of buttons on the tablet that was connected to the projector and speakers, and the sounds of Samirah's rapping filled the room.

I looked toward Michael to see if I could gauge his reaction. The blank stare was still pasted onto his face, but there was also a slight movement to his head, like he wanted to bop along to the beat but didn't want to divulge more about his mental calculations in the meeting.

I looked toward Nina for reassurance, and she gave me a small nod. I pulled in a breath, thought about how there was nowhere else to go except forward, so I kept going, and I would not stop until I had won them over.

"This song, which Samirah premiered on her Instagram, made over two hundred and fifty thousand impressions and garnered thousands of likes. And when she performed it for the first time to a live crowd, the response was electric. People were dancing, people were humming the melody, people were filming and going live on social media. It's a testament to how great of an artist Samirah is. Her songs are relatable, they're fun, they're deep, they're inspiring, but most of all, they are resonant."

"Thanks, Billie. Okay, Samirah," Michael said as he leaned farther in, folded his hands together, placed his elbows on the table. "Show us what you've got."

I looked to Nina, who nodded at me, and I cued up the track for "Two Ways" and waited for Samirah to make her moment.

"Billie, you know what to do," she said, rising from the table. She looked at me, then quickly pulled out her chair, all eyes focused in her direction. She walked over to the mic stand. I timed the bass to the second she pulled the mic toward her and began to rap. One hand on the mic, one hand stretched out to the room in front of her, she rapped about money and might. How she would always need money to survive and how she ain't ever had enough of it. How she needed might to bear through it, to help her achieve.

With the surging beat behind her and her quick melodic vocals, I snuck a look around the table and hoped that they would understand the gravity of what we were witnessing. This was the beginning of something, and whether they were on board with it or not, I knew, no matter what they said about her after, that I had been right all along: She was the kind of artist we wouldn't forget, someone we wouldn't come across again so easily if we let her go.

As she moved across the small space in the room and bounced on her knees like nineties Lil' Kim or Megan Thee Stallion on any stage, Michael had tapped his fingers against the hardwood, but as Samirah spat the second verse, the lyrics powerful, her voice reaching its crescendo as she sang the last four bars, the interest swelled, and Michael leaned forward and squinted. Gary and Sam watched, smiled, and nodded their heads at each other. I looked toward Nina again, hoping, but she was fixed on the performance.

Once Samirah had stopped her singing and rapping, her enthusiastic dancing as she demonstrated her prowess, I had expected people to be a little more enthusiastic that I'd found someone who could be a star. But the energy in the room wasn't palpable and strong like an electrical current, it was more like watching lightning through binoculars from my bedroom window.

Still, after Samirah's performance had ended, everyone in the meeting clapped, smiled too, eager to display their interest in her.

Nina had warned me about this reaction days earlier, how in these meetings they would work to keep their faces neutral, stoic, because they didn't want artists to expect too much. They wanted to keep the power in their hands as they contemplated how much they were willing to invest without pressure from artists with their concerns of advance level and percentage points.

"Okay, well, thank you so much, Samirah. That was quite a performance," Michael said. He stood and buttoned his suit jacket. "We'll be in touch soon."

Everyone else seated at the table stood too and began saying their goodbyes, giving out handshakes and exchanging small talk. Quincy was busy shaking Gary's hand, telling him that he was Samirah's manager and that he could give them anything additional they'd need on her, when Nina cut in.

"Yes, thanks, everyone, for attending the meeting. Samirah, Quincy—Billie and I will walk you out," Nina said.

"Yes, thanks so much, everyone. I appreciate you taking the time," I said. I left them with a weak smile, and the four of us crowded together as we walked toward reception.

"So how ya think that went? Hard to tell what they was thinking," Quincy started.

"Yeah, it's a little hard to tell," I said. "But! What we should be focusing on is how great you and Samirah were. I'm so proud. No matter what happens, I want ya to remember that."

"Yeah. I'm feeling good about what I did. Ima try to live in that. Still, I'm nervous now that we gotta wait to see what they say. When do you think we'll hear back?" Samirah looked around and lowered her voice so that Erykah, whose desk was a few feet away, couldn't hear.

"I think we should hear back in the next few days," Nina said. "Either way, like Billie said, I'm proud of us. Both of you should stay by your phone so we can be in touch in case anything comes up in the next week or so."

"A'ight, bet," Quincy said.

"Cool," I said. I looked down at my phone and saw a few missed calls from my office phone that I'd forwarded to my cell before the meeting. I still had my assistant job to do, the one that was actually paying the bills—well, at least some of the bills—so I needed to wrap this up.

"I've gotta get back to my desk, but I should be in touch soon," I said.

Quincy and Samirah nodded, and Nina, who stood beside me, gave Samirah a shoulder squeeze before the two of us walked back to our desks.

“So,” I said to Nina once they were safely on the elevator on the way out of the building, “how did that actually go?”

“I can’t say for sure, but I think it might have gone well,” she said. “This is the way Michael usually acts when he’s thinking of making an offer. Ask him about it before he leaves. But listen, Billie. I have something else to tell you. Do you have, like, five minutes to dip into a conference room?”

What more news could she have for me beyond this? Still, the urgency in her voice made me want to hear what she had to say.

We walked to one of the phone-booth rooms, where Nina quickly shut the door and invited me to sit.

“So what’s going on?” I asked.

“Okay, so you know how I’ve been in and out of the office for a few weeks now?” Nina said.

I nodded, remembering all those afternoons I had looked over to her desk and she wasn’t there. I had assumed she was meeting with or working on stuff for her artists.

“Yeah, so. I haven’t told many people here, because you know we can’t trust everybody. But when I turned down that lateral position Ultimate offered me, that wasn’t the only offer I had on the table. This other label has been tracking me for a while and has been trying to poach me since this whole merger has gone down, and I think they were hoping I was ready to make a move. Turns out they were right. Yesterday G.O.O.D Music Group offered me a job. They want me to be A&R director of a new imprint they’re building.”

Nina was usually calm as she delivered advice or cracked a joke, but now she was radiant, practically bursting with joy as she relayed the news. It was the most animated I had ever seen her, and it made me squeal in response, momentarily forgetting how nervous I felt about Samirah—all I felt was happy for my friend. “Oh my god, Nina, that’s amazing. Huge congrats. You so deserve this,” I said, tugging my lips into a smile.

“Yeah. I’m excited. I start in a couple weeks. My last day here is Friday. I wanted to be out of here by the time Ultimate was all moved into the building. Plus, I wanted to give myself some time off in between because you already know how burned out I’ve been. Anyway, I wanted to let you know soonest.

I'm glad we had a chance to work together. Whatever happens, I hope you stay in this industry. You've got a good ear," she said.

I had wanted more of this. Years of this. Nina's praise. Nina's guidance. Access to her brain, hoping to pick it for useful information, for her wisdom. But now it was gone. All I had left was Samirah.

I tried not to let it show, but I could feel disappointment welling up in my eyes. I cleared my throat quietly. I didn't want Nina to know that I was overcome with loss, that her leaving would mean something was missing from the Lit equation, from me.

I didn't want to seem like a hater when I was genuinely happy for her. This industry was and would always be hard, so her finding a place to grow, to put down roots of her own, was a rare beauty. I decided to play it cool. I blinked rapidly, trying to keep the tears in place. When I was sure I could trust myself, I spoke.

"Thanks. I'm really glad we had a chance to work together too. You were the best mentor I could have ever asked for. Truly. I'm gonna miss you," I said. I jokingly made a sniffling sound like I was on the verge of crying, but that wasn't so far from the truth.

"Well, it doesn't have to be goodbye," she said. She had a curious smirk on her face as she said it. There was more to this news.

"What do you mean?" I asked.

"Well, they're letting me bring someone with me to G.O.O.D., and if you're up for it, I'd love to bring you on as my assistant."

My mouth hung open in shock as I silently evaluated her offer. On one hand, I was touched that Nina felt strongly enough about me to bring me to her new place. She had been wary of me in the beginning, but now her interest was plain. She liked me and saw me doing things with her, alongside her. She saw what I always hoped she had seen in me.

But with everything that I'd been building here, with Samirah, I wasn't sure what the right decision would be. I wasn't sure I was ready to leave it all behind for a smaller label that might not have the space for me when I was ready to build on my own roster.

Over the last almost year, Nina had helped me survive Lit. Had made everything about this experience better. I could only imagine what it would be like to be her assistant, the opportunities that could come with a label willing to take a chance on diverse artists and treat them right. But it had also always been my dream to work at Lit. Even with all that had gone on, was I willing to give that up so soon?

"Nina, thanks so much. I'm flattered, really. But can I have some time to think about it? It's a big decision, and I want to make sure I'm making the right one," I said.

"Yeah," she said softly. "I know I've given you a lot to think about. But could you get back to me by Friday?"

"Will do," I said.

She gave a smile and pressed her hand to my shoulder before she returned to her desk. I stayed in the phone booth a little longer, trying to rearrange my thoughts.

When I returned to my cube, I was calmer, but I was still eager to hear Michael's verdict about Samirah and hoped that his decision would give me some clarity.

I looked toward Michael's office. He wasn't on the phone or occupied with a meeting. I knocked on his door and poked my head in.

"Hi, Michael, sorry to bother you," I started.

He looked up from his computer and waited. I moved farther into his office, and he motioned for me to sit.

"I wanted to check in after the meeting with Samirah. I'd love to know your thoughts . . ."

He pushed his chair back and folded his right leg over the left and leaned back.

"Yeah, Billie, I thought she was good. Really good. There's talent there. I think we can mold her. Why don't you and Nina draft an offer and send it to me for review when it's done," he said.

For once Michael had said something nice to me, but then I remembered who Michael was.

"Thanks so much, Michael," I said.

"But," he continued, "I want you to know, you can't ever do something like this again. This time you had the support of Nina, but still, you are not an A&R rep yet. You are an assistant. You make my appointments, you schedule and coordinate travel, you file expense reports, you get my coffee. It is not your job to find talent. It is your job to be my assistant and to support the team. Until you've paid your dues and been promoted, you need to do the job that you get paid to do. Do you understand?"

"Yes, Michael. I understand," I said.

I suddenly felt the urge to retch, nauseous because it was this very behavior Michael rewarded in Connor. According to Nina, Connor had gotten an assistant role at Lit with no internships or inherent connection to music. He was simply rewarded with it because of proximity and pedigree.

Connor's uncle had played golf with Michael for a decade. Because of his family connections, Connor was able to sign artists well before any other assistant had the opportunity. He fell upward and was promoted two years faster than some of the other reps who had been there years before him. At the thought of it, my mouth went thick with saliva, and I wished I could let it out all over Michael's desk so he could see how it feels to be embarrassed, to be ruined by something noxious.

Instead, I stood up, smoothed my pants, and quickly walked to the bathroom. I locked myself in the last stall from the door. My chest heaving and my makeup on the verge of being ruined, I tried to calm myself down. I tried not to think about what Lit would be like if I signed Samirah but continued working with Michael, if I would feel depleted by his hostility, if everything would be worth it once the Ultimate merger was finalized, or if I took that job with Nina instead. But mostly, I was nervous about how I would tell Quincy and Samirah that I had done it. That everything we had been working toward would be real. I went back to my cube and started to prepare the offer.

•

After work, Lucas and Alicia met me near the office so we could celebrate the Samirah news. I booked a private room located on the subway level of the Forty-Seventh Street–Rockefeller D Train station for fifty dollars an hour. The eight-hundred-square-foot room was decorated with Times Square–themed art and was equipped with free Wi-Fi, a flat-screen, a small sectional, a round coffee table, a sound system, two mics for karaoke, a pool table, and various board games.

I could have taken them somewhere else with better decor and food options, but I couldn't trust the emotions that could leak out of me. I was feeling too many things at once and was as liable to burst into tears as I was to scream excitedly into the sky now that I'd gotten approval to make an offer to Samirah. But there was also Nina's coming departure and offer, Michael's speech about me being an assistant, the fucked-up things I'd heard about Lit and how they might treat their artists, Mama and whether she might need my help again. I didn't have the mental space to be around other people. So we kept it to a party of three. As soon as we sat down, I started putting the karaoke versions of songs from YouTube in the queue, knowing that the two-hour block I booked for the room would be over before we knew it. Lucas cracked open a bottle of something he'd brought with him—a red nutcracker concoction he poured into plastic cups filled with ice. I picked up a cup and started a speech.

"I am so happy it all worked out. It took months of hard work. Mad sleepless nights and early mornings. But I did it. My first artist is about to be signed. Ah, I can't believe it. I just want to thank y'all for your help—Lucas for the photo shoot we did that went viral, Alicia for that article that put Samirah on the map. All of that really made a difference. I don't know if I could've done it as well without y'all."

"We're happy to do it, girl. That's what we're here for. We love you, Billie, there is nowhere to go but up from here, sis," Alicia said.

"Word, babe. Don't let nothing stop you. I'm so proud of you," Lucas said.

We cheersed our cups, and I smiled, grateful that I had the support of the two people who loved me best.

We sang along, karaoke-style, to pop and rap and R&B until our voices went hoarse.

I was tipsy when Lucas and I made it home. I wobbled to the kitchen table to take off my shoes, when I noticed the white envelope still sitting there. It was the envelope with the money Lucas wanted me to give to Mama. I had planned to give it to her this evening, and I was feeling contemplative as tequila settled in my stomach. Now that my career was going somewhere, I considered what I wanted for the rest of the future. Did I want to continue lending Mama money until the end of time? Did I want the extra stress Mama gave me when there was already so much at Lit, in this industry ahead of me?

I stewed in thoughts at the table for a couple of minutes before I put my shoes back on. "I'll be right back," I said, turning to Lucas as he slipped into the shower.

•

"Mama. We need to talk," I said as Mama opened her front door.

She wiped her eyes and nodded. "It's late, baby. But come in," she said, opening the door wider. Now here we were standing in the foyer, unsure of what to say next.

I walked to the kitchen and went to the cabinets for wine glasses. I knew Mama barely liked red, so I pulled the bottle I had bought for her months ago from the top of the fridge and poured a glass, and then sat on the sofa and took a sip. We sat for a while, staring at the TV and waiting for the words to come. After we'd watched a young white couple decide to stay in their newly renovated home over a new build on some HGTV show, I couldn't stand the silence any longer.

"Mama, I did it."

"What are you talking about?"

"With Samirah, with Nina. With Lit. I did everything I thought I would do. I'm signing my first artist that I discovered," I said, smiling.

"I always knew you would, Lili." She turned to me and looked somberly into my eyes. "I knew you'd accomplish whatever you set your mind to."

"Thanks, Mama." I put my hand over hers that sat on her lap. "But that's not why I'm here." I took a deep breath. "I never wanted to be a selfish person. You raised me to be a good woman. To put others before myself. And I've been doing that. My whole life I put everyone before me. I put *you* before me. But I think, in order for me to move forward, for me to really be free to go for what I want, I need to let that part of me go. I can't keep saving you when it's you who keeps letting things happen with Marvin in the first place. I can't let this get to a place where saving you is going to hurt me in a way I can't come back from. So here." I placed the envelope on the table in front of her.

"This is the last money I can give you to help cover any expenses. I can't do it anymore. I can't sacrifice myself because you need Marvin in your life. I can't stop everything to help you when you're the one who's supposed to be in my corner. I can't be the person I'm meant to be if I'm always holding you up. Until Marvin is gone, this is how it'll have to be." My voice broke as tears started rolling down my cheeks. It was the first time I'd said this out loud to her. It was the first time I had been real about how she had hurt me, about the cost of my relationship with her. But she needed to know that I could not do it anymore. I had my own life to live, and I needed boundaries if I was ever going to thrive.

"I never meant for this to happen, Billie. I never meant for Marvin to affect your life like this. I've just been so lost, you know. It was so hard being a single mother without my parents or anyone to guide me. Then Marvin was there for me, and he felt like everything I thought was missing. I thought maybe, when he fucked up, that it could be fixed. Like, one day he would realize what we had, and we could all be happy. I only had to get him to be good again. But it hasn't happened. He's only proved the opposite over and over. I sat by and let it happen. I see now how much damage I've done. I see how you've felt it all came on you. That pressure should have never even been yours to hold." She took my hands in hers. "I understand about the money, baby. I do. And I want you to know that I'm proud of you. Despite what you've been through in your life, you did it. What a strong, smart girl you turned out to be."

I smiled back at her, feeling lighter now that I had released the words I'd wanted to say for the last decade. It was almost midnight, so we got up, and Mama walked me to the door.

"Thanks, Mama. I hope one day you will be enough for you. You deserve it," I said.

She smiled at me sadly as I walked down the stairs and into a new era.

24

I had sent the offer details for Samirah to Michael for review before I left the office. By three in the afternoon the next day, the contracts team, who was used to handling deals overnight, had sent along the deal memo to Samirah and copied Michael. It came through in his email I had access to. I tried to open the memo attached to the email, but it was locked. I needed a password to get in. Still, without knowing the details, I knew that things were in motion. I had to tell Samirah and Quincy the good news. I walked to the bathroom and pulled out my phone to FaceTime them.

"I saw the deal memo in Michael's email. I can't see the details yet, but I know that they've made an offer. I am so happy for you! Huge congrats, y'all. We did it," I said.

Samirah screamed into the phone so loud I instinctively snatched one of my earbuds from my ears. I turned down the volume before I put it back in. "Oh my god, it's really happening. Wow. Thank you, Billie, for everything. Oh my god, I gotta call my mom," she said.

Quincy was in his studio when he answered. "Ayeee. Shout out to you, Samirah. I knew you had this shit in the bag since day one."

"Ah, I'm really happy this all worked out. Want to meet up for drinks later to celebrate? On me?" I said.

•

We agreed to meet at the speakeasy Nina had taken me to last year.

I didn't have a corporate card like she did, but I figured the wait to be reimbursed was worth this momentous occasion—my first artist as a budding A&R rep.

I'd ordered three glasses of champagne, and they were already at the table by the time Samirah and Quincy slid into the booth. As soon as they sat across from me, I held one glass up, waiting for them to grab theirs as well, but they didn't look excited.

In fact, they looked pissed, almost scowling as a red light passed across their faces on its way to light the stage where the jazz band had started to play. Samirah dug into her purse beside her and placed the deal memo on the table. I looked between them, confused as they stayed quiet. No one spoke for a few seconds, the silence of it loud, muting the music and chatter of others around us until it was only us breathing.

"What's wrong? I thought y'all would be happy to finally have the deal with Lit. I put together the offer terms myself, so I know you're getting the best a debut artist could get."

"Are you sure?" Quincy said. "Because if you did see what was in here, then you'd be real fucked up, Billie."

I looked at them, puzzled because I knew that what I had put together was fair. I had cribbed from an offer Nina had recently made to one of her artists. I wondered what it said for them to react this way. "Can I take a look?" I asked, reaching out for the papers.

The first thing I noticed was that it was a 360 deal, where essentially Lit would own Samirah's image, social media, promotion, and royalties far into the future. The recording commitment had been changed from twenty songs, roughly enough songs for at least two albums, to thirty. The royalty split was ninety–ten in places it should have been eighty–twenty, and, most disturbingly, MHCP LLC had been added into the document as the owner of all of Samirah's masters.

My mouth popped open as I read, and I started to get hot the closer I looked at the terms. I picked up a napkin from the table and fanned.

"So," Samirah said finally. "Billie, I know you worked so hard to get us this deal. But I can't take it. I can't agree to these terms. Plus, I talked to some people. You know, asked around. And I know that if I take this, it's going to kill my career before it really takes off. You seem as shocked as I was."

"I am. I don't know what to say. These are not the terms I sent to my team and definitely not what I wanted to happen," I said.

"Well, it is what it is," Quincy said. "At the end of the day, Billie, we appreciate everything you did to help. But this? It's bigger than you. If you figure it out, let us know. But for now, we gotta look at other options."

"Thanks for everything. Good luck," Samirah said.

They got up and walked out of the bar.

I understood their choice. Samirah had to do what was best for her and her music, Quincy what was best for his reputation, the artists he worked with. But I was devastated. It felt like someone had taken a sledgehammer to my chest, gutting me entirely.

I closed the bill, signing my name while staring at the three full glasses of Moët, grabbed my purse from beside me, and stood to leave.

•

The devastation turned to anger the more I thought about Michael, Connor, how close I'd gotten, how unfair it all was, how I'd eaten all of Michael's shit, this industry's shit, just so I could eventually be in the room to show artists that there were people fighting for them on the inside. I had held out on the hope that because I had looked over things carefully and I had the support of Nina, Lit would do the right thing. But the threat of Michael's deceitful business dealings always lurked beneath. In truth, Michael had probably always planned on offering Samirah a bad deal, as he'd done to so many artists before. I shouldn't have let my optimism and passion blind me to that possibility. I wouldn't let it happen again. After our failed celebration, I had originally intended on going home. But this feeling, like fire blazing through a dry forest, carried me to the office. Exposing Michael would be my retribution.

I wore all black clothing, with a hoodie over my head, and an N95 mask to disguise my mouth area. When I got to the office, it was late enough that no one was there. I looked around for the security guard, but thankfully, he was outside, smoking a cigarette. I let myself into the Lit lobby right as a crew of contractors, who had rearranged conference rooms and put up Ultimate signage above Erykah's desk, was leaving. I slid open the glass door to Michael's office. I scooted under his desk and took the key taped to the underside. I plugged the flash drive into Michael's computer and looked through each folder in the MHCP LLC file one by one. I emailed Alicia artist files—Juda, Samirah, Kyrie Kash, Yung Curren$y, among others—from the WeTransfer website so it couldn't be traced back to me, then I slipped out of the office in the dark night.

Alicia texted me as I walked home from the train station.

Alicia:

Did you do this?

Billie:

You didn't hear it from me.

Go get that full-time job sis.

Alicia:

Copy

At home, I stuffed myself with snack food and blues music and told Lucas what I had done.

"Do you think I'm gonna get fired?" I said as Lucas rubbed my back on the sofa. I rested my head on my knees. "Worse, do you think I can get arrested? What if it gets back to me?"

"You know what you did, babe? You finally stood up for yourself today. You stood up on behalf of artists today. People like you and me, everyday people with goals, dreams. You shouldn't ever feel ashamed or bad about that. Whatever comes will come, and we'll handle it together. But I'm proud of you. I knew that one day you would come back to yourself," he said.

We shared soft kisses until the tenderness made tears streak down my face. I turned the music up and filled myself with melancholic harmonies and bucolic chants and hollers against choked guitar strings and thought about the consequences my actions would bring, blues music the soundtrack of my dreams as Lucas's hands massaged me to sleep.

25

When I arrived at the office the next day, things looked different, like I was looking with new eyes. Plants and printers and conference rooms had been moved and reconfigured. Erykah and I had exchanged side-eyes at the signage at reception that was put in last night that included Ultimate's name. Either way, this was it. The move-in following the merger would happen today, and things were going to change around here, especially now that Trent took over as director of four Lit imprints that had been combined with Ultimate's to form a new division. There was a meeting later today that would explain it all. As I sat down at my desk, I wondered if what I'd sent to Alicia had had any impact.

Oddly enough, as I wondered, Alicia texted me with a link. Then she sent another text that said,

YOU NEED TO READ THIS NOW.

I clicked on the article, and there Michael was in the central image, a big red circle with a line through it on top of him, and next to that, a graphic stack of money that looked like it was being blown up by a firecracker. The title of the article was "Reverse Robin Hood? How Michael Hemley, A&R Director at Lit Music Productions, Embezzled Millions from Black and Brown Artists to Boost Careers of White Artists."

Alicia had stayed up the night before, typing an article that would burn Michael to the ground. Alicia had looked through the files I'd sent her thoroughly and then corroborated every story from the artists she had contact with. Unbeknownst to me, she'd been researching the story since the dancer had given her the scoop, and the files were the final evidence she needed. She got the full picture from Hanif, whose lyrics and vocals had helped mold Juda's career while Hanif's faltered. It finally made sense to me why Juda's flow and beats had seemed so outdated and inauthentic when Connor played the songs for me last year. The whole vibe had been Hanif's all along. Alicia interviewed her dance-captain friend's man, who had explained that he had received the same kind of 360 deal that Michael had offered Samirah. Alicia even talked to a member of Deliverance Desired who had signed over the rights to their masters, but also unknowingly locked themselves into multi-album recording deals that would bar them from performing their songs and profiting off their music and personas. The worst part, though all of it was tragic for the artists, was that Michael had been stealing a portion of the advances using his MHCP LLC and redirecting the funds to his personal offshore account. The sheer amount of evidence against Michael was damning, and even a man of his stature might not be able to fight everything that came to light.

When I finished the article, I felt a pang in my chest, feeling like I was now the one with a target on my back. Did people in the office think I was the leak? What would happen if it all came back to me?

As I wondered, looking off into the skyline through the windows, Michael was making his way to his office. The executives who usually sat inside their offices were all standing in their doorways, their eyes turned to Michael. They were quiet as they watched him go into his office and shut the door.

Michael put his coat on the hook, sat down, and fired up his desktop, which usually opened on a Google search page that showed snippets of the news of the day. And then he pulled the desktop phone from the wires and hurled it across the room. "Fuck!" he said loud enough for the whole office to hear.

In almost no time, three security officers were at Michael's office door along with Trent.

Michael looked from the officers to Trent. "You can't do this to me. I have spent my whole fucking career here, and I'll be god fucking damned if I'm going to let you take this from me." He looked around the office. "Connor, get in here. Tell them," he said frantically, looking out into the main office space. "Tell them that this is all a part of business. That they have it all wrong." But Connor wasn't there.

Connor Penchant hadn't come in that day. I suspected that he wouldn't be back in until this all blew over. While he was involved in the MHCP LLC schemes, Michael was the one who had officially signed off on the deals, and the Penchant family, worth millions, wouldn't let one of their own ruin their name, so it was whispered that they'd used their money to remove any trace of Connor as an accomplice.

"Michael, I'm sorry, buddy, that it has to end this way. It was a hell of a ride, though, right?" Trent said.

Michael, who had turned red from his yelling, lunged at Trent, who had backed up in time. Security tackled him, then held Michael tight as they made their way, him struggling against them, to the exit. Executives watched on, mouths agape, eyes wide with shock.

When the scene was over, Stanley, our CEO, who we hadn't seen in person since the last merger meeting, arrived on our floor.

"Hello, everyone. On behalf of Lit Music Productions, I'd like to apologize for that outburst you've witnessed. I'll be addressing this situation now in the New York conference room. Trent, join me," he added before they walked over together.

Shell-shocked, we all made our way. Stanley and Trent sat at the front.

"So I know that tensions are high today. You all may have seen that article about Michael's misdeeds at this label, and I want to assure you that Lit will not tolerate that kind of behavior. Michael has been terminated, effective immediately, and we're working with our team on next steps to rectify contracts with the affected artists. Going forward, I want to ensure transparent communication and leadership as we forge a new path in this industry and as a company." Stanley signaled toward Trent with his hand. "And our future is in Trent. That future is in fair deals, investing in and supporting our diverse roster and our employees."

Trent bowed his head. "Thanks, Stanley. And I want to echo those sentiments. I'm proud to be the new director here at Lit, and I look forward to working with all of you and leading you into a new future."

When the meeting was done, everyone scrambled out of the conference room, looking dazed. The office would be buzzing with this news for hours. I wasn't sure how to feel. There was still a chance I would get fired too. I was thinking as much on my way to my desk when Trent called out my name.

"Hi, Billie. Would you mind stepping into my office?" he asked.

I jumped at the sound of his voice, and worry ran through me like static. I wrung my hands as we walked over to his office.

Trent sat behind his desk.

"Door open or closed?" I asked as I stepped in.

"Closed. Please. Have a seat." He gestured with his hands to the two black leather chairs in front of him that looked like they had been worn in exactly the right amount.

He looked youthful here as his thick sandy-brown hair and hazel eyes shone in the light. I took a seat, folded my hands together to stop their fidgeting, and waited for him to speak.

"Billie, I called you in here today to talk about some changes in the company." He paused and straightened his tie.

My stomach started rumbling from nerves. I grabbed it to quiet the sounds and tried not to panic.

He continued, "So you've probably seen the article from *Kulture Magazine* about Michael's conduct at Lit. As you know, Michael will no longer be with the company, and I'll be taking over as director. Anyway, I'm a pretty straightforward guy, so I'll cut to the chase."

This was the moment I'd feared all along. I was going to be fired for my insolence and my outsized ambition. I held my breath as he delivered what I thought would be the final blow.

"We had our eyes on Nina for a role at this new division. But since today is her last day, she told me that I should look into you. She said you had a good ear. Said that I should give you a chance."

He leaned forward in his chair, coming closer to me, and I could see the lines in his face hinting at his middle age.

"We know that what Michael has done isn't what we want the label to stand for going forward. I've always been in the business of supporting artists, helping them make music, change the world. It's the whole point of me even allowing Ultimate to become a part of this place. Under my leadership, I think this is the kind of place where artists will feel seen. Heard. Respected. I plan to revolutionize the culture here, make sure it's artists first. And I think there's some space for you to be a part of that."

Excitement started to build inside me as I realized what could be happening. But I stopped myself before I let it get too far, in case this could still go bad. I apologized about Michael even though I wasn't sorry in the slightest. Michael had gotten exactly what he deserved. I only wished we could get rid of everyone else who held the same ideologies. But this was a small step. Small steps became big ones eventually. "Thanks so much, Trent. But what are you saying exactly?"

"Well, we wouldn't be bringing you in at Nina's level since you don't have the requisite experience yet. But I was hoping that you would be my assistant. I think you'd be perfect for this as Ultimate and Lit change."

I felt like I had runner's high, delicious endorphins coursing through my veins, fixing me where I had been broken. I held in a smile and nodded, eager to hear what he said next.

"You wouldn't be able to start finding talent right away. But unlike Michael, under me you would be able to start finding talent in addition to your regular assistant duties in about six or nine months. You'd come to all the meetings. You'd go to more shows. You'd really get a chance to be in the middle of it all. Anyway, you don't have to answer now. Think about it and get back to me on Monday, yeah?"

"Okay, I think I can do that. Thanks so much for the opportunity, Trent."

"No problem, Billie. Now if you don't mind," he said, motioning toward the desktop monitor.

"Oh yes. Of course," I said.

•

I went back to my desk and stared off into space, thinking. I started this day hoping I wouldn't get fired. But now I had two job offers, and Nina was expecting my answer soon.

I stacked everything up in my head. Lit versus G.O.O.D Music Group. In my heart, I knew the right decision.

I had to tell Nina.

I walked over to Nina's desk, where she was busy packing personal items into a box.

"Hey, Nina, do you have a sec?" I asked.

She nodded and walked with me to a phone booth room. Before I had a chance to get anything out, she cut in.

"So what's it going to be?" Nina said.

I took in a deep breath and folded my hands together in case they decided to shake from the nerves. "First, I wanted to say how much I appreciate everything you've done for me here. You have been the best thing about my time at Lit. And I'm so happy that you landed this new position. It's so well deserved, and I know you're going to kill it over there."

"Let me guess," Nina said. "You're not coming with me."

I shook my head. "I can't come with you," I said. "Trent offered me a job too, just a few minutes ago. And . . ." I paused, feeling that familiar cry in my throat. I cleared it and tried not to let my emotions get the better of me before I could get the rest out. "I feel like my work here at Lit isn't done. I know things will be different on the Ultimate side. I don't know what it will be like to work for Trent, but I'm excited about the possibilities. And you've already laid the groundwork. I want to follow in your footsteps, do what you did here. I want to build the roster of my dreams, then open the door for people like me who can come in behind me and do similar things. I . . . I hope you understand."

Nina dusted off her pants even though there was nothing there. "I understand, Billie. We all have to make the best choices for our own careers. Listen . . ." She grabbed hold of my shoulders and said, "Good luck with everything. I'm only a call away if you ever need anything—advice or an ear to vent, anything."

"Hey, I mean, since you said anything . . . if the new label would be interested, maybe you could try to pitch Samirah over there? Even though I won't get the chance to work with her, I know you would do right by her."

Nina shot me a knowing smile. "I'll see what I can do," she said.

She pulled me in for a hug. I would miss her every time I walked past her empty cube. I'd miss her, period. I hugged her back tighter.

•

I texted Lucas and Alicia to meet me after work to celebrate my decision.

We met at a crowded, brightly lit Irish bar on East Forty-Third Street that constantly texted me those happy-hour deals—the ones where I got to drink watered-down well drinks for free and my guests drank half-price if I brought enough friends with me—and Alicia, Lucas, and I squeezed into a booth.

I drank a sip of rum and Coke as Alicia continued her story about how she secured a job as a staff writer at *Kulture*.

"As soon as you sent me the info, I got to work. I was up all night writing it. It was the best thing I'd written in my life. You know once that dancer mentioned it, I had to look deeper."

I smiled at her because I knew she wouldn't have let it go so easily.

"I didn't even send it to Janet over email. I didn't want anyone to steal my scoop. I printed it out and dropped it onto Janet's desk. I sat down, crossed my arms, and just said, 'Read it.' I thought she was going to kick me out of her office. But after she'd looked at the first paragraph, she read the whole article. When she finished, she basically hired me full-time on the spot."

"Ayeee, Leesh. I'm proud of you. You are so brave to put your name on that. When I think back on what I did, I get scared. Like, wow. This could've really fucking blown up in my face," I said.

"Yeah, well. It didn't, girl. And now I'm employed. And, Lucas, you got your show. Billie, two job offers. It's crazy how we're finally getting what we wanted for so long," she said.

"Yeah, the Sunsetlandia deal is nearly finalized. They agreed to my terms. They're letting me keep all creative control. And they started a fund for the 'Create Your Niche' classes for my kids. New facility, guest speakers, new cameras, and all that!"

"That's dope, Lucas," Alicia said. "I'm so happy for you."

"Yeah, this is just gonna let me take my shit to the next level. Help me give back to my community. Build that generational wealth we're always talking about," he said.

I reached my hand to Lucas's cheek and rubbed gently. "I'm proud of you too, babe," I said.

"But, Billie," Alicia said, changing the topic. "What did you decide? Nina or Lit?"

"I thought about it like this: On one hand, working with Nina and working closely with her artists on music I care about would be amazing. But I wasn't sure if there would be space for me to shine or break out from her shadow once I'm known as her assistant. Beyond that, it's a smaller label, and while Nina is going to head a division, for me, it could also feel like a step back."

"Well then, what are the advantages to staying at Lit?" Alicia said. "Do you even know if this Trent guy is for real?"

"He says I'd eventually get to sign artists I wanted. And much sooner. It also really seems like things will be different with Trent there. If I left now I'd lose out on what could be a better opportunity."

The waitress stopped by the table to drop off the happy-hour-priced garlic fries we had ordered to share, and Alicia popped one into her mouth.

I took a fry too and tried to put on a brave face, but I was starting to feel I had made the wrong choice.

"Babe," Lucas said, looking straight into my eyes, "You got into this industry to do great things. You always said you wanted to forge your own legacy. Which label will give you that chance?"

I sat with that for a while, absentmindedly picking fries from the basket as the sounds of early tens pop warbled from the speakers overhead. I put the fries on my plate but they went uneaten.

26

On Monday, the official christening of the Ultimate and Lit union would happen.

At the eleven o'clock meeting, we'd meet our new colleagues and draw lines in the sand, making sure that they knew that this was Lit Music Productions and that the people who worked here would remain once the dust settled.

But for now, on this bright Saturday morning, I looked at Lucas as he snored in bed, drained from his morning workout, and gave him a kiss before I went to stare out of my window. As I looked out at the Bronx neighborhood, I thought about it all—Nina and Mama, Quincy and Samirah, and Lucas and Alicia, about how hard we all had to fight to thrive in this world.

I thought about how music had been my anchor, the thing that helped me when nothing else could. I thought about how I wanted to help bring music into the world to give others the same salvation music had given me. How I could be the one to give artists a chance to make music that felt true to themselves. When I accepted the job on Monday, I would soon be able to do all of that. All I needed was patience. For real this time.

I peered out the window, the Bronx set aglow in the morning hour, and I smiled.

I was on my way.

ACKNOWLEDGMENTS

There are so many people to thank, but I'll start with my wonderful editor, Chelcee Johns. Thank you, Chelcee, for your incisive and brilliant editing. This book would not be half as good without you. To Wendy Wong, thank you for your enthusiasm and for taking this book across the finish line. Thank you to the whole team at Ballantine: Jennifer Hershey, Abby Duval, Laura Petrella, Debbie Glasserman, Michael Morris, Brianna Kusilek, Jordan Hill Forney, Kim Hovey, Sydney Collins, Anusha Khan, Pam Alders, and Chanler Harris.

To Jennifer Herrera, thank you for your words at a lunch we had early in my career—that gave me the spark of inspiration I needed to write this book. To my first agent, Rachel Kim, thank you for your guidance and for believing in this book from the very beginning. Your vision and the way you immediately saw and understood the heart of my book meant the absolute world to me. To Angeline Rodriguez, my fabulous, rock star agent, thank you for your endless support and incredible advocacy—I am so grateful to be in your care. Thank you to Megan Muralles and the whole team at WME.

To my writing group, Anna Montague, Imani Gary, and Vedika Khanna, thank you for being my community and for keeping me accountable. I couldn't have done it without y'all!

To the Hurston/Wright Foundation, thank you for providing a space for me to focus on my craft and writing.

To my husband, Leo Kubota, thank you for being my number-one supporter and the most caring and creative person I've ever met. You are the best partner I could ever ask for. I love you.

Thank you to my big sister, Janelle aka Naomi Spratley, for always being there when I needed you. P.S. Aren't you happy I finally called you my big sister?

Thank you to my little sisters, Meg Green and Madison Green. Y'all are the future and I'm rooting for you!

Thank you to my mother, Nicole Green, for passing on your fun-loving and funny nature to me.

Thank you to my best friends, Jasmine Phillips, Latora Evans-Ashe, and Jahaira Escarraman, for your twenty years of friendship. I am eternally grateful to have you in my life.

To Dylan Gray, Dorian Randall, and other beta readers, thank you for your support and for your friendship.

And, lastly, thank you to my Oliver family and everyone else who has helped me on my journey.

ABOUT THE AUTHOR

AMBER OLIVER is a writer and book editor. Born and raised in the Bronx, New York, she currently resides in Harlem. *When the Music Hits* is her first novel.

Instagram: @ambero007
X: @Amber_Oliver007

ABOUT THE TYPE

This book was set in Fournier, a typeface named for Pierre-Simon Fournier (1712–68), the youngest son of a French printing family. He started out engraving woodblocks and large capitals, then moved on to fonts of type. In 1736, he began his own foundry and made several important contributions in the field of type design; he is said to have cut 147 alphabets of his own creation. Fournier is probably best remembered as the designer of St. Augustine Ordinaire, a face that served as the model for the Monotype Corporation's Fournier, which was released in 1925.